THE INVISIBLE EYE

COLLINS CHILLERS

·THE·INVISIBLE·
·EYE·

TALES OF TERROR BY
EMILE ERCKMANN
& LOUIS ALEXANDRE
CHATRIAN

Edited, with an Introduction, by

HUGH LAMB

HarperCollins*Publishers*

HarperCollins*Publishers*
I London Bridge Street
London SE1 9GF
www.harpercollins.co.uk

This edition 2018

First published in Great Britain by Ash-Tree Press 2002

Selection, introduction and notes © Hugh Lamb 2018

A catalogue record for this book
is available from the British Library

ISBN 978–0–00–826538–0

Typeset by Palimpsest Book Production Ltd,
Falkirk, Stirlingshire

Printed and bound in Great Britain by
CPI Group (UK) Ltd, Croydon CR0 4YY

MIX
Paper from
responsible sources

FSC
www.fsc.org   FSC™ C007454

This book is produced from independently certified FSC™ paper
to ensure responsible forest management.

For more information visit: www.harpercollins.co.uk/green

CONTENTS

To my wonderful family:
Richard and Maggie
My grandson Jack
Andrew, Tamar, Dylan and Ezra

INTRODUCTION

It is still uncommon to find the names of Erckmann–Chatrian in studies of Continental literature, a sad reflection on the obscurity suffered by these fine writers for more than a century.

While their main writing efforts – military history and fiction – are now unread and unavailable, their tales of terror have managed to survive in part, even seeing a revival in the early 1970s. *The Invisible Eye* – the first collection of their stories in Britain since 1981 – will, I hope, introduce more readers to their masterful talent for the macabre.

Emile Erckmann (b. 20 May 1822) and Louis Alexandre Chatrian (b. 18 December 1826) were both natives of Alsace–Lorraine, the border region for so long a bone of contention between France and Germany. Erckmann was born in Phalsbourg, the son of a bookseller, and it is possible that his being surrounded by books from an early age did much to inspire him to his own imaginative works. Chatrian was born in Soldatenthal, the son of a glass-blower. He did not follow his father's trade, instead becoming a teacher at Phalsbourg college.

It was here that Erckmann met Chatrian, while the former was studying law (a profession he never followed), and the two hit it off very well. It seems that Erckmann was the more literary and imaginative of the two, while Chatrian was of a much more practical and energetic mind. Their writing style seems to have been adapted to this difference between them, with Erckmann writing and Chatrian revising (a working system which was later to produce the most awful trouble).

They started writing together almost immediately, and had the distinction of seeing one of their first efforts, a play on the invasion of Alsace in 1814, banned in 1848 because of its effects on the volatile state of public opinion in the province at the time. They did manage to publish *Histoires et Contes Fantastique* in 1849, two years after their writing partnership commenced. It was ironic that the first work by the dynamic duo should so neatly sum up their writing career and later obscurity. It was an awful failure, and must have made them wonder if it was all worth the effort. They fared so badly in those early years that, by all accounts, they nearly starved. Thoroughly discouraged, Erckmann resumed his legal studies, and Chatrian took a job in the Eastern Railway Company in France.

It took some time, but they finally cracked the market in 1859 with their novel *The Illustrious Doctor Matheus*. Four years later, they struck the vein that was to bring them national renown with *Madame Therese,* a novel about Alsace at the time of the French revolution. They specialised in French history, particularly of the Napoleonic era; a time still alive in the memories of older French citizens, who supplied them with much detail. The books flowed out: *Waterloo* (1865), *La Guerre* (1866), *Le Blocus* (1867), *Histoire d'un Paysan* (1868) – the list was impressive.

As well as military fiction, they tried their hand at drama, and one result was the interesting *Le Juif Polonais*, published in English in 1871 as *The Polish Jew*. This was high drama on the psychological decline of a murderer. It became the stage play *The Bells,* and gave Sir Henry Irving his most celebrated role. Oddly, it also gave Boris Karloff one of his first horror film roles (five years before *Frankenstein*) as a hypnotist in the 1926 Chadwick production, directed by James Young from his own screenplay based on the Erckmann–Chatrian work.

Their most interesting book, *Contes Fantastiques* (not to be confused with their first collection), appeared in 1860. It contains some of their finest tales of terror (several of which are included here), and remains their best work in the genre.

The pair were known as 'the twins' at the height of their fame. According to one source, they worked out the plots of their stories while they sat drinking and smoking; and there is certainly plenty of both activities in their tales.

In Britain they fared very well. Their first book appeared in 1865 – Smith Elder's translation of *The Conscript* – and the same firm issued *The Blockade* four years later. Various publishers issued Erckmann–Chatrian books, including Richard Bentley, J. C. Hotten and Tinsley Brothers, but the writers really struck gold with Ward, Lock & Co. Starting with *The Great Invasion of 1813–14* (1870), Ward, Lock & Co. were to publish nineteen of their titles, fourteen of them between 1871 and 1874, which were big sellers. Luckily for us, Ward, Lock's catalogue was to include nearly all of Erckmann–Chatrian's short story collections.

Their happy working relationship did not last, however. In 1889 they quarrelled violently and it seems that Chatrian arrogantly claimed the copyright of their work. (Remember that Chatrian had spent the past forty years as the revising half of the partnership.) Erckmann went to court and recovered damages from Chatrian's secretary (I am unable to find out exactly why). Chatrian went into an immediate decline and died on 3 September 1890. Erckmann lived on for nine years, dying on 14 March 1899. They must have been rather sad years; he does not seem to have written anything of importance on his own following the split.

Within a few years of their deaths, the two writers had

slipped into obscurity in Britain. The golden era of Ward, Lock had ended around 1880, and no new title by Erckmann–Chatrian appeared in Britain after 1901. There was a Blackie edition (in French) of *Contes Fantastique* in 1901 (somewhat late in the day, it must be said), and there were one or two French study editions of their novels, including one, *Le Blocus* (1913), with a fine introduction by Arthur Reed Ropes, a friend of M.R. James and himself the author of a splendid macabre novel, *The Hole of the Pit* (1914). But that was it for eighty years.

However, Erckmann–Chatrian did live on, even if only as pale and wan shapes in the corner, thanks to weird fiction. They had attracted the attention of two famous writers in the genre, as different as two authors could ever be – H. P. Lovecraft and M. R. James.

It is entirely due to these two that this book exists at all. If I may be allowed a little personal history, I first encountered the names Erckmann–Chatrian in M. R. James's *Collected Ghost Stories*. Being very scared of spiders, I was fascinated to read in his introduction that 'Other people have written of dreadful spiders – for instance, Erckmann–Chatrian in an admirable story called *L'Araignée Crabe*'. I spent many years wondering what terrors lay hidden behind that French title. Then, much later, I came across H. P. Lovecraft's *Supernatural Horror in Literature* (a superlative researcher's primer), and was fascinated to read more about Erckmann–Chatrian. Lovecraft noted that '"The Owl's Ear" and "Waters of Death" are full of engulfing darkness and mystery, the latter embodying the familiar over-grown spider theme so frequently employed by weird fictionists'. It was a good bet that 'Waters of Death' was the same story as that mentioned by M. R. James. But how to get a copy? The British Museum catalogue did not mention either title, and I found that the Lovecraft version only appeared in an obscure American edition from the turn of the century, which was impossible to obtain. However, the British Museum catalogue did list several books of short stories by Erckmann–Chatrian and, on the assumption that one of them would contain this intriguing spider story, I set about tracking them down.

I never found an English book version of 'L'Araignée Crabe', much to my annoyance (in the end I got the French translated). What I did find was a set of splendid stories, forgotten for a century, which I duly reprinted in several of my anthologies. Then a chance encounter in 1978 with Thomas Tessier, who was an editor at Millington, led to his suggestion of an Erckmann–Chatrian collection. That Millington book was the original of this much expanded edition.

Erckmann–Chatrian stand apart from most of their contemporaries in European fiction who wrote in this vein. They did not essay the *conte cruel*, like Villiers de l'Isle Adam, or go in for paranoid fantasies, like Guy de Maupassant. Their tales are simple and straightforward, with all the effects up front. By rights, they should have dated severely. The pleasant surprise for modern readers is that they haven't.

They wrote two fine, long tales: 'The Wild Huntsman', an essay on teratology with a sunshine-filled forest for a setting, and 'The Man-Wolf', a chilling story of lycanthropy, set in a winter-shrouded Black Forest castle. Their weirdest tales deal with metaphysics. 'The Three Souls' postulates that man is made up of three stages of development: vegetable, animal, and human. An enterprising Heidelberg scholar decides to bring them all out in the hero by starvation. Another seeker after wisdom tries to eavesdrop on the whole world through a freak of geology called 'The Owl's Ear'. In neither case are the results successful or happy.

'The Invisible Eye' is a remarkable tale of an old woman who induces suicide in the tenants of a hotel room through dummies on which she bestows magical powers. Like all of Erckmann–Chatrian's work, the story's florid style (probably exaggerated by the awkward translation of the day) only adds to the marvellous atmosphere. Their most memorable tale is 'The Crab Spider', and it is easy to see why M. R. James liked it so much. He borrowed its structure – mysterious deaths, terrible cause discovered, fiery climax – for his 'The Ash-tree'.

In the works of Erckmann–Chatrian, we are able to step back over one hundred and fifty years, to the lost world of mid nineteenth century Europe, full of eminently believable characters – young men wooing, old men reminiscing, drinkers, smokers, noblemen, woodmen, peasants, witches, monsters, murderers, ghosts. Nothing like this is written today. Compared to their contemporaries – authors like Le Fanu or Bulwer-Lytton – Erckmann–Chatrian offer an easy target to critics, with their light touch and often bucolic tales. But these are stories with imagination second to none, and modern readers will not be disappointed. Welcome to the world of Erckmann–Chatrian.

Hugh Lamb
Sutton, Surrey
January 2018

THE INVISIBLE EYE

I

When I first started my career as an artist, I took a room in the roof-loft of an old house in the Rue des Minnesängers, at Nuremberg.

I had made my nest in an angle of the roof. The slates served me for walls, and the roof-tree for a ceiling: I had to walk over my straw mattress to reach the window; but this window commanded a magnificent view, for it overlooked both city and country beyond.

The old second-hand dealer, Toubec, knew the road up to my little den as well as I knew it myself, and was not afraid of climbing the ladder. Every week his goat's head, surmounted by a rusty wig, pushed up the trap-door, his fingers clutched the edge of the floor, and in a noisy tone he cried: 'Well, well, Master Christian, have we anything new?'

To which I answered: 'Come in: why the deuce don't you come in? I'm just finishing a little landscape, and want to have your opinion of it.'

Then his long thin spine lengthened itself out, until his head touched the roof; and the old fellow laughed silently.

I must do justice to Toubec: he never bargained with me. He bought all my pictures at fifteen florins apiece, one with the other, and sold them again at forty. He was an honest Jew.

This kind of existence was beginning to please me, and I was every day finding in it some new charm, when the city of Nuremberg was agitated by a strange and mysterious event.

Not far from my garret-window, a little to the left, rose the *auberge* of the Boeuf-gras, an old inn much frequented by the country-people. The gable of this *auberge* was conspicuous for the peculiarity of its form: it was very narrow, sharply pointed, and its edges were cut like the teeth of a saw; grotesque carvings ornamented the cornices and framework of its windows. But what was most remarkable was that the house which faced it reproduced exactly the same carvings and ornaments; every detail had been minutely copied, even to the support of the signboard, with its iron volutes and spirals.

It might have been said that these two ancient buildings reflected one another; only that behind the inn grew a tall oak, the dark foliage of which served to bring into bold relief the forms of the roof, while the opposite house stood bare against the sky. For the rest, the inn was as noisy and animated as the other house was silent. On the one side was to be seen, going in and coming out, an endless crowd of drinkers, singing, stumbling, cracking their whips; over the other, solitude reigned.

Once or twice a day the heavy door of the silent house opened to give egress to a little old woman, her back bent into a half-circle, her chin long and pointed, her dress clinging to her limbs, an enormous basket under her arm, and one hand tightly clutched upon her chest.

This old woman's appearance had struck me more than once; her little green eyes, her skinny, pinched-up nose, her shawl, dating back a hundred years at least, the smile that wrinkled her cheeks, and the lace of her cap hanging down upon her eyebrows – all this appeared strange, interested me, and made me strongly desire to learn who this old woman was, and what she did in her great lonely house.

I imagined her as passing there an existence devoted to

good works and pious meditation. But one day, when I had stopped in the street to look at her, she turned sharply round and darted at me a look the horrible expression of which I know not how to describe, and made three or four hideous grimaces at me; then dropping again her doddering head, she drew her large shawl about her, the ends of which trailed after her on the ground, and slowly entered her heavy door.

'That's an old mad-woman,' I said to myself; 'a malicious, cunning old mad-woman! I ought not to have allowed myself to be so interested in her. But I'll try and recall her abominable grimace – Toubec will give me fifteen florins for it willingly.'

This way of treating the matter was far from satisfying my mind, however. The old woman's horrible glance pursued me everywhere; and more than once, while scaling the perpendicular ladder of my lodging-hole, feeling my clothes caught in a nail, I trembled from head to foot, believing that the old woman had seized me by the tails of my coat for the purpose of pulling me down backwards.

Toubec, to whom I related the story, far from laughing at it, received it with a serious air.

'Master Christian,' he said, 'if the old woman means you harm, take care; her teeth are small, sharp-pointed, and wonderfully white, which is not natural at her age. She has the Evil Eye! Children run away at her approach, and the people of Nuremberg call her Fledermausse!'

I admired the Jew's clear-sightedness, and what he had told me made me reflect a good deal; but at the end of a few weeks, having often met Fledermausse without harmful consequences, my fears died away and I thought no more of her.

One night, when I was lying sound asleep, I was awoken by a strange harmony. It was a kind of vibration, so soft, so melodious, that the murmur of a light breeze through foliage can convey but a feeble idea of its gentle nature. For a long time I listened to it, my eyes wide open, and holding my breath the better to hear it.

At length, looking towards the window, I saw two wings beating against the glass. I thought, at first, that it was a bat imprisoned in my chamber; but the moon was shining clearly, and showed the wings of a magnificent night-moth, transparent as lace. At times their vibrations were so rapid as to hide them from my view; then for a while they would lie in repose, extended on the glass pane, their delicate articulations made visible anew.

This vaporous apparition in the midst of the universal silence opened my heart to the tenderest emotions; it seemed to me that a sylphid, pitying my solitude, had come to see me; and this idea brought the tears to my eyes.

'Have no fear, gentle captive – have no fear!' I said to it; 'your confidence shall not be betrayed. I will not retain you against your wishes; return to heaven – to liberty!'

And I opened the window.

The night was calm. Thousands of stars glittered in space. For a moment I contemplated this sublime spectacle, and the words of prayer rose naturally to my lips. But then, looking down, I saw a man hanging from the iron stanchion which supported the sign of the Boeuf-gras; the hair in disorder, the arms stiff, the legs straightened to a point, and throwing their gigantic shadow the whole length of the street.

The immobility of this figure, in the moonlight, had something frightful in it. I felt my tongue grow icy cold, and my teeth chattered. I was about to utter a cry; but by what mysterious attraction I know not, my eyes were drawn towards the opposite house, and there I dimly distinguished the old woman, in the midst of the heavy shadow, squatting at her window and contemplating the hanging body with diabolical satisfaction.

I became giddy with terror; my strength deserted me, and I fell down in a heap insensible.

I do not know how long I lay unconscious. On coming to myself I found it was broad day. Mingled and confused noises rose from the street below, I looked out from my window.

The burgomaster and his secretary were standing at the door of the Boeuf-gras; they remained there a long time. People came and went, stopped to look, then passed on their way. At length a stretcher, on which lay a body covered with a woollen cloth, was brought out and carried away by two men.

Then everyone else disappeared.

The window in front of the house remained open still; a fragment of rope dangled from the iron support of the sign-board. I had not dreamed – I had really seen the night-moth on my window-pane – then the suspended body – then the old woman!

In the course of that day Toubec paid me his weekly visit.

'Anything to sell, Master Christian?' he cried.

I did not hear him. I was seated on my only chair, my hands upon my knees, my eyes fixed on vacancy before me. Toubec, surprised at my immobility, repeated in a louder tone, 'Master Christian! – Master Christian!' then, stepping up to me, tapped me smartly on the shoulder.

'What's the matter? – what's the matter? Are you ill?' he asked.

'No – I was thinking.'

'What the deuce about?'

'The man who was hung—'

'Aha!' cried the old broker; 'you saw the poor fellow, then? What a strange affair! The third in the same place!'

'The third?'

'Yes, the third. I ought to have told you about it before; but there's still time – for there's sure to be a fourth, following the example of the others, the first step only making the difficulty.'

This said, Toubec seated himself on a box and lit his pipe with a thoughtful air.

'I'm not timid,' said he, 'but if anyone were to ask me to sleep in that room, I'd rather go and hang myself somewhere else! Nine or ten months back,' he continued, 'a wholesale furrier, from Tubingen, put up at the Boeuf-gras. He called for supper, ate well, drank well, and was shown up to bed in the room on the third floor which they call the "green chamber". The next day they found him hanging from the stanchion of the sign.

'So much for number one, about which there was nothing to be said. A proper report of the affair was drawn up, and the body of the stranger buried at the bottom of the garden. But about six weeks afterwards came a soldier from Neustadt; he had his discharge, and was congratulating himself on his return to his village. All the evening he did nothing but empty mugs of wine and talk of his cousin, who was waiting his return to marry him. At last they put him to bed in the green chamber, and the same night the watchman passing along the Rue des Minnesängers noticed something hanging from the signboard-stanchion. He raised his lantern; it was the soldier, with his discharge-papers in a tin box hanging on his left thigh, and his hands planted smoothly on the outer seams of his trousers, as if he had been on parade!

'It was certainly an extraordinary affair! The burgomaster declared it was the work of the devil. The chamber was examined; they replastered its walls. A notice of the death was sent to Neustadt, on the margin of which the clerk wrote – "Died suddenly of apoplexy".

'All Nuremberg was indignant against the landlord of the Boeuf-gras, and wished to compel him to take down the iron stanchion of his signboard, on the pretext that it put dangerous ideas in people's heads. But you may easily imagine that old Nikel Schmidt didn't listen with the ear on that side of his head.

'"That stanchion was put there by my grandfather," he said; "the sign of the Boeuf-gras has hung on it from father to son, for a hundred and fifty years; it does nobody any harm, it's more than thirty feet up; those who don't like it have only to look another way."

'People's excitement gradually cooled down, and for several months nothing happened. Unfortunately, a student from Heidelberg, on his way to the University, came to the Boeuf-gras and asked for a bed. He was the son of a pastor.

'Who would suppose that the son of a pastor would take into his head the idea of hanging himself to the stanchion of a public-house sign, because a furrier and a soldier had hung themselves there before him? It must be confessed, Master Christian, that the thing was not very probable – it would not have appeared more likely to you than it did to me. Well—'

'Enough! Enough!' I cried; 'it is a horrible affair. I feel sure there is some frightful mystery at the bottom of it. It is neither the stanchion nor the chamber—'

'You don't mean that you suspect the landlord? – as honest a man as there is in the world, and belonging to one of the oldest families in Nuremberg?'

'No, no! Heaven keep me from forming unjust suspicions of anyone; but there are abysses into the depths of which one dares not look.'

'You are right,' said Toubec, astonished at my excited manner; 'and we had much better talk of something else. By-the-way, Master Christian, what about our landscape, the view of Sainte-Odile?'

The question brought me back to actualities. I showed the broker the picture I had just finished. The business was soon settled between us, and Toubec, thoroughly satisfied, went down the ladder, advising me to think no more of the student of Heidelberg.

I would very willingly have followed the old broker's advice, but when the devil mixes himself up with our affairs he is not easily shaken off.

II

In solitude, all these events came back to my mind with frightful distinctness.

The old woman, I said to myself, is the cause of all this; she alone has planned these crimes, she alone has carried them into execution; but by what means? Has she had recourse to cunning only or really to the intervention of the invisible powers?

I paced my garret, a voice within me crying, 'It is not without purpose that Heaven has permitted you to see Fledermausse watching the agony of her victim; it was not without design that the poor young man's soul came to wake you in the form of a night-moth! No! all this has not been without purpose. Christian, Heaven imposes on you a terrible mission; if you fail to accomplish it, fear that you yourself may fall into the toils of the old woman! Perhaps at this moment she is laying her snares for you in the darkness!'

During several days these frightful images pursued me without cessation. I could not sleep; I found it impossible to work; the brush fell from my hand, and shocking to confess, I detected myself at times complacently contemplating the dreadful stanchion. At last, one evening, unable any longer to bear this state of mind, I flew down the ladder four steps at a time, and went and hid myself beside Fledermausse's door, for the purpose of discovering her fatal secret.

From that time there was never a day that I was not on the watch, following the old woman like her shadow, never losing sight of her; but she was so cunning, she had so keen a scent that without even turning her head she discovered that I was behind her, and knew that I was on her track. But nevertheless, she pretended not to see me – went to the market, to the butcher's, like a simple housewife; only she quickened her pace and muttered to herself as she went.

At the end of a month I saw that it would be impossible

for me to achieve my purpose by these means, and this conviction filled me with an inexpressible sadness.

'What can I do?' I asked myself. 'The old woman has discovered my intentions, and is thoroughly on her guard. I am helpless. The old wretch already thinks she sees me at the end of the cord!'

At length, from repeating to myself again and again the question, 'What can I do?' a luminous idea presented itself to my mind.

My chamber overlooked the house of Fledermausse, but it had no dormer window on that side. I carefully raised one of the slates of my roof, and the delight I felt on discovering that by this means I could command a view of the entire antique building can hardly be imagined.

'At last I've got you!' I cried to myself; 'you cannot escape me now! From here I shall see everything. You will not suspect this invisible eye – this eye that will surprise the crime at the moment of its inception! Oh, Justice! It moves slowly, but it comes!'

Nothing more sinister than this den could be imagined – a large yard, paved with moss-grown flagstones; a well in one corner, the stagnant water of which was frightful to behold; a wooden staircase leading up to a railed gallery, to the left, on the first floor, a drain-stone indicated the kitchen; to the right, the upper windows of the house looked into the street. All was dark, decaying, and dank-looking.

The sun penetrated only for an hour or two during the day the depths of this dismal sty; then the shadows again spread over it – the light fell in lozenge shapes upon the crumbling walls, on the mouldy balcony, on the dull windows.

Oh, the whole place was worthy of its mistress!

I had hardly made these reflections when the old woman entered the yard on her return from market. First, I heard her heavy door grate on its hinges, then Fledermausse, with her basket, appeared. She seemed fatigued – out of breath.

The border of her cap hung down upon her nose, as, clutching the wooden rail with one hand, she mounted the stairs.

The heat was suffocating. It was exactly one of those days when insects of every kind – crickets, spiders, mosquitoes – fill old buildings with their grating noises and subterranean borings.

Fledermausse crossed the gallery slowly, like a ferret that feels itself at home. For more than a quarter of an hour she remained in the kitchen, then came out and swept the stones a little, on which a few straws had been scattered; at last she raised her head, and with her green eyes carefully scrutinised every portion of the roof from which I was observing her.

By what strange intuition did she suspect anything? I know not; but I gently lowered the uplifted slate into its place, and gave over watching for the rest of that day.

The day following Fledermausse appeared to be reassured. A jagged ray of light fell into the gallery; passing this, she caught a fly, and delicately presented it to a spider established in an angle of the roof.

The spider was so large, that, in spite of the distance, I saw it descend then, gliding along one thread, like a drop of venom, seize its prey from the fingers of the dreadful old woman, and remount rapidly. Fledermausse watched it attentively; then her eyes half-closed, she sneezed, and cried to herself in a jocular tone: 'Bless you, beauty! – bless you!'

For six weeks I could discover nothing as to the power of Fledermausse: sometimes I saw her peeling potatoes, sometimes spreading her linen on the balustrade. Sometimes I saw her spin; but she never sang, as old women usually do, their quivering voices going so well with the humming of the spinning-wheel. Silence reigned about her. She had no cat – the favourite company of old maids; not a sparrow ever flew down to her yard, in passing over which the pigeons seemed to hurry their flight. It seemed as if everything were afraid of her look.

The spider alone took pleasure in her society.

I now look back with wonder at my patience during those long hours of observation; nothing escaped my attention, nothing was indifferent to me; at the least sound I lifted my slate. Mine was a boundless curiosity stimulated by an indefinable fear.

Toubec complained.

'What the devil are you doing with your time, Master Christian?' he would say to me. 'Formerly, you had something ready for me every week; now, hardly once a month. Oh, you painters! As soon as they have a few kreutzer before them, they put their hands in their pockets and go to sleep!'

I myself was beginning to lose courage. With all my watching and spying, I had discovered nothing extraordinary. I was inclining to think that the old woman might not be so dangerous after all – that I had been wrong, perhaps, to suspect her. In short, I tried to find excuses for her. But one fine evening, while, with my eye to the opening in the roof, I was giving myself up to these charitable reflections, the scene abruptly changed.

Fledermausse passed along her gallery with the swiftness of a flash of light. She was no longer herself: she was erect, her jaws knit, her look fixed, her neck extended; she moved with long strides, her grey hair streaming behind her.

'Oh, oh!' I said to myself, 'something is going on!'

But the shadows of night descended on the big house, the noises of the town died out, and all became silent. I was about to seek my bed, when, happening to look out of my skylight, I saw a light in the window of the green chamber of the Boeuf-gras – a traveller was occupying that terrible room!

All my fears were instantly revived. The old woman's excitement explained itself – she scented another victim!

I could not sleep at all that night. The rustling of the straw of my mattress, the nibbling of a mouse under the floor, sent a chill through me. I rose and looked out of my window

– I listened. The light I had seen was no longer visible in the green chamber.

During one of these moments of poignant anxiety – whether the result of illusion or reality – I fancied I could discern the figure of the old witch, likewise watching and listening.

The night passed, the dawn showed grey against my window-panes, and, slowly increasing, the sounds and movements of the re-awakened town arose. Harassed with fatigue and emotion, I at last fell asleep; but my repose was of short duration, and by eight o'clock I was again at my post of observation.

It appeared that Fledermausse had passed a night no less stormy than mine had been; for, when she opened the door of the gallery, I saw that a livid pallor was upon her cheeks and skinny neck. She had nothing on but her chemise and a flannel petticoat; a few locks of rusty grey hair fell upon her shoulders. She looked up musingly towards my garret; but she saw nothing – she was thinking of something else.

Suddenly she descended into the yard, leaving her shoes at the top of the stairs. Doubtless her object was to assure herself that the outer door was securely fastened. She then hurried up the stairs, three or four at a time. It was frightful to see! She rushed into one of the side rooms, and I heard the sound of a heavy box-lid fall. Then Fledermausse re-appeared in the gallery, dragging with her a life-size dummy – and this figure was dressed like the unfortunate student of Heidelberg!

With surprising dexterity the old woman suspended this hideous object to a beam of the over-hanging roof, then went down into the yard to contemplate it from that point of view. A peal of grating laughter broke from her lips – she hurried up the stairs, and rushed down again, like a maniac; and every time she did this she burst into fresh fits of laughter.

A sound was heard outside the street door, the old woman sprang to the dummy, snatched it from its fastening, and carried it into the house; then she reappeared and leaned over the balcony, with outstretched neck, glittering eyes, and eagerly listening ears. The sound passed away – the muscles of her face relaxed, she drew a long breath. The passing of a vehicle had alarmed the old witch.

She then, once more, went back into her chamber, and I heard the lid of the box close heavily.

This strange scene utterly confounded all my ideas. What could that dummy mean?

I became more watchful and attentive than ever. Fledermausse went out with her basket, and I watched her to the top of the street; she had resumed her air of tottering age, walking with short steps, and from time to time half-turning her head, so as to enable herself to look behind out of the corners of her eyes. For five long hours she remained abroad, while I went and came from my spying-place incessantly, meditating all the while – the sun heating the slates above my head till my brain was almost scorched.

I saw at his window the traveller who occupied the green chamber at the Boeuf-gras; he was a peasant of Nassau, wearing a three-cornered hat, a scarlet waistcoat, and having a broad laughing countenance. He was tranquilly smoking his pipe, unsuspicious of anything wrong.

About two o'clock Fledermausse came back. The sound of her door opening echoed to the end of the passage. Presently she appeared alone, quite alone in the yard, and seated herself on the lowest step of the gallery-stairs. She placed her basket at her feet and drew from it, first several bunches of herbs, then some vegetables – then a three-cornered hat, a scarlet velvet waistcoat, a pair of plush breeches, and a pair of thick worsted stockings – the complete costume of a peasant of Nassau!

I reeled with giddiness – flames passed before my eyes.

I remembered those precipices that drew one towards them with irresistible power – wells that have had to be filled up because of persons throwing themselves into them

– trees that have had to be cut down because of people hanging themselves upon them – the contagion of suicide and theft and murder, which at various times has taken possession of people's minds, by means well understood; that strange inducement, which makes people kill themselves because others kill themselves. My hair rose upon my head with horror!

But how could this Fledermausse – a creature so mean and wretched – have made discovery of so profound a law of nature? How had she found the means of turning it to the use of her sanguinary instincts? This I could neither understand nor imagine. Without more reflection, however, I resolved to turn the fatal law against her, and by its power to drag her into her own snare. So many innocent victims called for vengeance!

I hurried to all the old clothes-dealers in Nuremberg; and by the evening I arrived at the Boeuf-gras, with an enormous parcel under my arm.

Nikel Schmidt had long known me. I had painted the portrait of his wife, a fat and comely dame.

'Master Christian!' he cried, shaking me by the hand, 'to what happy circumstance do I owe the pleasure of this visit?'

'My dear Mr Schmidt, I feel a very strong desire to pass the night in that room of yours up yonder.'

We were on the doorstep of the inn, and I pointed up to the green chamber. The good fellow looked suspiciously at me.

'Oh! don't be afraid,' I said, 'I've no desire to hang myself.'

'I'm glad of it! I'm glad of it! for frankly, I should be sorry – an artist of your talent. When do you want the room, Master Christian?'

'Tonight.'

'That's impossible – it's occupied.'

'The gentleman can have it at once, if he likes,' said a voice behind us; 'I shan't stay in it.'

We turned in surprise. It was the peasant of Nassau; his large three-cornered hat pressed down upon the back of his neck, and his bundle at the end of his travelling-stick. He had learned the story of the three travellers who had hung themselves.

'Such chambers!' he cried, stammering with terror; 'it's – it's murdering people to put them into such! – you – you deserve to be sent to the galleys!'

'Come, come calm yourself,' said the landlord; 'you slept there comfortably enough last night.'

'Thank Heaven! I said my prayers before going to rest, or where should I be now?'

And he hurried away, raising his hands to heaven.

'Well,' said Master Schmidt, stupefied, 'the chamber is empty, but don't go into it to do me an ill turn.'

'I might be doing myself a much worse one,' I replied.

Giving my parcel to the servant-girl, I went and seated myself among the guests who were drinking and smoking.

For a long time I had not felt more calm, more happy to be in the world. After so much anxiety, I saw approaching my end – the horizon seemed to grow lighter. I know not by what formidable power I was being led on. I lit my pipe, and with my elbow on the table and a jug of wine before me, and sometimes rousing myself to look at the woman's house, I seriously asked myself whether all that had happened to me was more than a dream. But when the watchman came, to request us to vacate the room, graver thoughts took possession of my mind, and I followed, in meditative mood, the little servant-girl who preceded me with a candle in her hand.

III

We mounted the window flight of stairs to the third storey; arrived there, she placed the candle in my hand, and pointed to a door.

'That's it,' she said, and hurried back down the stairs as fast as she could go.

I opened the door. The green chamber was like all other inn bedchambers; the ceiling was low, the bed was high. After casting a glance round the room, I stepped across to the window.

Nothing was yet noticeable in Fledermausse's house, with the exception of a light, which shone at the back of a deep obscure bedchamber – a nightlight, doubtless.

'So much the better,' I said to myself, as I re-closed the window-curtains; 'I shall have plenty of time.'

I opened my parcel, and from its contents put on a woman's cap with a broad frilled border; then, with a piece of pointed charcoal, in front of the glass, I marked my forehead with a number of wrinkles. This took me a full hour to do; but after I had put on a gown and a large shawl, I was afraid of myself; Fledermausse herself was looking at me from the depths of the glass!

At that moment the watchman announced the hour of eleven. I rapidly dressed the dummy I had brought with me like the one prepared by the old witch. I then drew apart the window-curtains.

Certainly, after all I had seen of the old woman – her infernal cunning, her prudence, and her address – nothing ought to have surprised even me; yet I was positively terrified.

The light, which I had observed at the back of her room, now cast its yellow rays on her dummy, dressed like the peasant of Nassau, which sat huddled up on the side of the bed, its head dropped upon its chest, the large three-cornered hat drawn down over its features, its arms pendant by its sides, and its whole attitude that of a person plunged in despair.

Managed with diabolical art, the shadow permitted only a general view of the figure, the red waistcoat and its six rounded buttons alone caught the light; but the silence of night, the complete immobility of the figure, and its air of terrible dejection, all served to impress the beholder with irresistible force; even I myself, though not in the least taken by surprise, felt chilled to the marrow of my bones. How, then, would a poor countryman taken completely off his guard have felt? He would have been utterly overthrown; he would have lost all control of will, and the spirit of imitation would have done the rest.

Scarcely had I drawn aside the curtains than I discovered Fledermausse on the watch behind her window-panes.

She could not see me. I opened the window softly, the window over the way softly opened too; then the dummy appeared to rise slowly and advance towards me; I did the same, and seizing my candle with one hand, with the other threw the casement wide open.

The old woman and I were face to face; for, overwhelmed with astonishment, she had let the dummy fall from her hands. Our two looks crossed with an equal terror.

She stretched forth a finger, I did the same; her lips moved, I moved mine; she heaved a deep sigh and leant upon an elbow. I rested in the same way.

How frightful the enacting of this scene was I cannot describe; it was made up of delirium, bewilderment, madness. It was a struggle between two wills, two intelligences, two souls, one of which sought to crush the other; and in this struggle I had the advantage. The dead were on my side.

After having for some seconds imitated all the movements of Fledermausse, I drew a cord from the folds of my petticoat and tied it to the iron stanchion of the signboard.

The old woman watched me with open mouth. I passed the cord round my neck. Her tawny eyeballs glittered; her features became convulsed.

'No, no!' she cried, in a hissing tone; 'no!'

I proceeded with the impassibility of a hangman.

Then Fledermausse was seized with rage.

'You're mad! you're mad!' she cried, springing up and clutching wildly at the sill of the window; 'you're mad!'

I gave her no time to continue. Suddenly blowing out my

light, I stooped like a man preparing to make a vigorous spring, then seizing my dummy slipped the cord about its neck and hurled it into the air.

A terrible shriek resounded through the street; then all was silent again.

Perspiration bathed my forehead. I listened a long time. At the end of an hour I heard far off – very far off – the cry of the watchman, announcing that midnight had struck.

'Justice is at last done,' I murmured to myself; 'the three victims are avenged. Heaven forgive me!'

I saw the old witch, drawn by the likeness of herself, a cord about her neck, hanging from the iron stanchion projecting from her house. I saw the thrill of death run through her limbs and the moon, calm and silent, rose above the edge of the roof, and shed its cold pale rays upon her dishevelled head.

As I had seen the poor young student of Heidelberg, I now saw Fledermausse.

The next day all Nuremberg knew that 'the Bat' had hung herself. It was the last event of the kind in the Rue des Minnesängers.

THE OWL'S EAR

On a warm evening in July 1835, Kasper Boeck, a shepherd of the small village of Hirchwiller, presented himself before the burgomaster, Pétrus Mauerer, who had just finished his supper and was having a glass of Kirsch to help his digestion.

The burgomaster, tall and wiry, with his upper lip covered with a huge grey moustache, had in days gone by served in the armies of the arch-duke Charles. His was a bantering disposition, he had the village under his thumb, it was said, and ruled it with a rod of iron.

'Mr Burgomaster!' exclaimed the shepherd.

But Pétrus Mauerer, without waiting for the end of his speech, frowned and said to him: 'Kasper Boeck, start by removing your hat, remove your dog from the room, and then speak clearly, intelligibly, without stammering, so that I can understand you.'

Kasper took out his dog and returned with his hat off.

'Ah well!' said Pétrus, seeing him silent. 'What's going on?'

'What's going on is that the "ghost" has appeared again in the ruins of Geierstein!'

'Ah! I suspected it. Did you get a good look at it?'

'Very good, Mr Burgomaster.'

'Without shutting your eyes?'

'Yes, Mr Burgomaster. I had my eyes wide open. It was a fine moonlit night.'

'What shape did it have?'

'That of a small man.'

'Good!' And turning towards a glass door on his left, 'Katel!' the burgomaster shouted.

An old female servant half-opened the door.

'Sir?'

'I am going to take a walk on the hill. You will wait for me till ten o'clock. Here is the key.'

'Yes, master.'

Then the old soldier took down a gun from above the door, checked its priming, and slung it across his shoulder; then addressing Kasper Boeck: 'You will alert the constable to meet me in the small holly bush lane behind the mill,' he said. 'Your "ghost" must be some marauder . . . but if it turns out to be a fox, I will have myself a magnificent hat with long flaps made of it.'

Mauerer and the humble Kasper went out. The weather was splendid, the stars clear and innumerable. While the shepherd went and knocked at the constable's door, the burgomaster disappeared up a small lane of alder trees, which wound its way behind the old church. Two minutes later Kasper and the constable Hans Goerner, a pistol at his hip, ran to join Master Pétrus in the holly-lined lane. The three of them proceeded together to the ruins of Geierstein.

These ruins, situated some twenty minutes from the village, seemed quite insignificant; they were some pieces of dilapidated walls, four to six feet high, which stretched out in the midst of the heather. Archaeologists call them the aqueducts of Seranus, the Roman camp of the Holderlock, or the remains of Théodoric, according to their whim. The only thing which was really remarkable in these ruins was the stairway of a chamber hewn from the rock.

In a manner contrary to spiral stairs, instead of concentric circles narrowing at each step, the spiral of this one got wider, so that the bottom of the cistern was three times wider than the entrance. Was it a whim of architecture, or rather some other reason which gave rise to this bizarre structure? Little does it matter! The fact is that there resulted from it in the cistern this vague roaring such as can be heard by pressing a seashell to one's ear, and that one can hear the steps of the travellers on the gravel, the stirring of the air, the rustling of the leaves, and even the distant words of those passing along at the foot of the hill.

And so our three characters climbed the little path, between the vines and the kitchen-gardens of Hirchwiller.

'I can see nothing,' said the burgomaster, raising his nose mockingly.

'Nor I,' repeated the constable, imitating the tone of the other.

'It is in the hole,' murmured the shepherd.

'We shall see, we shall see,' took up the burgomaster.

Thus it was that after a quarter of an hour they arrived at the entrance to the chamber. The night was bright, clear, and perfectly calm. As far as the eye could see the moon outlined nocturnal landscapes of bluish lines, studded with slender trees, whose shadows seem sketched in black pencil. The heather and the broom in blossom perfumed the air with their sharp smell and the frogs of a neighbouring pool sang their full-throated chorus, interrupted with silences. But all these details escaped our fine countrymen. Their sole thoughts were of catching the 'spirit'.

When they reached the stair, all three stopped and listened, then looked into the darkness. Nothing appeared, nothing stirred.

'Confound it,' said the burgomaster. 'We have forgotten to bring a candle. You go down, Kasper, you know the way better than me. I'll follow.'

At this suggestion the shepherd stepped back suddenly. If left to his own devices the poor man would have taken flight. His woeful countenance made the burgomaster burst out laughing.

'Ah well, Hans, since he doesn't want to go down, you show me the way,' he said to the constable.

'But, master burgomaster,' said the latter, 'you are well aware that there are steps missing. We would risk breaking our necks!'

'Well then, what are we to do?'

'Yes, what are we to do?'

'Send your dog,' resumed Pétrus.

The shepherd whistled for his dog, showed him the stairs, urged him down; but he was no more willing than the rest to try his luck.

At that moment a bright idea struck the constable.

'Hey, Mr Burgomaster,' he said. 'If you were to fire a shot into it . . .'

'Indeed,' exclaimed the other, 'you are right. One will see clearly, at least.'

And without hesitation the good fellow approached the stair, levelling his gun.

But because of the acoustic effect described earlier, the 'spirit', the marauder, the individual, who was actually in the chamber, had heard everything. The idea of being shot at didn't appeal to him, for in a piercing, high-pitched voice he shouted out: 'Stop! Don't shoot! I'm coming up!'

Then the three dignitaries looked at each other, chuckling, and the burgomaster, leaning forward again into the opening, exclaimed in a coarse voice: 'Hurry up, you rogue, or I'll shoot! Hurry up!'

He cocked his gun. The click appeared to hasten the ascent of the mysterious character. Stones could be heard rolling. However it took another minute before he appeared, the chamber being over sixty feet deep.

What was this man doing in the midst of such darkness? He must be some great criminal! Thus at least thought Pétrus Mauerer and his assistants.

At last a vague shape emerged from the shadow, then slowly a small man, four and a half feet tall at the most, thin, in rags, his face wizened and yellow, his eyes sparkling like those of a magpie and his hair untidy, came out shouting:

'What right have you to come and trouble my studies, you wretches?'

This grandiloquence hardly matched his clothes and his appearance, so the indignant burgomaster replied: 'Try and show some respect, you rogue, or I'll start by giving you a thrashing.'

'A thrashing!' said the little man, hopping with anger and standing right under the burgomaster's nose.

'Yes,' resumed the former, who couldn't help but admire the courage of the pygmy, 'if you don't answer satisfactorily the questions that I am going to put to you. I am the burgomaster of Hirchwiller, here is the village constable and the shepherd with his dog. We are stronger than you . . . be sensible and tell me who you are, what you are doing here, and why you don't dare appear in broad daylight. Then we can see what shall be done with you.'

'All that's none of your business,' answered the little man in his curt voice. 'I shall not answer you.'

'In that case, march,' said the burgomaster, grasping him by the nape of the neck. 'You'll spend the night in prison.'

The little man struggled but in vain. Completely exhausted, he said (not without some nobility), 'Let me go, sir. I yield to force. I shall follow you.'

The burgomaster, who wasn't lacking in manners himself, became calmer in his turn.

'Your word?' he said.

'My word!'

'Fine . . . Quick march!'

And that is how on the night of 29 July 1835 the burgomaster captured a small red-haired man, as he emerged from the cave of Geierstein.

On their return to Hirchwiller, the vagabond was double-locked in, not forgetting the outside bolt and the padlock. Afterwards everyone went to recover from their exertions. Pétrus Mauerer, once in bed, pondered over this strange adventure till midnight.

The next day, about nine o'clock, Hans Goerner, the constable, having received orders to bring the prisoner to the town-hall, so that he could undergo a new examination, went with four sturdy lads to the cell. They opened the door, quite curious to look at the will-o'-the-wisp. They saw him hanging by his tie from the bars of the skylight. Several say that he was still kicking . . . others that he was already stiff. Whichever it was, someone ran off to get Pétrus Mauerer, to inform him of the fact. What is certain is that at the arrival of the latter, the little man had breathed his last.

The magistrate and the doctor of Hirchwiller drew up a formal report of the catastrophe. The unknown man was buried and all was settled.

Now about three weeks after these events, I went to see my cousin Pétrus Mauerer. I am his closest relative and, consequently, his heir. This circumstance maintains an intimate relationship between us. We were dining together, chatting of this and that, when the burgomaster told me the little story as I have just related it.

'It's strange, cousin,' I said to him, 'really strange. And you have no other information on this unknown man?'

'None.'

'Have you found anything that could put you on the track of his intentions?'

'Absolutely nothing, Christian.'

'But after all, what could he have been doing in the chamber? What was he living on?'

The burgomaster shrugged his shoulders, filled our glasses, and answered me: 'Your health, cousin.'

'And yours.'

We remained silent for some moments. It was impossible for me to accept the sudden end of the adventure. In spite of myself I gloomily pondered over the sad fate of certain men who appear and disappear in this world, like the grass in the fields, without leaving the slightest memory or the slightest regret.

'Cousin,' I resumed, 'how long would it take from here to the ruins of Geierstein?'

'Twenty minutes at the most. Why?'

'Because I would like to see them.'

'You know that today we have a meeting of the town council and I cannot accompany you.'

'Oh! I shall be able to find them on my own.'

'No, the constable shall show you the way, he has nothing better to do.' My dear cousin called his servant.

'Katel, get Hans Goerner . . . make him hurry up . . . It's two o'clock. I must go.'

The servant went out and the constable wasn't long in coming. He received orders to guide me to the ruins.

While the burgomaster was making his way solemnly to the council chamber, we were already going up the hill. Hans Goerner pointed out the remains of the aqueduct. At this point the rocky ridges of the plateau, the bluish distances of the Hundsrück, the dismal dilapidated walls, covered in a dark ivy, the tolling of the bell of Hirchwiller, summoning the dignitaries to the meeting, the constable panting, clinging to the brush- wood . . . took on in my eyes a sad, harsh hue. It was the story of this poor hanged man which stained the horizon.

The stairway to the chamber appeared very strange, its spiral elegant. The prickly bushes in the clefts of each step, the deserted appearance of the surroundings, all were in harmony with my sadness. We descended. Soon the bright point of the opening which seemed to grow narrower and narrower and to assume the form of a star with curved rays, alone sent us its pale light.

When we reached the bottom of the chamber what a superb view awaited us of those stairs lit up underneath, throwing their shadows with wonderful regularity. Then I heard the buzzing which Pétrus had told me about; the huge granite conch had as many echoes as stones!

'Since the little man, has anyone come down here?' I asked the constable.

'No, sir. The peasants are afraid. They think that the hanged man will return.'

'And you?'

'Me, I'm not curious.'

'But the magistrate . . . his duty was . . .'

'Humph! What would he be doing in the "Owl's Ear"?'

'They call this the Owl's Ear?'

'Yes.'

'It is almost that,' I said, looking up. 'This inverted vault forms the outer ear very well, the underneath part of the steps represents the drum, and the bends of the stairway the cochlea, the labyrinth and the opening of the ear. That then explains the murmuring that we can hear: we are at the bottom of a colossal ear.'

'That is very possible,' said Hans Goerner, who seemed to understand nothing of my observations.

We were on our way back up. I had already taken the first steps when I felt something snap beneath my foot. I bent down to see what it could be and I noticed at the same time a white object in front of me. It was a sheet of torn paper. As for the hard matter that had been pulverized, I recognized a sort of pot made of glazed stoneware.

'Ho! Ho!' I said to myself, 'this will be able to throw some light on the burgomaster's story for us.'

And I joined Hans Goerner, who was by now waiting for me at the kerb of the cistern.

'Now, sir,' he shouted to me, 'where would you like to go?'

'First of all let us sit down a little, we shall see presently.'

And I found a place on a large stone, while the constable let his hawk-like eyes gaze all around the village, to discover marauders in the gardens, if there were any.

I carefully examined the stoneware vessel, of which no more than a fragment remained. This fragment took the shape of a funnel, lined with down on the inside. It was impossible for me to make out its purpose. Next I read the piece of paper, which was written on in a very steady hand. I transcribe it here according to the text. It seems to be a continuation of another sheet, for which I have since searched in the vicinity of the ruin, but in vain.

My 'microeartrumpet' has therefore the double advantage of multiplying ad infinitum the intensity of sounds, and of being able to fit the ear, which in no way impedes the observer. You cannot imagine, my dear master, the charm that one feels on hearing these thousands of imperceptible sounds which, on fine summer days, blend into one mighty buzzing. The bee has his song like the nightingale, the wasp is the warbler of the mosses, the cicada is the lark of the tall grasses, in this the mite is the wren – it has only a sigh, but this sigh is melodious!

This discovery which, from the sentimental point of view, makes us live the life of universal nature, surpasses in its importance all that I could say about it.

After so many sufferings, privations, and worries how happy it is in the end to gather the rewards of our labours! With what leaps the soul rises up to the divine author of these microscopic worlds, whose splendour is revealed to us. What then are these long hours of anguish, hunger, scorn which overwhelmed us in the past? Nothing, sir, nothing! Tears of gratitude wet our eyes. One is proud to have bought through suffering new joys for humanity and to have contributed to its improvement. But however vast, however admirable are the first results of my 'microeartrumpet', its advantages are not limited to that alone. There are others more positive, more material in some respects, and which can be translated into figures.

Just as the telescope causes us to discover myriads

of worlds, completing their harmonious revolutions in the infinite, so too my 'microeartrumpet' extends the sense of hearing beyond all the limits of possibility. Thus, sir, I shall not stop at the circulation of the blood and vital fluids in the living body; you hear them running with the impulsiveness of cataracts, you perceive them with a distinctness which terrifies you, the slightest irregularity in the pulse, the lightest obstacle strikes you and has on you the effect of a rock against which break the waves of a torrent.

It is undoubtedly a tremendous conquest for the development of our physiological and pathological knowledge, but it is not on this point that I insist.

By pressing your ear to the ground you hear the hot springs surging at immeasurable depths, you assess their volume, the currents, the obstacles.

Would you like to go any further? Enter an underground chamber sufficiently large to pick up a considerable quantity of sounds; then, at night, when all is asleep, when nothing disturbs the inner sounds of our globe, listen!

Sir, all that it is possible for me to tell you at present, because in the midst of my abject misery, my privations, and often my despair, I have only a few lucid moments left to gather together geological observations, all that I can assert for you is that the bubbling incandescent lava, the glow of boiling substances is something terrifying and sublime, and which can only be compared to the impression of the astronomer sounding the endless depths of the universe with his telescope.

However, I must admit that these impressions need to be studied further and classified methodically, so as to draw from them fixed conclusions. Consequently as soon as you condescend, my dear and worthy master, to send to me at Neustadt the small sum that I ask to provide for my basic needs, we shall see that we agree

with a view to establishing three subterranean obser-
vatories, one in the valley of Catania, the other in
Iceland, and the third in one of the valleys of Capac-
Uren, Songay, or Cayembé-Uren, the deepest of the
Cordilleras, and as a consequence . . .

Here the letter stopped.

I was dumbfounded. Had I read the ideas of a madman,
or rather the fulfilled inspirations of a genius? What was I
to say? or think? Thus this man, this wretch, living at the
bottom of a den like a fox, dying of hunger, had perhaps
been one of those chosen people, whom the Supreme Being
sends to earth, to enlighten future generations.

And this man had hanged himself out of disgust and
despair! His request had not been answered when he only
asked for a piece of bread in exchange for his discovery. It
was horrible.

A long time, a very long time, I stayed there, dreaming,
thanking heaven for having limited my intelligence to the
everyday needs for life, for not having wanted to make
myself superior to the common crowd. Finally the constable
seeing me staring, my mouth wide open, ventured to touch
my shoulder: 'M. Christian,' he said to me, 'look it is getting
late. The burgomaster must have returned from the meeting.'

'Ah! That's right!' I exclaimed, crumpling up the paper.
'On our way.'

We climbed down the hill again.

My worthy cousin received me, his face beaming, on the
threshold of his house: 'Well, well! Christian! Have you
found anything of this idiot who hanged himself?'

'No.'

'As I suspected. He was some madman who escaped from
Stefansfeld or elsewhere. Indeed he did well to hang himself.
When one is good for nothing, it's the simplest thing.'

The following day I left Hirchwiller. I shall never go back.

THE WHITE AND THE BLACK

I

At that time we passed our evenings at Brauer's alehouse, which opens upon the square of Vieux-Brisach. After eight o'clock there used to drop in, one by one, Frederick Schultz the notary; Frantz Martin the burgomaster, Christopher Ulmett the magistrate; the counsellor Klers; the engineer Rothan; the young organist Theodore Blitz; and some others of the chief townsfolk, who all sat around the same table and drank their foaming *bok-bier* like brothers.

The apparition of Theodore Blitz, who came to us from Jena with a letter of recommendation from Harmosius – his dark eyes, his brown dishevelled hair, his thin white nose, his metallic voice, and his mystic ideas – occasioned us some little disquiet. It used to trouble us to see him rise abruptly and pace two or three times up and down the room, gesticulating the while, mocking with a strange air the Swiss landscapes with which the walls were adorned – lakes of indigo-blue, mountains of an apple-green, paths of brilliant red. Then he would seat himself down again, empty his glass at a gulp, and commence a discussion about the music of Palestrina, about the lute of the Hebrews, about the introduction of the organ into our churches, about the shophar, the sabbatic epochs, etc. He would knit his brows, plant his sharp elbows on the edge of the table, and lose himself in deep thought. Yes, he perplexed us not a little – we others who were grave and accustomed to methodical ideas. However, it was necessary to put up with it; and the engineer Rothan himself, in spite of his bantering spirit, in the end grew calm and no longer continued to contradict the young organist when he was right.

Theodore Blitz was plainly one of those nervously organised beings who are affected by every change of temperature. The year of which I speak was extremely warm; we had several heavy storms towards the autumn, and folk began to fear for the wine harvest.

One evening all our little world was gathered, according to custom, around the table, with the exception of the magistrate Ulmett and the organist. The burgomaster talked about the weather and great hydraulic works. As for me I listened to the wind gamboling without amongst the plane-trees of the Schlossgarten, to the drip of the water from the spouts, and to its dashing against the windows. From time to time one could hear a tile blown off a roof, a door shut to with a bang, a shutter beat against a wall. Then would arise the great clamour of the storm, sweeping, sighing, and groaning in the distance, as if all the invisible powers were seeking and calling on one another in the darkness, while living things hid themselves, sitting in corners, in order to escape a fearful meeting with them.

From the church of Saint-Landolphe nine o'clock sounded, when Blitz hurriedly entered, shaking his hat like one possessed, and saying in his husky voice: 'Surely the Evil One is about his work! The white and the black are having a tussle. The nine times nine thousand nine hundred and ninety thousand spirits of Envy battle and tear themselves. Go, Ahriman! Walk! Ravage! Lay waste! The Amschaspands are in flight! Oromage veils her face! What a time, what a time!'

And so saying he walked round the room, stretching his long skinny limbs, and laughing by jerks.

We were all astounded at such an entry, and for some seconds no one spoke a word. Then, however, the engineer Rothan, led on by his caustic humour, said: 'What nonsense is that you are singing there, M. Organist? What do Amschaspands signify to us? or the nine times nine thousand nine hundred and ninety thousand spirits of Envy? Ha! ha! ha! It is really comic. Where on earth did you pick up such strange language?'

Theodore Blitz stopped suddenly short in his walk and shut one eye, while the other, wide open, shone with a diabolic irony.

When Rothan had finished: 'Oh, engineer,' said he; 'oh! sublime spirit, master of the trowel, and mortar, director of stones, he who orders right angles, angles acute, angles obtuse, you are right – a hundred times right.'

He bent himself with a mocking air, and went on: 'Nothing exists but matter – the level, the rule, and the compass. The revelations of Zoroaster, of Moses, of Pythagoras, of Odin – the harmony, the melody, art, sentiment, they are all dreams, unworthy of an enlightened intellect such as yours. To you belongs the truth, the eternal truth. Ha! ha! ha! I bow myself before you: I salute you; I prostrate myself before your glory, imperishable as that of Nineveh and of Babylon.'

Finishing his speech, he made two little turns on his heels, and uttered a laugh so piercing that it was more like the crowing of a cock at daybreak.

Rothan was getting angry, when at the moment the old magistrate Ulmett came in, his head protected by a great otter-skin cap, his shoulders covered by his bottle-green greatcoat bordered with fox-skin. His hands hung down beside him, his back was bent, his eyes were half-closed, his big nose was red, and his large cheeks were wet with rain. He was as wet as a drake.

Outside the rain fell in torrents, the gutters gushed over, the spouts disgorged themselves, and the ditches were swollen into little rivers.

'Ah, heavens!' cried the good fellow. 'Perhaps it was foolish to come out on such a night, and after such work too – two inquests, verbal processes, interrogatories! The *bok-bier* and old friends, though, would make me swim across the Rhine.'

And muttering these words he put off his otter-skin cap and opened his great pelisse to take out his long tobacco-pipe and his pouch, which he carefully laid down upon the table. After that he hung his greatcoat and his hat up beside the window, and called out: 'Brauer!'

'Well, M. Magistrate, what do you want?'

'You would do well to put to the shutters. Believe me, this storm will wind up with some thunder.'

The innkeeper went out and put the shutters to, and the old magistrate, sitting down in his corner, heaved a deep sigh.

'You know what has happened, burgomaster?' he asked in a solemn voice.

'No. What has occurred, my old Christopher?'

Before he replied M. Ulmett threw a glance around the room.

'We are here alone, my friends,' said he, 'so I am able to tell you. About three o'clock this afternoon some one found poor Gredel Dick under the sluice of the miller at Holderloch.'

'Under the sluice at Holderloch?' cried all.

'Yes; a cord round her neck.'

In order to understand how these words affected us it is necessary that you should know that Gredel Dick was one of the prettiest girls in Vieux-Brisach; a tall brunette, with blue eyes and red cheeks; the only daughter of an old anabaptist, Petrus Dick, who farmed considerable portions of the Schlossgarten. For some time she had seemed sad and melancholy – she who had beforetime been so merry in the morning at the washing-place, and in the evening at the well in the midst of her friends. She had been seen crying, and her sorrow had been ascribed to the incessant pursuit of her by Saphéri Mutz, the postmaster's son – a big fellow, thin, vigorous, with an aquiline nose and curling black hair.

He followed her like a shadow, and never let her off his arm at the dances.

There had been some talk about their marriage, but old Mutz, his wife, Karl Bremer his son-in-law, and his daughter Saffayel, were opposed to the match, all agreeing that a 'heathen' should not be introduced into the family.

For three days past nothing had been seen of Gredel. No one knew what had become of her. You may imagine the thousand different thoughts which crowded upon us when we heard that she was dead. No one thought any longer of the discussion between Theodore Blitz and the engineer Rothan touching invisible spirits. All eyes were fixed on M. Christopher Ulmett, who, his large bald head bent, his heavy white eyebrows knit, gravely filled his pipe, with a meditative air.

'And Mutz – Saphéri Mutz?' asked the burgomaster. 'What has become of him?'

A slight flush coloured the cheeks of the old man as he answered, after some seconds of thought: 'Saphéri Mutz? He has gone.'

'Gone!' cried little Klers. 'Then he acknowledges his guilt?'

'It certainly seems so to me,' said the old magistrate simply. 'One does not scamper off for nothing. As for the rest, we have searched his father's place, and found all the house upset. The folk seemed struck with consternation. The mother raved and tore her hair; the daughter wore her Sunday clothes, and danced about like a fool. It was impossible to get anything out of them. As to Gredel's father, the poor fellow is in the deepest despair. He does not wish to say anything against his child, but it is certain that Gredel Dick left the farm of her own accord on Tuesday last in order to meet Saphéri. The fact is attested by all the neighbours. Now the gendarmes are scouring the country. We shall see, we shall see!'

Then there was a long silence. Outside the rain fell heavily.

'It is abominable!' cried the burgomaster suddenly.

'Abominable! To think that every father of a family, even such as bring up their children in the fear of God, are exposed to such misfortunes.'

'Yes,' replied Ulmett, lighting his pipe. 'It is so. They say, no doubt rightly, that heaven orders all things; but the spirit of darkness seems to me to meddle a good deal more than is necessary in them. For one good fellow how many villains do we find, without faith or law? And for one good action how many evil ones? I tell you, my friends, if the Evil One were to count his flock—'

He had not time to finish, for at that moment a terrific flash of lightning glared in through the chinks of the shutters, making the lamp burn dim. It was immediately followed by a clap of thunder, crashing, jerky – one of those claps which make you tremble. One might have thought that the world was coming to an end.

The clock of the church of Saint-Landolphe just then struck the half-hour. The tolling bells seemed to be just hard by one. From far, very far off, there came a trembling plaintive voice, crying: 'Help! Help!'

'Some one cries for help,' said the burgomaster.

'Yes,' said the others, turning pale, and listening.

While we were all thus in fright, Rothan, curling his lips in a joking fashion, broke out: 'Ha! ha! ha! It is Mademoiselle Roesel's cat singing its love story to Monsieur Roller, the young first tenor.'

Then dropping his voice and lifting his hand with a tragic gesture, he went on: 'The time has sounded from the belfry of the chateau!'

'Ill-luck to those who laugh at such a cry,' said old Christopher, rising.

He went towards the door with a solemn step, and we all followed him, even the fat innkeeper, who held his cotton cap in his hand and murmured a prayer very low. Rothan alone did not stir from his seat. As for me, I was behind the others, with outstretched neck, looking over their shoulders.

The glass door was scarcely opened when there came another flash of lightning. The street, with its white flags washed by the rain, its flushed gutters, its multitude of windows, its old gables, its signboards, glared out from the night, and then was swallowed up in the darkness.

That glance of the eye allowed me to see the steeple of Saint-Landolphe with its innumerable little carvings all clothed in white light. In the steeple were the bells hanging to black beams, with their clappers, and their ropes hanging down to the body of the church. Below that was a stork's nest, half torn in pieces by the wind – the young ones with their beaks out, the mother at her wits' end, her wings extended, while the male-bird flew about the shining steeple, his breast thrown forward, his neck bent, his long legs thrown out behind as if defying the thunder peals.

It was a strange sight, a veritable Chinese picture – thin, delicate, light, something strange, terrible, upon a black background of clouds broken with streaks of gold.

We stood, with open mouths, upon the threshold of the inn, and asked: 'What did you hear, M. Ulmett? What can you see, M. Klers?'

At that moment a lugubrious mewing commenced above us, and a whole regiment of cats set to work springing about in the gutter. At the same time a peal of laughter filled the room—

'Ah well! ah well!' cried the engineer. 'Do you hear them? Was I wrong?'

'It was nothing,' murmured the old magistrate. 'Thank heaven, it was nothing. Let us go in again. The rain is recommencing.'

As we took our places again, he said: 'Is it astonishing, M. Rothan, that the imagination of a poor old fellow, such as myself, goes astray at a time when earth and heaven confound themselves, while good and bad are struggling together, while such mysterious crimes occur around us even at this day? Is it strange?'

We all took our places with a feeling of annoyance with the engineer, who had alone remained quiet, and had seen us disconcerted. We turned our backs on him as we emptied our glasses without saying a word, while he, his elbow on the edge of the window-ledge, hummed between his teeth I know not what military march, the time of which he beat with his fingers on the ledge, without deigning to notice our ill-humour.

So things went on for some minutes, when Theodore Blitz said laughingly: 'Monsieur Rothan triumphs. He does not believe in invisible spirits. Nothing troubles him. He has a good foot, good eye, and good ear. What more is wanting to convict us of ignorance and folly?'

'Ha,' replied Rothan, 'I should not have dared to say it, but you express things so well, Monsieur Organist, that one cannot disagree with you, especially in any matter that concerns yourself. As for my old friends Schultz, Ulmett, Klers, and the others, it is different, very different. Any one may at times be led astray by a dream, only one must see that it does not become a custom.'

Instead of answering to this direct attack, Blitz, his head bent down, seemed to be listening to some noise without.

'Hush,' said he, looking at us. 'Hush.'

He lifted his finger, and the expression of his face was so striking that we all listened with an indefinable feeling of fear.

The same instant heavy steps were heard in the street without; a hand was laid on the catch of the door, and the organist said to us in a trembling voice: 'Be calm – listen and see. Heaven be with us.'

The door opened and Saphéri Mutz appeared.

Should I live to be a thousand years old the figure of that man will never be erased from my memory. He is there – I see him. He advances reeling, pale – his hair hanging about his face – his eye dull, glassy – his blouse tight to his body – a big stick in his hand. He looks upon us without seeing us, like a man in a dream. A winding track of mud is left behind him. He stops, coughs, and says in a low voice, as if speaking to himself: 'Well! what if they arrest me! What if they kill me! I would rather be here!'

Then, recollecting himself, and looking at us, one after another, he cried with a movement of terror: 'I have spoken! What did I say? Ah! the burgomaster – the magistrate Ulmett.'

He made a bound as if he would fly, and I know not what he saw in the darkness of the night without which drove him once more from it into the room.

Theodore Blitz slowly arose. After he had looked at us, he walked up to Mutz, and, with an air of confidence, he asked him in a low voice, pointing to the dark street: 'Is it there?'

'Yes,' said the man, in the same mysterious tone.

'It follows you?'

'From Fischbach.'

'Behind you?'

'Yes, behind me.'

'That is so, it is surely so,' said the organist, throwing another look upon us. 'It is always thus. Well then, stop here, Saphéri; sit down by the fire. Brauer, go and look for the gendarmes.'

At the word gendarmes the wretched fellow grew fearfully pale, and seemed to think again of flight, but the same horror beat him back once more, and he sank down at the corner of a table, his head between his hands.

'Oh! had I but known – had I but known!' he moaned.

We were more dead than alive. The innkeeper went out. Not a breath was heard in the room. The old magistrate had put down his pipe, the burgomaster looked at me with a stupefied air. Rothan no longer whistled. Theodore Blitz, sitting at the end of a bench, looked at the rain streaking the darkness.

So we remained for a quarter of an hour, fearful all the

time that the man would take it into his head to attempt to fly. But he did not stir. His long hair coiled from between his fingers, and the rain dripped from his clothes on to the floor.

At length the clatter of arms was heard without, and the gendarmes Werner and Keltz appeared upon the step. Keltz, darting a side glance at the man, lifted his great hat, saying: 'Good evening, Monsieur Magistrate.'

Then he came in and coolly put the handcuffs on Saphéri's wrists, while Saphéri covered his face with his hands.

'Come, follow me, my son,' said he. 'Werner close up.'

A third gendarme, short and fat, appeared in the darkness, and all the troop set off.

The wretched man made no resistance.

We looked at one another's pale faces.

'Good evening, gentlemen,' said the organist, and he went off.

Then each of us, lost in his own thoughts, rose and departed to his home in silence.

As for me, I turned my head more than twenty times before I came to my door, fearful that I should see the *other* that had followed Saphéri Mutz ready to lay its hands upon me.

And when at last, thank heaven, I was safe in my room, before I got into bed and blew out my light I took the wise precaution of looking under my bed to convince myself that *it* was not hidden there. I even said a prayer that *it* would not strangle me during the night. Well, what then? One is not a philosopher at all times.

II

Until then I considered Theodore Blitz as a species of visionary imbecile. His maintaining the possibility of holding correspondence with invisible spirits by means of the music composed by all the sounds of nature, by the rustling of the leaves, by the murmur of the winds, by the hum of the insects, had appeared to me very ridiculous, and I was not the only one in that opinion.

It seemed all very well to tell us that if the grave sound of the organ awoke in us religious sentiments, that if martial music swept us on to war, and the simple melodies led us into reveries, it was because the different melodies were the invocation of the genii of the earth, who came suddenly into our midst, acted on our organs, and made us participants of their own proper essence. All that, however, appeared to me to be very obscure, and I had never doubted that the organist was just a little mad.

Now, however, my opinions changed respecting him. I said to myself that man is not a purely material being, that we are composed of body and soul; that to attribute all to the body, and to endeavour to ascribe all significance to it, is not rational; that the nervous fluid, agitated by the undulations of the air, is almost as difficult to comprehend as the direct action of occult powers; that we know not how it is that even a mere tickling of our ears, regulated by the rules of counter points, excites in us a thousand agreeable or terrible emotions, elevates the soul to heaven, melts us, awakens in us the ardour of life, enthusiasm, love, fear, pity. No, the first theory was not satisfactory. The ideas of the organist appeared to me more sublime, more weighty, more just, and more acceptable, looking at things all round.

Then how could one explain, by means of mere nervous sensation, the arrival of Saphéri Mutz at the inn; how could one explain the terror of the unhappy man, which forced him to yield himself up; and the marvellous foresight of Blitz when he said to us: 'Hush! Listen! He comes! Heaven be with us!'

In the end all my prejudices against an invisible world disappeared, and new facts occurred to confirm me in this fresh manner of thinking.

About five days after the scene I have described, Saphéri Mutz had been transported by the gendarmes to the prison of Stuttgart. The thousand tales which had been set afloat respecting the death of Gredel Dick died away. The poor girl slept in peace at the back of the hill of the Trois-Fontaines, and folk were busied in looking after the wine harvest.

One evening about nine o'clock, as I left the great warehouse of the custom-house – where I had been tasting some samples of wine on behalf of Brauer, who had more confidence in my judgment in such a matter than in his own – my head a little heavy, I chanced to direct my steps towards the great Alley des Plantanes, behind the church of Saint-Landolphe.

The Rhine displayed to my right its azure waters, in which some fishermen were letting down their nets. To my left rose the old fortifications of the town. The air began to grow cool; the river murmured its eternal song; the fir trees of the Black Forest were softly ruffled; and as I walked on the sound of a violin fell on my ear.

I listened.

The black-headed linnet never threw more grace, more delicacy, into the execution of his rapid trills, nor more enthusiasm into the stream of his inspiration. It was like nothing I had heard. It had no repose, no measure. It was a torrent of notes, delirious, admirably symphonising, but void of order or method.

Then, clashing with the thread of the inspiration, came some sharp incisive notes, piercing the ear.

'Theodore Blitz is here,' said I to myself, putting aside the high branches of an elder hedge at the foot of a slope.

I looked around me, and my eyes fell upon a horse-pond covered with duck-weed, where the big frogs showed their flat noses. A little farther off rose some stables, with their big sheds, and an old dwelling-house. In the court, surrounded by a wall breast-high in which was a worm-eaten door, walked five or six fowls, and under the great stall ran the rabbits, their croups in the air, their tails up. When they saw me they disappeared under the gate of the grange like shadows.

No noise save the flow of the river and the bizarre fantasy of the violin could be heard.

Where on earth was Theodore Blitz?

The idea occurred to me that he was perhaps making trial of his music on the family of the Mutzes, and, curiosity impelling me, I glided into a hiding-place beside the wall to see what would happen in the farm.

The windows were all wide open, and in a room on the ground floor, long, with brown beams, level with the court, I perceived a long table furnished with all the sumptuousness of a village feast. Twenty or thirty covers were there. But what most astonished me was to see but five persons in front of this grand display. There was old Mutz, sombre and thoughtful, clad in a suit of black velvet with metal buttons. His large osseous head, grey, his forehead contracted in fixed thought, his eyes sunken, staring before him. There was the son-in-law, thin, insignificant, the neck of his shirt coming up almost to his ears. There was the mother in a great tulle cap, with a distracted look; the daughter – a rather pretty brunette – in a cap of black taffeta with spangles of gold and silver, her bosom covered with a silk neckerchief of a thousand colours. Lastly, there was Theodore Blitz, his three-cornered hat over his ear, the violin held between his shoulder and chin, his little eyes sparkling, his cheeks standing out in relief from a deep wrinkle, and his elbows thrown out and drawn in, like a grasshopper scraping its shrill aria on the heath.

The shades of the setting sun, the old clock with its delf dial with red and blue flowers, and above all the music, which grew more and more discordant, produced an indefinable impression upon me. I was seized with a truly panic terror. Was it the effect of my having breathed too long the *rudesheim*? Was it the effect of the pale tints of the falling night? I do not know; but without looking farther I glided away as quietly as possible, bending down, creeping by the wall in order to regain the road, when all of a sudden a large dog darted the length of his chain towards me, and made me utter a cry of surprise.

'Tirik!' cried the old postmaster.

And Theodore, perceiving me, jumped out of the room, crying: 'Ah! it is Christian Species! Come in, my dear Christian! You have come most opportunely.' He strode across the court, and came and took my hands.

'My dear friend,' said he to me, with strange animation. 'This is a time when the *black* and the *white* engage with one another. Come, in come in.'

His excitement frightened me, but he would accept none of my excuses, and dragged me on without my being able to make any resistance.

'You must know, dear Christian,' said he, 'that we have this morning baptized an angel of heaven, the little Nickel Saphéri Brêmer. I have celebrated her coming into the world by the chorus of the "Séraphins". Nevertheless, you may imagine that three-fourths of those who were invited have not come. Ha! ha! ha! Come in then! You will be welcome.'

He pushed me on by the shoulders, and willing or unwilling, I stepped across the threshold.

All the members of the Mutz family turned their heads. I should have liked not to have sat down, but those enthusiasts surrounded me.

'This will be the sixth!' cried Blitz. 'The number six is a good number!'

The old postmaster took my hands with emotion, saying: 'Thanks, Monsieur Species, thanks for having come! They say that honest folk fly from us! That we are abandoned alike by God and by man! You will stop to the end?'

'Yes,' mumbled the old woman, with a supplicating look. 'Surely Monsieur Species will stay to the end. He will not refuse us that?'

Then I understood why the table was set in such grand fashion, and why the guests were so few. All of those invited to the baptism, thinking of Gredel Dick, had made excuses for not coming.

The idea of a like desertion went against my heart.

'Oh, certainly,' I said. 'Certainly! I will stay – with pleasure – with great pleasure!'

The glasses were refilled, and we drank of a rough strong wine, of an old *markobrünner*, the austere flavour of which filled me with melancholy thoughts.

The old woman, putting her long hand upon my shoulder, murmured: 'Just a drop more, Monsieur Species, just a drop more.'

And I dared not say no.

At that moment Blitz, passing his bow over the vibrating cords, made a cold shudder pass through all my limbs.

'This, my friends,' said he, 'is Saul's invocation to the Pythoness.'

I should have liked to run away, but in the court the dog was lamentably howling, the night was coming on, and the room was full of shadows. The harsh features of old Mutz, his keen eyes, the sorrowful compression of his big jaws, did not reassure one.

Blitz went on scraping, scraping away at that invocation of his, with great sweeps of his arm. The wrinkle which ploughed itself deep down his left cheek grew deeper and deeper, the perspiration stood on his forehead.

The postmaster filled up our glasses again, and said to me in a low imperious voice: 'Your health.'

'Yours, Monsieur Mutz,' responded I, trembling.

All of a sudden the child in the cradle commenced to cry, and Blitz, with a diabolical irony, accompanied its shrill wailing with piercing notes, saying: 'It is the hymn of life – ha! ha! ha! Really, little Nickel sings it as if he were already old – ha! ha! ha!'

The old clock at the same time commenced to strike in

its walnut-tree case; and when I raised my eyes, astonished by the noise, I saw a little figure advance from the background, bony, bald, hollow-eyed, a mocking smile on its lips – Death, in short.

He came out a few steps and set himself to gather, by jerks, some bits of flowers painted in green on the edge of the clock-case. Then, at the last stroke of the hour, he turned half round and went back to his den as he had come out.

'Why the deuce did the organist bring me here?' said I to myself. 'This is a nice baptism! And these are merry folk – ha! ha! ha!'

I filled my glass and drank it in order to gain courage.

'Well, let us go on, let us go on. The die is cast. No one escapes his destiny. I was destined before the commencement of the ages to go this evening to the custom-house; to walk in the alley of Saint-Landolphe; to come in spite of myself to this abominable cut-throat place, attracted by the music of Blitz; to drink *markobrünner* which smacks of cypress and vervain; and to see Death gathering painted flowers! Well, it is droll – truly droll!'

So I dreamed, laughing at men who, thinking themselves free, are dragged on by threads attached to the stars. So astrologers have told us, and we must believe them.

I laughed then amongst the shadows as the music ceased.

A great silence fell around. The clock alone broke the stillness with its regular tick-tack; outside the moon, slowly rising over the Rhine, behind the trembling foliage of a poplar, threw its pale light over innumerable ripples. I noticed it, and saw a black boat pass along in the moon's reflected light. On it was a man, all dark like the boat. He had a loose cloak around him, and wore a large hat with a wide brim, from which hung streamers.

He went by like a figure in a dream. I felt my eyelids heavy.

'Let us drink,' cried the organist.

The glasses clattered.

'How well the Rhine sings! It sings the air of Barthold Gouterolf,' said the son-in-law, '*ave-ave-stella!*'

No one made reply.

Far off, far off, we could hear the rhythmic beat of two oars.

'Today,' cried the old postmaster suddenly, in a hoarse voice, 'Saphéri makes expiation.'

No doubt he had long been thinking, thinking of that. It was that which had rendered him so sad. My flesh crept.

'He thinks of his son,' said I to myself, 'of his son who dies today!'

And a cold shiver ran through me.

'His expiation,' cried the daughter with a harsh laugh, 'yes – his expiation!'

Theodore touched my shoulder, and, bending to my ear, said: 'The spirits are coming – they are at hand!'

'If you speak like that,' cried the son-in-law, whose teeth were chattering. 'If you speak like that I shall be off!'

'Go then, go then, coward!' said the daughter. 'No one has need of you.'

'Very well, I will be off,' said he, rising.

And taking his hat off the hook in the wall, he went away with long strides.

I saw him pass rapidly before the windows, and I envied him.

How could I get away?

Something was walking upon the wall in front. I stared – my eyes wide open with surprise, and at length saw that it was a cock. Far off between the old palings the river shone, and its ripples slowly beat upon the sand of the shore. The light upon it danced like a cloud of sea-gulls with great white wings. My head was full of shadows and weird reflections.

'Listen, Peter,' cried the old woman, at the end of a moment. 'Listen, you have been the cause of all that has happened to us.'

'I,' cried the old man huskily, angrily, 'I! of what have I been the cause?'

'Yes,' she went on. 'You never took pity on our lad. You forgave nothing. It was you who prevented his marrying that girl!'

'Woman,' cried the old man, 'instead of accusing others, remember that his blood is on your own head. During twenty years you have done nought but hide his faults from me. When I punished him for his evil disposition, for his temper, for his drunkenness, you – you would console him, you would weep with him, you would secretly give him money, you would say to him, "your father does not love you; he is a harsh man!" And you lied to him that you might have the greater portion of his love. You robbed me of the confidence and respect that a child should have for those who love him and correct him. So then, when he wanted to marry that girl, I had no power to make him obey me.'

'You should have said "yes",' howled the woman.

'But,' said the old man, 'I had rather say no, because my mother, my grandmother, and all the men and women of my family would not be able to receive that pagan in heaven.'

'In heaven,' chattered the woman. 'In heaven!'

And the daughter added in a shrill voice: 'From the earliest time I can remember, our father has only bestowed upon us blows!'

'Because you deserved them,' cried the old man. 'They gave me more pain than they did you.'

'More pain! Ha! ha! ha! more pain!'

At that moment, a hand touched my arm. It was Blitz. A ray of the moon, falling on the window-panes, scattered its light around. His face was white, and his stretched-out hand pointed to the shadows. I followed his finger with my eyes, for he evidently was directing my attention to something, and I saw the most terrible sight of which I have a memory – a shadow, motionless, appeared before the window, against the light surface of the river. This shadow had a man's shape, and seemed suspended between heaven and earth. Its head hung down upon its breast, its elbows stood out square beside the body, and its legs straight down tapered to a point.

As I looked on, my eyes round, wide opened with astonishment, every feature developed in that wan figure. I recognised Saphéri Mutz; and above his bent shoulders I saw the cord, the beam, and the outline of the gibbet. Then, at the foot of this deathly apparition, I saw a white figure, kneeling, with long dishevelled hair. It was Gredel Dick, her hands joined in prayer.

It would seem as though all the others, at the same time, saw that strange apparition as well as myself, for I heard them breathe: 'Heaven! Heaven have mercy on us!'

And the old woman, in a low choking voice, murmured: 'Saphéri is dead!'

She commenced to sob.

And the daughter cried: 'Saphéri! Saphéri!'

Then all disappeared, and Theodore Blitz, taking me by the hand, said: 'Let us go.'

We set off. The night was fine. The leaves fluttered with a sweet murmur.

As we went on, horrified, along the great Alley des Plantanes, a mournful voice from afar off sang upon the river the old German song:

> 'The grave is deep and silent,
> Its borders are terrible!
> It throws a sombre mantle
> It throws a sombre mantle
> Over the kingdom of the dead.'

'Ah!' said Blitz, 'if Gredel Dick had not been there we should have seen the *other* – the fearful one take Saphéri. But she prayed for him! The poor soul! She prayed for him. What is *white* remains *white*!'

The voice afar off, growing feebler and feebler, answered the murmur of the tide:

> 'Death does not find an echo
> For the song of the thrush,
> The roses which grow on the grave,
> The roses which grow on the grave,
> Are the roses of grief.'

The horrible scene which had unfolded itself to my eyes, and that far-off melancholy voice which, growing fainter and fainter, at length died away in the distance, remain with me as a confused mirage of the infinite, of that infinite which pitilessly absorbs us, and engulfs us without possibility of our escape. Some may laugh at the idea of such an infinity, like the engineer Rothan; some may tremble at it, as did the burgomaster; some may groan with a pitiable voice; and others may, like Theodore Blitz, crane themselves over the abyss in order to see what passes in the depths. It all, however, comes to the same thing in the end, and the famous inscription over the temple of Isis is always true:

> I am he that is.
> No one has ever penetrated the mystery
>   which envelops me.
> No one shall ever penetrate it.

THE BURGOMASTER IN BOTTLE

I have always professed the highest esteem, and even a sort of veneration for the Rhine's noble wine; it sparkles like champagne, it warms one like Burgundy, it soothes the throat like Bordeaux, it fires the imagination like the juice of the Spanish grape, it makes us tender and kind like lacryma-christi; and last, but not least, it helps us to dream – it unfolds the extensive fields of fancy before our eyes.

In 1846, towards the end of autumn, I had made up my mind to perform a pilgrimage to Johannisberg. Mounted on a wretched hack, I had arranged two tin flasks along his hollow ribs, and I made the journey by short stages.

What a fine sight a vintage is! One of my flasks was always empty, the other always full; when I quitted one vineyard, there was the prospect of another before me. But it quite troubled me that I had not any one capable of appreciating it to share this enjoyment with me.

Night was closing in one evening; the sun had just disappeared, but one or two stray rays were still lingering among the large vine-leaves. I heard the trot of a horse behind me. I turned a little to the left to allow him to pass me, and to my great surprise I recognised my friend Hippel, who as soon as he saw me uttered a shout of delight.

You are well acquainted with Hippel, his fleshy nose, his mouth especially adapted to the sense of taste, and his rotund stomach. He looked like old Silenus in the pursuit of Bacchus. We shook hands heartily.

The aim of Hippel's journey was the same as mine; in his quality of first-rate connoisseur he wanted to confirm his opinion as to the peculiarities of certain growths about which he still entertained some doubts.

So we continued our route together. Hippel was extremely gay; he traced out our route among the Rhingau vineyards. We halted occasionally to devote our attention to our flasks, and to listen to the silence which reigned around us.

The night was far advanced when we reached a little inn perched on the side of a hill. We dismounted. Hippel peeped through a small window nearly level with the ground. A lamp was burning on a table, and by it sat an old woman fast asleep.

'Hallo!' cried my comrade; 'open the door, mother.'

The old woman started, got up and came to the window, and pressed her shrunken face against the panes. You would have taken it for one of those old Flemish portraits in which ochre and bistre predominate.

As soon as the old sybil could distinguish us she made a grimace intended for a smile, and opened the door for us.

'Come in, gentlemen – come in,' cried she with a tremulous voice; 'I will go and wake my son; sit down – sit down.'

'A feed of corn for our horses and a good supper for ourselves,' cried Hippel.

'Directly, directly,' said the old woman assiduously.

She hobbled out of the room, and we could hear her creeping up stairs as steep as a Jacob's ladder.

We remained for a few minutes in a low smoky room. Hippel hurried to the kitchen, and returned to tell me that he had ascertained there were certain sides of bacon by the chimney.

'We shall have some supper,' said he, patting his stomach; 'yes, we shall get some supper.'

The flooring creaked over our heads, and almost

immediately a powerful fellow with nothing but his trousers on, his chest bare, and his hair in disorder, opened the door, took a step or two forward, and then disappeared without saying a word to us.

The old woman lighted the fire, and the butter began to frizzle in the frying-pan.

Supper was brought in; a ham put on the table flanked by two bottles, one of red wine, the other of white.

'Which do you prefer?' asked the hostess.

'We must try them both first,' replied Hippel, holding his glass to the old woman, who filled it with red.

She then filled mine. We tasted it; it was a strong rough wine. I cannot describe the peculiar flavour it possessed – a mixture of vervain and cypress leaves! I drank a few drops, and my soul became profoundly sad. But Hippel, on the contrary, smacked his lips with an air of satisfaction.

'Good! very good! Where do you get it from, mother?' said he.

'From the hillside close by,' replied the old woman, with a curious smile.

'A very good hillside,' returned Hippel, pouring himself out another glass.

It seemed to me like drinking blood.

'What are you making such faces for, Ludwig?' said he. 'Is there anything the matter with you?'

'No,' I answered, 'but I don't like such red wine as this.'

'There is no accounting for tastes,' observed Hippel, finishing the bottle and knocking on the table.

'Another bottle of the same,' cried he, 'and mind, no mixing, lovely hostess – I am a judge! *Morbleu*! this wine puts life into me, it is so generous.'

Hippel threw himself back in his chair; his face seemed to undergo a complete transformation. I emptied the bottle of white wine at a draught, and then my heart felt gay again. My friend's preference for red wine seemed to me ridiculous but excusable.

We continued drinking, I white and he red wine, till one o'clock in the morning.

One in the morning! It is the hour when Fancy best loves to exercise her influence. The caprices of imagination take that opportunity of displaying their transparent dresses embroidered in crystal and blue, like the wings of the beetle and the dragon-fly.

One o'clock! That is the moment when the music of the spheres tickles the sleeper's ears, and breathes the harmony of the invisible world into his soul. Then the mouse trots about, and the owl flaps her wings, and passes noiselessly over our heads.

'One o'clock,' said I to my companion; 'we must go to bed if we are to set off early tomorrow morning.'

Hippel rose and staggered about.

The old woman showed us into a double-bedded room, and wished us goodnight.

We undressed ourselves; I remained up the last to put the candle out. I was hardly in bed before Hippel was fast asleep; his respiration was like the blowing of a storm. I could not close my eyes, as thousands of strange faces hovered round me. The gnomes, imps, and witches of Walpurgis night executed their cabalistic dances on the ceiling all night. Strange effect of white wine!

I got up, lighted my lamp, and, impelled by curiosity, I went up to Hippel's bed. His face was red, his mouth half-open, I could see the blood pulsating in his temples, and his lips moved as if he wanted to speak. I stood for some time motionless by his side; I tried to see into the depths of his soul, but sleep is an impenetrable mystery; like death, it keeps its secrets.

Sometimes Hippel's face wore an expression of terror, then of sadness, then again of melancholy; occasionally his features contracted; he looked as if he was going to cry.

His jolly face, which was made for laughter, wore a strange expression when under the influence of pain.

What might be passing in those depths? I saw a wave now and then mount to the surface, but whence came those frequent shocks? All at once the sleeper rose, his eyelids opened, and I could see nothing but the whites of his eyes; every muscle in his face was trembling, his mouth seemed to try to utter a scream. Then he fell back, and I heard a sob.

'Hippel! Hippel!' cried I, and I emptied a jug of water on his head.

This awoke him.

'Ah!' cried he, 'God be thanked, it was but a dream. My dear Ludwig, I thank you for awakening me.'

'So much the better, and now tell me what you were dreaming about.'

'Yes, tomorrow; let me sleep now. I am so sleepy.'

'Hippel, you are ungrateful; you will have forgotten it all by tomorrow.'

'*Morbleu*,' replied he, 'I am so sleepy, I must go to sleep; leave me now.'

I would not let him off.

'Hippel, you will have the same dream over again, and this time I shall leave you to your fate.'

These words had the desired effect.

'The same dream over again!' cried he, jumping out of bed. 'Give me my clothes! Saddle my horse! I am off! This is a cursed place. You are right, Ludwig, this is the devil's own dwelling-place. Let us be off!'

He hurried on his clothes. When he was dressed I stopped him.

'Hippel,' said I, 'why should we hurry away? It is only three o'clock. Let us stay quietly here.'

I opened the window, and the fresh night air penetrated the room, and dissipated all his fears. So he leaned on the window-sill, and told me what follows.

'We were talking yesterday about the most famous of the Rhingau vineyards. Although I have never been through this part of the country, my mind was no doubt full of impressions regarding it, and the heavy wine we drank gave a sombre tinge to my ideas. What is most extraordinary, in my dream I fancied I was the burgomaster of Welcke' (a neighbouring village), 'and I was so identified with this personage, that I can describe him to you as minutely as if I was describing myself. This burgomaster was a man of middle height, and almost as fat as I am. He wore a coat with wide skirts and brass buttons; all down his legs he had another row of small nail-headed buttons. On his bald head was a three-cornered cocked hat – in short, he was a stupidly grave man, drinking nothing but water, thinking of nothing but money, and his only endeavour was to increase his property.

'As I had taken the outward appearance of the burgo-master, so had I his disposition also. I, Hippel, should have despised myself could I have recognised myself, what a beast of a burgomaster I was. How far better it is to lead a happy life, without caring for the future, than to heap crowns upon crowns and only distil bile! Well, here I am, a burgomaster.

'When I leave my bed in the morning the first thing which makes me uneasy is to know if the men are already at work among my vines. I eat a crust of bread for breakfast. A crust of bread! what a sordid miser! I who have a cutlet and a bottle of wine every morning! Well, never mind, I take – that is, the burgomaster takes his crust of bread and puts it in his pocket. He tells his old housekeeper to sweep the room and have dinner ready by eleven. Boiled beef and potatoes I think it was – a poor dinner. Well, out he goes.

'I could describe the road he took, the vines on the hill-side, to you exactly,' continued Hippel; 'I see them before me now.

'How is it possible that a man in a dream could conceive such an idea of a landscape? I could see fields, gardens, meadows, and vineyards. I knew this belongs to Pierre, that to Jacques, that to Henri; and then I stopped before one of these bits of ground and said to myself: "Bless me, Jacob's clover is very fine." And farther on, "Bless me, again, that acre of vines would suit me wonderfully." But all the time I felt a sort of giddiness, an indescribable pain in the head. I hurried on, as it was early morning. The sun soon rose, and the heat became oppressive. I was then following a narrow path which crossed through the vines towards the top of the hill. This path led past the ruins of an old castle, and beyond it I could see my four acres of vineyard. I made haste to get there; as I was quite blown when I reached the ruins, I stopped to recover breath, and the blood seemed to ring in my ears, while my heart beat in my breast like a hammer on an anvil. The sun seemed on fire. I tried to go on again, but all at once I felt as if I had received a blow from a club; I rolled under a part of a wall, and I comprehended I had a fit of apoplexy. Then the horror of despair took possession of me. "I am a dead man," said I to myself; "the money I have amassed with so much trouble, the trees I have so carefully cultivated, the house I have built, all, all are lost – all gone into the hands of my heirs. Now those wretches to whom in my lifetime I refused a kreutzer will become rich at my expense. Traitors! how you will rejoice over my misfortune! You will take the keys from my pockets, you will share my property among yourselves, you will squander my gold; and I – I must be present at this spoliation! What a hideous punishment!"

'I felt my spirit quit the corpse, but remain standing by it.

'This spiritual burgomaster noticed that its body had its face blue, and yellow hands.

'It was very hot, and some large flies came and settled on the face of the corpse. One went up his nose. The body stirred not! The whole face was soon covered with them, and the spirit was in despair because it was impotent to drive them away.

'There it stood. There, for minutes which seemed hours.

Hell was beginning for it already. So an hour went by. The heat increased gradually. Not a breath in the air, nor a cloud in the sky.

'A goat came out from among the ruins, nibbling the weeds which were growing up through the rubbish. As it passed my poor body it sprang aside, and then came back, opened its eyes with suspicion, smelt about, and then followed its capricious course over the fallen cornice of a turret. A young goatherd came to drive her back again; but when he saw the body he screamed out, and then set off running towards the village with all his might.

'Another hour passed, slow as eternity. At last a whispering, then steps were heard behind the ruins, and my spirit saw the magistrate coming slowly, slowly along, followed by his clerk and several other persons. I knew every one of them. They uttered an exclamation when they saw me: "It is our burgomaster!"

'The medical man approached the body, and drove away the flies, which flew swarming away. He looked at it, then raised one of the already stiffened arms, and said with the greatest indifference: "Our burgomaster has succumbed to a fit of apoplexy; he has probably been here all the morning. You had better carry him away and bury him as soon as possible, for this heat accelerates decomposition."

'"Upon my word," said the clerk, "between ourselves, he is no great loss to the parish. He was a miser and an ass, and he knew nothing whatever."

'"Yes," added the magistrate, "and yet he found fault with everything."

'"Not very surprising either," said another, "fools always think themselves clever."

'"You must send for several porters," observed the doctor; "they have a heavy burden to carry; this man always had more belly than brains."

'"I shall go and draw up the certificate of death. At what time shall we say it took place?" asked the clerk.

'"Say about four o'clock this morning."

'"The skinflint!" said a peasant, "he was going to watch his workmen to have an excuse for stopping a few sous off their wages on Saturday."

'Then folding his arms and looking at the dead body: "Well, burgomaster," said he, "what does it profit you that you squeezed the poor so hard? Death has cut you down all the same."

'"What has he got in his pocket?" asked one.

'They took out of it my crust of bread.

'"Here is his breakfast!"

'They all began to laugh. Chattering as they were the groups prepared to quit the ruins; my poor spirit heard them a few moments, and then by degrees the noise ceased. I remained in solitude and silence. The flies came back by millions.

'I cannot say how much time elapsed,' continued Hippel, 'for in my dreams the minutes seemed endless. However, at last some porters came; they cursed the burgomaster and carried his carcass away; the poor man's spirit followed them plunged in grief. I went back the same way I came, but this time I saw my body carried before me on a litter. When we reached my house I found many people waiting for me, I recognised male and female cousins to the fourth generation! The bier was set down – they all had a look at me.

'"It is he, sure enough," said one.

'"And dead enough too," rejoined another.

'My housekeeper made her appearance; she clasped her hands together and exclaimed: "Such a fat, healthy man! who could have foreseen such an end? It only shows how little we are."

'And this was my general oration.

'I was carried upstairs and laid on a mattress. When one of my cousins took my keys out of my pocket I felt I should like to scream with rage. But, alas! spirits are voiceless; well, my dear Ludwig, I saw them open my bureau, count my

money, make an estimate of my property, seal up my papers;
I saw my housekeeper quietly taking possession of my best
linen, and although death had freed me from all mundane
wants, I could not help regretting the sous of which I was
robbed.

'I was undressed, and then a shirt was put on me; I was
nailed up in a deal box, and I was, of course, present at my
own funeral.

'When they lowered me into the grave, despair seized
upon my spirit; all was lost! Just then, Ludwig, you awoke
me, but I still fancy I can hear the earth rattling on my
coffin.'

Hippel ceased, and I could see his whole body shiver.

We remained a long time silent, without exchanging a
word; a cock crowing warned us that night was nearly over,
the stars were growing pale at the approach of day; other
cocks' shrill cry could be heard abroad, challenging from the
different farms. A watchdog came out of his kennel to make
his morning rounds, then a lark, half awake only, warbled
a note or two.

'Hippel,' said I to my comrade, 'it is time to be off if we
wish to take advantage of the cool morning.'

'Very true,' said he, 'but before we go I must have a
mouthful of something.'

We went downstairs; the landlord was dressing himself;
when he had put his blouse on he set before us the relics
of our last night's supper; he filled one of my flasks with
white wine, the other with red, saddled our hacks, and
wished us a good journey.

We had not ridden more than half a league when my
friend Hippel, who was always thirsty, took a draught of the
red wine.

'P-r-r-r!' cried he, as if he was going to faint, 'my dream
– my last night's dream!'

He pushed his horse into a trot to escape this vision, which
was visibly imprinted in striking characters on his face; I

followed him slowly, as my poor Rosinante required some consideration.

The sun rose, a pale pink tinge invaded the gloomy blue of the sky, then the stars lost themselves as the light became brighter. As the first rays of the sun showed themselves, Hippel stopped his horse and waited for me.

'I cannot tell you,' said he, 'what gloomy ideas have taken possession of me. This red wine must have some strange properties; it pleases my palate, but it certainly attacks my brain.'

'Hippel,' replied I, 'it is not to be disputed that certain liquors contain the principles of fancy and even of phantasmagoria. I have seen men from gay become sad, and the reverse; men of sense become silly, and the silly become witty, and all arising from a glass or two of wine in the stomach. It is a profound mystery; what man, then, is senseless enough to deny the bottle's magic power? Is it not the sceptre of a superior incomprehensible force before which we must be content to bow the head, for we all some time or other submit to its influence, divine or infernal, as the case may be?'

Hippel recognised the force of my arguments and remained silently lost in reverie. We were making our way along a narrow path which winds along the banks of the Queich. We could hear the birds chirping, and the partridge calling as it hid itself under the broad vine-leaves. The landscape was superb, the river murmured as it flowed past little ravines in the banks. Right and left, hillside after hillside came into view, all loaded with abundant fruit. Our route formed an angle with the declivity. All at once my friend Hippel stopped motionless, his mouth wide open, his hands extended in an attitude of stupefied astonishment, then as quick as lightning he turned to fly, when I seized his horse's bridle.

'Hippel, what's the matter? Is Satan in ambuscade on the road, or has Balaam's angel drawn his sword against you?'

'Let me go!' said he, struggling; 'my dream – my dream!'

'Be quiet and calm yourself, Hippel; no doubt there are some injurious qualities contained in red wine; swallow some of this; it is a generous juice of the grape which dissipatés the gloomy imaginings of a man's brain.'

He drank it eagerly, and this beneficent liquor re-established his faculties in equilibrium.

He poured the red wine out on the road; it had become as black as ink, and formed great bubbles as it soaked in the ground, and I seemed to hear confused voices groaning and sighing, but so faint that they seemed to escape from some distant country, and which the ear of flesh could hardly hear, but only the fibres of the heart could feel. It was as Abel's last sigh when his brother felled him to the ground and the earth drank up his blood.

Hippel was too much excited to pay attention to this phenomenon, but I was profoundly struck by it. At the same time I noticed a black bird, about as large as my fist, rise from the bushes near, and fly away with a cry of fear.

'I feel,' said Hippel, 'that the opposing principles are struggling within me, one white and the other black, the principles of good and evil; come on.'

We continued our journey.

'Ludwig,' my comrade soon began, 'such extraordinary things happen in this world that our understandings ought to humiliate themselves in fear and trembling. You know I have never been here before. Well, yesterday I dreamt, and today I see with open eyes the dream of last night rise again before me; look at that landscape – it is the same I beheld when asleep. Here are the ruins of the old château where I was struck down in a fit of apoplexy; this is the path I went along, and there are my four acres of vines. There is not a tree, not a streamlet, not a bush which I cannot recognise as if I had seen them hundreds of times before. When we turn the angle of the road we shall see the village of Welcke at the end of the valley; the second house on the right is the burgomaster's; it has five windows on the first floor and four below, and the door. On the left of my house – I mean the burgomaster's – you see a barn and a stable. It is there my cattle are kept. Behind the house is the yard; under a large shed is a two-horse wine-press. So, my dear Ludwig, such as I am you see me resuscitated. The poor burgomaster is looking at you out of my eyes; he speaks to you by my voice, and did I not recollect that before being a burgomaster and a rich sordid proprietor I have been Hippel the *bon vivant*, I should hesitate to say who I am, for all I see recalls another existence, other habits and other ideas.'

Everything was in accordance with what Hippel had described. We saw the village at some distance down in a fertile valley between hillsides covered with vines, houses scattered along the banks of the river; the second on the right was the burgomaster's.

And Hippel had a vague recollection of every one we met; some seemed so well known to him that he was on the point of addressing them by name; but the words died away on his lips, and he could not disengage his ideas. Besides, when he noticed the look of indifferent curiosity with which those we met regarded us, Hippel felt he was entirely unknown, and that his face, at all events, sufficed to mask the spirit of the defunct burgomaster.

We dismounted at an inn which my friend assured me was the best in the village; he had known it long by reputation.

A second surprise. The mistress of the inn was a fat gossip, a widow of many years' standing, and whom the defunct burgomaster had once proposed to make his second wife.

Hippel felt inclined to clasp her in his arms; all his old sympathies awoke in him at once. However, he succeeded in moderating his transports; the real Hippel combated in him the burgomaster's matrimonial inclinations. So he contented himself with asking her as civilly as possible for a good breakfast and the best wine she had.

While we were at table, a very natural curiosity prompted

Hippel to inquire what had passed in the village since his death.

'Madame,' said he with a flattering smile, 'you were doubtless well acquainted with the late burgomaster of Welcke?'

'Do you mean the one that died in a fit of apoplexy about three years ago?' said she.

'The same,' replied my comrade, looking inquisitively at her.

'Ah, yes, indeed, I knew him!' cried the hostess; 'that old curmudgeon wanted to marry me. If I had known he would have died so soon I would have accepted him. He proposed we should mutually settle all our property on the survivor.'

My dear Hippel was rather disconcerted at this reply; the burgomaster's *amour propre* in him was horribly ruffled. He nevertheless continued his questions.

'So you were not the least bit in love with him, madame?' he asked.

'How was it possible to love a man as ugly, dirty, repulsive, and avaricious as he was?'

Hippel got up and walked to the looking-glass to survey himself. After contemplating his fat and rosy cheeks he smiled contentedly, and sat down before a chicken, which he proceeded to carve.

'After all,' he said, 'the burgomaster may have been ugly and dirty; that proves nothing against me.'

'Are you any relation of his?' asked the hostess in surprise.

'I! I never even saw him. I only made the remark some are ugly, some good-looking; and if one happens to have one's nose in the middle of one's face, like your burgomaster, it does not prove any likeness to him.'

'Oh no,' said the gossip, 'you have no family resemblance to him whatever.'

'Moreover,' my comrade added, 'I am not by any means a miser, which proves I cannot be your burgomaster. Let us have two more bottles of your best wine.'

The hostess disappeared, and I profited by this opportunity

to warn Hippel not to enter upon topics which might betray his incognito.

'What do you take me for, Ludwig?' cried he in a rage. 'You know I am no more the burgomaster than you are, and the proof of it is my papers are perfectly regular.'

He pulled out his passport. The landlady came in.

'Madame,' said he, 'did your burgomaster in any way resemble this description?'

He read out: 'Forehead, medium height; nose, large; lips, thick; eyes, grey; figure, full; hair, brown.'

'Very nearly,' said the dame, 'except that the burgomaster was bald.'

Hippel ran his hand through his hair, and exclaimed: 'The burgomaster was bald, and no one dare to say I am bald.'

The hostess thought he was mad, but as he rose and paid the bill she made no further remark.

When we reached the door Hippel turned to me and said abruptly: 'Let us be off!'

'One moment, my friend,' I replied; 'you must first take me to the cemetery where the burgomaster lies.'

'No!' he exclaimed – 'no, never! do you want to see me in Satan's clutches? I stand upon my own tombstone! It is against every law in nature. Ludwig, you cannot mean it?'

'Be calm, Hippel!' I replied. 'At this moment you are under the influence of invisible powers; they have enveloped you in meshes so light and transparent that one cannot see them. You must make an effort to burst them; you must release the burgomaster's spirit, and that can only be accomplished upon his tomb. Would you steal this poor spirit? It would be a flagrant robbery, and I know your scrupulous delicacy too well to suppose you capable of such infamy.'

These unanswerable arguments settled the matter.

'Well, then, yes,' said he, 'I must summon up courage to trample on those remains, a heavy part of which I bear about me. God grant I may not be accused of such a theft! Follow me, Ludwig; I will lead you to the grave.'

He walked on with rapid steps, carrying his hat in his hand, his hair in disorder, waving his arms about, and taking long strides, like some unhappy wretch about to commit a last act of desperation, and exciting himself not to fail in his attempt.

We first passed along several lanes, then crossed the bridge of a mill, the wheel of which was gyrating in a sheet of foam; then we followed a path which crossed a field, and at last we arrived at a high wall behind the village, covered with moss and clematis; it was the cemetery.

In one corner was the ossuary, in the other a cottage surrounded by a small garden.

Hippel rushed into the room; there he found the grave-digger, all along the walls were crowns of *immortelles*. The gravedigger was carving a cross, and he was so occupied with his work that he got up quite alarmed when Hippel appeared. My comrade fixed his eyes upon him so sternly that he must have been frightened, for during some seconds he remained quite confounded.

'My good man,' I began, 'will you show us the burgo-master's grave?'

'No need of that,' cried Hippel; 'I know it.'

Without waiting for us he opened the door which led into the cemetery, and set off running like a madman, springing over the graves and exclaiming: 'There it is; there! Here we are!'

He must evidently have been possessed by an evil spirit, for in his course he threw down a cross crowned with roses – a cross on the grave of a little child!

The gravedigger and I followed him slowly.

The cemetery was large; weeds, thick and dark-green in colour, grew three feet above the soil. Cypresses dragged their long foliage along the ground; but what struck me most at first was a trellis set up against the wall, and covered with a magnificent vine so loaded with fruit that the bunches of grapes were growing one over the other.

As we went along I remarked to the gravedigger; 'You have a vine there which ought to bring you in something.'

'Oh, sir,' he began in a whining tone, 'that vine does not produce me much. No one will buy my grapes; what comes from the dead returns to the dead.'

I looked the man steadily in the face. He had a false air about him, and a diabolical grin contracted his lips and his cheeks. I did not believe what he said.

We now stood before the burgomaster's grave. Opposite there was the stem of an enormous vine, looking very like a boa-constrictor. Its roots, no doubt, penetrated to the coffins, and disputed their prey with the worms. Moreover, its grapes were of a red violet colour, while the others were white, very slightly tinged with pink. Hippel leaned against the vine, and seemed calmer.

'You do not eat these grapes yourself,' said I to the gravedigger, 'but you sell them.'

He grew pale, and shook his head in dissent.

'You sell them at Welcke, and I can tell you the name of the inn where the wine from them is drunk – it is The Fleur de Lis.'

The gravedigger trembled in every limb.

Hippel seized the wretch by the throat, and had it not been for me he would have torn him to pieces.

'Scoundrel!' he exclaimed, 'you have been the cause of my drinking the quintessence of the burgomaster, and I have lost my own personal identity.'

But all on a sudden a bright idea struck him. He turned towards the wall in the attitude of the celebrated Brabançon Männe-Kempis.

'God be praised!' said he, as he returned to me, 'I have restored the burgomaster's spirit to the earth. I feel enormously relieved.'

An hour later we were on our road again, and my friend Hippel had quite recovered his natural gaiety.

MY INHERITANCE

At the death of my worthy uncle, Christian Haas, mayor of
Lauterbach, I was already music conductor to the Grand
Duke Yeri Peter, and I had fifteen hundred florins as salary.
That did not prevent me from being in very low water. Uncle
Christian, well aware of my position, never sent me a penny,
so I cannot help shedding a few tears in learning his post-
humous generosity. I inherited from him, alas! . . . two
hundred and fifty acres of good plough-land, vineyards,
orchards, a bit of forest, and his fine mansion of Lauterbach.

'Dear uncle,' I said to myself with much feeling, 'now I
see the extent of your wisdom, and glorify you for keeping
your purse-strings tied up. If you had sent me any money,
where would it be now? In the hands of the Philistines! Little
Kate Fresserine alone could have given any news about it.
But now, by your caution, you have saved the situation. All
honour to you, dear Uncle Christian! . . . All honour to you!'

And having said all this and much more, not less touching
or less sincere, I set off on horseback for Lauterbach, It was
very odd! The demon of avarice, with whom I never had
any dealings, almost made himself master of my soul.

'Kasper,' he whispered in my ear, 'now you're a rich man.
Up to the present you have only pursued vain phantoms.
Love and pleasure and the arts are only smoke. A man
must be mad to think anything of glory. There is no solidity
about anything except lands, houses, and money out on first

mortgages. Give up your illusions! Push forward your fences, widen your fields, heap up your money, and you will be honoured and respected. You will become mayor like your uncle, and the people, when you approach, will take off their hats a mile away, saying, "Here comes Herr Kasper Haas . . . the rich man . . . the warmest gentleman in the country!"'

These ideas came and went in my head like figures from a magic lantern, and I found they had a reasonable, serious look, and I was much taken with them.

It was in mid-July. In the heavens the lark poured out his unending music; the crops undulated in the plain; the warm puffs of light wind carried to me the love-cries of the quail and the partridge in the corn; the foliage twinkled in the sunlight; the Lauter murmured in the shadow of the large old willows. But I saw or heard nothing of all that. I wished to be the mayor, I stuck out my abdomen; I puffed out my cheeks, and I repeated to myself, 'Here comes Herr Kasper Haas . . . the rich man . . . the warmest gentleman in the country! Ho! Ho! Ho!'

And my little mare galloped on. I was anxious to try on the three-cornered hat and the great red waistcoat of my Uncle Christian, for I thought that if they suited me it would save me buying others. About four in the afternoon the little village of Lauterbach appeared, nestling in the valley; and it was with some emotion that I looked at the large fine mansion which was to be my residence, the centre of my estate and my power. I admired its picturesque situation on the dusty highway, the immense roof of grey tile, the sheds with their vast wings brooding over carts and wagons and crops, with a farmyard behind, then the kitchen garden, the orchard, the vineyards on the hill slope, the meadows in the distance. I thrilled with pleasure at the spectacle.

And as I went down the main road of the village, old women, with nose and chin meeting like nut-crackers, bare-headed, rumpled children, men in big otter-skin hats, a pipe with a silver chain in their mouths – all these good folks looked at me and greeted me: 'Good day, Herr Kasper! Good day, Herr Haas!'

And all the little windows fill with astonished faces. I already feel at home. It seems to me I have always been a great landowner of Lauterbach. My life as a musical conductor is no more than a dream – my enthusiasm for music a folly of youth. How money does alter a man's way of looking at things!

However, I stopped before the house of Notary Becker. He has the deeds of my property, and must give them to me. Tying my horse to the ring by the door, I jumped on the step, and the old lawyer, his bald head uncovered, his thin spine clad in a long green dressing-gown with a flower pattern, came out to welcome me.

'Herr Kasper Haas! I have much honour in greeting you!'

'Your servant, Master Becker!'

'Will you deign to enter, Herr Haas?'

'After you, Master Becker, after you.'

We crossed the hall, and I saw at the end a little bright airy room, a well-set out table, and, near the table, a pretty girl, graceful and sweet, her cheeks touched with a modest blush.

'Herr Kasper Haas!' said the venerable notary.

I bowed.

'My daughter Lothe!' added the worthy man.

While I was feeling my old artistic inclinations revive within me, and admiring the little nose, the scarlet lips, and large blue eyes of Fräulein Lothe, her slender waist, and her little dimpled plump hands, Master Becker invited me to take my place at the table, saying that, as he knew I was about to arrive, he had had a little meal prepared for me.

So we sat down and talked about the beauties of nature. I thought of the old father, and began to calculate what a notary would earn in Lauterbach.

'Fräulein, may I have the pleasure of helping you to the wing of a chicken?'

'Sir, you are very good. With pleasure.'

Lothe lowered her eyes. I filled her glass, and she moistened her red lips with the wine. Father was joyful, and talked about hunting and fishing.

'You will no doubt take up the pleasures of a country life. Our rabbit warrens are splendid, and the streams are full of trout. There is some fine hunting in the forest, and in the evening there is good company at the tavern. The inspector of woods and waters is a charming young man, and the magistrate is an excellent hand at whist.'

I listened, and thought this calm and peaceful sort of life was delicious. Fräulein Lothe seemed to me charming. She talked little, but her smile was so sweet and frank that she must be very loving, I fancied.

At last the coffee and the liqueur arrived. The young lady retired, and the old lawyer got on to serious business affairs. He spoke to me of my uncle's estate, and I listened very attentively. No will, no legacies, and no mortgage! Everything clear, straightforward, regular! 'Happy Kasper!' I said to myself. 'Happy Kasper.'

Then we entered the study to deal with the title-deeds. The closeness of the air, the piles of documents, the rows of law books, quickly chased away the day-dreams of my amorous fantasies. I sat down in a big armchair, and Master Becker thoughtfully fixed his horn spectacles on his long curved nose.

'Here are the title-deeds to your Eichmatt meadowlands, a hundred acres of the best soil in the parish, and splendidly watered. Three crops of hay in a year. It will bring you in four thousand francs. Here are the deeds for your Grünerwald farms, and those for your Lauterbach mansion. It is by far the largest in the village, dating from the sixteenth century.'

'The devil! Master Becker, that is nothing in its favour.'

'On the contrary. It is in a perfect state of repair. It was built by Hans Burckart, the Count of Barth, as his hunting-house. It is true, a good many generations have passed since then, but the upkeep and repair have never been neglected.'

With more explanations, Master Becker handed me the

title-deeds of my other properties; and having put the parchments in a bag lent to me by the worthy man, I took leave
of him, more convinced than ever of my new importance.
Arriving at my mansion, I inserted the key in the lock, and
kicking the step, I cried, 'This is mine!' I entered the hall,
'This is mine!' I opened the wardrobes, and seeing the linen
piled to the top, 'This is mine!' I mounted to the first floor,
repeating always like a madman, 'This is mine! This is mine!
Yes, I am the owner!'

All my cares of the future, all my fears for the morrow
are dissipated. I figure in the world, no longer by the feeble
merit men allow me, by the caprice of the fashion of the
day, but by the possession of things that everybody covets.
Oh, poets! . . . Oh, artists! . . . what are you beside this stout
owner of land, who nourishes you by the crumbs from his
table? You are only the ornament of his banquet . . . the
distraction of his moods of boredom . . . the songbird on his
hedgerow . . . the statue decorating his garden . . . You exist
only by him and through him . . . Why should you envy
him the fumes of pride and vanity . . . he who owns the
only realities in this world!

If in this moment the poor Musical Conductor Haas had
appeared before me, I should have looked at him over the
shoulder, and asked myself, 'Who is this fool? What has he
in common with me?'

I opened the window. Night was falling. The setting sun
gilded my orchards, my vineyards that lost themselves in the
distance. On the summit of the hill a few white stones indicated the cemetery. I turned round. A vast Gothic hall, the
ceiling adorned with heavy mouldings, took my eye. I was
in the hunting-lodge of Hans Burckart, the Count of Barth.
An antique spinet was placed between two of the windows.
I passed my fingers over the keys absent-mindedly. The slack
wires knocked together with the strange, twangling, ironic
voice of teethless old women humming over the melodies
of their youth.

At the end of the hall was the half-vaulted alcove, with great red curtains and a four-poster bed. The sight reminded me that I had been six hours in the saddle. And, undressing with a smile of unspeakable satisfaction, 'This is the first time,' I said, 'I have slept in my own bed.' And lying down, my eyes bent on the immense plain, already bathed in shadows, I felt my eyelids grow heavy in pleasant fashion. Not a leaf murmured; the noises of the village died one by one away . . . the sun had sunk . . . some golden gleams marked his trail in infinite space . . . I soon fell asleep.

It was night, and the moon shone in all her glory when I awoke with no apparent cause. The vague fragrances of summer came through the window to me. The air was filled with the sweet scent of the new hay. I stared around in surprise, for when I tried to get up to close the window, by some inconceivable thing, my body slept on, heavy as lead, while my head was perfectly free. With all my efforts to rise, not a muscle responded. I felt my arms by my side completely inert . . . my legs were stretched out, motionless; my head moved in vain. The deep, cadenced breathing of my body frightened me . . . my head fell back on the pillow, exhausted by its efforts. 'Am I paralysed in my limbs?' I asked myself. 'Kasper Haas, the master of so many vineyards and fat pasturages, cannot even move this clod of clay that he really owns? O God! . . . What does it mean?'

And as I was thinking in this melancholy way, a slight sound attracted my attention. The door of my alcove opened; a man dressed in some stiff stuff like felt, as the monks of Saint Gualber in Mayence are . . . a large grey felt hat with a hawk's plume in it . . . his hand buried to the elbow in hide gloves . . . entered the hall. His bell-shaped boots came above his knees; a heavy gold chain, charged with decorations, hung from his neck. His tanned, bony face, with hollow eyes, wore a look of keen sadness, and there were horrible greenish tints on it.

He walked the hall with hard, firm step, like the tick-tack

of a clock; and with his hand on the guard of an immense sword, striking the floor with his heel, he cried, 'This is mine! . . . Mine . . . Hans Burckart. . . Count of Barth!'

It was like an old rusty machine grinding out necromantic words. It made my flesh creep. But at the same time the door at the other end opened, and the Count of Barth disappeared through it. I heard his automatic step descend a stair that never seemed to come to an end. The sound of his footfall on each step grew fainter and fainter, as though he were descending to the fiery depths of the earth.

As I still listened, hearing nothing, lo! suddenly the great hall was filled with many people. The spinet sounded . . . they danced . . . they sang . . . made love and drank good wine. I saw against the blue background of the moon, young ladies loll round the spinet; their cavaliers, clad in fabulous lace, and numberless knick-knacks, sat with crossed legs on gold-fringed stools, leaning forward, tossing their heads, waddling about, making themselves pleasant. The little withered fingers of an old lady, with a nose like a parrot's beak, clicked on the keys of the spinet; bursts of thin laughter rocketed left and right, ending in a mad rattle that made the hairs stand up in my neck.

All this society of folly and grace and fine manners exhaled a smell of rose water and mignonette soured by old age. I made again some superhuman efforts to get rid of this nightmare. Impossible! But at the same moment one of the young ladies said: 'Gentlemen, make yourselves at home . . . This domain—'

She did not have the time to finish. A silence of death followed her words. I looked around. The phantasmagoria had disappeared.

Then the sound of a horn struck my ears. Outside, horses were prancing, dogs barking, and the moon, calm, contemplative, shone into my alcove. The door opened, as by a wind, and fifty hunters, followed by young ladies, two hundred years old, with long trailing gowns, filed majestically from one hall to the other. Four serfs also passed, bearing on their stout shoulders a stretcher of oak branches on which rested – bleeding, frothy at the mouth, with glazed eyes – an enormous wild boar. I heard the sound of the horn still louder outside. Then it died away in the woodlands like the sleepy cry of a bird . . . and then . . . nothing!

As I was thinking of this strange vision, I looked by chance in the silent shadows, and was astonished to see the hall occupied by one of those old Protestant families of bygone days, calm, dignified, and solemn in their manners. There was the white-haired father, reading a big Bible; the old mother, tall and pale, spinning the household linen, straight as a spindle, with a collar up to her ears, her waist bound by fillets of black ratteen; then the chubby children with dreaming eyes leaning on the table in deep silence; the old sheep dog, listening to his master; the old clock in its walnut case, counting the seconds; and farther away, in the shadow, the faces of girls and the features of lads in drugget jackets and felt hats, discussing the story of Jacob and Rachel by way of declaring their love.

And this worthy family seemed to be convinced of the holy truths; the old father, with his cracked voice, continued the edifying story with deep emotion:

'This is your promised land . . . the land of Abraham and Isaac and Jacob . . . which I have designed for you from the beginning of the world . . . so that you shall grow and multiply there like the stars of the sky. And none shall take it from you . . . for you are my beloved people, in whom I have put my trust.'

The moon, clouded for a few moments, grew clear again, and hearing nothing more I turned my head. The calm cold rays lighted up the empty hall; not a figure, not a shadow . . . The light streamed on the floor, and, in the distance, some trees lifted their foliage, sharp and clear, against the luminous hillside.

But suddenly the high walls were hidden in books. The

old spinet gave way to the desk of a learned man, whose big wig showed to me above an armchair of red leather. I heard the goose-quill scratching the paper. The writer, lost in thought, did not stir. The silence overwhelmed me. But great was my surprise when the man turned in his chair, and I recognised in him the original of the portrait of the Jurist Gregorius that is No. 253 in the Hesse-Darmstadt Picture Gallery. Heavens! how did this great person descend from his frame? That is what I was asking myself when in a hollow voice he cried, 'Ownership, in civil law, is the right to use and abuse so far as the law of nature allows.' As this formula came from his lips, his figure grew dimmer and dimmer. At the last word he could not be seen.

What more shall I tell you, my dear friends? During the following hours I saw twenty other generations succeed each other in the ancient castle of Hans Burckart . . . Christians and Jews, lords and commoners, ignorant people and learned, artists and philistines, and all of them claimed the place as their legitimate property. All thought themselves the sovereign masters of the property. Alas! the wind of death blew them out of the door. I ended by becoming accustomed to this strange procession. Each time one of these worthy persons cried, 'This is mine!' I laughed and murmured, 'Wait, my friend, wait, you will vanish like the rest.'

I was weary when, far away, very far away, a cock crowed, and with his piercing voice awoke the sleeping world. The leaves shook in the morning wind, and a shudder ran through my body. I felt my limbs were at last free, and rising on my elbow I gazed with rapture over the silent countryside . . . But what I saw was scarcely calculated to make me rejoice. All along the little hill-path that led to the graveyard climbed the procession of phantoms that had visited me in the night. Step by step they advanced to the lich-gate, and in their silent march, under the vague grey shadowy tints of the rising dawn, there was something terrible. As I looked, more dead than alive, my mouth gaping, my forehead bathed in a cold sweat, the leaders of the procession seemed to melt into the old weeping willows. There remained only a little number of spectres. And I was beginning to recover my breath, when my uncle Christian, the last figure in the procession, turned round under the old gate, and motioned to me to come with him. A voice, far away . . . ironical, cried: 'Kasper . . . Kasper . . . Come . . . This land is ours!'

Then everything disappeared, and a purple line, stretching across the horizon, announced the dawn. I need not tell you that I did not accept the invitation of Master Christian Haas. It will be necessary for someone more powerful than he to force me to take that road. But I must admit that my night in the castle of Burckart has singularly altered the good opinion I had conceived of my own importance. For the strange vision seemed to me to signify that if the land, the orchards, the meadows do not pass away, the owners vanish very quickly. It makes the hair rise on your head when you think on it seriously.

So, far from letting myself slumber in the delight of an idle country life, I took up music again, and I hope next year to have an opera produced in Berlin. The fact is that glory, which common-sense people regard as moonshine, is still the most solid of all forms of ownership. It does not end with life. On the contrary, death confirms it, and gives it a new lustre. Suppose, for example, that Homer returned to this world. No one would think of denying him the merit of having written the *Iliad*, and each of us would hasten to render to this great man the honours due to him. But if by chance the richest landowner of his age returned to claim the fields, the forests, the pasturages, which were the pride of his life, it is ten to one he would be treated as a thief, and perish miserably under the blows of the Turks.

THE WILD HUNTSMAN

I

In those happy days of youth, when the sky appears of a deeper blue and the foliage of a more vivid green, when mountain-torrents rush down with greater impetuosity and noise, when lakes are calmer, and their limpid depths more clear; when Nature is clothed in unspeakable grace, and all things sing to us in our hearts, and whisper of love, of art, of poetry – in that happy time I wandered alone through the grand old forest of Hundsrück.

I wandered from town to town, from one forester's house to the next; singing, whistling, looking about me, without any definite object; fancy-led, seeking ever a deeper depth still more distant and more leafy, where no sound but the whisperings of the wind and the music of trees could ever reach me.

One morning I stepped out before daylight from the door of the Swan hostelry at Pirmasens to cross the wooded hills of Rothalps to the hamlet of Wolfthal. The boots came to arouse me at two o'clock, as I had requested; for towards the end of August it is best to travel at night, as the heat during the day, concentrating at the bottom of the gorges, becomes insupportable.

Picture me, then, on the way at night, my hunting-jacket buttoned closely to my figure, my knapsack depending from my shoulders, my stick in my hand. I walked at a good pace. Vines succeeded to vines, hemp-fields to hemp-fields; then came fir-trees, amongst which the darkened pathway wended; and the pale moon overhead seemed to plough an immense furrow of light beyond.

The excitement of the walk, the deep silence of the solitude, the twittering of a bird disturbed in its nest, the rapid passage through the trees of an early squirrel going to drink at a neighbouring spring, the stars glinting between the hills, the distant murmur of the water in the valley, the first clear notes from the thrush uttered from the topmost spray of the pine-tree, and crying to us that far, far away there was a streak of light, that the day was breaking, and at length the pale crepuscule, the first purple tint on the horizon, appeared across the dark coppices – these numerous impressions of the journey insensibly led up to the birth of the day.

About five o'clock I came out upon the other side of the Rothalps, nine miles from Pirmasens, into a narrow winding gorge.

I can always recall the sensation of freshness and delight with which I welcomed this retreat. Below me a little torrent, clear as crystal, rushed over its moss-grown stones; on the right, as far as the eye could reach, extended a forest of birch; and to the left, beneath the lofty pine-trees' shade, the sandy path meandered to the deep roads.

Below the road the heather and the heaths sprang up with golden drops; still farther away some briars, and then a streak of water with its clustering green cresses.

Those who during their youth have had the happiness to light upon such a place in the forest depths, at that hour when Nature comes forth from her rosy bath and in her robe of sunshine, when the light plays amongst the foliage, and drops its golden tears into the untrodden depths, when the mosses, the honeysuckle, and all climbing plants burn incense in the shade, and mingle their perfumes under the canopy of the lofty palm-trees, when the parti-coloured tomtits hop from branch to branch in search of insects, when the thrush, the bullfinch, and the blackbird fly down to the rivulet and drink their fill, with wings outstretched over the tiny foaming falls, or the thieving jays, crossing above the trees in flocks, direct their flight towards the wild cherry-trees – at the hour, in short, when all Nature is animated, when everything is enjoying love, and light, and life – such people as those to whom I have referred alone can understand my ecstasy.

I seated myself upon the root of an ancient moss-grown oak, my stick resting idly between my knees; and there, for the space of an hour, I abandoned myself, child-like, to endless day-dreams.

By degrees the light increased; the humming of insects grew louder, while the melancholy notes of the cuckoos, repeated by the echoes, marked in a curious way the measure of the universal concert.

While I was thus meditating, a distant sharp note, skilfully modulated, struck upon my ear. From the moment of my arrival at this spot I had heard, without paying any attention to, this note; but so soon as I had distinguished it from the numerous forest noises I thought: 'That is the note of a bird-catcher, his hut cannot be far away, and there must be some forester's house close by.'

I arose and looked about me. Towards the left hand, in the direction of the rising ground, I quickly distinguished a penthouse roof whose dormer windows and white chimneys glistened amid the innumerable branches of the forest pines. The house was quite half an hour's walk from my resting-place, but that did not prevent me saying aloud, 'Thank Heaven!'

For it is no small matter, I may tell you, to know where to find a crust of bread and a flask of *kirchenwasser*. So I once again shouldered my knapsack, and cheerfully struck into the path which promised to lead me to the house.

For some few minutes longer the bird-catcher's call

continued its cheery notes; then, all of a sudden, it ceased. Towards seven o'clock the small birds would have finished their morning 'grub', and the day, waxing hotter and brighter, would discover the lurking enemy behind the thick leafy screen of his hiding-place; it was time to take up the bird-lime.

All these thoughts passed through my mind as I continued to advance, regretting that I had not sooner resumed my journey, when about fifty or sixty paces to the left I caught sight of the bird-catcher, a fine old forester, tall, sinewy, and muscular, clad in a short blue blouse, an immense game-bag depending from his shoulder, the silver badge upon his chest, and the small peaked cap placed jauntily upon his head. He was in the act of taking up his nets, and at first I only caught sight of his broad back, his long muscular limbs arrayed in cloth gaiters reaching up above the knee beneath his blouse; but as he turned I perceived the wiry profile of a regular old huntsman, the grey eyes shaded by long lashes; a long white moustache shrouded the lips; snowy eyebrows, an honest profile, somewhat stem, yet with something of a thoughtful, even a rather ingenuous cast; but the silver-grey hair, and a certain indescribable look in the depths of the eyes, corrected the easy-going impression which struck one at first sight. And if the broad back was somewhat bent, the thin shoulders were so wide that one could not help feeling a certain respect for this fine old forester.

He moved about in all directions, sometimes in the light, sometimes in the shadow, stretching out a hand here, stooping there, perfectly at home. Resting upon my stick, I watched him narrowly, and thought what a capital subject for a picture he would make.

Having taken up his nets and twigs, and wrapped them carefully, he proceeded to string together by the beaks the birds he had captured, the smallest first, garland fashion. At length, having arranged them to his liking, he plunged them all into his game-bag; then swinging it upon his shoulders, he took up the great holly staff that was lying upon the ground beside him, and struck out towards the path.

Then for the first time he noticed me, and his face assumed an official expression consistent with his dress, but involuntarily his sternness disappeared, and his grey eyes beamed kindly upon me.

'Ha, ha!' he exclaimed in French, but with a curious German accentuation, 'good morning, *monsieur*; how are you this morning? Is it to your taste?'

'Yes, pretty well,' I replied in the same language.

'Ha, ha!' said the brave fellow, 'you are a Frenchman, then; I saw that at once!' and he saluted like an old soldier. 'Are you not a Frenchman?' he added.

'Well, not exactly, I come from Dusseldorf.'

'Ah! from Dusseldorf; but it is all the same,' he said, as he lapsed into the old German tongue; 'you are a good fellow nevertheless.'

He placed his hand lightly upon my shoulder as he spoke.

'You are *en route* early,' he said.

'Yes, I come from Pirmasens.'

'It is nine good miles from here; you must have set out at three o'clock this morning.'

'At two o'clock, but I halted for an hour in the dell yonder.'

'Ah! yes, near the source of the Vellerst. And, if not impertinent, may I inquire your destination?'

'My destination! Oh! I go anywhere. I walk about, look around me—'

'You are a timber contractor, then?'

'No, I am a painter.'

'A painter – good. A capital profession that. Why you can make three or four crowns a day, and walk about with your hands in your pockets meanwhile. Painters have been here before. I have seen two or three in the last thirty years. It is a capital calling.'

We pursued our way towards the house together, he with bent back, stretching out his long limbs, while I came trudging after, congratulating myself on having pitched upon a resting-place. The sun was getting very warm, and the ascent was steep. At intervals long vistas opened out to the left, and mingled together in deep gorges; the blue distance trended down towards the Rhine, and beyond the hazy horizon mingled with the sky and passed into the infinite.

'What a splendid country!' I cried as I stood wrapped in contemplation of this wonderful panorama.

The old keeper stopped as I spoke; his piercing eyes took in the prospect, and he replied gravely: 'That's true! I have the most beautiful district of all the mountain as far as Neustadt. Every one who comes to see the country says so; even the ranger himself confesses as much. Now look yonder. Do you see the Losser descending between those rocks? Look at that white line – that is the foam. You must see that closer, sir. You should hear the roar of the cataract in the spring when the snows are melting; it is like thunder amongst the hills. Then look higher up; do you see the blossom of the heather and the broom? Well, there is the Valdhorn; the flowers are falling just now, but in the spring you would perceive a bouquet that rises to heaven. And if you are fond of curiosities, there is the Birckenstein; we must not forget that. All the learned people – for one or two such do come here during the year – never fail to go and read the old inscriptions upon the stones.'

'It is a ruin, then?'

'Yes; an old piece of wall upon a rock enveloped in nettles and brambles – a regular owl's nest. For my own part, I like the Losser, the Krapenfelz, the Valdhorn; but as they say in France, every one has his own taste and colour. We have everything here, high, medium-sized, and young forest trees, brushwood and brambles, rocks, caverns, torrents, rivers—'

'But no lakes,' I said.

'Lakes!' he exclaimed. 'No lakes! As if we had not just beyond the Losser a lake a league in circumference, dark and deep, surrounded by rocks and the giant pines of the Veierschloss! They call it *The Lake of the Wild Huntsman*!'

And he bent his head as if in reflection for some seconds. Then suddenly rousing himself, he resumed his route without uttering a word. It appeared to me that the old keeper so lately enraptured had suddenly struck upon a melancholy chord. I followed him musing. He, bending forward, wearing a pensive air, and learning on his great holly staff, took such long and vigorous strides that it seemed as if his limbs would burst through his blouse every moment!

The forester's house came into sight between the trees in the midst of a verdant meadow. At the end of the valley the river could be perceived following the undulations of the hills; farther still in the gorge were clusters of fruit-trees, some tilled ground, a small garden surrounded by a low wall, and finally on a terrace having the wood for a background was the house of the old keeper – a white house, somewhat ancient in appearance, with three windows, and the door on the ground floor, four windows above with little diamond-shaped panes, and four others in the garrets amid the brown tiles of the roof.

Facing the wood in our direction was an old worm-eaten gallery with a carved balustrade, the winding staircase outside being fastened to the wall. A lattice trellis-work occupied two sides upon which the honeysuckles and vines clambered and hung back in festoons from the roof. Across the green sward the small black window-panes glittered in the shade. On the wall of the kitchen garden an old chanticleer was proudly strutting in the midst of his hens; upon the mossy roof a flock of pigeons were moving about; in the stream a number of ducks were swimming, and from the threshold we could have perceived the length of the sloping dell, the extensive valley, and the leafy forest shades as far as the eye could reach.

Nothing so calm and peaceable as this house, lost in the solitudes of the mountains, can be imagined; its very appearance touched one more than you might fancy, and made one feel inclined to live and die there – if possible.

Two old hounds ran out to welcome us. A young girl was

hanging some linen out to dry upon the balustrade, and seeing the dogs running out, looked up. The old keeper smiled as he pressed forward.

'You are at home here,' I said.

'Yes, this is my house.'

'May I ask for a crust and a glass of wine?'

'Of course, man, of course. If the keepers sent people away I wonder to what inn the travellers could go. You are right welcome, sir.'

At this moment we reached the gate in the palings of the little garden; the dogs jumped upon us, and the girl in the balcony waved her hand in welcome. At the end of the garden another gate gave us admission to the yard, and the keeper, turning to me, exclaimed in a joyous tone: 'You are now at the house of Frantz Honeck, gamekeeper to the Grand Duke Ludwig. Come into the parlour. I will just get rid of my game-bag, take off my gaiters, and join you there.'

We traversed a narrow passage. Talking as we advanced, the keeper pushed open the door of a low square whitewashed room, furnished with beechwood chairs, having a heart-shaped ornament cut in the back of each, a high walnut-wood press, with glittering hinges and rounded feet, and at the farther end was an old Nuremberg clock. In the corner to the right stood the stove, and by the lattice-windows was a firwood table; these made up the furniture of the room. On the table were a small loaf of bread and two glasses.

'Sit down. Make yourself comfortable,' said the old keeper. 'I will return in a few moments.'

He left the room as he spoke.

I heard him enter the next room. Then, delighted to find myself in such good quarters, I took off my great-coat. The dogs stretched themselves on the floor.

'Louise! Louise!' cried out old Frantz.

The young girl passed the windows, and her pretty rosy face put aside the plants to look into the room. I bowed to her. She blushed, and hastily retired.

'Louise!' cried the old man again.

'I am here, grandfather, I am here,' she replied gently as she came into the passage.

Then I could not help hearing their conversation.

'There is a traveller come, a fine lad; he will breakfast here. Go and draw a flask of white wine, and put on two plates.'

'Yes, grandfather.'

'Go and fetch my woollen jacket and my *sabots*. The birds have turned out well this morning; the young man comes from the Swan at Pirmasens. When Caspar returns send him in.'

'He is tending the cows, grandfather, shall I call him?'

'No, an hour hence will do.'

Every word reached me distinctly. Outside dogs barked, hens cackled, the leaves rustled gently in the breeze; everything was cheerful, fresh, and green.

I placed my knapsack upon the table and sat down thinking of the happiness of living in such a place without any care beyond the daily work.

'What a life!' I thought. 'One can breathe freely here. This old Frantz is as tough as an oak notwithstanding his seventy years. And what a charming little girl his granddaughter is!'

I had scarcely finished these reflections when the old man, clad in his knitted vest and his iron-tipped *sabots*, came in laughing, and cried out: 'Here I am. I have finished my morning's work. I was up and about before you, sir; at four o'clock I had gone my round of the felled timber. Now we are going to rest ourselves, you and I; take a quiet glass and smoke another pipe – pipes again! But tell me, do you wish to change? You can go up to my room.'

'Thank you, Père Frantz, I have need of nothing but a little rest.'

This title of Père Frantz appeared to please the old man; his cheeks betrayed a smile.

''Tis true that my name is Frantz,' he said, 'and I am old

enough to be your father – ay, your grandfather. But may I ask your age?'

'I am nearly twenty-two.'

At this moment the little Louise entered, carrying a flask of white wine in one hand, and in the other some cheese, upon a beautiful specimen of Delft ware, ornamented with red flowers. Frantz ceased to speak as she came in, thinking, perhaps, it is better to hold his tongue about age in the presence of his granddaughter.

Louise was about sixteen years of age; she was fair as an ear of corn, of good height and figure. Her forehead was high, her eyes were blue, her nose straight, with a tendency to turn up at the end, with delicate nostrils; her curving lips were as fresh as two cherries, and she was shy and retiring. She wore a dress of blue cloth striped with white, braced-up Hundsrück fashion. The sleeves of her dress scarcely descended below the elbow, and left her round arms displayed, though somewhat burnt by exposure in the open air. One cannot imagine a creature more soft and gentle or more artless, and I am persuaded that the maidens of Berlin, Vienna, or elsewhere, would have lost by the comparison.

Père Frantz, seated at the end of the table, appeared very proud of her. Louise placed the cheese and the flask upon the table without a word. I was quite silent – dreaming. Louise having left the room, quickly returned with two plates, beautifully clean, and two knives. She then appeared about to leave us, but her grandfather, raising his voice, said: 'Remain here, Louise; remain here, or they will say you are afraid to meet this youth. He is a fine young fellow too. Ha! what is your name? I never thought of asking your before.'

'My name is Théodore Richter.'

'Well, then, Monsieur Théodore, if you feel so disposed, help yourself.'

He attacked the cheese as he spoke. Louise sat down timidly near the stove, sending now and then a quick glance in our direction.

'Yes, he is a painter,' continued old Honeck, as he went on eating; 'and if you would not mind our seeing your pictures it will give us great pleasure, will it not, Louise?'

'Oh, yes, grandfather,' she replied; 'I have never seen any.'

For some moments I had been cogitating how best I could propose to remain in the neighbourhood and study the environs, but I did not know how to broach this delicate subject. Here was now the opportunity ready made.

'Well,' I replied, 'I desire no better, but I warn you I have nothing very first-rate. I have only sketches, and it will take me a fortnight at least to complete them. There is no painting, only drawing, as yet.'

'Never mind, *monsieur*; let us see what you have got.'

'With great pleasure,' I said as I unfastened my knapsack. 'I will first show you the neighbourhood of Pirmasens, but what is that to be compared to your mountains? Your Valdhorn, your Krapenfelz, those are what I should like to paint; those *are* scenes and landscapes!'

Père Honeck made no immediate reply to this. He took gravely the picture I handed to him, the high tower, the new temple, and a background of mountains. I had finished this in water-colours.

The good man having studied this for a few minutes with arched brows and open mouth, selecting the best light by the window, said gravely: 'That is splendid – capital; that's right!'

He appeared quite affected by it.

'Yes,' he said, 'that's the place; that's well done; one can recognise it all. Louise, come here, look at that. Wait, take it this side; is not that the old market itself, with the old fruiterer, Catherine, in the corner? And the grocer Froelig's house, and there is the church porch and the baker's shop. They are all there – nothing is wanting. Those blue mountains behind are near Altenberg. I can see them almost. Capital!'

Louise, leaning upon the old man's shoulder, appeared quite wonder-stricken. She said not a word. But when her grandfather asked: 'What do you think of that, Louise?'

'I think as you do, grandfather; it is beautiful,' she replied in a low voice.

'Yes,' exclaimed the old man, turning to me, and looking me full in the face. 'I did not think you had it in you. I said to myself, "Here is a young fellow walking about for amusement." Now I see you *do* know something. But mind, it is easier to paint houses and churches than woods. In your place I should stick to houses! Since you have begun I should go on if I were you: that's certain.'

Then smiling at the ingenuous old man, I showed him a little sketch I had finished at Hornbach – a sunrise on the outskirts of the Howald. If the former had pleased him this threw him into ecstasies. After the lapse of a moment he raised his eyes and exclaimed: 'Did you do that? It is marvellous – a miracle! There is the sun behind the trees; we can recognise the trees, too, and there are birch, beech, and oak. Well, Master Théodore, if you have done that I admire you.'

'And suppose I were to suggest, Père Frantz,' I said, 'to remain here for a few days – and pay my way, of course – to look about me and paint a bit, would you turn me out of doors?'

A bright blush crossed the old keeper's face.

'Look here,' he said, 'you are a good lad; you want to see the country – a most beautiful country it is, too, and I should think myself a brute to refuse you. You shall share our table, eggs, milk, cheese, a hare on occasion; you shall have the room we keep for the ranger, who will not visit us this year; but as for payment, I cannot take your money. No; I will not take a farthing. Besides, I am not an innkeeper – yet—'

Here the good man paused.

'Yet,' he continued, 'you might, perhaps – after all, I do not like to ask; it is too much.'

He glanced at Louise, blushing more and more, and at length said: 'That child yonder, *monsieur*. Is she difficult to paint?'

Louise at these words quite lost countenance.

'Oh, grandfather!' she stammered.

'Wait a bit,' cried the good man; 'don't imagine I am asking for anything very grand – not a bit; a bit of paper will do as big as my hand only. Look you, Louise, in thirty or forty years, when you have grown grey, you will be glad to have something like your young self to look at. I will not hide from you, Monsieur Théodore, that if I could see myself in uniform once again, helmet on my head, and my sword in my hand, I should be too delighted.'

'Is that all?' I exclaimed; 'that's easy enough, I am sure.'

'You agree, then?'

'Do I agree? Not only will I paint Mademoiselle Louise in a large picture, but I will paint you also, seated in your armchair, your musket between your knees, your gaiters and jack-boots on. *Mademoiselle* shall also be depicted leaning over the chair, and so that the picture may be complete, we will put in that rascal yonder.'

I indicated the dog which lay stretched upon the floor asleep, his muzzle resting upon his paws.

The old keeper gazed at me with tearful eyes.

'I knew you were a good fellow,' he said after a short silence. 'It will give me great pleasure to be painted with my little granddaughter; she at least shall see me as I am now. And if in time she should marry and have children, she will be able to say: "That is Grandfather Frantz, just as he used to be."'

Louise at this moment quitted the room. The old keeper wished to call her back, but his voice was husky, and he could not. A few moments afterwards, having coughed two or three times behind his hand, he resumed, pointing to the dog: 'That, Monsieur Théodore, is a good greyhound, I do not deny; he has a good nose and strength of limb, but there are others as good. If you do not mind, we will put the other in the picture.'

He whistled, and the terrier bounded into the room; the greyhound also got up, and both dogs came wagging their tails to rub their noses against their master's knees.

'They are both good animals,' he said as he caressed them. 'Yes, Fox has good qualities; he has a good nose still, notwithstanding his age. I should wrong him were I to deny it. But if you want a rare dog, look at Waldine there. She has a nose as fine, ay, finer than, the other, she is gentle, never tires, and has all the qualities a good dog ought to have. But this is all beside the question, M. Théodore; what we have to look for in animals is good sense and "ready wit".'

'Rest assured, Père Frantz,' I replied, 'we will put both of them in!'

Père Frantz then invited me to see my room. I took up my knapsack, and we went outside to ascend to the gallery. Two doors opened upon the balcony; we passed the first, pushing aside the clustering ivy which stretched across the balustrade, and Père Honeck opened the farther door.

One can scarcely picture my happiness when I reflected that I was about to pass a fortnight – a month – perhaps the whole of the beautiful season – in the midst of these verdant scenes of nature far from the busy hum of men.

The shutters of the room had been closed since the departure of the ranger the preceding autumn. Honeck threw back the shutter into the plants which clambered over the wall alongside.

'There, M. Théodore,' he said, 'look at that.'

In the subdued light that entered the room through the clustering creepers I perceived that the apartment was of good height and extent, the two windows opening directly full over the valley. So, notwithstanding the foliage, the light penetrated the room in all its strength, making patterns of the vine-leaves and honeysuckle on the wall. Between the windows was one of those antique chests of drawers of carved oak of great size. On the right in a sort of alcove was a bed with three mattresses. Four chairs of the same style as the chest of drawers occupied the embrasure of the smaller windows, and to the left in an old black frame was an engraving of Frederick II. On the chest of drawers were a water-bottle and two goblets of Bohemian glass.

'Why, you lodge me like a prince, Père Honeck,' I cried enthusiastically.

'You are satisfied, then?'

'Am I satisfied? Why a prince could not be better treated. Yes, I am content, quite content, I assure you. I have never been better lodged. I am in the seventh heaven,' I exclaimed, as I seated myself at a window and let my eyes roam from the yard to the garden, from the garden to the orchard, from the orchard to the meadow, and the river as far as the eye could reach. What a view it was! Ah! how I *could* work, how freely I could breathe, how truly I could give myself up to the contemplation of those woods, those dells, those mountains!

'Very well,' said the old man; 'all right; so much the better if everything is to your liking; but just see that you have all that you require.'

'What more can I require? Everything seems as if it had been specially prepared for me. But – one moment – wait – is there—?'

'Well – out with it!'

'By Jove! It is not so easy to find what I want here!'

'What is it, then?'

'An easel.'

'What on earth is that?'

'A sort of desk on which I rest my pictures.'

'I have never seen one,' replied the keeper, becoming uneasy.

'After that, Père Frantz, we must put up with the loss, only it is not so convenient.'

'If I had known – if I had only seen it – perhaps—'

'I will show you the kind of thing it is.'

Then opening my knapsack, with four strokes of a pencil I sketched an easel. The keeper understood it at once.

'Is that all?' he exclaimed, laughing. 'You may rest assured you will have one in the morning. I am something of a workman, M. Théodore, in all branches of trade. One must be so when one lives in the woods. My granddaughter often gives me a bit of carpentering to do. Let me go to work. I will take my saw and plane. You will help me, and we will settle it together.'

'All right; that's understood.'

And full of energy I set about unpacking my colours, my pencils, my palette, explaining to the old keeper as I did so the uses of all these things, which astonished him mightily, and he was quite impatient that I should set to work. I also unrolled my canvas, after arranging the dimensions of the picture which he was desirous I should paint. Père Honeck undertook to make the frame himself.

All these arrangements occupied us quite two hours; we were still in the room chatting and arranging matters when the blast of a horn announced the return of the youthful Caspar.

'Hullo! time flies in your society,' said the old keeper, rising. 'It is midday already. The cows are returning. Let us go down, and after dinner we can set to work again.'

'By all means,' I replied. And we descended in high spirits.

II

It was exactly twelve o'clock when we came out upon the old gallery. The heat was almost insupportable.

It was the hour when everything seeks the shade; the cattle retire beneath the great trees, with bending limbs and closed eyes; the deer seek the coolest ferny retreats, the birds hide in the most leafy branches. All are silent except the insects, whose unceasing hum only renders the depth of silence more profound.

Young Caspar, his yellow hair hanging over his forehead like a tuft of grass, his face the colour of gingerbread, his little thin arms showing sunburnt to the elbow beneath his short-sleeved linen vest, once blue, and wearing trousers of threadbare linen ragged and hanging about his legs – this little Caspar, with his naked feet and his nose in the air, advanced proudly blowing his horn. Behind him came five or six goats with well-filled udders, an old male and three kids bringing up the rear. They appeared to be quite broiled by the sun, and meanwhile Caspar blew long blasts upon his horn which echoed to the very depths of the forest.

'Hi, Caspar!' cried the old keeper from the top of the staircase, 'take your goats in first – you can blow that horn of yours in the evening as much as you please.'

The youthful goatherd made no reply. He wiped his nose with the back of his hand, opened the gate into the yard, and looking at me all the time from the corner of his eye, he admitted the goats, which disported themselves in a frolicsome manner as they advanced to the stable. Then Père Frantz, looking at me with a smile, said: 'We must keep these young people up to their work, eh?'

We then descended the staircase, and turning the corner we entered the darkened parlour, which felt so cool in consequence of the luxuriant growth surrounding the window. Louise entered and laid a white cloth at one end of the table. In the centre were placed a small soup-tureen and three plates. I cannot deny that I was very much pleased to think that Louise was to dine with us.

'We must have some air at dinner-time,' said the old keeper as he threw open the lattice-casement. 'I would rather suffer a little greater heat than be unable to breathe freely. Sit down yonder, M. Théodore; now that you are one of us that shall be your place.'

I sat down against the wall. Louise appeared almost immediately with a bottle of clear water all covered with glittering air-bubbles, and a decanter of white wine.

As she placed them on the table she raised her eyes timidly, and encountered my steadfast gaze. She blushed deeply. I felt somewhat discomfited too.

'Well, Louise, what is there for dinner?' asked Père Honeck.

'You know very well, grandfather, that there is no meat in the house. I have made an omelette.'

She took the cover off the tureen, and the smell of some very excellent white soup pervaded the room. The soup having been served, we took it with great gusto, Frantz and I.

'What excellent soup!' I exclaimed when I had finished.

'Well, yes, it is not so bad,' said the old man, as he licked his moustache.

Louise having gone out to fetch the omelette, he leaned over towards me, and whispered: 'She can make soup as well and better than Mother Grédel at The Swan; it is a miracle.'

Louise re-entered at the moment, and he stopped.

After the omelette we had cheese by way of dessert, and a bumper of wine terminated the repast.

'I have had a good dinner,' said the keeper as he got up from the table; 'and you, M. Théodore?'

'I have dined capitally – could not be better,' I replied.

He then entered the kitchen, lit his pipe, and came out again, saying: 'Now then to work.'

It was nearly one o'clock; the shadows were beginning to lengthen in the yard; the dogs were sleeping on the doorstep, the fowls on the coping of the wall beneath the vines.

We turned round by the yard. As we passed I saw Louise through the small panes of glass washing the plates at the sink in the kitchen, and I could not help giving her a friendly nod. Beneath the staircase of the old gallery a sort of cavern opened, to which we descended by three steps. In the midst of this room we found a massive carpenter's bench, and the walls were hung around with saws, planes, and other tools.

Frantz took off his jacket, rolled up his sleeves, and, lifting up a pine plank, said: 'I think this will do for us. Now give me the measurements, M. Théodore.' So we began our work.

And thus it happened, my dear friends, that in the year of grace 1839, in the lovely month of August, I found myself installed with the old keeper, Frantz Honeck, in the depths of the forest of Rothalps.

III

To this day I can recall with pleasure the first hours of my sojourn at the house in the forest. Père Honeck came to wake me very early in the morning.

'Come along, M. Théodore,' he said, placing the lanterns on the chest of drawers. 'Day is breaking; it is time to get up.'

I hesitated, and began to stretch my arms.

'Ah, Père Frantz, if you only knew how I have slept!'

'Slept at your age! Bah! you told me the other day that I was not to attend to you; it was only joking on your part. Now get up; it is a splendid morning.'

Then, taking my courage in both hands, I jumped up, had a hasty wash, half dressed myself, and, very chilly, I pushed aside the creepers to take a look at the prospect without.

The misty rain was falling thickly, and all was grey, vague, and confused. The keeper left the room; his lantern was on the chest of drawers. I dressed, and put on my thick leather boots to walk in the rain. Five minutes afterwards Waldine and Fox burst in upon me, jumping up and wagging their tails.

Pressing my felt hat over my ears I glided past Louise's chamber and descended to the yard, where I found Master Honeck standing beneath the cart-shed, his fowling-piece slung over his shoulders.

'Here you are, then; let us be off,' he said.

He opened the garden gate, and we took the path leading to Grinderwald. We proceeded at a good pace, Père Frantz in advance with bent back, his limbs as steady as a young man's. I came behind, still somewhat sleepy; but very soon the fresh morning air, the movement, the feeling of satisfaction at having conquered my laziness, dissipated all unpleasant impressions. After the lapse of a few minutes I felt comfortable and vigorous, and could have accomplished my fifteen leagues without fatigue.

Oh, that night march! The solitude of the woods, the freshness, the perfume of the giant pines and the wild plants – how all this invigorates one, clears the brain, and sets the pulses of life bounding afresh!

We did not speak; we walked along, given up to our own reflections without any need to communicate them one to the other. We were bound for the distant 'felling villages' of Grinderwald, amongst the forest population.

Have you, my readers, ever heard, very early in the morning, the hatchet of the woodcutter striking the oak with measured cadence? Have you ever heard in the distance, in the far distance, the sharp blows which are prolonged by the echoes? Then the creaking of the falling tree, the warning shout, the rustling of the leaves, and the dull thud of the giant measuring his length upon the earth, crashing among the brushwood? Have you ever beheld the fire of the charcoal-burner under the dark shade of the green boughs, tinting with a red glow the briars and moss, and throwing a ruddy tinge even upon the tops of the lofty fir-trees, then drawing the luminous belt closer only to spread it out wider than before? And the charcoal-burner standing out in strong relief, squatting by the flame, his great felt hat flattened upon his back, smoking a short pipe, and turning the potatoes in the embers; have you ever seen this behind the underwood? Well, it was in the centre of such a strange world as this that Père Honeck and I were to travel for days in the forest of Rothalps.

Thanks to these morning rambles I became thoroughly acquainted with the locality in about three weeks; the rocks, torrents, ravines, felling stations, charcoal-burners, the old roads of *schlitte* – in fact, all the best points of view, except, perhaps, the Lake of the Wild Huntsman, of which the old keeper declined to speak.

I recollect quite well, as we were going to Grinderwald, the fancy that, for the twentieth time, possessed me to revert to this subject.

'Ah, by-the-bye, there is the Lake of the Wild Huntsman, Père Honeck; when shall we go thither?'

He was, as usual, on in front, and, turning slowly, would gaze at me with a peculiar expression; then, raising his hand and pointing towards the north, he would reply brusquely: 'The lake is yonder, M. Théodore, between those high peaks; you can go there if you like.'

'How? Will you not guide me?'

'You want a guide to the Wild Huntsman's Lake. No, no; every one is free to do as he pleases. I will not prevent you from going since you are bent upon it, but Frantz Honeck does not go up that side of the mountain – not he.'

The old man said this in such a mysterious manner that it impressed me; my desire to see this lake naturally increased; yet a sort of deference to my host's opinion prevented my going thither; so I waited a favourable opportunity.

But we returned from our expeditions to Grinderwald between seven and eight o'clock. Louise had laid the cloth; the omelette, the wine, and the water awaited us. We sat down gladly and ate with good appetite, drank our wine, then smoked our pipes leaning from the window and watching little Caspar opening the stabledoor, then cracking his whip as his long line of cows and goats filed in. This was still the pleasantest time of the day, one of those calm, sweet rural scenes whose remembrance fades not.

Sometimes I went alone to the borders of the Howald, to the banks of the Losser, to paint a rock, a cluster of oaks, a corner of the forest; or to the opposite hills to study the long perspectives. I never worked so well in my life. And the portrait – I made great progress with that.

I can fancy I see Père Honeck now seated clad in his grand green uniform, with yellow braid, his forage-cap tilted over one ear, buttoned up, brushed very solemn, his carbine between his knees, his pouch and haversack on one side, his game-bag on the other; his heavy grey moustache turned up at the ends. Behind him Louise, red as a turkey-cock, her pretty fair hair crowned with a little cap of black hair with pink and gold ornaments, the little sky-blue silk *fichu* crossed over her bosom, and her pretty arms, naked to the elbow, crossed over the back of the chair.

I had, above all things needful, capital light, that tempered by the leafy screens overhead. The foliage on the right, the small lattice-window, the pretty face of Louise, her rounded arms, her pretty plump hands, her peasant costume, so neat and picturesque, and the sunburnt wrinkled face of the old keeper, with his grey piercing eyes beneath his bushy white eyebrows, all harmonised wonderfully in this darkened light.

And then I did all I could myself; I painted with all my soul, all my love, all my enthusiasm, arising from my life in the open air, my admiration for the mountains, my happy existence, centered thus in the forest; there was all this in the picture, the most complete and the best executed portrait I had ever done.

As the picture advanced towards completion Père Honeck appeared to like me more and more. Often-times when returning from my rambles in the evening I found him in my room contemplating the portrait in a sort of ecstasy.

'Ah, there you are, M. Théodore!' he used to say; 'I am in the humour to have a peep at myself.'

'And does it suit? Are you contented with it?'

'Monsieur Théodore, do you require the opinion of such a poor old fellow as I? You are an artist, and I am only an old ignorant keeper. You know that you were right to put in the grey, the red, and the brown, and all sorts of colours necessary. You are a true artist. And that picture, let me tell you, though it is only the portrait of Frantz Honeck and his granddaughter Louise, ought to be placed in a castle, and not in the poor dwelling of a forester.'

Thus the old keeper spoke in a tone of conviction that

charmed me. But more than all I wished to hear Louise's opinion, and I did not dare to ask it.

'What sense that girl has!' said Frantz to me one day. 'Yesterday morning, as we were returning from Grinderwald, I was thinking very much of our portrait, and I was wondering how a few patches of green, yellow, or red on the grey could represent people so exactly, so that they appeared to exist long after their deaths. The more I pondered the less I understood it. As I came into the yard I found Louise feeding the fowl. "Ah, Louise," I cried, "can you tell me how it is that our portrait is more beautiful than the picture of Saint Catherine at Pirmasens?" "Why, grandfather, it is because it lives." "Lives!" "Why of course it is not your face, not mine, that M. Théodore is painting, nor the vine-leaves at the window, nor the daylight: it is our souls!" 'Do *you* understand this fine distinction?' said the old man. 'She found out the reason at once. There are no children now-a-days – no children now.'

And Père Frantz laughed heartily. For my part I was very glad to know Louise's opinion at last. The old keeper had no misgivings respecting my increasing affection for his grand-daughter; and myself – had I seriously considered the question? Day by day Louise identified herself more and more with those I held dearest in the world. In the house I could not catch her dainty footfalls or the rustle of her dress without listening for her approach. Out of doors there was Louise. I could see her before me in the path; her graceful figure, her fair hair, her springing step appeared to me amid the shade of the brushwood. And in the evening, as I hastened homewards towards the house whose roof peeped amid the trees, it was not Père Honeck whom I first descried, it was always Louise in the gallery, in the garden, or perhaps at one of the upper windows, framed in the ivy or honeysuckle.

'Well, M. Théodore, have you found a good subject?' she would exclaim in her pleasant voice. 'Are you satisfied with your work?'

'Yes, Louise, yes, I am, quite so. Everything is so beautiful here.'

I should have liked to say more, but that calm, clear gaze of the girl inspired more respect than love.

Nevertheless, one evening, when we were in the old galley watching the glorious autumn sunset, and both Louise and I were silent in admiration of the beauty of the sight, suddenly, and as it were in spite of myself, I exclaimed sadly: 'Oh, why cannot I always remain here? Why must I leave this place?'

Louise looked at me in surprise.

'Do you wish to go away, M. Théodore?' she said, a slight blush overspreading her countenance as she spoke.

'Yes, Louise, I must go. They are expecting me at Dusseldorf, and besides, the picture is finished now.'

My voice trembled. Louise, who was watching me, dropped her head without making any answer. After a long pause she murmured as if to herself: 'Great Heaven, I never thought of that!'

For more than a quarter of an hour we remained silent, leaning over the balcony, and not daring to look at one another. I was conscious of a voice within saying to me, 'Speak; tell her you love her.' But another and a more powerful voice replied, 'No, Théodore, do not do that; remember the hospitality you have enjoyed; remember that the old man has treated you like his own son. You may not be able to carry out your promise to Louise.'

And as I listened to these two voices young Caspar appeared with his file of goats; then Louise, lifting her eyes like one awakening from a dream, said: 'It is seven o'clock, M. Théodore; grandfather will soon be back. I must go and attend to the cooking.'

She descended the staircase with bowed head and abstracted air. I entered my room, and sitting down by the window I rested my head between my hands and reflected on the consequences until the cheery voice of Père Honeck reached me: 'M. Théodore, come down; the cloth is laid.'

I went and sat down at table. Père Frantz had that day shot a splendid grouse, and intended to take it himself to the ranger at Pirmasens. He told us how, when returning from the stubble-field, a herd of wild boar had crossed the track, and that one of these fine mornings he would pay them a visit so that I might taste boar's-head. All these incidents had made him very cheerful, and he took a glass more than usual; then, caressing his moustaches, he said to Louise: 'My child, the night is fine; let us go outside and sit upon the bench and sing the hymn "Oh Lord, the Author of our holy thoughts".'

Louise blushed, and said she did not feel inclined to sing.

'Bah!' said the old man, taking her by the arm; 'you must come out, and the singing will come too. M. Théodore, you have never heard Louise sing; she has a voice – a voice – well, I have never heard anything to equal it!'

So we went out.

Little Caspar was cutting a whip-handle from the hedge in the garden. We sat down upon the old moss-covered stone seat, and Père Honeck struck up the hymn.

Louise's sweet voice took up the tune and mounted to heaven so purely that all the fibres of my heart responded tremblingly.

The voices harmonised so perfectly that I could not remember ever having listened to anything more beautiful; it was like the ivy clinging in graceful festoons around the topmost branches of an ancient oak in Grinderwald. Then the night was so lovely; the streaks of the sunset glow extended from one valley to the other; a gentle breeze agitated the leaves.

Gravely absorbed in my reflections I listened, and at length, impelled by a mysterious impulse, I united my voice to those of the old keeper and his granddaughter.

Little Caspar, in a neighbouring bramble, stretched forth his neck, and with wide-open eyes gazed at us in delight. When we had finished Honeck cried out: 'Well, Caspar, what do you think of that, eh?'

The youth only struck his cheek with the back of his hand in reply.

Never shall I forget that evening; we remained out there singing, chatting of the picture, of hunting on distant expeditions, of lovely landscapes, until nearly ten o'clock.

The stars were shining out in thousands overhead, when at length the old keeper said, as he rose up: 'We must start for Pirmasens tomorrow morning at three o'clock; we ought to go to bed now. Good night, M. Théodore.'

'Good night, Père Frantz; good night, Mademoiselle Louise.'

And I mounted the staircase thankful for all the blessings I had received.

IV

Once alone in my room I was in the habit of pondering upon the affairs of the day, and a melancholy feeling took possession of me. I had no desire to sleep, so I sat down, leaning my elbow upon the window-sill, and gazed out between the large leaves which were silvered by the moon's rays.

The various sounds of our forest residents had one by one died away, the old keeper was in bed, the dogs had stretched themselves comfortably in their corners, the silence, a profound silence, fell upon everything, and was scarcely broken by the murmur of the wind through the trees, and I thought, 'In a few days I shall be leaving here, knapsack on shoulder, *bâton* in hand; Louise will say in her sweet voice, "Adieu, M. Théodore, adieu!" Père Honeck will accompany me some distance on my journey, to the fork of the river perhaps, and will then shake my hand, saying: "Well, well, we must part. I wish you a pleasant journey, M. Théodore; Heaven be with you!" And that would be the end of all these days of peace and love – nothing but a memory henceforth!'

Thinking of these things, I felt a sad swelling of the heart.

'Ah! if you could only live by your work, or if your aunt Catherine would make you a nice little allowance, you could decide this question. But as things are at present you must go, and as your voice trembles each time you speak to Louise you must avoid being alone in her society, so that Père Frantz may think you a man of honour, and you may think the same of yourself!'

So I determined to set out next day to the Lake of the Wild Huntsman as soon as Père Honeck had left us for Pirmasens; and about eleven o'clock I went to bed satisfied with the resolutions I had taken.

But other things occurred in the course of that night, such strange events as will never be effaced from my mind.

Philosophers think that there is nothing in this world that does not come under the control of our senses, and such men when dying gaze in an affrighted manner into the gloom as if they could perceive something terrible which they fear to meet in a closer inspection. Then some one says, 'What do they perceive yonder? are there other beings in existence which are visible only to the dying?'

The fly, fluttering towards the sunlight, does not see the spider which is watching for him in his web; he does not perceive him until it is too late to escape his clutches. But what can one say upon such a subject as that to which I have referred? These beings either exist or they do not exist. We shall know one day, and the later the better!

I slept quietly enough until about one o'clock, when the plaintive howling of Waldine and Fox awoke me suddenly. I raised myself upon my elbow and listened intently. The moon was shining brilliantly just opposite my window, the trellis-work with the leaves and climbing plants crossed its disc in black relief, as did the little hexagonal panes, and farther away five or six sprays of the fir-trees cut the shining surface.

Just awakened from sleep as I was, this effect of light and

shade had a most peculiar appearance, but the howling of the dogs had a most depressing effect; they gave forth their yells in full cry slowly, and in a prolonged howl, from a low note to the highest sharp of which a canine throat is capable.

I now remembered that Spitz, the old dog belonging to my aunt Catherine, had howled in just such a manner while my uncle Matthias was dying; and this thought made my blood run cold.

Soon the lowing of the cows, the cries of the goats, and the grunting of the pigs mingled with the howling of the dogs in a most dreadful *ensemble*. Then Père Honeck jumped out of bed, the window underneath was opened hastily, and the rattle of a gun being loaded struck upon my ear. I waited for the shot, and my blood chilled as I listened, but the dogs continued to howl, the cattle to low without cessation, and just as the blood was leaving my flushed cheeks, I heard the old keeper call out: 'Fox, Waldine, keep quiet there!'

It was a great relief to me to hear his voice, and I may confess that the superstitious fears I had experienced dispersed; it seemed as if the dread influence had passed away, and I arose full of courage.

From the old gallery I immediately perceived Père Honeck, gun in hand, standing upright before the low wall of the yard. He was only half-dressed; his head was raised, his hair was dishevelled; he had all the appearance of a person listening intently for something.

I hurriedly descended the staircase.

'In the name of Heaven what is this all about?' I asked in a low voice.

'Ah!' he replied, turning his head, and pointing towards the gorge of the Losser, 'it is that brute who is passing with his band. Listen! It is the Wild Huntsman.'

I listened, but no sound except the distant murmur of the river broke upon my ears. I was surprised. 'But, Père Frantz,' I said after a pause, 'I do not hear anything.'

Then the old keeper, as one who is awaking from a dream,

turned very pale, and fixing his grey eyes upon mine, said with a strange look in his face: 'It is a wolf – yes, the old wolf of the Veierschloss with his cubs. Every year that beast prowls about the house. The dogs even are aware of his presence; they are afraid of him.'

Then approaching the hounds he said, as he patted their heads to reassure them: 'Come, come, old fellow; Waldine, lie down; that cursed beast is far away by this time; he will not return.'

The dogs, trembling still, rubbed themselves against their master's legs, at the same time the goats and cows ceased to bleat and bellow.

Père Honeck, rising, grounded his gun, and with a forced smile said: 'I am sure you were afraid, M. Théodore; is it not so? Those sounds at the dead of night always produce a very curious sensation; so many ideas crowd upon one's brain. But you see dogs are like human creatures; when they get old they dote – a poor wretched wolf frightens them; instead of attacking him they cry like blind animals, and attempt to save themselves. Well, well, they are quiet now, and the cattle also; so we may go to bed and have a good sleep.'

As he spoke he opened the door of his room, and shivering, I once again ascended to my own.

All this appeared to me very unnatural; the tone of the old keeper's voice, his pallor, the curious expression of his grey eyes as he spoke of wolves and their cubs, all seemed to me equivocal. I was quite upset and nervous. Was this the effect of the chill night-air, the sudden interruption of my sleep, or what other cause had rendered me so excited? I could not understand, but for the first time the conviction of invisible influences, of supernatural beings, took possession of my mind.

I jumped into bed and hid my head beneath the clothes up to my ears; then with wide-open eyes I kept looking at the lattice and thinking of all these things. The moon had passed away from the window; she was now lighting up the side of the house and the fir plantation below. While I slept I fancied I could hear the dogs growling again from time to time like the distant muttering of a storm; these animals were as nervous as I was.

At length all was quiet, and my brain being worn out by these strange occurrences, I fell fast asleep.

V

When I awoke it was broad daylight, the fowls were cackling in the yard, the dogs were running about, and all else was quiet and peaceful around our forest home. I dressed quietly and went downstairs into the large dining-room. There I found Père Honeck walking up and down in a 'brown study'. The breakfast was laid as usual upon the white cloth.

'What! still here, Père Honeck!' I exclaimed. 'Why I thought you were halfway to Pirmasens by this time!'

'Caspar has gone instead, M. Théodore,' he replied. Then after a pause he added as we seated ourselves: 'I must remain here; Louise is not very well, and cannot get up this morning.'

The occurrences of the night came to my recollection, and I now remembered that Louise had not appeared during the alarm, and that struck me as strange. I would gladly have mentioned the subject to Père Frantz, but towards the end of our meal the old keeper became unusually silent, and appeared less inclined to converse than usual; he evidently was concealing something, and I did not think it prudent to question him.

'Well, that is not very serious, Père Honeck,' I said as we rose from table.

'Let us hope it may not be,' he replied gravely. 'Are you going out anywhere today, M. Théodore?'

'Yes, I think of going to sketch the "Thrushes' Retreat" in the Howald.'

'Good – go,' he said, as if glad to be rid of me.

I nodded and went out. Soon afterwards I took my sketch-book and the path to the Howald.

'It is quite time I went,' I said to myself sadly. 'The picture is finished, the girl is ill. Père Frantz has some secret lurking in his mind. I shall become a nuisance in the house. Everything in this mundane sphere must have an end. I have been well received and lodged, and I ought to be content. Now it is "Farewell, M. Théodore; take care of yourself."'

I was thoroughly unhappy.

The image of Louise – that soft pink and white face – gripped my heart 'with hooks of steel'. The somewhat reserved tone of the old keeper when speaking to me respecting his granddaughter gave me sufficient food for reflection. Was Louise really ill, or was Père Honeck doubtful about my affection for her? What ideas was I picturing to myself on this subject! I went on at random; a distant gleam in the brushwood, the profile of an aged tree, the grey form of a decaying old trunk covered with moss and ivy, arrested my footsteps: I wished to go on, and take the memory of the place with me everywhere, but I had no fancy for anything; the fair maiden face occupied me entirely.

About three o'clock the weather became overcast, and up to that time I had never yet seen the grand old forest without the sunbeams. A fine mist began to fall. I turned back and retraced my steps. Autumn was upon us, I realised. I determined to tell Père Honeck that I was about to return to Dusseldorf.

About six o'clock I drew near the house once again, and I could perceive the old keeper at the door. He waved his hand to me, apparently glad at my return, but it was only a momentary brightness, and his face resumed its serious expression.

'Have you a change of clothes, M. Théodore?' he said as I came up.

'Yes, I have all that I require.'

'All right; run upstairs; I will wait for you; dinner is laid.'

'Very well; I will be down in five minutes.'

He entered the passage, and I ascended to my room, changed, and came down to dinner. As the afternoon was gloomy, Frantz Honeck lighted the lamp. We supped together without speaking. He was in a reverie, his eyes fixed upon his plate, while I was irritated by his silence, to which I was unaccustomed.

This kind of thing lasted for half-an-hour. The solemn ticking of the old Nuremberg clock and the loud patter of the unceasing rain upon the leaves appeared to lengthen that period indefinitely, and forced me to count the quarters of the seconds. I shall never forget that evening. How was I to announce my approaching departure? It was easy enough. I had only to say, 'Père Honeck, I must leave you tomorrow.' Yes, but what would he think of such a sudden determination? Would he not attribute it to the discontent with which I experienced his reserve, to the irksomeness of Louise's absence, perhaps even to the discovery of the secret he wished to conceal? What do I know? In uncertainty everything stops one.

I kept gazing at the old keeper, who sat with knitted brows, and appeared scarcely conscious of my presence.

However, as he pushed back his chair to the window and took up his pipe, according to custom, suddenly, in a loud voice, I said: 'Père Frantz, look at the rain; it may continue for some days. The picture is completed. My aunt Catherine expects me at Dusseldorf. I must tell you at once tomorrow I leave here.'

Then he, fixing his grey eyes on me, and looking as if he would read my very soul, replied, after a pause: 'Yes, yes, I expected as much. You are going away, and will carry with you a false impression concerning Frantz Honeck and his granddaughter.'

'A false impression! Why I have never experienced such hospitality as yours, Master Frantz, so cordial, so frank, so—'

'Oh, that is not my meaning. You cannot conceal anything from me, M. Théodore; you have too open a countenance to conceal your thoughts. I saw it last night, and I see it now in your eyes, that you have something on your mind; you suspect Frantz Honeck of keeping secrets.'

I could not help blushing, and he continued as he filled his pipe: 'Well, you cannot deny it, so you see I am right. But it shall never be said that a straightforward fellow like you, a man of feeling, a true artist, quitted this house with any suspicions of us. No, no, that shall never be. You shall know all; you shall know why I have refused to guide you to the Lake of the Wild Huntsman; why the dogs howled so last night, why Louise is ill – everything. I have been thinking of this since the morning. It is not to every one that one would confide family matters, sacred confidences touching religion and honour. No; one must know and esteem the person to whom we confide such things.'

'Master Honeck, your esteem and friendship touch me deeply, but if it be in the least unpleasant—'

'No, not the least; it is not as if you were a scamp. Listen, M. Théodore. I will just go down to the cellar and fetch a bottle of wine, and since you wish to leave us, well, we will drink a parting glass.'

And without waiting for my reply he descended to the cellar.

My readers can picture my astonishment; the grave manner in which Père Frantz spoke announced the serious nature of his confidence. The strange occurrence of the preceding night, the lugubrious howling of the dogs, the indisposition of Louise, the refusal of the old keeper to conduct me to the Lake of the Wild Huntsman – how could he explain all these? What mysterious narration could reconcile such widely-different occurrences? I confess all this excited my curiosity to a very high pitch.

When Père Honeck returned his face had undergone a change; the preoccupied expression of the day before had given way to a sort of exultation. He put the bottle on the table; then, seating himself and filling the glasses, he said: 'Fill your pipe first; this will be a long story, but as we are about to part for an indefinite period, we must not grudge passing a night together. Your health, M. Théodore.'

'Yours, Master Frantz.'

We drank the toast respectively. The old keeper, leaning out of the window, gazed around. Night had fallen; the rain had ceased; no sound, save the regular drip, drip, of the water, was heard as it fell from leaf to leaf. He then returned to his seat with a preoccupied air, and commenced his narrative as follows:

'Four hundred years ago there existed in this country a race of wolves. When I say wolves, I mean a savage race who delighted in hunting and fighting, and who believed that plants, animals, and men had been created solely for their enjoyment and food. This race is named the Wild Huntsmen, and in our old forest charts they are known by no other name. They themselves lay claim to the ancient stock of the *Burckar* kings of Suabia. Whether they were right or not I cannot say, but one thing is very certain, that they were thickset and broad-shouldered and entirely covered with hair; that they all, young and old, had low flat foreheads, yellow eyes, hook noses, enormous mouths, garnished with immense regular white teeth, and massive chins, bristling with shaggy beards which extended as high as the temples. Their arms were so long that they could reach below their knees without stooping, and this attribute gave them a great advantage in the handling of the sword, axe, or other instruments of warfare, in the use of which they were great adepts.

'On the other hand, it must be confessed that on the Rhine, from Strasburg to Cologne, and even farther, there were no such warriors and no more famous hunters than those wild men; they passed all their time on horseback, either hunting the deer, or in burning, pillaging, and sacking the smaller *châteaux*, the convents, the churches, and the hamlets in the vicinity.

'This race of nobly-born robbers had their headquarters for centuries in a fortress built upon the living rock, on the border of the lake bearing their name. The smallest blocks used in building this stronghold were ten feet square. Plants grew around in abundance, and even shrubs like the holly, the briar, and the hawthorn flourished. One would have fancied it an unbroken precipice, but behind the brushwood were embrasures through which the archers discharged their bolts upon the passers-by, as a party of sportsmen would fire upon defenceless game.

'A deep moat filled with water from the lake surrounded the castle, and above it rose four high square towers, whereon used to swing at the end of the long iron rods the bodies of the unhappy peasants who were caught poaching upon the territory of the Wild Huntsmen.

'Naturally the ravens, owls, and hawks enjoyed themselves immensely in a spot where flesh was never wanting. These birds might have been seen in the nooks of the Veierschloss cleaning their beaks, pluming themselves as they awaited their horrible banquet, or ranged in long files, their heads on their shoulders, with still sanguinary beaks, sitting, gorged and lethargic after their disgusting meals, upon the line of ramparts. At night their horrible cries filled the valley, and mingled with the songs of the robbers, just as in a farmyard the twittering of the sparrows is mingled with the "tic-a-tack" of the threshers in the barn after the harvest. Such, M. Théodore, is the manner in which these Burckars lived among the ruffians they had assembled round them to carry out their nefarious schemes, and it threatened to last for years. Fortunately, when misery is greatest Providence comes to our rescue, and by means such as those brigands cannot comprehend.

'The last of the race was called Vittikâb; he was just like the rest in appearance, in his love of gold, of hunting, of dogs and horses.

'And since I am on the subject I may tell you that these Wild Huntsmen had succeeded in obtaining, by cross-breeding the collie, the Danish dog, and the wolf, a race of dogs unrivalled in hunting, so hardy, so untiring were they. These were the wolf-dogs, thin muscular animals with upright ears, red eyes, jaws as firm as iron, long tails, strong haunches like all savage animals, and black claws. In all old hunting narrations they speak of these dogs, and wish that the breed could be restored, for they are sadly needed in wild-boar hunts; but the breed is extinct, and will never be resuscitated.

'Vittikâb, then, had the same tastes, and character as the other Burckars; he was the greatest hunter and the most accomplished robber of his time. I remember having seen, when I was a youth, a picture of him in an old almanac, in which he was represented as pillaging Landau. Every house was burning; people were clustered on the roofs, and extending their hands in supplication to Heaven, or casting their furniture from the windows. The Trabans at the end of the street had two or three children impaled upon their lances like frogs; enough to make your hair stand on end to look at the picture only; and when one thinks that there were men who actually committed such barbarities it makes one shudder. Underneath was written, "Sacking of Landau in the year 1409". And on the opposite page was a likeness of Vittikâb, very stern, a sort of helmet upon his head, with a protruding beak which extended almost as far as his nose. To look at him one would say he deserved to be burned alive – he was the most cruel brute on the earth.'

Père Frantz, pale with anger, lit his pipe at the candle; he closed his eyes and waited until the tobacco was properly lighted, a thoughtful expression upon his face. I kept looking at him in a dreamy fashion. At length he pushed the candle to the centre of the table again, and recommenced:

'Now I am compelled to admit that amongst this troop of Vittikâb's was my ancestor Zaphéry. That is a most painful reflection for me; I would rather have been descended from the poorest peasant who had suffered indignities at the hands of those rascals, for that would cause me to dwell upon the fortunes of my ancestors – now I can only blush for them. As I am powerless to change them, I consider that it is intended as a punishment for my pride, if I had any; but you know very well, M. Théodore, that I have none, and that I only pride myself upon my rank in the service, as all men ought to do who have got what they really deserved.

'This Honeck was at that time chief huntsman of the Veierschloss. If you will go near the Wild Huntsman's Lake tomorrow you will see the ruins of the castle; it is a great pile of rubbish which covers at least three acres. Two towers are still standing. Between them the portal can still be perceived, and above the door, on the right, near to the aperture, whence protruded one of the girders of the draw-bridge, is still a round-shaped window. There Zaphéry Honeck lived in a kind of vault above the guard-room. You can no longer get up there, because the staircase is broken away; but in my young days I very well remember my grandfather Gottlieb brought me there to tell me this history I am now telling you.

'In this vault Zaphéry could see from one side the opposite mountain, from the other the courtyard of the Veierschloss; for there were two courts, surrounded by high walls, and dark as cisterns. In the first were all the dog-kennels, ranged side by side, and a staircase to the right leading to the apartments of the chief Wild Huntsman himself; on the left a similar staircase led up to the resting-place of the commoner robbers; and beneath were the kitchens, the bakery, and the butcher's stalls. In the other court were the stables and the wood-house. You can go there tomorrow and you will see how solidly built it is.

'Honeck slept in that vault, and all day he hunted in the mountain. I do not know whether he actually took part in Vittikâb's expeditions, but he could not have been much better than the rest of them, because the Wild Huntsman liked him very much, and never went out hunting without him; they rushed together through the woods like the wind; they both thoroughly understood every trick and turn of the game they pursued. There never was such a fellow to sound the horn like Honeck, except Vittikâb, whose horn was three times larger, and whose blast almost tore the atmosphere asunder. When they sounded the *fanfare* together you might have heard them from the Howald to Steinberg; the old woods shook at the sound.

'Honeck had something cheerful in his disposition, but Vittikâb was as gloomy as night itself; his yellow eyes always appeared to be looking for something to kill; he never smiled. Every evening, in his want of occupation, he would compel Master Honeck to enter the upper cavern, hung with battle-axes, two-handed swords, antlers, and all kinds of defensive weapons, and pointing to the table, he would say: "Eat, drink; your master commands you!"

'And the huntsman, who desired nothing better, would seat himself before the venison and eat and drink abundantly as desired. The wine had been taken from Marmoutier cellars. They hobnobbed together. Honeck carried his wine like a mere bottle; he only made his cheeks and nose red. But the more Vittikâb drank the paler he became, the more he scowled, and the more absorbing became his desire for destruction.

'Then at times as night advanced and the numerous owls hooted all along the cornices flapping their wings, and rapping with their beaks, then the Wild Huntsman would stare for half an hour at a time at his friend Honeck without moving an eyelid, his lips closed, and his nose curved with a terrible expression. And when the other least expected it he would exclaim suddenly: "Why do you laugh, you rascal?"

'Honeck, like all old sportsmen, had a habit of closing the eye without knowing it. It was a nervous affection; he could not help it.

'"I was not laughing, my lord," he would reply.

'"I say you were!" roared the Burckar.

'"Well, since you wish it, I *was*, then," said Honeck; "but I couldn't help it."

'"Then why did you laugh?" repeated the count furiously.

'"I was thinking of the hunting, and—"

'"You lie! You were thinking – you were thinking of something very different."

'"What the devil should I be thinking of, then?" exclaimed Zaphéry. "If you would only say once and for all what you wish me to think about, I will tell you whenever you like to ask me, and then perhaps you will be satisfied."

'These words usually pacified Vittikâb when he had a gleam of sense left, but on other occasions his rage was much increased thereby, his yellow eyes gleamed instead of looking bloodshot; then it was high time for Honeck to get out of his reach, for when he appeared like that, the Burckar always attempted to kill his huntsman. So without losing any time in polite speeches and saying goodnight, at the very first gleam in his chief's eyes he made for the door; the count would follow him in a terrible rage, stammering out, "Stop, stop, or I will have you hanged." But Zaphéry paid no attention; he hurried down the staircase as if he were a robber. The dogs howled, the robbers rushed out of the guard-room to see what was the matter, and the count at once got calmer; the howling of the dogs somewhat sobered him, and he re-entered the room staggering, and muttering confusedly to himself.

'Honeck barricaded himself in his vault, and lay down upon a bearskin to sleep off the effects of the wine he had taken. In this manner those two drunkards passed their days and nights. This happened every night, except when a storm was raging without; then Vittikâb was in his glory. He listened with delight to the thunder resounding through the gorges of the Howald; and when the rain, the wind, and hail rushed through the air, when the whole surface of the lake was white with foam, he went out upon the ramparts of the Veierschloss; while all the birds were torn from their nests and dispersed by the furious tempest like leaves in a storm, then the Wild Huntsman rose up and said, "Let us be off."

'And they would descend, Honeck and he, staggering one against the other, and saddle their horses. The robber-band hearing them coming down would hasten to lower the drawbridge; they would rush out together like a thunderbolt into the fearful storm. Then Vittikâb would laugh at the crashing of the trees and at the driving rain. At daybreak they would return through the distant hamlet, and he would say: "Honeck, I can sleep a little this morning, I fancy. I have not done such a thing for a long time."

'The poor inhabitants of those forest villages, the woodcutters, the charcoal-burners, often out of work and destitute, their cabin roofs penetrated by the rain, their wives and children shivering with cold, standing haggard at the door of their wretched dwellings, and seeing the terrible Burckar pass by with paler cheeks and eyes more sunken even than theirs, would say: "How is it that such a grand personage as he, with plenty of money, and land, and corn, can be wretched? Ah! if we were only in his place, if we had but the hundredth part of his riches, or even the crumbs that fall from his table, how happy we should be! – we should be thankful indeed."

'Yes, it is all very well to say, "We should be happy," but one should see to the bottom of people's hearts before they wish to be like them. The sparrows are cold enough during the winter and seek for food in a most pitiable plight, but they become gay enough and twitter from branch to branch when spring comes. What good would it do me to have spring always here if I did not enjoy anything? What use would it be to me to possess the best land in the district if the dew of heaven never descended and if the grass dried up? What good would it be were I very strong, very powerful, and very rich, if no ray of tenderness ever warmed my heart, and the remembrance of no good action ever roused my better feelings? Every one knows where his own shoe pinches, but he does not carry other people's burthens. Before desiring a change he ought to look round him a little.'

The old keeper at this point winked at me and smiled. He then filled our glasses, and said: 'Your health, M. Théodore.'

'Yours, Père Frantz.'

'You may think, perhaps, that it was remorse for all his wicked actions that made the Burckar miserable. On the contrary, he regretted he had not committed more evil deeds. What made him so inveterate against human nature you shall soon hear, and you will see whether there is not a Providence on the earth; you shall see whether poor and honest men have not the best reasons to rejoice; although rich people may appear outwardly prosperous and happy, a worm is preying upon their hearts.

'Twenty years before that period, when Vittikâb was thirty years old, he married a daughter of the noble house of Lichtenberg, named Ursula. The count was much attached to this young lady, who was very beautiful and religious. He listened to her supplication sometimes when she begged the life of some poor creature whom he would have hanged. He trusted to have a son to continue the noble race of the Burckars, who would have also the inheritance in the Lichtenberg, because Ursula was an only child; these things had a softening influence upon his character.

'But when the child was born, you can picture his rage at finding it was absolutely a monster, a hideous being which had no resemblance to humanity. Instead of acknowledging that this was the natural consequence of the ferocity of the Burckars, who had behaved like wild beasts for generations, instead of submitting to the decrees of Providence, he snatched the infant from its mother's arms to strangle it. The young wife, who, notwithstanding all defects, loved her offspring – for you know, M. Théodore, that mother's love is deepened in proportion to the helplessness, weakness, or faults of the children – well, the poor mother threw her arms around her husband and implored him to spare the child with such touching appeals and copious tears that he, the greatest monster of his race, was moved, and yielded somewhat to her entreaties. But he put away his wife and interned her in her room at the other end of the gallery. And as he passed along the gallery and saw all the hunters, all the beaters, and the *reiters* below in the yard waiting the birth of the infant Burckar, to salute him with a martial flourish like his ancestors, he exclaimed in a terrible tone: "The burckar is dead. Let Goëtz come up. The rest of you may go to the devil!"

'He then returned to his lair.

'This Goëtz whom he had summoned was an old hunter of fifty years of age, still robust, and who had educated Vittikâb himself. He was the most devoted servant that the family ever had. In days gone by this man wished to kill a wild boar at bay, and while on the point of attack had missed his aim. The furious animal had then, by a single blow on the hip, rendered the hunter lame for life. He was rough in appearance and manner, but that did not prevent his being a fairly good-hearted fellow all the same.

'Two minutes afterwards he entered the private apartment of his chief, who, indicating the poor infant stretched upon the table, said: "There, look at that; that is a Burckar."

'The other recoiled, and the count, laughing like a hyena, said: "He is of thy master's blood. At first I thought of killing him, but the breed deserves better treatment. Listen, old friend; you are lame; you cannot walk; it is with difficulty you can mount a horse. Well, you shall take this descendant of Virimar, and shall hide him with you in the Martens' Tower, where you can live together. Perhaps he may improve as he grows older."

'Goëtz made an attempt to speak.

'"I am ashamed of my offspring," interrupted Vittikâb; "he must be concealed. I can depend upon nobody but you. If you refuse I will throw the thing into the lake, but woe to you if I repent afterwards!"

'"I will obey you," said Goëtz.

'That very day a report was spread that the child would be buried. Goëtz and Vittikâb descended into the cavern of Virimar, the first of the Burckars, with a small coffin, and were followed by a band of *reiters* carrying torches. He interred the coffin in the tomb of Virimar. Then Goëtz departed to the Martens' Tower with the child and with Hatvine, Vittikâb's old nurse, who used to follow the expeditions on a mule to tend the wounded and to watch over the spoils. Hatvine was directed to carry the food of these two isolated beings. Every morning she went up to the tower with a large saucepan, high up to the Martens' tower, the highest pinnacle of the Veierschloss.

'The poor mother, who did not cease night and day to mourn for her child, at length died of grief, and the women of Lichtenberg who had been attending upon her disappeared without any one knowing what became of them, all but one old woman who had attended the countess in her confinement; she was devoured by two of the great Danish dogs one evening when she was crossing the courtyard. These dogs were seldom let loose because of their ferocity, except when an occasional attack was to be made upon a wolf and her young. That night they chanced to be at liberty, and the poor old midwife was devoured by them; such was her fate!

'After these events Vittikâb could no longer contain himself; he nursed a spite against every one, particularly against children. About this time he entered upon his great wars against Trèves, Lutzelstein, Schirmeck, and Landau. The whole of the Hundsrück, from Alsace to the Vosges, rang with these startling tidings, and the remembrance of them has been transmitted through four centuries as a testimony of the extent to which men without honesty, religion, or honour can go. No savage beasts could supply a more cruel history.

'After these conflicts, which lasted eight years, Vittikâb came to the Veierschloss again, no longer ruddy as heretofore and reserved in manner; no longer the boon companion of his captain, Jacobus, and his lieutenant, Krapt, and the kind-hearted master to his old nurse, Hatvine. He could endure the society of no one except Honeck, for they ever were hunting and drinking together.

'But he was continually thinking about the child; sometimes he was anxious to have it killed, sometimes he was tempted to have it proclaimed a Burckar, notwithstanding its appearance, and to exterminate all those who would not confess its suitability; for the reflection, that his next of kin, the Geroldsek, the Dagsbourg, the Lutzelstein, savages like himself, hunters, man-slayers seeking only each other's destruction – to think that these relatives of his, whom he wished dead at least, should one day inherit his property, that they should divide his woods, his dogs, his horses, and the treasure amassed during past centuries by the Burckars in the caverns of the Veierschloss – to think that this must happen sooner or later, made his eyes glisten with fury. He would shake with rage, and perambulate the galleries with flashing eyes, his red beard stiff with anger, and with a dreamy, fearsome aspect such as an untamed tiger wears in his cage.

'How to obviate this, how could it be obviated, that was the question.

'The more he pondered over it the less he saw his way to an accomplishment. He was minded to burn it all – the castle and the wood together; but the ground would still remain, and gold and the ruins; his cousins would rebuild the Veierschloss!

'What was to be done? He got very tipsy by way of sharpening his intellect; then one night he made his way towards the Martens' Tower. He was going to see the "monster", whom old Goëtz had christened Hâsoum, in the expectation that he would prove something human after all; but he always returned more disgusted than ever.

'The old nurse and Goëtz only were in the secret; the other inhabitants of the castle had no doubt something took place in the tower, yet no one had sufficient courage to go and find out, and if by chance Vittikâb had encountered any one upon the staircase he would have cleft him to the chine.

'For twelve years things went on in this manner, in which period expeditions were organised against the castles of Triefels, Haut-Bar, Fénétrange, and many others, for in these unhallowed days all the landed proprietors in the chain of the Vosges and Mont Tonnere waged perpetual war.

'Vittikâb succeeded in all his undertakings, but to what purpose! If in returning from the chase he happened to remark the beautiful trees around, he would think, "All these lovely woods will revert to my cousins." Did his serfs come with their tribute of corn, barley, oats, hay, fowls, butter, or eggs when the rent was due, instead of being satisfied he would think, "My cousins will be rich." Had he made a successful foray, and returned with plunder, he would hold aloof from his jolly captain, Jacobus, and his *reiters*. Alone in the rear of the party, pale and worried, he would mutter between his clenched teeth, "Must I still risk my neck to benefit Geroldsek or Dagsbourg, and fill my coffers for them to empty?" So thus the older he grew the more the world troubled him.

'And then from time to time, and particularly at night after Honeck's departure, a fearful retrospection assailed him. He would recall to mind that during the burning of Landau, as an old smith endeavoured to escape, bearing his grandchild on a mattress in the expectation of saving him from the slaughter, he (Vittikâb) had commanded that both the fugitives should be thrown into the flames, and that the old man, standing erect in the midst of the burning piles, and holding his grandchild up at arm's length to preserve him as long as possible, exclaimed: "Thou merciless Burckar, without feeling or compassion, thou shalt one day need pity, and shalt not receive it. Thou destroyer of children, thou shalt desire children, and shalt not have them. *Cursed mayst thou be – ay, cursed as Herod!"*

'All this came back to him in the gloom – the old man's face, his flashing eyes, the voice, and, notwithstanding his intoxication, he quailed and stammered out: "You lie, you lie! I shall have children!" And the old man seemed to reply: "It is thou thyself that liest; thou shalt never have children; they will be but monsters!"

'Nevertheless this dream did not prevent the reflection that he was still young, and could, if he chose, marry a lady of noble lineage who would regenerate the tainted stock of the Burckars, and then he would have children born to him.

'One evening, when he and his huntsman were busily employed in getting tipsy as usual – they scarcely spoke except with a shrug of the shoulders or a wink occasionally – Vittikâb, cold and reserved, was listening to an owl which was hooting at regular intervals in a neighbouring loophole. Suddenly starting from his reverie he said: "Tomorrow morning early you shall saddle a pair of horses, and we will ride together. You understand?"

'"For hunting?" asked Honeck.

'"No, to see the Roterick at Birkenstein at the other side of the Losser."

'He was silent and Honeck, bowing, said:

'"Good, my lord; it shall be done."

'But he did not quite comprehend the Wild Huntsman's meaning, for the barons of Roterick had been enemies of the Burckars for centuries, and hitherto Vittikâb, too far distant to molest them, had treated them with contempt.

'You must know, M. Théodore, that the barons of Roterick belong to the old nobility of Germany. They were really more noble and more courageous than the Burckars, but poor and ruined. These barons had always been deceived and despoiled by the Burckars without ever having been conquered by them. They had defended their religion against the Saracens, and their mother country against the Turks, the Spaniards, and Italians. They had joined the crusades, and in the taking of the Holy Sepulchre, and the emperors too, at any time when they found it necessary to avenge an insult or to defend their ancient rights against any one, no matter who.

'The Burckars all this time remained in their native fastnesses; they laid hands upon everything that came in their way; and the Roterick, on their return from their distant campaigns, would always find that these robbers had taken a corner of a wood, a valley, a pond, or some villages. This made them very angry; they disputed, fought; but as people are usually weakened on their return from a campaign, men and money both wanting, the Roterick could not fight it out, and the Burckars remained masters of the possessions they had annexed.

'Thus it came to pass that the Roterick were spoiled most completely, and the Burckars, who always stood in fear of them, could not get rid of them by fair means, so had finished by burning their *château* of Birkenstein.

'After all this you can imagine the feelings of the last Roterick for the last Burckar, who he declared was nothing but a bandit. Vittikâb, on his part, treated the other as a beggar, a "tatterdemalion", because he was really very poor, and his ancient castle was built in the side of the mountain, where it lay surrounded by palisades, and the whole place looked more like a half-burnt farm than the residence of a noble family.

'But all this did not detract from the pride of the owner, who was as haughty as if he had a thousand retainers at his back, and while he bestrode his old pony with his sword buckled on his thigh he looked down upon Vittikâb with great disdain. He lived wretchedly, it is true, with only his daughter Vulfhild and his old squire Péters; the rents of a small village and a little hunting scarcely sufficed for the requirements of the occupants of the castle; but inasmuch as the blood of the Wild Huntsman was thin and vitiated, so much was that of the Roterick pure and good. Throughout

Germany it was said, "Roterick has rich blood. Burckar's has a wolfish tinge."

'Vittikâb knew that very well; he had for a long time thought of this subject, and had taken his resolution to have children with human faces, to marry Vulfhild, and to give the old baron every satisfaction that he might demand.

'He said nothing of all these resolutions overnight, but left home very early next day with Honeck for Birkenstein. Roterick, wearing a red leather cap, looked tall, thin, and worn, and had clear grey eyes; his hair was white as snow, but he was still upright and stood firmly, notwithstanding his great age. Roterick was at the door of the old castle; the arch stood out against the clear sky; the walls at the other side had fallen down; he was gazing with pride upon his heather when Vittikâb and his huntsman made their appearance. At first his indignation knew no bounds. He signed to them not to approach, and old Péters ran up with a halberd, but Vittikâb appeared as one who had come to repair the ill-usage his ancestors had committed, and to form with the Roterick a lasting alliance. The old noble, astonished at such proposals, permitted the Burckar to enter the courtyard.

'He and Vittikâb then entered into the armoury, the only chamber which had escaped unhurt in all the pile, and held a council for two long hours.

'Goodness only knows what the wild count promised the old baron. He promised, no doubt, all that he would have exacted had he been capable and powerful enough to demand his rights, sword in hand: the rebuilding of his castle, the restitution of his domain, his stables, and his pack of hounds. That must have been so, for at the termination of the conference they were reconciled.

'Vittikâb, accompanied by the baron, then went to visit Vulfhild, who occupied a moss-grown tower, and amused herself in working tapestry in the company of two old women. Notwithstanding the sinister appearance of the

Burckar, the daughter of Roterick consented to become the mistress of the Veierschloss, and permitted the Wild Huntsman to kiss her white hands.

'But one thing is very certain – that on his return the Count Vittikâb rode with loose rein, and looked twenty years younger; his pale cheeks glowed once more, he laughed loudly, and in a clear strong voice he addressed himself to his companion, saying: "Zaphéry, all goes well. We shall have children this time – proper children. We will bring them up for hunting – ha, ha! they will have long arms and hairy, but they will be men."

'"I quite believe it, my lord," replied the other without the least understanding what his master said.

'"Yes," said Vittikâb, "the old Burckar race is not extinct. The Geroldsek and the Dagsbourg shall never handle the gold of the Virimar; they shall never hunt our game nor mount our horses."

'And, rising in his stirrups, he threw his arms aloft, and his long sallow face beamed with enthusiasm; he uttered cries of triumph which echoed through the woods for an immense distance.

'Honeck had never seen his master so joyous but on one occasion previously, and that was at the assault of Landau, when he scaled the walls and cut off the lance-points with his battle-axe like grass. He was terrible in his joy!

'But as they drew near the Veierschloss he became more grave, but was quite as happy. He blew his horn as a signal to the retainers to let down the drawbridge, and the pair entered the castle.

'In the courtyard they found Captain Jacobus, Lieutenant Krapt, and many soldiers. Vittikâb, ere he dismounted, addressed them all in a pithy speech thus: "I wish you all to understand that I, Vittikâb, Count and Lord of Veierschloss, and the noble lady Vulfhild of Roterick, are affianced, and that the marriage will be celebrated in three weeks from this day. I wish all around me to be happy as on an occasion of a victory and a distribution of spoil. We shall not stint the wine. He who will not rejoice will deserve to be hanged, and he who gainsays what I tell you will have to settle accounts with me. So make yourselves happy. I desire it."

'He regarded the astonished assembly with a piercing gaze, and then hastened up to the gallery amid shouts of "Long live the count! Long live Vulfhild!", cries which have been in use for centuries to toady those who are masters.'

At this point the old forester paused; he knocked the ashes from his pipe and placed it on the window-sill to cool. Then after a pause, during which he gazed at me with favour, he said: 'M. Théodore, I am sure that you have never brought tears to the eyes of any human being. I can say as much for myself too, although my hair is white and my life is almost sped. That is why we are so quiet and calm in the middle of the night, that is why nothing troubles us: we have placed our hopes in Providence. The spirit of darkness may hover around us as he pleases; he cannot take possession of our hearts, he cannot inspire evil thoughts in us.

'But, M. Théodore, every one is not so. If the spirit of darkness has no power over the good man, he has a fearful influence upon the wicked. His heart is an open dwelling for him, it is his house of call, his place of amusement, and his dwelling. Thus when a bad man looks at you, you can see behind his eyes that wicked being who goes and comes at will, who watches you and seeks to discover the least sign of yielding, that he may destroy you. The face of great sinners is like the reflection of this terrible fiend. The worst of all that is, that once this being has established himself he is never content; the master of the house may well condemn himself; he may, indeed, cry for pity, and exclaim, "I did not intend to do so"; from the moment that he has become bound to him he must obey him.

'Now this was just Vittikâb's case. He had committed every crime, save one, the greatest of all, from which he had shrunk hitherto; but, as is always the case, the devil must have his way after all.

'That day, from the return of the count until midnight, the Veierschloss resounded with shouts, drinking-songs, the clinking of goblets, as if it were a regular tavern. Six casks of wine were broached in the courtyard; every one could draw for himself and drink his fill.

'Soon nothing could be seen along the ramparts, in the corners, on the steps in the old galleries, or anywhere, but retainers, soldiers, huntsmen stretched like logs right and left, with extended limbs and purple faces, hanging lips, flask in hand, dead drunk. That is how they celebrated the engagement of Vittikâb in a manner worthy of him.

'While these things were taking place in the lower part of the Veierschloss, Goëtz, Hâsoum's guardian, was growing very old and worn out in the Martens' Tower, like an old snail in his shell; he asked himself: "What was going on yonder in the castle? What was making them all so jolly? Had they won a battle, and got plenty of loot?" And the old man listened, but did not know what to think of it all. For twenty years he had known everything connected with the castle from tower to basement. He could distinguish the head of the sentinel upon the outworks, the passage of the soldiers through the yard, in the galleries, on the staircases. He knew, by intuition almost, every brood of rooks or owls in the ramparts, the openings they frequented for their morning fights, the crevices in which they built their nests, and the number of their young. And this sharpness of hearing increased in proportion as his power of vision diminished, as it had done during the last years; and he had no resource, as in past days, in walking upon the battlements at night and keeping watch, gazing far away into the mountains, the dells, the rising ground in the distance, the clumps of trees which he had seen more closely in happier days, the tracks he had followed, the springs at which he had quenched his thirst.

'Goëtz was almost bald; there scarcely remained a lock of hair on his head, and that was white as snow; his features were shrunken, he was obliged to close his eyes in any strong light, and his eyes were now generally half shut. His hands, formerly so muscular, were now weak, and the blue veins stood up prominently in them; his knees were "shaky"; he spoke with effort, and scarcely addressed more than a few sentences to Hatvine during the day, and occasionally a few words with Vittikâb, when the Wild Huntsman came up to the tower.

'But he become fonder and more attached to the unfortunate Hâsoum; he loved him as his own child; he looked upon him as almost beautiful, and every night he ascended to the highest storey of the tower to look at him as he lay asleep. "Poor thing," he thought, "descended from such an illustrious stock, and from such a famous race, your father detests you; but I love you, for you have no faults. You are strong, and if strength of mind be wanting, it will come sooner or later, perhaps when old Goëtz shall have passed away, and had no opportunity to instil it. You do not talk, 'tis true; you are dumb, but your eyes can speak, and they tell me that you love me. Ah! how I love you too! But I am growing old, and when Goëtz shall have departed what will become of you, dear child, what will become of you, what will they do to you?"

'The poor old man was touched by his own thoughts; a tear ran down his cheek; he brought a heavy heart away with him, and he who in former days had been no better than a Burckar, he who imbrued his hands in blood at Trèves, at Lutzelstein, and Landau, and who cared little for God when he was well and strong, now prayed and invoked a blessing upon Hâsoum.

'So on that evening Goëtz wondered why they rejoiced, why did they sing, what extraordinary event had happened, and why Hatvine had not told him that morning, when she brought him his breakfast, what it was all about. But she could not have told him, because Vittikâb and Honeck had not then returned; nevertheless this reflection disquieted him.

'As night fell the castle became quiet, and silence supervened. Some embers still glowed upon the hearth, and Goëtz, seated with his back to the wall, with bowed head and closed eyes, began to doze.

'At length, about eleven o'clock, the sound of the trumpet of the watchman passed over the lake like a sigh; the echoes of the Howald awoke for an instant, and all was quiet.

'Goëtz roused himself, and was about to retire; he was in the act of lighting his torch when he fancied he heard something stealthily approaching.

'"It is Vittikâb," he muttered; "he is coming now."

'In fact, in a moment or two steps were heard ascending the staircase, and the count appeared, his visor thrown open, his stooping shoulders clad in a sort of cassock of red leather; his dagger was suspended at his thigh.

'"Where is Hâsoum?" he demanded.

'"He is asleep, my lord," replied Goëtz, pointing to the floor above.

'"Good," replied Vittikâb.

'And, turning, he glanced round the terrace, which was not his custom; he then entered, drew the bolt, and indicating the bench near the oaken table, said rudely to the old man: "Sit there!"

'Goëtz obeyed wonderingly, for this was the first occasion during twenty years that Vittikâb had visited him sober. He was calm, cold, and gloomy.

'What passed between those two Heaven only knows. That it was something important was evident, for about an hour afterwards they went out together upon the battlements. The Burckar was pale as death; his nose seemed to curve over his lips; his chin was firmly set. Goëtz was bareheaded; the two grey tufts of hair bristled with fear; his eyes were suffused with tears. The moon shone brilliantly in the blue vault of heaven, bringing out the heavy masonry of the battlements in strong relief. At the angle of the great staircase above the darkened courtyard stood Vittikâb, his hand upon the hilt of his poignard. He turned sharply round, and said in a stern voice: "You have heard what I say?"

'"You shall be obeyed, my lord," replied the old man in the same mysterious accents.

'The count then descended, and Goëtz, supporting himself by the balustrade, regarded him for a few seconds with dim eyes; then, when his master had disappeared, he clasped his hands upon his head with a gesture of indescribable agony, and re-entered the tower, moaning aloud, but stifling the sound as much as possible for fear of awaking Hâsoum; but he could not altogether stifle the utterance of his grief, and he trembled from head to foot like a leaf. Fortunately his unhappy charge slept soundly, for all day he was continually moving about, climbing from beam to beam up to the roof of the tower a hundred and twenty feet high, and gazing through its narrow loopholes upon the surrounding country, the lake, and the fertile valleys beneath. His whole life consisted in this. He slept well. Goëtz might sob and groan as much as he chose.

'You will very likely think it odd, M. Théodore, that in the midst of all the preparations which were being made for Vittikâb's wedding no one troubled about Goëtz, and that he was completely passed over in silence. But there was a Higher Power at work, and the hour was approaching.

'Early next morning Vittikâb sent thirty of his retainers in various directions to hasten the coming of the carpenters and other workmen from fifty villages round; others to hasten up vendors of silks and satins, cooks and confectioners from Strasburg even, or from Spires and Mayence. Some carried invitations to the margraves, counts, and barons of the Rhenish Provinces, the Meuse and the Moselle.

'Jerome de Spire, the celebrated architect, came about two days afterwards, and set about constructing immense arcades above the grand courtyard, which was to serve as a banqueting-room at this Balthazar's feast, and from that time nothing was heard but the grating of saws and the sound of blows of hammer and hatchet.

'The surrounding woods, now filled with woodcutters, resounded day and night with the noise of falling trees and the grinding of the wheels of the waggons drawn by oxen three abreast, and almost crushed by the weight of the enormous trunks.

'Then scaffolding was erected around the walls, cranes rose up from the tops of the towers, with their ropes and pulleys to hoist up the beams to the ramparts, and the ant-like crowd of workmen worked the levers, turned the cranks, screw-jacks, quarried and fixed the stone-blocks in their places.

'The foundations were soon fixed, and the arcades quickly sprang up upon them.

'But in all this bustle perhaps the man most occupied of all was Zaphéry Honeck, for if the count was anxious to show off his new buildings, he would be still more celebrated for his great hunting exploits.

'Now Master Honeck, as chief huntsman, was charged with this part of the entertainment. The count had placed all the hounds and huntsmen at his disposal.

'Honeck was in the enjoyment of such a mission; for he was the most skilful hunter of his time, notwithstanding his habits of drunkenness and gluttony.

'Without loss of time he collected his force of prickers and set off to the mountains with the view to track the animals to their lairs, so that each part of the forest might be thoroughly explored, and recommended that they should follow up the herds of wild-boar or wolves rather than isolated animals, "for," he said, "to set two hundred men and three hundred dogs upon the trail of one animal is like throwing a net to catch one fish; every man must, at least, have one chance of distinction."

'So the day of the feast drew nigh.

'Frequently, at night, Honeck, tired out and covered with mud – for he was obliged to follow his game even into the marshes of the Losser – often when returning thus serious and thoughtful he would hear Vittikâb cry out: "Hollo, Zaphéry! Zaphéry! You pass one like an arrow. Come here."

'The huntsman would then ascend, and the Burckar, showing him the arcade, would say: "That is getting on well, is not it?"

'Then taking him by the arm, he would display the rich stuffs from Flanders, the gold and silver ornaments piled up in the great hall to be put in position on the last day before the *fête*. Honeck, who was thinking only of the game, would reply: "Ah! oh! Beautiful! Splendid!" till Vittikâb got him upon the subject of his hunting by explaining: "Well, but you have told me nothing about your hunting; are you contented?"

'Then Honeck would brighten up, and reply: "Yes, my lord, yes, I think all goes well."

'"Good, good," Vittikâb would reply; "that is all I desire to know; I have no time to go into details. I depend upon you."

'Instead of putting himself out and commanding his dependant, he had become suddenly a pleasant companion, and, indeed, he ought to have been, for he had all he wanted, and whatever he wanted done appeared to do itself, as it were.

'Meanwhile the wedding-day drew nigh; the alterations were all finished, and the work of decoration was begun.

'There never had been such a beautiful autumn as that year; the sun shone brightly, and generally in a cloudless sky. Women and children, summoned from the neighbouring villages, carried boughs and moss to the castle to cover the walls, for green is always pretty; it is the colour which attracts our eyes most, and in which Providence has clothed the earth.

'Above the arcades some workmen were stretching silken coverings and draping them with flags, and others set out the tables beneath. The principal gateway, the drawbridge, and the whole frontage of the ramparts were clothed with firs, the tops of which reached almost as high as the embrasures. The gloomy Veierschloss had never presented such a sight; it had become like Vittikâb, cheerful and smiling; the nest of the sparrow-hawk is lined with moss, as is that of the warbler.

'But what was the use of all this decoration when the fiat had gone forth?

'Two days before the wedding-day, one morning when Honeck was putting his game-bag over his shoulder in anticipation of the hunting-party, the door of the room opened, and the under-keeper, Kaspar Rébock, appeared. Rébock had passed the night in the forest. He was a true hunter, and all real huntsmen are like hounds, they never leave a trail until they are actually obliged; they frequently pass two or three nights in the wood with only a crust of bread in their wallet. So Rébock entered, covered with mud to his shoulders.

'"You here!" exclaimed Honeck, who was impatient to be off. "You have tracked a slot, and you come to make your report. All right; we can talk about that this evening."

'"That's true, Master Honeck," replied the other, "I *have* come to talk to you about a trail, but I have never seen the like of it before."

'He opened his wallet and produced some grass covered with moss, upon which was the impression of a long narrow paw, with four claws in front, and another at the side. Honeck perceived at a glance that it was something out of the common, but he said nothing, and taking the tuft from Rébock he took it to the window in order to see it better. Rébock, leaning upon his staff, gazed at him steadfastly. For some minutes Honeck examined the impression steadily; at length he said: "Yes, this is something rather unusual. At first I fancied that Blac or Spitz was playing you a trick, but they are not sharp enough to place the claws in this way on the toes. It must be really the slot of some animal. It might be that of an Alpine bear if all the claws were in the same direction, but to tell you the truth, Rébock, I do not know what it can be."

'And he looked at the under-keeper, whose face beamed with self-satisfaction.

'"Where the devil did you find this?" said Honeck. "Come now, sit down and tell me the whole history of it."

'They seated themselves at a corner of the table, and Rébock, quite delighted at having discovered a slot which Master Honeck could not recognise, plunged at once into the details of this astonishing discovery. He said that on the previous day, between nine and ten o'clock, when following up the trail of the deer, he noticed this impression upon a crab-tree, and at once suspecting some practical joke, he knelt down to examine it more closely, as he was convinced it was the track of no ordinary animal. Then, leaving the deer to take care of themselves, he followed his new trail, which led him from the high ground of the Kirschberg into the marshes of the Losser, and lost itself in the mud. That, in his ardour, he had pressed on, and had advanced as far as the pollards which lined the bank of the stream, but there he lost his boots, and the ground giving way beneath his feet, he was obliged to return and make a *dètour* round the marsh so as to strike the trail at the other side. Unfortunately the marshes of the Losser are nine good miles in circumference, and one cannot make very rapid progress when one is obliged to seek a trail in the reeds and rushes, so it had occupied Rébock five hours in getting round, and it was only at the farther side in the heath in the Hasenbruck that he had fortunately succeeded in finding the trail ascending towards the rock of Trois Epis.

'One thing surprised Honeck very much, and this was that the huntsman informed him that he had passed a wood-cutter's fire on the way, and had noticed that the animal, instead of avoiding it as all wild animals do, had actually stopped beside it and walked round it, leaving traces of his large paws firmly printed in the sand alongside the thick boot-prints and *sabots* of the woodcutters; and, finally, he had halted within a few paces of the fire, so the depth of his foot-marks was easily recognised.

'"Are you quite sure that the fire was actually burning?" inquired Honeck.

'"I placed my hands over the embers," replied Rébock; "they were quite warm then, and as the animal had been there long before I came up, the fire must have been burning brightly when he reached it."

'"This is very strange," said Honeck: "very strange indeed."

'He had good reason for his surprise, for even the fiercest of the forest animals are afraid of fire, so this one must have appeared more ferocious than all the rest!

'Rébock said, in continuation, that he had kept on the trail, and about seven o'clock in the evening he had reached the plateau of the Trois Epis, and after a long quest he had discovered the animal's lair, which was a cavern in a recess, deep and dark, between the rocks. He had not dared to enter for fear of those terrible claws, for had he discovered the animal he would have been doubtless torn to pieces, an opinion which Master Zaphéry fully endorsed.

'Such was Rébock's narrative, and we can imagine how glad Master Honeck was on the eve of the grand hunting party to hear of such a novelty.

'"Good," he said, rising; "very good indeed. I will go and investigate this. But mind, Rébock, say nothing about this to any one. If it be large game like the bear, the boar, or stag, we shall get him right enough. But we must leave to the count the pleasure of the surprise. Everybody must be astonished, margraves, burgraves, and all, so that they may go back to their homes and report that we have game here such as exists nowhere else."

'"You may rest assured, Master Honeck," replied Rébock,

"that I shall hold my tongue. If my superiors are content, that is quite enough for me."

'He then retired to get some rest, and Zaphéry set out upon the trail at once. He remained out all day. It was only at nightfall that he returned to the Veierschloss. He had not only verified Rébock's account, but had discovered further proofs that the animal was of a nature very different from all others in that region in his resting-places, his retreats, his cunning, his habits and instincts. What could it be? Whence did it come? How was it that it had never been previously observed in the Howald? How had it been able during all these years to roam about and satisfy its hunger by preying upon the inhabitants of the forest without leaving the least trace of its existence? This was what puzzled the huntsman, and he could not fathom the mystery. But his business was to be able to set the hounds on the track of this beast, and to astonish Vittikâb's guests with something unusual.

'"What a hunting party we shall have! What a hunt! Fifteen herd of deer, twelve packs of wild boars, six litters of wolves, with foxes and hares *ad libitum*, besides this beast, of which no one has ever seen the like."

'Thus did Honeck reason as he approached the Veierschloss with hasty strides. From a great distance he could perceive the grand entrance open, and the courtyard lighted up with torches. Many noble personages, the counts of Simmeringen, of Loetenbach, and Triefels had arrived, accompanied by their numerous suites, and the domestics of the castle standing in the open air ready to conduct them to their several apartments, and to supply them with refreshment according to Vittikâb's orders.

'Zaphéry Honeck made his way through the assemblage, and succeeded in obtaining a morsel of food and a cup of wine before he ascended to his bedroom to sleep and to prepare for the fatigues of the next day.

'Now, M. Théodore, you can understand the astonishment of the landgraves, the burgraves, and margraves of the district when they heard that the "Wild Count" was about to wed a Roterick. It was not only because he was old, grey, and a twenty years' widower that they were surprised, that he only cared for hunting and pillage, and that he got drunk regularly every day, but they were chiefly astonished that Vulfhild had consented, for the Rotericks had been enemies of the Burckars for centuries, and the races appeared irreconcilable.

'But Vittikâb, in his pride, laughed at all these things; he was sure beforehand that everybody would come to his wedding; some out of curiosity, some for love of the good cheer, some to be present at the grand hunting display, and all of them so that at a future time it might be in their power to say, "We attended those sumptuous feasts of Balthazar – we never saw anything like them, and never shall witness such again."

'And Vittikâb was quite right.

'When these grandees heard what great preparations were being made at Veierschloss, what an assemblage of architects, goldsmiths, velvet and silk merchants, and the most celebrated cooks in Germany, they all set out with their wives, children, and a grand retinue, falcon on wrist and dogs in leash. Every path in the Hundsrück was crowded with the guests, and the poor people of the neighbourhood followed them in their rags, as if performing a pilgrimage, hoping to pick up the crumbs from the rich men's tables. Such was the condition of things when at the very last day of preparation Zaphéry Honeck came back from the cliffs of the Trois Epis.

'Honeck in his little room above the guard-house could not sleep a wink that night; he was obliged to toss about from side to side on his bearskin rug; sleep would not come to him, because his brain was troubled with a thousand anxious and worrying thoughts which he could not banish from his mind.

'In fact, Honeck had not a moment's rest all night; the

strange animal he had tracked would keep returning to his mind; sometimes he fancied he was tracing its slot in the marshes of the Losser, sometimes beneath the brush-wood of the Howald, sometimes amongst the *débris* of the rocks of the Trois Epis, within two paces of the cave, and from this trail he sought to gather some idea of the strength and size of the animal. Then he wondered how it was that he never had noticed the trail before, as he had for the last thirty years been conversant with every trail in the forest, and in a twinkling could discover the trace of a squirrel amongst the leaves. He then came to the conclusion that this particular beast must have come from underground, or across the sea, or had arrived from Poland or some even more distant territory. He was very pleased to think that the count would have the first trial at this strange beast, and yet his heart smote him a little. But he got up, and leaning his elbows upon the window-sill, which was, like all the others, decorated with leafy drapery, he gazed into the dark courtyard, and inhaled the perfume of the leaves and flowers with which the walls were covered. Groups of workmen were dimly discernible upon ladders on the ramparts and in the galleries, fixing up flags, banners, and garlands. Torches, which appeared to move about like fireflies, illuminated the gloom for a moment, and then disappeared in the distance.

'The courtyard, with its arcades a hundred and fifty feet high, now resembled an immense cathedral; the slightest sound was perceptible from one end to the other. Jérôme de Spire stood in the centre and gave his orders to press on with the work.

'At length the grey dawn appeared; the sounds subsided one by one, the workmen left off, and old Jérôme retired. Then the huntsman sought his bed again and endeavoured to get some repose; this time he succeeded, and "slept like a top!".

'Now he slept soundly and long; the sun was peeping through the banners and standards that decorated the great courtyard, when suddenly the blare of trumpets broke like thunder upon his ears and awoke him with a start. He raised himself upon his elbow and listened. From the courtyard, the bridge, the glacis, and the covered way arose a mighty murmuring as of the sea, and above this was heard the clang of arms, the neighing of horses, and the voices of the riders. Honeck comprehended at once that the *fêtes* had commenced. He got up, somewhat alarmed, and leaned out of his dormer window; the most dazzling sight met his gaze; all along the galleries, the stairs, and the terraces one could see nothing but rows of heads piled up one behind the other; on the right hand beneath were the *reiters*; on the left the Trabans, at the farther end and on a daïs was Vittikâb seated upon his throne.

'The cuirasses and accoutrements of the *reiters* glinted like mirrors; at their head opposite the throne was the captain, Jacobus; his great plume almost touched the banners overhead, his scarlet cloak almost covered the crupper of his horse, and he looked at least six feet high.

'All the *reiters* wore their long flat swords at their hips. The Trabans were clad in coats of mail; their headdresses, made like the heads of wolves, protruded over their foreheads, they held their maces at the shoulder; Krapt, in a similar dress, and wearing a leather helmet, stood opposite the throne with Jacobus, and looked quite as big, as proud, and as terrible as his companion.

'Between the *reiters* and the Trabans, stretched from the principal entrance up to the steps of the throne, was a carpet of the skins of animals; bears, wolves, wild boars, badgers, stags, deer, and foxes, some of all kinds, and it was a magnificent display. Only Burckars could have produced such a carpet, for the furs extended two hundred paces in length and thirty in width across the paved court. Even Honeck was astonished. But what struck him more than all was Vittikâb himself seated on his throne.

'Picture to yourself, M. Théodore, a kind of heathen deity,

solidly made and thickset, his neck almost buried in his shoulders, full of fierceness, strength, and arrogance; a sort of wild joy in his expression which seemed to say, "I am the most terrible deity of all." Picture such a being, with a wolfish head, seated on high in a massive iron throne of ancient make, clothed in the robes of Herod, his beard falling over his chest, and wearing the diadem of the Wild Huntsman upon his short red hair. That was just the sort of being Vittikâb appeared.

'He had dressed himself in the state clothes of his great-grandfather, Zweitibolt, and so old that they were as stiff as pasteboard, and the red velvet was scarcely perceptible beneath the gold lace; epaulets of old-fashioned pattern drooped below his shoulders; his cuirasse of silver curved outwards between the epaulets; upon this cuirasse thick chains of gold rattled; a species of tunic of wild-boar skins reached below his hips, and his sandals were laced up with embroidered straps which were continued up to the knee. He held a mace, spangled with diamonds, in the shape of a sceptre; his crown sparkled on his forehead like a cluster of stars.

'Honeck, while looking down upon all this display of arms and grandeur, upon the banners and decorations, and the hundreds of nobles and ladies assembled beneath, said to himself, "Truly the Burckars are a mighty race; they are a great people superior to all these nobles here assembled as the oak is above the birch." And he felt a reverence for his master such as he had never before experienced, and he could almost have worshipped him.

'Thus while the huntsman for the space of half an hour remained gazing in ecstasy, suddenly the master of the ceremonies, Erhard, clothed in a long tunic of grey plush, carrying a small ivory wand, advanced gravely between the *reiters* and the Trabans to the steps of the throne; then, turning round, he uplifted his wand with a most important air. Immediately the trumpets blared forth, and from the farther end of the temporary hall advanced a knight holding his

lady by the hand. The lady's train was so long as to neces-
sitate its being upheld by a foot-page as she advanced. When
they had reached the foot of the throne the trumpets ceased,
and the major-domo cried out in a voice as hoarse as a crane
in a fog: "The high and mighty Margrave Von Romelstein
and his noble spouse!"

'Then Vittikâb descended three steps, while the margrave
and his lady ascended to meet him, and Jacobus and Krapt,
standing right and left, bowed humbly, lowering their
weapons with a haughty grace that was magnificent to
behold. Vittikâb, who was in his glory, smiled graciously;
then the trumpets sounded again, the margrave, his lady
and child, descended and passed up into the right-hand
gallery.

'For three mortal hours this ceremony was prolonged; the
trumpets sounded every moment, a gentleman and lady
advanced, the major-domo proclaimed their names and titles,
and Vittikâb descended two, three, or four steps, according
to the rank of those presented. Then the trumpets sounded
again, and that was all.

'"Well," thought Honeck, "if this is going to last all day I
will have a stoup of wine meantime."

'He had made this observation about a hundred times,
when a tremendous noise was heard in the borders of the
forest where the poor people were enjoying the scraps of
the entertainment.

'"Long live Roterick! Long live Vulfhild! Long live the
lovely maiden!"

'These cries came nearer and nearer, and were prolonged
by the echoes of the Howald. Shortly afterwards the rapid
trot of a cavalcade was heard, and the challenge of the
advanced sentinel. The uproar gained strength every moment.

'Honeck, now very much excited, leaned half out of a
window, and as he did so the escort clattered over the bridge;
then came the noise of wheels, then the sound of hoofs
upon the pavement was heard, and the trumpets sounded.

'The news travelled along the galleries, terraces, and all over the immense building. Every one rose and leaned forward to gaze upon the bride-elect.

'But Honeck paid no attention to these things. He looked down when the two first trumpeters appeared, advancing slowly, and sounding the fanfare as they marched, with distended cheeks; then appeared a long file of white horses, caparisoned with golden trappings, and preceding a purple daïs, which the huntsmen recognised as having been pillaged by the Burckars at Trèves from Bishop Werner twelve years previously; four tufts of ostrich feathers waved at the corners; the fringe descended to the ground, and the handles were of solid silver.

'Beneath the canopy Vulfhild was seated on a magnificent throne.

'At length the cavalcade entered, headed by the ancient Roterick, whose armour and tall red crest betokened nobility. You may imagine that cries of "Long live Roterick! Long live Vulfhild! Long live the Burckar!" resounded through the hall.

'Vittikâb rose, triumph beaming in his eyes and in his face; his beard bristled with pride. He descended from his throne, hastened towards his bride with the quick light step of a wolf without looking to the right or left, without noticing the salutations he received. In a second he had reached the triumphal car, and his long arms, from which dangled his brocaded sleeves, were extended beneath the daïs; he lifted Vulfhild like a swan in his long hairy hands, and deposited her gently on the ground.

'Then all the assembly were able to see her as, tall, lithe, and proud, she stood clothed in a dress of dark green velvet, the boar's head of the Burckars embroidered on her corsage, and her magnificent auburn hair, curling in long ringlets over her snowy neck, transfixed with a golden dart. Every one admired the strings of pearls which fell in folds over her rounded bust, her high wide forehead, her aquiline nose,

her great grey eyes, her thin lips, and her firm chin. She
was just the wife for the Wild Count.

'Vittikâb smiled without speaking, and led Vulfhild to his
throne, in the midst of a storm of applause. He placed her
upon a seat on the left of his throne, and standing up with
his hand upon the shoulder of the young girl, who appeared
honoured by his touch, he cried out in a loud voice, like
thunder rolling amid the storm: "Behold the wife of the
fortieth descendant of the Burckar, Vittikâb the Wild Count,
Burgrave of Veierschloss, Margrave of Howald and Hasser;
evil to him who condemns him!"

'He then sat down with a wild, shy air, and the whole
assemblage was agitated like leaves in a storm. A dozen
Trabans, the wolf's head badge on their foreheads, the skin
falling down to their waists and over the cruppers of their
horses, and wearing cuirasses of ox-hide, though with legs
and arms naked, advanced to the foot of the throne. They
carried straight, wide-mouthed trumpets about six feet long,
the red pennon fluttering almost to their stirrups, and,
turning their faces towards the assembly, they played the
hymn of Virimar, an air which went back to the time when
the Burckars were living in the marshes of the Losser – an
air so wild and terrible that your hair would stand up upon
your head had you heard it; it was called the Marseillaise
of the Wild Count, and was never played except on the
occasion of the marriage of a Burckar, or when they went
into battle. When it was sounded even the wounded got up
and began to fight anew; it was enough to make one's flesh
creep!

'When the music had ceased the silence became oppressive. Vittikâb and Vulfhild rose up and descended from the
daïs; they then advanced slowly between the ranks of the
reiters and the Trabans; the doors of the two side-galleries
were opened at the same time, and all the nobles, and their
ladies, the barons, margraves, and burgraves got up and
followed the Wild Count in the order of precedence. The

entire *cortège* passed before Honeck and ascended the great staircase which led to the banqueting-hall.

'Honeck then roused himself as from a dream, and was about to retire, when, raising his eyes for a last look around, he perceived above the platform a white, pale face looking out of a bay-window. The distant features seen through an opening in the roof of the extemporised building, and in relief against the sky, had something weird about it, and the huntsman stayed to regard it more steadfastly. He then recognised old Goëtz, but how changed! his thin cheeks, his hollow eyes; he was quite upset at the sight.

'"Good Heavens!" he exclaimed, "how old the poor fellow looks! and yet Hatvine always said that he was wonderfully well preserved notwithstanding his great age. However, there is the fact! such a brave hunter too, a good man, and one who twenty years ago could run like a stag through the forest. Well, Honeck, my lad, perhaps in fifteen or twenty years you will be so yourself, an old owl nailed upon the barn door!"

'Zaphéry was right. Goëtz had grown old, very old, since the last visit of Vittikâb. There are weeks sometimes which count like years!

'However, the sight of the old huntsman had suddenly reminded Honeck that the chase was to take place the next day, and thinking that all these grand personages whom he had seen would look to him on this important occasion, he was much troubled in consequence of misgivings that he would not justify the confidence placed in him by his master, and the enthusiasm which at the same time even gave him hopes that he had done better than usual. "How fortunate it is," he thought, "that we have a strange animal to hunt! After such grand ceremonies as these it is only right that we should have something better than wild boars and stags; we wanted some rare beast which had never been seen in the Vosges and in Hündsruck before; and now Saint Hubert has sent it."

'Instead of losing his time gossiping with his friends from

the Triefels, Geroldseck, and Bamberg, as he would have
done at any other time, he went to seek his assistants to
couple the hounds and to choose the relays for the hunt in
the direction of the Losser and of the cliffs of the Trois Epis.
And while all along the galleries of the Veierschloss was
heard the clinking of glasses, goblets, and cups, mingled with
drinking songs and shouts of laughter, and while all the
guests of the Wild Count, as well as the *reiters*, Trabans, and
other retainers, were giving themselves up to festivity, he
thought of nothing but the responsibility of his hunting, and
took all his measures with that view. He was thus occupied
for the rest of the day, and even during part of the night,
but then everything was arranged and the triumph of the
Burckar assured.

'It was a goodly sight next morning to behold the grand
courtyard of the Veierschloss before the departure of the
hunting party, the long ranks of the most beautiful horses
in Germany, brought even from Poland, the least of which
was worth its weight in gold to the Wild Count; it was goodly
to see them waiting by the wall in a long line extending
from the bottom of the court almost up to the grand entrance,
neighing, champing their bits, looking from one to the other
impatiently, and shaking their heads with sudden jerks. It
was indeed a fine sight.

'And then the dogs coupled up in leashes of six, eight,
and ten; these terrible beasts, with tawny hides, large flat
heads, yellow eyes, long backs, and trailing tails, regular wolf
dogs, yawning widely, stretching themselves, extending their
paws, and uttering melancholy and sinister howls – they
were worth seeing.

'Behind them came the huntsmen clothed in leather, their
nervous legs encased in gaiters with bone buttons, their felt
hats ornamented with a heron's plume at the back of the
head, the double-coiled horn worn crosswise, the leashes
wound round their arms as far as the elbow, and their
cowhide whips ready for use in the other hand.

'Further still, the beaters, the margraves, burgraves, land-graves, and all the gallants, sturdy as oaks, magnificently dressed in their masters' liveries, held the magnificent horses by the bridle, for in that age it was the ambition of their masters to surpass each other in the quality of their horses.

'Every moment the impatience became greater, the horses grew restless, the dogs strained at their leashes, and howled dismally. A few blows of the whip imposed silence for a few seconds, but they soon afterwards began again as loudly as before.

'Honeck walked up and down, his great red whiskers bristling with agitation, gazing at the gallery every moment. The quivering of his eyebrows seemed to say, "Come along, come along! The dew is passing off, the sun is rising, the scent will not lie; he is late." Then, addressing the huntsmen, he said: "Yokel, haul in that leash. Must I tell you for ever that the longer your leash the less power you have over the dogs? Kaspar, is that the way to carry your horn? If you think to gain distinction that way you are very much mistaken."

'And he resumed his promenade, muttering to himself. At length, about seven o'clock, the great door of the state apartments opened widely. All the guests in hunting costume came forth along the gallery, Vittikâb at their head.

'He alone of all had retained the ancient hunting costume: the vest of thick leather, the tunic of buckskin; his legs were naked; he had also resumed his iron headpiece with the peak behind. He seemed glad, and the wine-drops glistened in his great tawny beard. At his right hand advanced the lovely Vulfhild, holding her head as erect as a white eagle, while Vittikâb, with his thick neck and high shoulders, looked more like an old "lammergeyer" which appears to laugh as he darts from his rocky perch to make sure of his prey.

'As he descended the grand staircase he saw his dogs and horses over the balustrade, and cried out: "Honeck!"

'"My lord?" replied the huntsman, advancing with head

uncovered, and the plumes of his cap sweeping the ground as he came forward.

'"What have you got for us, eh?" asked his master in a good-humoured tone. "You have not forgotten that we hunt today with the best sportsmen of the Black Forest, the Ardennes, and the Vosges, our rivals and our masters?"

'He said this in politeness, looking, as he spoke, towards the forest margraves and landgraves, such as the ancient Hatto, the Triefels, Lazarus Schwendi of Haut-Landsberg, and others who were renowned in hunting, and who were flattered by this compliment from a Burckar. Honeck bowed and said nothing. Vittikâb resumed: "Yes, we shall have critics this time, so speak out. Can you promise us game worthy of our guests and ourselves?"

'Then Honeck, standing upright, replied gravely: "My lord, I can dare to promise you that the chase shall be a worthy one. St Hubert has sent us a quarry worthy of the race of Burckar and their noble guests."

'He did not wish to anticipate events, believing that the surprise should be pleasant and sudden. Everybody thought that he referred to some wild boar of more than usual size, and Vittikâb, smiling, said: "Very good; since it is so, go you and sound the departure yourself; that shall be your recompense. Now, gentlemen, to horse!"

'All the guests immediately descended into the courtyard; some assisted the ladies to mount, and then sprang upon their own horses. Then each one took his place, Roterick and Vulfhild in the first rank, Vittikâb in front to lead the party. Honeck, on horseback, stood on one side to witness the passage of the cavalcade; the huntsmen brought up the rear with the hounds.

'When Master Zaphéry saw that all was in order he sounded the departure as he and Vittikâb only could sound it. The Veierschloss and the mountains rang out like bells, and the distant echoes replied. The cavalcade set out amid the baying of the packs.

'But something very strange occurred – an incident, M. Théodore, which should have caused the spectators to reflect, for it was a warning such as Heaven sends us on great occasions. It was fated that the Burckar should be punished, and so a token was sent beforehand, as every one remembered afterwards, and confessed that there is no such thing as *chance*.

'Now as Vittikâb, the best horseman of his time, and who all his life had been accustomed to mount untrained animals, was about to cross the bridge, his horse stopped short.

'This at first astonished his rider, for the horse was a well-trained animal which he had ridden frequently, and had himself chosen it for this occasion. That is why he wished to go forward quietly, but the horse would not stir. The count then spurred him fiercely, but the animal only reared and tried to unseat his rider, and the entire cavalcade pulled up to avoid the plungings of the animal. Vittikâb became white with rage, and with his strong hand he reined the animal back on his haunches, and made him stand almost upright, so that the count's plume nearly touched the teeth of the portcullis; then, bending forward upon the animal's neck, like the wolf he was, the Burckar drove his spurs into his side with all his force, and now the furious animal darted out like a thunderbolt, and all the rest followed.

'Those who stood beneath the drawbridge between the bays of the guardhouse saw nothing but a confused assemblage of horses, waving tails, and hoofs on the pavement, with long robes fluttering about like flags. That only lasted for a second or two between the walls of the outworks, but it was a terrible sight, and long afterwards, in the midst of the howling of the dogs and the braying of Honeck's horn, the noise made by the galloping of the hunting party over the bridge was heard a long way off, like the noise of a hundred hammers beating on an anvil.

'Then Honeck in his turn spurred his horse forward, and

the other hunters followed on foot, dragged onward by their dogs.

'Once outside the glacis the cavalcade ascended directly to the opposite side of the Gaisenberg so as to reach the wood. Robert, the under-huntsman, was galloping alongside, having received orders to put the hunters on the tracks of the animal, and to sound his horn three times when all was ready so as to warn Honeck to uncouple the hounds.

'Zaphéry led the pack through the valley on the right; by crossing the lake he ought to gain the defile of Sureaux, then the marsh of the Losser, whence the trail was visible in the direction of the plateau of Trois Epis.

'The weather was lovely; not a cloud crossed the vault of heaven. The impatient "yapping" of the hounds could have been heard a mile away. Honeck, galloping about all this time, returned to view the hunting party; it was visible above the brush-wood and briars like streamers of many colours; it was a beautiful sight but in a few minutes it disappeared beneath the trees. Then the huntsman followed up the pack more closely, and exclaimed: "All goes well, all goes well; in an hour or two we shall have good fun. Now go ahead and hold your tongues, you brawling curs; a little patience, and you will have plenty of time to howl; those which cry the most do not always do best when it comes to the scratch!"

'The dogs, of course, redoubled their cries in proportion as they descended into the ravine.

'Honeck had never been more certain of his game; but when at the end of a quarter of an hour the light entered the defile, and the dogs having reached the weeds at the Losser scented the trail, they recoiled unmistakably, for the joyous yelping was all at once changed into the wildest howling, the most plaintive and furious lamentations possible.

'Honeck, then, hearing that death-cry, was afraid that the animal had got away out of reach before the hunters had taken up their positions.

'"The fiend choke you!" he exclaimed. "Have you never seen a trail before? Will you be silent, you brutes? Don't you see that the animal has cleared off?"

'But his indignation was thrown away. The dogs, head in air, and with melancholy eyes, continued their lugubrious howling. Zaphéry was a true huntsman, and now his training told. As he could not strike the hounds for fear of making them more noisy still, he ran as fast as he could before them, and cried out to his assistants: "Hold hard!"

'Then the dogs, believing that he was pursuing the prey, kept silence, and tugged at their leashes furiously. At that moment the three notes from Rébock's horn were heard from the mountain, and Honeck, delighted to perceive that the hounds turned to it at once, let them go! In two seconds there was not one of them left in the valley. To the right and left upon the rocks in the brushwood and the briars, three or four hundred feet up the hills, noses to the ground, the pack ran, glided, sprang forward, and rushed upon the trail.

'"I hope the animal did not get away before the men took up their stations," said Honeck.

'All the rest hoped so too.

'Zaphéry, in order to see the assemblage and to assure himself that the relays were all in order, hurried up to the top of the flat rock which overlooked the chain of hills. When he reached the summit he was able to see for an immense distance around over all the adjacent hills, the valleys, the rocky peaks, the plain of the Palatinate on his left as far as the eye can reach, and he was enabled to take in at a glance the conditions of the hunt.

'The foremost hounds had already passed the cavern of the Trois Epis, a proof that the animal was no longer there. But before coming to a definite conclusion the huntsman waited a few moments. He could perceive some hundreds of yards to the right the long line of the Burckar hounds carefully following the trail. Thus, one after the other, they reached the cavern into which the animal had entered, then coming out again they hastened with new ardour up the other slope of the mountain.

'Honeck, who had not a doubt respecting the departure of the animal, sounded his horn to warn the hunters. He had scarcely sounded it when Vittikâb himself replied from the depths of the defile, and he could perceive the Wild Count leave his post at full speed and follow the tracks of the hounds. Two or three "old hands", Hatto de Triefels, Lazarus Schwendi, Elias Rouffacher, followed the count with loose rein; then Vulfhild flew out in her turn like an eagle with outstretched wings, her long habit floating behind her, and by degrees all the rest took the same direction.

'Honeck then seeing the pack start off again, sounded the departure for the first relay, and the chase was continued by all together, sixty dogs in front and fifty horses behind. It was a marvellous sight.

'Having gazed at it for a few moments, and muttering to himself that his master was the first hunter in the empire, who could tell at a glance the true trail, and knew how to follow up the animal closely, Honeck's attention was naturally directed to the chase itself, and he was then quite confounded at its extraordinary tricks, resources, and tracks, different from any other animal he had ever seen.

'In the first place he noticed that the animal never ran in the open; he always kept in the woods, and more in the skirts than in the interior. This was easy enough to perceive, for every moment he saw the file of dogs enter the forest, then come out again without penetrating beyond the borders, and the hunters followed in the same direction. He made up his mind more than once that the beast, when he found himself hard pressed, had climbed up a tree, for sometimes the dogs would rush together as if sure of their trail, then suddenly stop, turn round, and howl, noses in air, and once again resume their course.

'After two long hours, after many turnings and windings,

the chase suddenly broke into greater speed than ever – they actually flew over the ground. Vittikâb was in front, in the direction of the hills bordering the plain. Then the sound of the horns grew more and more faint to his ears, and the upshot of it was that he found himself alone in the forest; now and then at long intervals the horn of the Wild Count was heard borne upon the breeze. At this time the troop was more than three miles beyond the Losser; two relays placed upon the Gaisenberg had been of no service.

'The day got hotter and hotter, and Honeck on his rock, not able to distinguish anything farther, was about to descend the mountain when he heard the sound of the count's horn far in the distance. He would have known it anywhere. He listened and continued to gaze intently; the baying of the dogs came up to him in a confused echo; then suddenly, at half a league distance, Vittikâb appeared alone, passing beneath the forest trees like a lightning flash. He sounded his horn again and again, a full clear note which made the woods ring again. Then some other horns more distant still took up the signal; the entire company was now returning by an immense circuit.

'"I'll bet that Vittikâb is alone on the trail," thought the huntsman, "although the devil himself could not distinguish anything at this distance. I am proud of that master of mine!" And what made him more glad, and went to his heart, was that the note of the old hound Tobie, which possessed the best nose in the pack, rose at regular intervals, and from time to time with this music were blended the notes of the horn, from which one could understand that the count was encouraging the old hound.

'In fact, some minutes afterwards Zaphéry perceived them passing one after the other two miles away behind the rocks, but Tobie was not unaccompanied; more than a hundred dogs were galloping with him, and so close together did they appear from the height on which Honeck stood, that they seemed as if he could cover them with his hand.

'A moment after old Hatto, and then Rouffacher, some other gentlemen, and then Vulfhild also, passed in view. At the head of a second band was old Roterick, easily distinguished by his height and the red plume in his cap.

'"Ha, ha," laughed Honeck to himself, "the hunt is up yonder!"

'And he became more and more attentive. As he continued to gaze, forgetting the heat, suddenly close to him, from the breach of a rock covered with briars, he distinguished the voice of Rébock calling him.

'"Master Honeck!"

'Turning round, he replied, "Ah, is that you, Rébock?"

'"Yes, it is I; I tethered my horse to yours. What a fine head of game we have given them, eh? He may boast of giving them a pretty race."

'"Yes, yes," replied Honeck brusquely, "I have seen it all. It is a fine run. I cannot be of the party myself, but it makes one proud of such a master as the Wild Count."

'"That's true, Master Honeck, but we may have something to fear for not having run down the beast."

'"Well, we can run him down tomorrow, but what we can have a long time afterwards is not worth the trouble of getting. Hush! The chase is up again. Listen!"

'Vittikâb's horn was heard like thunder in the valley. Honeck leaned over; he could not distinguish the count, but the whole pack were streaming towards a deep gorge five hundred or six hundred feet below the plateau; that was the Gorge of the Iron Pot, which is so called in consequence of its being terminated by a black rock a hundred feet high, flat at the base, and rounded something like a pot. The gorge itself, of horseshoe form, is bounded on two sides by sharp-pointed rocks. Honeck, seeing the hounds in that direction, exclaimed: "We have him now. He has gone to the Pot with a vengeance."

'"Master Honeck," said Rébock, "I wish I could think so, but, saving your presence, the game is too sharp for that."

'"It is a strange beast which is unacquainted with the country," replied Zaphéry, as he got down from his position.

'Rébock followed him but half convinced. At the foot of the elevation they mounted their horses, and traversing the ridge, in five minutes they came within fifty yards of the precipice. Honeck, who was particularly elated, dismounted, and, throwing the bridle to Rébock, said: "There now, d'ye hear? The struggle has commenced. What did I tell you?"

'And without waiting for a reply he ran through the brushwood, while Rébock dismounted in his turn, and hastened to tie up the horses. That done, he rejoined Honeck as he ran.

'A tremendous uproar arose from the gorge; it was easy to perceive from the howling, the gnashing of teeth, and the cries of every kind that came up from the abyss, that the whole pack was engaged, and that the prey was making a fight for it.

'The two huntsmen, quivering with excitement, advanced to the edge of the precipice, and leaned over to get a view of what was passing beneath, but they had scarcely glanced downwards when they became deadly pale. They had seen something which they had never seen before, M. Théodore, and which, please God, will never be seen again.

'Now just picture to yourself an immense gorge a hundred feet wide and sixty feet deep, studded with sharp rocks, glistening like bronze, whence trickled a stream of water cold as ice all the year round. If you looked to the bottom of the gorge you might discover a pile of sharp rocks, amongst which a stream of water threaded its way over its black pebbles.

'It was not a particularly inviting spot. There was no moss nor grass, nor any such thing; it was a regularly forsaken place. Occasionally a young wolf or a fox might be taken here, but old ones never, because once they got out of it they would never return to it again.

'Well, fifty or sixty yards to the left Rébock and Honeck

perceived in a sort of niche a creature something like a bear, about six feet high, which was neither man nor beast, for he had two legs as we have, spare limbs, and slightly crooked; he had claws, and if he had arms, he had also hands an ell long; if his head was something human, with eyes in front, he had the ears of a wolf, a flattened nose, a hare-lip which displayed a row of immense white teeth; he possessed an abundance of yellow hair, which fell from his shoulders like a mane. And if this creature was naturally repulsive, we can fancy his appearance when he was engaged in fighting the hounds, knocking them over with terrible force with a heavy branch torn from an old oak that overhung the precipice, rolling his eyes, drawing back his lips so as to display his teeth, and shouting in accents as melancholy as the winds of winter on the Krapenfels. We can picture the astonishment of the two hunters at the sight.

'As for the dogs they were furious, for you know that in proportion as dogs are taken by surprise the more savage they become when they *do* attack the prey, and that is why they did not give way before the monster they now encountered.

'It was a terrible struggle. The dogs sprang for fully fifteen feet upon the game, sometimes singly, sometimes together, and one could see nothing but their foaming jaws as they jumped up; then they fell back again, their ribs broken, their heads crushed, or dragging their paws after them, and howling so as to be heard a league away. Some of them, stretched almost lifeless in the stream, turned their heads to lap up a few drops of water; some merely gazed furiously round without having courage to renew the attack; some behind ran up with widely opened jaws, and without taking warning they pressed forward into the mass only to be flung back senseless and dying.

'The monster showered his blows like a woodcutter at work. Nothing could be seen but his two great shaggy arms in the air, his great head beneath his hair leaping from his shoulders at every stroke; his legs, torn and bleeding, were planted firmly apart.

'Honeck noticed that some old hounds were crawling stealthily along the rock instead of coming up boldly to the attack; above all, he noticed old Tobie, which, as usual, was about to take the game by the rear; he saw him crouch three or four times, then, as if he was sensible that the distance was too great, he would crawl a little nearer, his eyes glistening like two candles; he was at the same time glad and nervous, for to see the monster knock over his best hounds, and not to be able to tell whether it was a man or an animal, brought the perspiration to his temples; but he did not dare to wish him dead.

'In the midst of all this tumult Vittikâb's horn was heard. He entered at the other end of the defile, and the sound, prolonged by the instrument, echoed to the very bottom of the abyss, and overcame all other sounds. Very soon the gallop of his horse was heard amid the notes of his horn, but at the supreme moment, and as he arrived in front of the rock, a short hoarse sound made itself heard, and all were silent; nothing but the din of the combat was audible.

'Honeck and Rébock turned round, and what did they behold? Vittikâb at the bend of the gorge pale as death, struck dumb, his mouth wide open, his eyes staring, clutching his bridle with both hands; his horse reined back on his haunches, his haunches almost touching the ground. The Wild Count's face – that terrible face – expressed such dismay that the hunters could almost have believed they were gazing upon a ghost, and they both experienced a chilling of the blood as they looked.

'Just then the animal uttered a terrible cry of distress; they say that he called Vittikâb to his assistance, but too late! Tobie had by this time approached near enough; he leaped at the animal's throat, and the monster, hurled from his position, fell amongst the other dogs; then nothing was visible except his long arms endeavouring to defend himself from their devouring jaws; then they sank down, and nothing could be heard but the deep groans of the quarry and the grinding of teeth!

'Then a terrible cry echoed through the valley, and Vittikâb, his battle-axe raised, fell upon this mass of dogs like a lion amongst a pack of wolves, felling, maiming, and killing them with a fearful fury. In a second he was covered with the blood and brains, and, bending from his saddle, he seized the hunted animal by the hair, and, lifting him like a doll at arm's length, he exclaimed in a voice choked with emotion: "Hâsoum, Hâsoum, it is I!"

'But he only spoke to a corpse – a bleeding, lifeless body, which lay with open mouth and hanging limbs. He saw it was dead, and Vittikâb, with a sob, placed it on the saddle-bow before him, and galloped homewards at full speed.

'Honeck and Rébock looked at each other, they were so faint and pale that they hardly recognised each other.

'"Let us to the castle," said Honeck, shivering.

'They hurried to their horses and mounted quickly; then, taking a short cut, they descended the hill at speed in the direction of the Veierschloss.

'By the time they reached the foot of the mountain they could perceive the count already far along the path by the lake still holding the dead body across the saddle, while he himself, bending forward with tightly closed lips and cap awry, was staring between his horse's ears, riding like the wind amid the brushwood. Far, very far, behind him came his guests, the long habits of the ladies and the parti-coloured dresses floating in long rows; they had seen the Wild Count pass, and the consternation was universal.

'Just about the same time Captain Jacobus was keeping guard at the sally-port. He was walking up and down with his hands behind him when he perceived in the valley, just under the shade of the hill, all the long file of riders galloping round the lake, enveloped in a cloud of dust.

'"Hullo!" he said; "the hunting party is returning; the wedding feasts will soon commence."

He descended to warn the *Vachlimeister*, and he scarcely had had time to lower the drawbridge when Vittikâb came thundering over it, crying out: "Goëtz! Let Goëtz be brought hither at once," in a voice which reminded them of the war-cries of the Burckars.

'All the galleries and staircases were covered with *reiters* and Trabans as if in expectation of an assault; they saw the count leap from his horse and place the dead body on the table of honour in the midst of the flowers and the gold and silver plate. His face was so careworn they scarcely recognised him.

'Two or three *reiters* hastened at once to the Martens' Tower to fetch Goëtz at the same time that Honeck, Rébock, Hatto, Lazarus, Schwendi, Vulfhild, Roterick, and fifty others dashed through the gateway. In an instant all the castle was aroused. Cries, lamentations, and the clashing of arms echoed under the vaults of the castle.

'Vittikâb, standing by the table, threw his cap beside the body of the monster; then, with his red hair clinging damply on his forehead, his teeth clenched, his eyes almost starting from their sockets, looked round upon the assemblage as each individual was bending down to gaze upon the monster, and having seen him turned away shuddering, and asked the other whether they had ever beheld the like.

'The count, deadly pale, paid no attention to them; he looked without appearing to see anything; his lips trembled. But the sound of footsteps on the great staircase aroused him; he turned round suddenly, and as old Goëtz, leaning over the balustrade with staring eyes at sight of the monster, remained motionless and horror-stricken, the count exclaimed: "You have not obeyed orders, Goëtz."

'"My lord, I could not," replied the old man; "it is too much for me; I let him go. I thought the Lord would have pity on the poor creature. Do with me as you will!"

'"He had pity, then," said the count. "Yes, the servant had pity, the father had none."

'And seeing the surprise of his guests, he added in a harsh voice, as he pointed to the body: "That is my son; that is the last Burckar. Twenty years ago I imprisoned him in the Martens' Tower. I was ashamed of him. I wished to kill him. I confided my wishes to this old servant, but he begged and prayed me, on his knees, to relent. I was deaf to his entreaties. The old servant had more pity than the father, and he let him go free."

'As he spoke thus the Burckar was like a madman. The whole assembly grew pale.

'"Listen," he continued; "it is to my shame. I thought, 'He has wolf's ears. The Burckars are no longer men; they are wild beasts. I must hide this one.' It is Providence who has punished me thus. For twenty years I have lived in the hope to have children. I murdered those of other people out of envy and jealousy. It was breaking my heart to let the old race die out. At last I thought of Roterick. You know, Roterick, I went to see you, and I was cheerful. If I could I would have strangled you, for I am a Burckar, and hate you and yours! But I laughed. I promised everything, I gave up everything. I wanted your good blood. I wished for children with human faces – real children – and then gave orders to kill the other one."

'As he continued to speak he roused himself more and more, and his thick tones became more distinct.

'"It is horrible," he said, as if speaking to himself, "a father putting his son to death through a feeling of pride. Ah, what a cursed being I am – cursed for evermore! Yes, it is horrible! Have you ever heard of a similar instance?" he exclaimed. "No, you never have heard anything like it; there has been nothing like it since the commencement of the world. That old man at Landau who is the cause of all this – ah, the wretch! If I could only see him roasting once again!"

'And he then cried out at the top of his voice: "The priest spoke the truth!"

'No one understood to what he referred when he spoke
to his old henchman respecting Landau and the priest.
Honeck alone could recall the circumstances. The face of the
old man who was carrying his little grandson away upon
the mattress passed before his eye like a lightning flash, and
the image of the bishop Verner also rose up as he appeared
cursing the Burckar, and exclaiming as he stood on the steps
of the cathedral porch, with hands outstretched: "Cursed
may you be! May the Divine vengeance fall upon you all!
You are not men, you are monsters!"

'Honeck recalled this, and he understood the speech of
Vittikâb.

'The Wild Count himself continued to speak, and even
he was constrained to sob as he finished his address. It was
terrible to see a man such as he weep. More than one of
the spectators turned aside in dismay, but Vittikâb paid no
attention to anything.

'"I care not," he exclaimed; "you men are all cowards.
You are the cause of all this misfortune; you have left us to
do all this, to rob and burn, instead of hunting us out like
so many wild beasts. Yes, you *are* cowards; may you be all
cursed as well as we, you wretches! Had you not been the
cowards you are we should not have been as we are. But
the lad here – what has he done that he should be devoured
by dogs? Why should he have been shut up in the tower?
Why does not Providence have pity upon the poor creature?"

'And throwing himself upon the monster with outstretched
arms, he burst into tears and exclaimed: "Oh, my poor child,
you are suffering for the crimes of your fathers; you are
suffering for me, for Rouch, for Virimar, for all our accursed
race. Is it just? No, no; it is upon us, the real brutes, that
the punishment should fall!"

'For a long time he wept as if his heart would break.
Several of the *reiters*, seeing their chief, man of iron as he
was, so overpowered, went away, not wishing to witness his
grief. But he, suddenly raising himself up, and looking round

upon the astonished assemblage, exclaimed: "Have I wept? Vittikâb has wept! Oh! if I could exterminate you all to gain back one single day, I would never weep again!"

'Though his eyes gleamed fire his limbs were cold. Then, passing his hand over his face, he cried: "Ah! if you could only have seen him fight! He was a true Burckar, a real Burckar – one against them all. When I saw him, although I quailed at the sight, I was proud of him; yes, I was proud! If I could only bring him back to life! He would be your chief!"

'And raising his hands to heaven, he exclaimed: "Rouch, Virimar, Zweitibold, my ancestors, will you not come to revive him? Will you let the whole race die out?"

'He uttered this bitter cry in tones audible even across the lake!

'But the silence grew only more profound; no one moved; all were engrossed in expectation to see the old brigands emerge from their tombs to succour the monster before them; but after a pause Vittikâb, bowing his head, gazed intently at Hâsoum for a few seconds, and then said: "It is all over! This is how the grand old race of warriors dies out! They finish with a monster! Other families, the Foxes, the Geroldseck, the Dagsbourg, may live to inherit our spoils, the spoils we have won during the last thousand years. They may come now; they will no longer be affrighted by the cry of the wolf, which used to make them quail. That is all over now!"

'Then, turning to his retainers, he said: "Trabans and *reiters*, take all you can find; this gold and silver, the treasure amassed in the caves of Virimar, all is yours! I give it you freely; take it away. What has been obtained by pillage may be pillaged again!"

'Then waving his long arms over his head, he cried: "Now let the winds moan, let the night-birds croak; let the torrents rush down; let all the voices of heaven and earth recount, from age to age, this lamentable story! And when the peasantry, as they sit in the chimney-corner, shall hear these things they shall whisper, 'There is the hunt of the Savage Count crossing the mountain, there are the horns sounding, the horses neighing, and the dogs following the trail of Hâsoum!' They shall all hear it, and remember that Providence is over all, and does what seemeth Him good!"

'Then he lifted the body, and clasping it tightly in his arms he ascended the grand staircase, passing all the assembly in silence. They watched him traverse the gallery and disappear in the cavern beyond.

'Immediately the Trabans and *reiters* precipitated themselves upon the plate; they forced open the cave of Virimar, they loaded the horses, and fled away pell-mell. Margraves, burgraves, counts, barons, huntsmen, and beaters, even old Hatvine on her mule, and Goëtz made haste to quit the cursed place. After the lapse of an hour the Veierschloss was almost as deserted as it is at this day. Honeck alone had no desire to plunder, and remained in the courtyard, and fastened up the hounds, according to his custom as they returned to their kennels. He attributed all this evil to himself, and cursed himself for having ever conceived the idea of hunting any strange beast. He was attached to Vittikâb, and kept looking in the direction of his retreat as he thought of these things.

'At length, no longer able to contain himself, he went up to speak to the count. He entered the room and beheld his master stretched upon the corpse of his son. For a long time Honeck did not venture to speak. Vittikâb did not stir, and it was not for a full half-hour that, hearing Honeck move, he rose, his face bedewed with tears, and said: "What do you want here?"

'"Master, I have come to be with you."

'"Leave me!" replied the Burckar.

'"Master," replied Honeck, "all the rest have fled. I alone remain to serve you."

'"I have no need for service," replied the count as he opened the door and pushed the huntsman out.

'Honeck heard the bolts fastened, and then he descended. He encountered two dogs, which just then returned. He fastened them up in their kennels, and then he ascended to his room, took up his walking-staff, and departed. He thought to obtain employment easily enough as chief huntsman, for his accomplishments were well known in the entire district, but his heart was sad as he left the old castle of the Burckar where his youthful days had been passed, and where his forefathers for a thousand years had lived and died.

'He proceeded at random without looking whither he went. At length, at nightfall, he passed near the village of Gaisenberg, and wished to gaze once more upon the old tower which he had so often saluted with his horn as he came from the Howald. He climbed up to the right above the lake. At the summit of the ridge, amongst the brushwood, he sat down on a rock, and rested there far into the night, with his walking-staff between his knees, not being able to make up his mind to descend the other side of the hill. The melancholy moon rose in the blue vault of heaven, silence fell around, and still he did not stir.'

'"Behold, Honeck!" he muttered to himself; "look, there is your old home! Now you have quitted it, and who can tell if you will ever see it again?"

'While Honeck was thus lamenting, suddenly flame burst out in the Veierschloss; at first in the hayloft belonging to the stables, and in the woodhouse at the end of the yard. Masses of thick black smoke, streaked with sparks, rose in dark columns, and as the night was perfectly calm this smoke extended itself like a pall over the building. Then the old beams and the dry woodwork of the ancient castle caught fire like straw; the flame gaining ground rapidly soon enveloped the high towers as well. The lake beneath reflected the glare of the conflagration, and the shadows of thousands of birds passed swiftly from the old building across the blazing pile.

'Honeck comprehended in an instant that Vittikâb had set the castle on fire, and he did not move, knowing that he could be of no use. He kept gazing at the flames in dismayed silence; but his heart was wrung to hear the neighing of the horses which were in the stables, and the plaintive howling of the dogs which he had himself fastened up in their kennels; these sounds came up to him there in endless wailings, and he could picture their terrible sufferings in that still-increasing conflagration.

'Honeck became mad, and remained in that condition I know not how long. One thing is certain, and that is that the poor woodcutters of Lembach found him, and that after a time, having recovered his senses, and taking all these lessons to heart, he relinquished the idea of becoming a huntsman again, and became a woodcutter at Homât in the environs of Pirmasens; he chose a simple and hard-working life, married the daughter of a woodcutter like himself, and had children by her.

'I am descended from this Honeck.

'As he had, doubtless, grave faults to expiate, but not sufficiently great to bring upon his descendants the fate of the Burckars, our family has been only afflicted by a kind of chronic infirmity. Every autumn one of us falls into a kind of trance, which lasts two or three days, which corresponds to the duration of the great hunt in which Hâsoum perished, and the burning of the Veierschloss.

'And if you wish to hear the end of all this, M. Théodore, I may tell you that the Wild Count returns to earth in expiation of his crimes, and that he resumes in the Howald the chase of his son Hâsoum. This hunt starts from the Veierschloss, and thence into the plain of the Palatinate, makes the tour of the Hündsruck, including Mont Tonnerre; reaches the Vosges by way of Bitche, Lutzelstein, and Lutzelbourg; descends to the Jura, and terminates by plunging into the Lake.

'But the most extraordinary circumstance connected with

this is that the Burckar is accompanied by the souls of all the descendants of his former retainers. It comes upon you like a blast of wind, your spirit is swept away in a breath, your body sleeps while you are absent, tearing "over hill, over dale, through bush, through briar," in the train of those terrible phantom dogs, blowing blasts on the horn enough to split your cheeks, and shouting like incarnate devils. You pass by lakes, rivers, mountains, in a dazed sort of way during the two or three days' absence, and when you wake it appears to be a dream.

'That is what I underwent while I was a youth, and that is what Louise suffers now. If you look upon her, there her body is, her hands clasped, as white as wax. You would take her for a saint in her niche. It would not be right that you should behold her; you are too young, otherwise you should see her, and would pray to her yourself, for the sleep resembles death.

'The Burckar came to take her soul last night when those dogs began to howl so wildly. Where are they now? Oh! on the slopes of the Jura, in the gorges of the Vosges, in the recesses of the Black Forest – who can tell?'

Père Frantz ceased speaking, and I gazed on him stupefied at this strange recital.

'I decided to tell you all this, M. Théodore,' he said, 'for fear you might entertain some unjust suspicions concerning us. You might have harboured some unjust thoughts about us, and I was distrustful about you on that account.'

'Ah, Père Honeck!' I exclaimed, 'I never—'

'No,' he replied; 'frankness above everything; mysteries are for scoundrels. When there is nothing to be ashamed of one can tell everything.'

'Well, you are right,' I replied, 'and I thank you for your confidence. Your narrative carries a great lesson; it shows that if men can improve and get better by means of work and honest living, they can also descend to the level of the beasts by nourishing their animal passions. Those who think they can escape human justice, or overcome it, and commit crimes with impunity, find out their mistake sooner or later.'

The old keeper rose without replying.

Day was breaking, the dawn was streaked with rosy light, and the perfume of the woods enveloped all things around us. We went outside to inhale the fresh morning air. The birds were singing all around that house in the forest, and the sun was just peeping between the fir-trees.

'Do you still find it necessary to leave us, M. Théodore?' asked the old keeper.

'Yes; if I could but remain, Père Frantz, I should be the very happiest of men, but I must go and work to gain my living. I have now laid in a good stock of subjects. I must set to work. Ah, if I were only rich!'

'Well, then, come and lie down for a few hours. I shall not be sorry to have a little rest myself.'

He entered his room, and I ascended to my chamber. Two or three hours afterwards the old man came into my room, and seeing that I was awake, 'Well,' said he, 'have you rested?'

'Yes, Père Frantz, I think I have slept, but I am not quite certain.'

'Ah, well!' he said in a good-humoured tone, 'all is for the best.' Then, taking up my knapsack, he added, 'We will have a biscuit and a glass of wine before you start, and then I will accompany you as far as the Three Fountains.'

As we proceeded along the gallery I experienced quite a sinking of the heart when I reflected that I should not be able to bid Louise farewell. Père Frantz divined my thoughts apparently, for, stopping at her door, he said: 'Wait a moment.'

He entered the room; then returning, he signed to me to approach.

'As you are about to leave us,' he whispered, 'come here; it is only natural, after all, that you should see her.'

I approached the bed and gazed upon Louise sleeping

beneath the pretty blue curtains, as the old keeper had described her. She appeared to me to be more beautiful than I had deemed possible, and I then realised how deeply I loved her. After a pause the old man, who was close beside me, whispered: 'When you reflect that her soul is not so far away, it is very strange indeed, is it not?'

And he gazed at me with eyes full of tears.

'If her spirit were here,' he continued, 'Louise would wish you a pleasant journey and you would embrace her, no doubt. So kiss her now: there can be no harm in it.'

I pressed my lips tremulously upon the forehead of the fair young girl, and then, grave and thoughtful, with a sad and loving heart, I followed the old man and descended the steps of the old gallery for the last time.

After breakfast Père Frantz accompanied me as far as the Three Fountains. We were both greatly moved when the moment of separation arrived.

'A pleasant journey, M. Théodore,' said the old keeper as he clasped my hand. 'Think of us sometimes. And if you ever come in this direction again remember the house of old Père Frantz.'

I could only reply with a warm grasp of the hand, a clasp such as one exchanges when one is bidding a friend an eternal adieu. Then without trusting myself to speak, for my heart was beating almost to suffocation, I took the path from the Three Fountains and plunged into the pine-wood. But after walking for five minutes, and finding myself alone, I began to think of all I had left behind me, of that peaceable existence in the midst of the forest, of the good old man Honeck, of Louise, my dear little Louise; and dwelling upon these things I could not restrain myself. I burst into a flood of tears.

LEX TALIONIS

I

In 1845, said Dr Taifer, I was attached as assistant surgeon to the military hospital at Cairo.

The hospital is built within the Kasba, upon the top of a rock three or four hundred feet high. It commands a view of the town, of the governor's house, and of the wide-stretching plain which extends as far as the eye can reach.

The view is wild and grand. From my window, open to admit the evening breeze, I saw the crows and vultures as they wheeled around the rock or hid themselves, as the twilight darkened, in the fissures. I could from it easily throw my cigar into the Rummel, which glided like a snake at the foot of the gigantic wall.

Not a sound, not a murmur, disturbed the quiet of my studies till the time came when the bugle and drum awoke all the echoes in the fortress, calling the men to the barracks.

Garrison life never had charms for me. I had never been able to give myself up to absinthe, rum, and little glasses of cognac. At the time of which I speak, a man who would not do so was charged with being wanting in *esprit de corps*. My gastric faculties, however, would not permit me to be possessed of such a kind of spirit.

I gave myself up, therefore, to visiting the wards, to drawing up my prescriptions, to a rigorous attention to my duties. When I returned home, I amused myself by making notes, turning over the leaves of some of my books, registering my observations.

In the evening, at the hour when the sun slowly withdrew his rays from the plain, I would sit – my elbow upon the sill of my window – to watch that great natural spectacle, always the same yet ever varying. In the distance a caravan wound along the side of the hills. An Arab galloped away off into the extreme horizon, until he was lost to sight in the distance. Some cork-trees stood out against the background of purple sky; and far, far below me was a flock of birds of prey, sweeping on the darkening air with their flapping wings, or hovering immovable. All this interested me – had a charm for me. I would have sat there for hours together had not I been obliged to betake me to the dissecting-room!

No one troubled himself to criticise those tastes of mine, with the exception of a certain lieutenant of volunteers named Castagnac, whose portrait it is necessary I should draw for you.

When I arrived at Constantine, as I got out of the carriage, I heard a loud voice behind me.

'Hulloa! I wager that is our assistant-surgeon.'

I turned round, and found myself in the presence of a tall infantry officer, meagre, bony, red-nosed, grey-moustached, his kepi over his ear, its point cocked up towards the sky, his sabre between his legs. It was Lieutenant Castagnac.

As I was turning away from this strange figure the lieutenant seized me by the hand. 'Welcome, doctor,' said he, 'I am delighted to make your acquaintance. *Morbleu*! you are tired, are you not? Let us go in and I will introduce you to the assembly.'

The assembly at Constantine means, in truth, the company in the ale-house, the place where the officers meet.

We went in, for how could one resist the effusive sympathy of such a man? And yet I had read *Gil Blas*!

'Waiter – two glasses. What do you take, doctor? Cognac or rum?'

'No – curaçoa.'

'Curaçoa! Why not go the whole length? Ha! ha! ha! You have strange taste. Waiter, a glass of absinthe for me – and full up – lift your elbow in pouring it out! That's right! Your health, doctor.'

'Yours, lieutenant!'

I was already in the stranger's good graces.

It is hardly necessary for me to tell you that my liking for him did not last long. I was not long in observing that my friend Castagnac had a habit of being deeply absorbed in his newspaper when Rabelais' quarter-of-an-hour came – when it was time to pay. That shows you what kind of fellow he was.

As a compensation I made the acquaintance of several officers of the same regiment, who often laughed with me at this new species of Amphitryon. One of these was Raymond Dutertre, a fine fellow, certainly not wanting in ability, who told me that on his arrival he, too, had had just such a reception.

'Only,' said he, 'as I detest such low-spirited fellows, I told Castagnac I did so, before my comrades. He took the remark in bad part, and, my faith! we went for a turn without the walls, where I gave him a pretty little prick with my sword which did much to damage his reputation, for, thanks to some successful duels, he had a great name, and was respected as an executioner of swaggerers.'

Things went on thus until, in the middle of June, the fever made its appearance at Constantine. The hospital had in it not only soldiers, but also a good many of the townsfolk, and I was compelled to lay aside my studies in order to attend to the patients.

Amongst those who were ill at the same time were Castagnac and Dutertre. Castagnac was not, however, ill of a fever. He had that peculiar affection known as *delirium*

tremens, a species of delirium, accompanied by nervous tremblings, peculiar to persons who have given themselves up
to drinking. The attack is preceded by uneasiness and sudden
tremblings, and is characterised by the flushed appearance
of the face and the alcoholic scent of the breath.

Poor Castagnac would throw himself out of his bed, and
would run about on the floor on all fours, as if he were
hunting rats. He would mew in a terrible fashion, and would
at intervals pronounce a cabalistic word, like a fakir in an
ecstatic state: 'Fatima! O Fatima!'

From this I assumed that the poor fellow had once been
unhappy in love, and had afterwards betaken himself to
drink in order to find consolation.

This idea inspired me with a profound pity for him. It
was such a sad thing to see that tall thin fellow spring to
the right, to the left, then draw himself together stiff, as a
piece of wood, his face white, his nose blue, his teeth set.
One could not listen to his cries without shuddering.

At the end of half-an-hour, when he came to himself
again, he would always ask: 'What did I say, doctor? Did I
say anything?'

'No nothing, lieutenant.'

'But I must have said something! Tell me what it was, do
not keep it from me.'

'Bah! How can I remember, what you said? A few empty
words! Sick people will rave now and then.'

'A few empty words! What were they?'

'Ha! How can I tell you? If you wish it I will put them
down on the next occasion!'

Then he would grow pale and would look at me with a
fixed gaze which seemed to search the bottom of my soul.
He would close his loose-hanging eyelids, press his lips
together, and murmur to himself: 'A glass of absinthe would
do me good.'

Then he would stretch his arms down beside him and lie
perfectly still.

The next day, as I was going to Castagnac's room, I saw coming towards me, at the end of the passage, my friend Raymond Dutertre.

'Doctor,' he said, taking my hand in his, 'I have come to ask you to do me a favour!'

'Willingly, my dear fellow, provided I have the power.'

'I want you to give me permission in writing to go out for the day.'

'As to that do not think of it – anything you like, but not permission to go out.'

'But, doctor, it seems to me that I am all right – quite right. I have had no fever for the last four days.'

'That is true, but there is fever in the town and I do not want to expose you to a relapse.'

'Well then, give me a pass for two hours only – just time to go there and come back.'

'It is impossible, my dear fellow. Do not ask me for it. It would be useless. I know well enough how tired one gets of being in a hospital, and how impatient sick folk are to get out to breathe the fresh air, but you must have patience.'

'Well, are you determined?'

'Quite. In eight days, if the improvement continues, we will go—'

He went off in a very bad humour. I did not mind that, but on turning round, what was my surprise to see Castagnac, his great eyes wide open, staring after his comrade, with a strange look on his face.

'Well,' said I, 'how are you this morning?'

'All right, quite right,' he answered sharply. 'Is that Raymond who has just gone away?'

'Yes.'

'What did he want?'

'Oh, nothing! He wanted me to give him a written permission to go out, and I refused it.'

'Ah! you refused it?'

'Certainly – what else could I do?'

Castagnac drew a long breath, and, as it were, withdrawing within himself, appeared to fall into a state of somnolency.

I know not how it was, but a vague dread came over me. The voice of the man had somehow disturbed my nerves, and I went on my way full of thought.

On that day one of my patients died. I had his body carried to the dissecting-hall, and towards nine o'clock in the evening, leaving my lodging, I went down the stairs which led to the amphitheatre.

Picture to yourself a little vaulted room, fifteen feet high and twenty feet wide. Its two windows opening upon the precipice which skirts the highway to Philippeville. At the farther end is a sloping table on which is the body which I propose to dissect.

Having put down my lamp upon a stone ledge in the wall, made for the purpose, and having opened my case of instruments, I commenced work and was absorbed in it for more than two hours without interruption.

The recall had been sounded long ago. The only sound I heard was the step of the sentinel. Sometimes he would remain still, or his musket would rattle on the ground. Then, hour after hour, the patrol came round, and I heard the challenge, the distant whispering of the password, and saw the movement of the lantern casting a ray of light over the slope – brief noises, clatters, the gradual cessation of which seemed to make the silence oppressive.

It was past twelve, and I was beginning to feel tired, when, looking by chance to the side of the room where was the open window, I was startled by a strange sight. There was a row of little screech-owls, grey, their feathers puffed out, their eyes green and squinting, fixed upon my lamp. They pressed forward to the edge of the casement, struggling with one another, each seeking to obtain a place.

These hideous birds, attracted by the smell of flesh, were awaiting my departure so that they might pounce upon their feast.

It would be impossible for me to tell you how horrified I was by this sight. I sprang towards the window, and all the birds disappeared into the gloom without, like dead leaves carried away by the wind.

At the same moment a strange noise caught my ear, a noise almost imperceptible in the still night. I leaned forward, with my hand upon the edge of the window, looking out and holding my breath so as to be able to hear the better.

Above the amphitheatre was the room of Lieutenant Castagnac, and below, between the precipice and the wall of the hospital, ran a ledge about a foot wide, covered with pieces of broken bottles and earthenware, thrown there by the hospital attendants.

But, at that hour of the night, when the least sound, the lightest breath, could be heard, I could distinguish the steps and groping of a man proceeding along the ledge.

'Heaven grant,' I said to myself, 'that the sentinel does not see him! Should he hesitate one second he is lost!'

I had hardly finished when a husky choking voice, the voice of Castagnac, cried suddenly in the silence: 'Raymond! Where are you going?'

That exclamation went through me. It was a declaration of doom. At the same moment some debris fell down the slope, and then I heard some one clinging, with great gasps, to the narrow ledge. The cold sweat rolled down my face. I tried to see – to leave my room – to call for aid – my tongue was paralysed.

All of a sudden I heard a groan. I listened. Would nothing follow? I deceived myself. There was a burst of mocking laughter, and a window was shut to with such violence that I could hear the noise of broken glass. Profound continued silence threw its winding-sheet over the fearful drama.

How shall I go on, my friends? Terror drove me back to the farthest end of the room. There, trembling, my hair bristling, my eyes fixed on space before me, I remained for more than twenty minutes, listening to the beating of my heart and seeking to restrain its throbs with my hands. At the end of that time I mechanically closed the window, took the lamp, mounted the stairs, and went along the passage to my room. I lay down but I could not shut an eye. I heard those gasps – those long painful heavings of the victim – and then the laughter of his murderer.

'To kill a man upon the highway with a pistol in one's hand,' I said to myself, 'is no doubt dreadful, but to murder with a word – without any peril to oneself!'

Outside the sirocco was blowing. It was sweeping over the plain with low moaning, and dashing the sand and gravel of the desert even against the top of the wall. At last the violence of the feelings which possessed me made me feel the need of sleep. Fright alone kept me awake. I pictured to myself the tall Castagnac in his shirt, leaning out of his window, his neck stretched out, looking down into the profound shadowy depths of the precipice after his victim, and the thought made my blood run cold.

'It was he,' I said to myself, 'it was he! If he knew that I was here!'

Then I thought I heard the boards of the corridor creak under a stealthy step, and I lifted myself up upon my elbow, my mouth half open, listening.

At length, however, the necessity for sleep prevailed, and towards three o'clock I slept as sound as a bell.

It was full day when I awoke. The night wind had subsided. The sky was clear, and the calm was so profound that I doubted my recollection. Surely I must have had a terrible dream?

What was strange was that I felt afraid to set about ascertaining the truth. I performed my various duties, and it was not until I had visited all the rooms, and made a prolonged inquiry into the condition of each of my patients, that I betook myself to the chamber of Dutertre.

I knocked at his door. There was no answer. I opened it. His bed had not been slept in. I called the hospital assistants and asked where the lieutenant was. No one had seen him since the preceding evening.

Then summoning all my courage, I went to Castagnac's room.

A rapid glance at the window showed me that two of its panes were broken. I felt myself grow pale, but recovering myself I said, 'What a storm we had during the night! What did you think of it, lieutenant?'

He was calmly sitting with his elbows on the table, his long bony face between his hands, pretending to read a military work.

'*Parbleu!*' replied he, pointing to the window. 'Look at that!'

'It looks, lieutenant,' said I, 'as though this room must be more exposed than the others – or, perhaps, you left the window open?'

An almost imperceptible muscular contraction was visible around the jaws of the old soldier.

'Faith, no,' said he, looking at me strangely. 'It was closed.'

'Ah!'

I went to him to feel his pulse.

'And how are you going on?'

'Oh, so so.'

'Certainly! You are better – just a little disturbance! In five days, lieutenant, you will be all right. I promise you. Then, however, take care. No more of that green poison – or if you do, look to yourself.'

In spite of the cheerful tone I assumed, my voice was trembling. The arm of the old scoundrel, as I held it in my hand, seemed like a serpent. I should have liked to fly. Then his eye, fixed, yet restless, was never off me for an instant. It was terrible! Nevertheless I contained myself.

As I was leaving, turning suddenly as if I had forgotten something, I said: 'Bye the bye, lieutenant, has Dutertre been to see you?'

His grey hair seemed to bristle.

'Dutertre?'

'Yes. He is missing – missing since yesterday. No one knows what has become of him. I expect—'

'No one has called on me,' he replied, with a little dry cough, 'no one.'

He took up his book, and I left his room as assured of his guilt as I was it was day. Unfortunately, however, I had no proof of it.

'If I denounce him,' said I to myself, when I was in my room, 'he is sure to deny it, and if he does so what proof could I bring that my assertion is true? My own bare testimony would not be sufficient of itself. I should be made odious by the accusation, and should have made a terrible enemy.'

Again, such crimes as these are not recognised by the law. In the end I resolved to keep my eye upon Castagnac without his suspecting me, believing that he would ultimately betray himself. Then I went off to the commandant, and simply reported to him the fact of Lieutenant Dutertre's disappearance.

The next day some Arabs arrived, on their way to Constantine, their asses laden with gums, and they stated that on the way to Philippeville they had seen a uniform hanging high up in the rocks of the Kasba, and that the birds of prey flew around it in hundreds, filling the air with their clamour.

It was the body of Raymond.

The remains were recovered with infinite pains, men climbing along the rocks by means of cords and ladders.

For two or three days the officers in the garrison talked about this remarkable occurrence, and a thousand guesses were made as to what could have taken place. Then other affairs distracted their attention – bezique and piquet.

Men who are daily exposed to peril have not much sympathy to waste on others. Jacques dies, Pierre takes his place. The regiment itself is immortal. It is a personification of what is called the humanitarian principle. You are, then you shall be! By existence you participate in the eternal and infinite being! Yes, I shall exist, but as what? That is the question. Today as a lieutenant of hussars – and tomorrow as a clod of earth! Such a condition of things is worthy of a second thought.

II

My position, in the midst of the general indifference, was pitiable. Silence weighed upon me as if it were a crime. The sight of Castagnac filled me with indignation, with a sort of insupportable disgust. The gloomy look of that man, his ironical smile, chilled my blood. He would now and again look at me as if he would search to the bottom of my soul, and these furtive glances, full of malignity, did not at all add to my ease.

'He suspects something,' I said to myself. 'If he was only certain, I should be lost. Such a man shrinks from nothing.'

These thoughts imposed an intolerable restraint upon me. My work suffered in consequence of it. It was necessary I should put an end to such a state of things – but how?

Heaven came to my assistance.

One day as I passed through the wicket, about three o'clock in the afternoon, in order to go to the town, the corporal of the infirmary, running to me, gave me a piece of paper, which he had found in Raymond's tunic.

'It is a note from a certain woman named Fatima,' said the good fellow. 'It seems the girl was attached to Lieutenant Dutertre. I thought, major, that perhaps the letter would interest you.'

As I read the letter I was much astonished. It was very short, and indeed merely named a time and a place of meeting. But what a revelation was the signature!

'Then,' said I, 'the exclamations of Castagnac when he

had his severest fits, the exclamation "Fatima, Fatima," was the name of a woman, of a living woman, and she loved Dutertre! Who knows? Perhaps it was in order to keep this appointment that Raymond asked me to give him the written permission! Yes, yes! The note is dated the third of July. It must have been so. Poor fellow! As he could not slip out in the daytime, he ventured along that dreadful ledge at night; and then – Castagnac heard him!'

Turning these things over in my mind, I descended to the foot of the rock, and found myself in front of a low brick building, open to the wind, as is the custom in the East.

In the back of this place a certain Sidi Houmaïum, armed with a long wooden spoon and gravely sitting in his slippers, was stirring the perfumed powder of Moka in a vessel full of boiling water.

I must tell you that I had cured Sidi Houmaïum of a malignant skin affection, which had defied all the panaceas and all the charms of the native doctors and surgeons. The good fellow in consequence cherished quite an affection for me.

All around the room ran a bench covered with little rope mats, and upon this bench sat five or six Moors, each with his red fez with its blue tassel on his head, his legs crossed, his eyes half closed, his *chibouk* between his lips, silently inhaling the perfume of the Turkish tobacco and of the Arabian berry.

I do not know how it was, but the idea occurred to me to consult Sidi Houmaïum. It was one of those strange impulses which one is unable to account for, and of which one cannot explain the origin.

I went into the *botéga* with a solemn step, to the great surprise of the folk within, and took my place on the bench.

The *kaouadji*, without seeming to remember me, brought me a *chibouk* and a cup of hot coffee.

I sipped the beverage; I smoked my *chibouk*. Time went slowly on, and towards six o'clock the hypocritical tones of the *muetzin* were heard, calling the pious to prayer.

All rose, passed their hands over their beards, and set out for the mosque.

At last I was alone.

Sidi Houmaïum, casting around him an uneasy look, came to me and bent down to kiss my hand.

'Sir Taleb, what has brought you to my humble place?' he asked. 'What service can I do you?'

'You can introduce me to Fatima.'

'Fatima, the Moorish girl?'

'Yes, the Moorish girl.'

'Sir Taleb, in your mother's name, do not see that girl.'

'Why not?'

'She is the ruin of all who come near her. She has a deadly charm – do not see her.'

'Sidi Houmaïum, my resolution is unchangeable. Fatima possess a charm! Very well. I possess a charm – a more powerful one. Hers deals death; mine gives life, youth, beauty. Tell her, Sidi Houmaïum, tell her that the wrinkles of old age efface themselves as I approach. Tell her that I have found the pippins of the apple of Eve – that apple which has, for countless ages, condemned all to die; tell her I have set them, and that from them has sprung up the tree of life, the sweet fruits of which give the beauty of eternal youth. If one tastes of it, however old she be, though she be ugly and wrinkled like a witch, she becomes young again – her wrinkles disappear, her skin becomes white and sweet as a lily, her lips red and perfumed like the queen of flowers, her teeth sparkling as those of a young jackal.'

'But, Sir Taleb,' cried the Mussulman, 'Fatima is not old. She is young and pretty – so pretty that she would be worthy of a sultan.'

'I know it. She is not old, but she will become so. I want to see her. Remember, Sidi Houmaïum, remember your promises.'

'Since such is your desire, Sir Taleb, come here again

tomorrow at the same time. But remember what I tell you, Fatima makes a terrible use of her beauty.'

'Rest assured, I will not forget.'

And extending my hand to the *coulouglis*, I went out as I had come in, my head held high, and my step majestic.

You may imagine with what impatience I awaited the hour of my appointment with Sidi Houmaïum. I could hardly restrain myself. A hundred times I went over the great court awaiting the cry of the *muetzin*, taking off my hat to every one I met, and even chatting with the sentinel in order to kill time.

At last the verse of the Koran was heard in the high air, hovering on from minaret to minaret over the still city. I hurried along the street, and found Sidi Houmaïum closing his *botéga*.

'Well?' said I almost breathless.

'Fatima is waiting for you, Sir Taleb.'

He put up the bar, and without another word, led me on.

The sky was dazzling in its brilliancy. The tall white houses, a veritable procession of ghosts, clothed here and there with a ray from the sun, reflected their mournful pallor on the few passers-by.

Sidi Houmaïum walked on without looking aside, the long sleeves of his *bernous* almost sweeping the ground; and as we walked I could hear him reciting in Arabic, in a low tone, some prayers which sounded something like those of our pilgrims.

At length, leaving the great street, he plunged into the narrow Suma alley, so narrow that two people cannot walk abreast. There in the black mud of the gutter, under wretched sheds, grovels a crowd of cobblers, of embroiderers on morocco-leather, of sellers of Indian spices, aloes, dates, rare scents. Some come and go with an apathetic air, others are squatted down, their legs crossed, meditating on heaven only knows what, in an atmosphere of blue smoke exhaled from their mouth and nose.

The African sun penetrates the dark passage with its golden beams, lighting up here an old grey-beard with hooked nose, with his *chibouk* in his fat hand, the fingers of which are loaded with rings; farther on it rests on the graceful profile of a young Jewess, thoughtful and sad, within her shop; or perhaps, better still, it lights up an armourer's stall, with his slender *yataghans*, his long Bedouin guns with their stocks inlaid with mother-of-pearl. The smell from the ground struggles with the keen odour of the laboratory. The sunlight chases the shadows, carves them into grotesque shapes, lightens them up into dim gloom – never able to entirely banish them.

All of a sudden, in one of the intricate turns of the alley, Sidi Houmaïum stopped before a low door and knocked.

'You will follow me,' I said in a low voice. 'You can act as interpreter.'

'Fatima speaks French,' he answered, without turning his head.

At that moment the shining face of a negress appeared at the wicket. Sidi Houmaïum spoke some words in Arabic. The door opened and suddenly shut itself behind me. The negress went out by a side door I had not observed, and Sidi Houmaïum remained in the alley.

After having waited some minutes I began to grow impatient, when the side door opened, and the negress who had let me in signed to me to accompany her.

I went on some paces, and found myself in a small inner court, paved with mosaic work of little delf bricks. Several doors opened into the same court.

The negress led me on into a room, the open windows of which were hung with silk curtains of Moorish design. All around were cushions of violet chintz, a large amber-coloured reed mat covered the floor, interminable arabesques of flowers and of fantastic fruits were displayed on the ceiling. What, however, attracted all my attention was Fatima herself, as she leaned on her elbow on the divan, her eyes veiled by her eyelids with long black lashes, her lips slightly parted, her nose straight and fine, her arms loaded with heavy bracelets. She had little feet, and calmly played with her slippers embroidered with greenish gold, when I stood upon the threshold.

For some seconds the Moorish girl looked at me out of the corner of her eyes, and then, a slight smile parting her lips, said in a self-possessed voice: 'Come in, Sir Taleb. Sidi Houmaïum told me you were coming, and I know what brings you here. You are very good to interest yourself in poor Fatima, who is growing old, for she is now seventeen. Seventeen! It is an age of regrets and wrinkles! A time for late repentance! Ah, Sir Taleb, sit down and make yourself at home. You bring me the apple of Eve, do you not? The apple which keeps one youthful and beautiful. Ah! poor Fatima has need of it!'

I knew not what to answer. I was confused, but recalling to myself the errand on which I had come, my blood ceased to run so fast, and I became as cool as marble.

'You rally with much grace, Fatima,' said I, seating myself upon the divan. 'I have heard your wit praised no less than your beauty, and find that what was said of you is true.'

'Ah!' said she, 'and by whom?'

'By Dutertre.'

'Dutertre?'

'Yes – Raymond Dutertre, the young officer who fell down the precipice of the Rummel. He whom you loved, Fatima.'

She opened her big eyes in surprise.

'Who says I loved him?' she asked me with a strange look. 'It is not true. Did he tell you that?'

'No, but I know it. This note proves it to me; this letter which you wrote to him, and which has been the cause of his death; which led him to risk his life at night on the rocks of the Kasba.'

Hardly had I finished those words, when the girl rose abruptly, her eyes sparkling with a sombre fire.

'I was sure of it,' she said. 'Yes. When the negress came and told me that some one had been killed there, I said "Aissa, it is he who has done it. It is he! Ah! the wretch!"'

While I looked at her, astounded, not comprehending her words, she came to me and said in a low voice: 'Will he die for it? Will he die for it soon? I should like to see him cut to pieces.'

She took me by the arm, and looked at me as if she would read my soul. I shall never forget the livid pallor of that face, those great dark gleaming eyes, those trembling lips.

'Of whom do you speak, Fatima?' I asked, quite bewildered. 'Explain yourself. I do not know what you mean.'

'Of whom? Why, of Castagnac! You are Taleb in the hospital. Well then, poison him. He is a villain. He got me to write to the officer to come here. I did not wish him to come. I well knew that the young fellow had sought an introduction to me for a long time, but I knew that Castagnac contemplated some evil against him. When I refused to write he threatened to come from the hospital to beat me if I did not do so at once. See. There is his letter. I tell you, he is a villain.'

It would pain me, my friends, to repeat to you all that the Moorish girl told me about Castagnac. She told me the story of their love – how he had ill-used her, how he used to beat her.

When I left Fatima's house my heart was heavy.

Sidi Houmaïum waited for me at the gate, and we retraced our steps through the Suma alley.

'Take care,' said the *coulouglis*, looking at me out of the corner of his eyes, 'take care, Sir Taleb. You are very pale. The evil angel hovers over your head!'

I pressed the hand of the good fellow, and said: 'I fear nothing.'

My resolution was taken. Without losing a moment I went to the Kasba, entered the hospital, and knocked at the door of Castagnac's room.

'Come in.'

It would seem the sight of me was not very welcome, for when he looked round he gave a slight start.

'Hulloa! Is it you?' said he, with a forced smile. 'I was not expecting you.'

For an answer I showed him the letter he had written to Fatima.

He became pale, and when he had looked at it for some seconds he was about to throw himself upon me, but I stopped him with a gesture.

'If you move a step,' I said, laying my hand upon my sword hilt, 'I will kill you like a dog. You scoundrel! You have murdered Dutertre! I was in the amphitheatre and overheard all! Do not deny it. Your conduct towards that girl has been disgraceful. How could a French officer degrade himself to such a degree! Now, listen. I would give you up to justice, but your disgrace would also reflect upon us. If you have any courage kill yourself. I give you till tomorrow. If tomorrow, at seven o'clock, I find you alive, I will myself hand you over to the commandant.'

Having said these words, I left the room without waiting for his response, and hastened to order the sentinel not to allow Lieutenant Castagnac to leave the hospital on any pretence whatever. I also ordered the door-keeper to keep a sharp watch, and told him that I should hold him responsible for whatever might follow if he was negligent or cowardly. Then I calmly walked to my lodgings, as if nothing had happened. I was even more merry than usual, and prolonged my dinner till close upon eight o'clock.

Since Castagnac's criminality had been proved to me so certainly, I was pitiless. Raymond cried to me to revenge him.

When I had dined I went to the shop of a seller of resin and bought a pitch-torch, such as our *spahis* carry at their night carousals. After that, entering the hospital, I went direct to the amphitheatre, taking care to double lock the door behind me.

The voice of the *muetzin* announced the tenth hour; the mosques were empty; the night was dark.

I sat down in front of my window, breathing the lukewarm puffs of the breeze, and gave myself up to thoughts which had beforetimes been so dear to me. How much had I suffered, how much trouble had I not gone through during the last five days. In all my past life I could not find the like. It seemed to me as though I was escaping from the grasp of some malignant spirit to enjoy new freedom!

So time rolled on. The guard had already twice relieved the sentinels, when, all of a sudden, I heard quick stealthy footsteps upon the stair. A light knock echoed on the door.

I made no reply.

A nervous hand sought the handle.

'It is Castagnac,' I said to myself, astonished.

Two seconds passed.

'Open,' cried some one from outside.

I was not deceived. It was he.

I listened, and heard him try to force open the stout oak door with his shoulders.

All was silent. He listened. I remained perfectly quiet, holding my breath. Something was thrown down upon the stairs. I could hear his steps die away.

I had escaped death.

But what if he should return?

Fearing another and more fierce attempt upon the door, I put up the two great bars which made a veritable prison of the room.

It was labour thrown away, for on reseating myself I saw the shadow of Castagnac thrown upon the wall between the two bastions. The moon, which rose on the side of the town, threw the shadow of the hospital upon the precipice. A few stars sparkled on the horizon, not a breath of air was stirring.

Before committing himself to the dangerous path the old soldier halted, looking towards my window. He hesitated for a considerable time.

At the end of about a quarter of an hour he made the first step, proceeding with his back against the wall. He was come to the middle of the ledge, and no doubt flattered himself he would now be able to arrive at the slope which descends to the Kasba, when I uttered the death-cry: 'Raymond, where are you going?'

Although he was taken by surprise, he had, however, more coolness than his victim. The wretched fellow did not budge an inch, and answered me with an ironical laugh: 'Ah! ah! Are you there, doctor? I thought you were. Listen, I shall come back, and we shall have a little account to settle together.'

Lighting my torch and holding it over the precipice, I cried: 'It is too late. Look, you scoundrel, that is your tomb.'

The immense tiers of the abyss with their black rocks, glittering, bristling in grotesque shapes, were lighted up down to the very bottom of the valley.

The scene was titanic. The white light of the torch fell, step by step, between the rocks, making their enormous shadows dance in the profundity, and seemed to hew out endless shadowy forms.

I was overwhelmed by the scene myself, and recoiled a step, as if struck with giddiness.

But he – he who was not separated from the gulf by more than the space of a single foot, how great must his terror have been!

His knees shook, his hands clung to the wall. I advanced once more. An immense bat, attracted by the light, hovered in mystic circles around the huge walls, like a black rat, with sharp nails, swimming in a circle of light. Far off, very far off, glimmered the waters of the Rummel.

'Mercy!' cried the murderer, in broken tones. 'Mercy!'

I had not the courage to prolong his torture, and I threw my torch into space.

It fell slowly, carrying the scattered flame down into the deep shadows, lighting by turns the layers of rock, and sprinkling its dazzling sparks over the thorns.

It became no more than a speck in the night, falling, falling. Then a shadow shot between it and my eye like a thunderbolt.

I knew that justice had been done.

As I ascended the steps from the amphitheatre I trod upon something. I bent down. It was my sword. Castagnac, with his wonted treachery, had resolved to kill me with my own weapon, so that it might be believed I had committed suicide.

As to the rest – as I had foreseen, the door of my room had been broken open, my bed turned upside down, my papers scattered about. He had done his work well in my room.

This at once dissipated every feeling of pity which had occurred to me when I thought of the scoundrel's miserable end.

THE CRAB SPIDER

The hot springs at Spinbronn, situated in Hundsrück some leagues from Pirmesens, at one time enjoyed a magnificent reputation. All those who suffered from gout or kidney troubles in Germany used to congregate there. The wild aspect of the country did not deter them. They stayed in pretty cottages at the bottom of the pass and bathed in the waterfall, which fell in thick sheets of foam from a cave at the top of a cliff. They drank a decanter of mineral water or two a day, and the resident doctor, Daniel Hâselnoss, who gave out his prescriptions wearing a large wig and a chestnut-coloured suit, did excellent business.

Today the waters at Spinbronn feature no longer in the 'Codex'; in this poor village, you can see only wretched woodcutters, and, sad to relate, Dr Hâselnoss has long gone! All of which is the result of a series of very strange occurrences which Councillor Hans Bremer of Pirmesens related to me one summer evening.

'You of course know, Maître Frantz,' he said to me, 'that the spring at Spinbronn comes out of a sort of cave, approximately fifteen feet high and twelve to fifteen feet wide; the water has a temperature of 67°C and is briny. As for the cave, it is entirely covered on the outside with moss, ivy, and brushwood and no one knows its depth, since hot vapours prevent anyone from entering.

'However, a peculiar thing had been remarked since the last century, that some of the birds of the neighbourhood, thrushes, turtle-doves, and hawks, were often seen to fly in but never to come out. No one knew to what mysterious influence they should attribute this peculiarity.

'In 1801, during the watering season, perhaps owing to the unusually heavy rain that year, the spring became more abundant, and one day the bathers who were walking at the bottom on the lawn saw a human body, dead white, falling from the waterfall.

'You may judge for yourself, Maître Frantz, the general panic. Naturally it was thought that in years gone by a murder had been committed at Spinbronn, and that the body of the victim had been thrown into the spring. But the body weighed no more than twelve pounds, and Dr Hâselnoss deduced from this that it must have lain in the sands for more than three centuries, to have been reduced to this state of desiccation.

'This line of reasoning, though very plausible, did not prevent a crowd of bathers, who were naturally upset at having drunk from the salty water, from leaving at the end of that day. Those who were genuine sufferers with gout and their kidneys consoled themselves . . . but more breaking up inside the cavern occurred for all the debris, mud, and rubbish which was in the cave was disgorged over the ensuing days; a real charnel house came down from the mountain, skeletons of animals of every sort – quadrupeds, birds, reptiles – in short all the worst horrors imaginable.

'Hâselnoss immediately published a pamphlet pointing out that all these bones came from an antediluvian world, that they were fossil bones which had accumulated there in a sort of hollow during the deluge that is four thousand years before Christ, that as a consequence they could be considered genuine stones, that people should not be disgusted by them . . . But his work had scarcely reassured the gout sufferers, when, one fine morning, the corpse of a fox, then that of a hawk with all its feathers, fell from the waterfall.

'It was impossible to maintain any longer that these remains were previous to the flood. Consequently the feeling of disgust was so great that everyone hastened to pack his belongings and go off to take the waters elsewhere.

'"What a disgrace!" exclaimed the beautiful ladies . . . "What a horror!" "That's where the virtue of these mineral waters comes from . . . We would rather die from kidney stones than continue such treatment!"

'After eight days only a huge Englishman remained at Spinbronn, who had at the same time gout in both hands and the feet and who was known as Sir Thomas Haverburch, Commodore. He lived in great style, as was the custom of British people in a foreign country.

'This character, big and fat, with a florid complexion, but whose hands were literally knotted with gout, would have swallowed broth made with dead bodies if he thought it would cure his infirmity. He laughed a great deal at the departure of the other invalids and took up residence in the prettiest cottage, halfway up the hill, declaring his intention of spending the winter at Spinbronn.'

At this point Councillor Bremer slowly inhaled a generous pinch of snuff, as if to rekindle his memories; he shook the delicate lace of his shirt frill with the tips of his fingers and continued.

'Five or six years before the revolution of 1789, a young doctor from Pirmesens, called Christian Weber, had set off for San Domingo in the hope of there making his fortune. He had effectively amassed some one hundred thousand pounds in the exercise of his profession, when the revolt of the negroes broke out.

'There is no need for me to remind you of the barbaric treatment which our unfortunate compatriots suffered in Haiti. Dr Weber had the good fortune to escape the massacre and to save a part of his fortune. He then travelled to South America, and spent several years in French Guiana. In 1801 he returned to Pirmesens and established himself at

Spinbronn, where Dr Hâselnoss handed over his house and his dead practice.

'Christian Weber brought with him an old negress called Agatha – an awesome creature, with a short squat nose, lips as big as your fist, her head covered in a triple row of scarves in garish colours. This poor old woman loved red; she had hooped earrings which dangled as far as her shoulders, and the mountain people of Hundsrück would come from twenty miles around to stare at her.

'As for Dr Weber, he was a tall, gaunt man, invariably dressed in a sky-blue coat with swallow-tails and in buckskin breeches. He wore a pliable straw hat and boots with bright yellow tops, on the front of which dangled two silver tassels.

'He wasn't very talkative; his laugh had something of a nervous twitching in it, and his grey eyes, usually calm and meditative, shone with an unnatural glow at the slightest sign of contradiction. Each morning he would go for a walk on the mountain, letting his horse roam and whistling, always in the same monotone, the same melody from a negro song. This eccentric had brought back from his travels a number of boxes full of weird insects, some of them bronzy-black and as big as eggs, others small and scintillating like sparks. He seemed to be much more fond of these than of his patients and from time to time, on his way back from his strolls, he brought back some butterflies pinned to the band of his hat.

'He had hardly settled into Hâselnoss's huge house than he filled its farmyard with foreign birds, Barbary geese with scarlet cheeks, guinea-fowl, and a white peacock which usually perched on the garden wall and which shared with the negress the admiration of the mountain folk.

'If I am going into details, Maître Frantz, it's because they remind me of my early youth. Dr Weber turned out to be at the same time both my cousin and my tutor, and on his return to Germany, he had come to get me and install me in his home at Spinbronn. Black Agatha at first inspired in me some fear, and it was only with some difficulty that I could get used to her unusual features. She was a good woman, she could make spicy dishes well, she hummed strange songs in a guttural voice at the same time snapping her fingers and rhythmically raising her fat legs in turn, so that I ended up liking her very much.

'Dr Weber had, quite naturally, made friends with Sir Thomas Haverburch, who was in his eyes his most prominent patient, and I wasn't long in realizing that these two eccentrics had long sessions together. They chatted about various mysteries, like the transmission of energy, and they indulged in certain bizarre gestures which they had both observed in the course of their travels, Sir Thomas in the East and my tutor in the Americas. I found it very intriguing.

'As happens with children, I was always on the look-out for what they seemed to want to hide from me. But despairing in the end of discovering anything I resolved to ask Agatha. The poor old woman, after making me promise to say nothing about it, confessed to me that my tutor was a sorcerer. Moreover, Dr Weber exercised a peculiar influence over the negress's mind and this lady, normally so cheerful and always ready to amuse herself at the slightest thing, trembled like a leaf, when, by chance, her master's grey eyes fell on her.

'All this, Maître Frantz, seems to have no connection with the springs of Spinbronn . . . But, wait, just wait . . . You will see by what a strange string of circumstances my story is related to this.

'I told you that birds would go into the cave and not come out, and even other bigger animals. After the final departure of the bathers, some inhabitants of the village remembered that a young girl, called Loïsa Müller, who lived with her old invalid grandmother in a cottage on the slope of the hill, had suddenly disappeared about five years ago. She had set off one morning to look for grass in the forest, and since then no one had ever heard of her again, except that a few days later, some woodcutters who were coming down from the mountain had found her apron and her sickle a few paces from the cave.

'Since then it was obvious to everyone that the body that had fallen from the waterfall, and about which Hâselnoss had said such very nice things, was none other than that of Loïsa Müller. The poor young girl had undoubtedly been drawn into the cavern by the mysterious influence to which even weaker things were subjected almost daily.

'This influence, what was it? No one knew. But the inhabitants of Spinbronn, superstitious like all mountain folk, claimed that the devil lived in the cave, and the terror spread in the surrounding districts.

'Now, one July afternoon in 1802, my cousin was working on a new classification of the insects in his boxes. He had taken several quite curious ones from them the evening before. I was beside him, holding a lighted candle in my hand and in the other a needle that I heated.

'Sir Thomas, sitting down, his chair leaning against the edge of a window and his feet on a stool, watched us working and smoked a cigar.

'I was on very good terms with Sir Thomas Haverburch, and I used to accompany him every day to the woods in his barouche. He enjoyed listening to me chattering in English and wanted to make of me, he would say, a real gentleman.

'When he had labelled all his butterflies, Dr Weber at last opened the box of his biggest insects and said: "Yesterday I caught a magnificent stag-beetle, the great *Lucanus Cervus* of the oaks of Hartz. It has this peculiarity that its right claw forks into five branches. It's a rare species."

'At the same time I gave him the needle, and as he pierced the insect before fixing it on to the cork strip, Sir Thomas, who up to then was impassive, got up, and drawing near a box, began to consider the crab spider from Guiana that it contained with a feeling of horror that strikingly portrayed itself on his fat red face.

'"There," he exclaimed, "is the most hideous work of creation! I only have to see it and I feel myself shaking all over." In fact a sudden pallor spread all over his face.

'"Bah!" said my tutor, "all that's just a childish phobia. You heard your nurse cry out when she saw a spider, you were afraid, and you have retained the impression. But if you looked at the spider through a powerful microscope, you would be amazed at the perfection of its organs, at their admirable arrangement, and at their very elegance."

'"It disgusts me," cut in the Commodore abruptly. "Ugh!" He turned on his heel.

'"Oh! I don't know why," he said, "the spider has always made my blood run cold."

'Dr Weber started to laugh, and I, who shared Sir Thomas's feelings, exclaimed: "Yes, cousin, you should take this nasty creature out of the box. It is disgusting. It mars all the others."

'"You little animal," he said to me, his eyes sparkling, "who is forcing you to look at it? If it doesn't please you, off you go elsewhere!"

'Evidently he was angry. Sir Thomas, who was then in front of the window looking at the mountain, turned round suddenly, came and took me by the hand, and said to me in a kindly way: "Your tutor, Hans, loves his spider. We prefer the trees and the grass. Let's go for a walk."

'"Yes! Go!" shouted the doctor, "and return for supper at six." Then raising his voice, "No hard feelings, Sir Haverburch!"

'Sir Thomas wanted to drive himself and dismissed his servant. He made me sit beside him on the same seat and we set off for the Rothalps.

'While the carriage slowly climbed the sandy path, a sadness that I could not control took hold of my soul. Sir Thomas, for his part, was serious. He was aware of my sadness and said to me: "You don't like spiders, Hans, no more do I. But, thank Heaven, there are no dangerous ones in this country. The crab spider which your tutor has in his box comes from French Guiana. It lives for years, in the huge swampy forests constantly filled with humid vapours and burning gases; it needs this temperature to live. Its web, or to be more precise, its huge net, envelops an entire thicket. It captures birds in it, just like our spiders catch flies. I have seen others in the collections of those people who study such things but it could not live long in this cold climate. All those that ever escaped no doubt perished very quickly. But chase from your mind these revolting images and have a pull at my old Burgundy!"

'Then, turning round, he lifted up the lid of the second seat and took out of the straw a sort of a gourd, from which he filled to the brim a leather cup and handed it to me.

'The carriage, harnessed to a small horse from the Ardennes, thin and nervous as a goat, climbed up the precipitous path. Myriads of insects buzzed in the heather. On the right, a hundred paces at the most, stretched above us the dark edge of the forests of Rothalps, whose sinister depths, full of brambles and rank weeds, revealed now and then some clearings, flooded with light. On our left, tumbled the stream of Spinbronn. The higher we climbed the more the silvery sheets of water floating in the abyss took on an azure hue, and redoubled their thundering roar.

'I was enthralled by the spectacle. Sir Thomas, leaning back on his seat, his knees up to his chin, gave way to his customary dreaming, while the horse, straining with its legs and leaning its head on the harness, so as to balance the carriage, suspended us as it were from the edge of the rock. Soon, however, we reached a shallower slope, surrounded with shadows. I had still got my head turned and my eyes lost in the boundless view. At the sight of the shadows I turned around and saw, within a hundred paces, the cave of Spinbronn. The surrounding underwood was magnificently green, and the spring, which before falling from the plateau stretched over a bed of sand and black pebbles, was so limpid that one would have thought it frozen over, had not light wisps of steam covered its surface.

'The horse had just stopped of its own accord to breathe. Sir Thomas, standing up, gazed for a few seconds at the scenery.

'"How calm everything is," he said; then after a moment's

silence, "If you weren't here, Hans, I would willingly take a bathe in the pool."

'"But, Commodore," I said to him, "why not go for a bathe? I can very easily go for a short stroll roundabouts. There is on the mountain nearby a huge pasture all covered with strawberries. I shall go and pick some of them. I shall be back in an hour."

'"I'd really like to, Hans, it's a good idea. Dr Weber claims that I drink too much burgundy. You have to fight wine with mineral water. This sandy bed pleases me."

'Then both of us having climbed down, he tied the horse to the trunk of a small birch tree and shook my hand as if to say to me, "You can go."

'I saw him sit down on the moss and take off his boots. As I moved away he turned round and shouted: "In an hour, Hans!" These were his last words.

'An hour later I returned to the spring. The horse, the carriage, and Sir Thomas's clothes were the only things to be seen. The sun was setting. The shadows lengthened. There was no bird song under the foliage, not an insect buzzed in the tall grasses; a deathly silence hovered over the solitude.

'This silence terrified me. I climbed on to the rock which towers over the cave. I looked right and left. No one! I called out. No reply! The sound of my voice, repeated by the echoes, made me afraid. Night was coming down slowly. An indescribable anguish oppressed me. Suddenly the story of the young girl who had disappeared came to my mind; and I started to run down. But, having arrived in front of the cave, I stopped, overcome by an inexpressible terror. Glancing into the black shadow of the spring, I could see two motionless red blobs . . . then huge lines splashing about in a peculiar way in the midst of the darkness, and this at a depth where perhaps no human eyes had yet penetrated. Fear gave to my sight, to all my senses, a subtlety of perception unheard of. For some seconds I heard, quite clearly, a cicada singing its evening lament on the edge of the wood. Then my heart, for a moment stilled by emotion, started to beat furiously and I heard nothing else!

'Then, uttering a terrified cry, I ran off, leaving behind the horse, the carriage. In less than twenty minutes, leaping over rocks, brushwood, I had reached the threshold of our house, burst through the front door, and shouted in a choked voice: "Run! Run! Sir Haverburch is dead! Sir Haverburch is in the cave!"

'After these words, uttered in the presence of my tutor, old Agatha, and two or three people invited that evening by the doctor, I fainted. I have learned since that I was delirious for an hour.

'The entire village went off to look for the Commodore. Christian Weber had dragged them off. At ten o'clock in the evening, the entire crowd came back, bringing with them the coach and, in the coach, Sir Haverburch's clothes. They had discovered nothing. It was impossible to go ten steps into the cave without being suffocated by the hot vapours from the spring.

'During their absence Agatha and I had remained seated in the corner of the chimney. I, muttering in terror incoherent words, she, her hands crossed on her knees, her eyes wide open, going from time to time to the window to see what was going on, because one could see from the foot of the mountain torches running through the woods. One could hear voices, far away, hailing one another in the night.

'When her master approached, Agatha started to tremble. The doctor came in suddenly, pale, his lips tight, despair imprinted on his face. About twenty woodcutters followed him in confusion, with their large wide-rimmed felt hats, their weather-beaten faces, waving the remnants of their torches. Hardly were they in the room than the sparkling eyes of my tutor seemed to look for something. He saw the negress, and without a single word being exchanged between them, the poor woman started to cry out.

'"No! No! I don't want to!"

'"And I want to!" replied the doctor harshly.

'You might have said that the negress had been seized by an invincible power. She shuddered from head to toe and, Christian Weber pointing out a seat for her, she sat on it with a corpse-like rigidity.

'All those present, witnesses of this frightening spectacle, good-living people of coarse primitive manners, but full of pious sentiments, crossed themselves, and I, who didn't know then, even by name, the terrible magnetic power of the will, I started to tremble, thinking that Agatha was dead.

'Christian Weber had gone up to the negress and passed his hand over her brow in a rapid movement.

'"Are you there?" he said.

'"Yes, master."

'"Sir Thomas Haverburch?"

'At these words she had a renewed trembling fit.

'"Can you see him?"

'"Yes! Yes!" she said in a choking voice. "I see him."

'"Where is he?"

'"Up there! At the bottom of the cave! Dead!"

'"Dead!" said the doctor. "How?"

'"The spider! Oh, the dreadful crab spider! Oh!"

'"Calm yourself," said the doctor, quite pale. "Tell us clearly."

'"The crab spider has him by the throat . . . he is there . . . at the bottom . . . under the rock . . . swathed in cobwebs . . . Ah!"

'Christian Weber turned a cold look to those present, who, stooping in a circle, their eyes popping out of their heads, listened. I heard him murmur: "Horrible! Horrible!" Then he resumed.

'"Can you see him?"

'"I can see him."

'"And the spider. Is it big?"

'"Oh! Master, never . . . never have I seen one so huge, neither on the banks of the Mocaris nor in the lowlands of Konanama . . . It is as big as my head!"

'There was a lengthy silence. All those present looked at each other, their faces livid, their hair standing on end. Christian Weber alone appeared calm. Having passed his hands several times over the brow of the negress, he began.

'"Agatha, tell us how death struck Sir Haverburch."

'"He was bathing in the pool of the stream . . . The spider saw him from behind, his back naked. It was hungry, it had been fasting for a long time. It saw him, his arms on the water. Suddenly, it dashed out, as quick as lightning, and placed its claws around the Commodore's neck, and he shouted 'My God! My God!' It bit him and ran off. Sir Haverburch collapsed into the water and died. Then the spider came back and surrounded him with its web, and swam gently, gently as far as the bottom of the cave. It pulled the thread. Now it's completely black."

'The doctor turned towards me, no longer afraid. He said: "Is it true, Hans, that the Commodore went for a bathe?"

'"Yes, cousin."

'"At what time?"

'"At four o'clock."

'"At four o'clock. It was very hot, wasn't it?"

'"Ah, yes!"

'"That's it!" he said, beating his brow. "The monster could come out without fear!"

'He uttered some unintelligible words, then, looking at the mountain folk: "My friends!" he exclaimed. "That's where this mass of debris comes from . . . the body, the skeletons which frightened the bathers . . . that's what has ruined you all . . . It's a crab spider – God knows where it came from – but it's there . . . hiding in its web . . . and on the lookout for its prey from the bottom of the cave! Who can tell the number of its victims?"

'Then, filled with a sort of rage he left, shouting: "Bring faggots! Faggots!"

'All the woodcutters followed him in the utmost confusion. Ten minutes later, two big coaches laden with faggots slowly climbed the hill. A long procession of woodcutters, backs bent, axes over their shoulders, followed them into the middle of the dark night. My tutor and I walked in front, holding the horses by the bridle. The melancholy moon dimly lit up this funereal procession. From time to time the wheels creaked, then the carriages, raised up by the stony ruggedness of the path, fell back into the ruts with a heavy jolt.

'Drawing near the cave, our procession halted. The torches were lit and the crowd moved forward towards the abyss. The limpid water, flowing over the sand, reflected the bluish flames of the resinous torches, whose beams lit up the tops of the black pines leaning over the rock.

'"We must unload here," said the doctor. "Then we must block the entrance to the cave."

'And it was with a feeling of terror, that each one set to his task of carrying out their orders. The faggots fell from the top of the carts. Some stakes, placed below the opening of the spring, prevented the water from dragging them off.

'At about midnight the entrance to the cave was literally shut. The water whistling beneath, poured out right and left over the moss. The upper faggots were perfectly dry. Then Doctor Weber, seizing hold of a torch, set fire to them himself. The flames, rushing up from twig to twig, crackling angrily, soon leapt up to the sky, chasing before them clouds of smoke.

'It was a strange and wild spectacle, to see these huge woods with their quivering shadows lit up in this way.

'The cave disgorged a black smoke, which gradually increased until it was pouring out. All around waited the woodcutters, sombre and motionless, their eyes fixed on the entrance. And I myself, though fear made me tremble from head to toe, was unable to take my eyes away from it.

'We had already been waiting a quarter of an hour, and the doctor was beginning to get impatient, when a black object, with long hooked legs, suddenly appeared in the shadow and scuttled towards the opening.

'A general uproar resounded around the pile of faggots. The spider, chased by the fire, went back into its cave. Then, choked by the smoke, it returned to the charge and rushed to the middle of the flames. Its long hairy legs caught the flames and shrivelled up. It was as big as my head and a violet crimson; I can only describe it as a bladder full of blood – the blood of Sir Thomas Haverburch!

'One of the woodcutters, afraid of seeing it cross the fire, threw his axe at it, and hit it so well that its blood for a moment covered all the fire around it. But then the flames burned up more fiercely above and consumed the horrible insect.'

'Such, Maître Frantz, is the strange event that destroyed the fine reputation that the waters of Spinbronn previously enjoyed. I can assure you of the scrupulous accuracy of my account. But as far as explaining it to you, that would be impossible. However, it is not absurd to imagine that insects, subjected to the raised temperature of certain spring waters, which provide for them the same conditions of existence and development as the scorching climates of Africa and South America, can reach incredible sizes. Dr Weber was of the opinion that the spider must have escaped from someone's collection and found the hot cave before it was killed by the cold climate.

'Be that as it may, my tutor, thinking that it would be impossible after this event to revive the waters of Spinbronn, resold Hâselnoss's house, and returned to South America with his negress and his insect collections. I was sent to boarding school in Strasbourg, where I stayed till 1809.

'The chief political events of the era at this time absorbed the attention of Germany and France and the facts that I have just related to you went completely unnoticed.

'But nobody drinks the waters of Spinbronn even to this day.'

THE MYSTERIOUS SKETCH

I

Opposite the chapel of Saint Sebalt in Nuremberg, at the corner of Trabaus Street, there stands a little tavern, tall and narrow, with a toothed gable and dusty windows, whose roof is surmounted by a plaster Virgin. It was there that I spent the unhappiest days of my life. I had gone to Nuremberg to study the old German masters; but in default of ready money, I had to paint portraits – and such portraits! Fat old women with their cats on their laps, big-wigged aldermen, burgomasters in three-cornered hats – all horribly bright with ochre and vermilion. From portraits I descended to sketches, and from sketches to silhouettes.

Nothing is more annoying than to have your landlord come to you every day with pinched lips, shrill voice, and impudent manner to say: 'Well, sir, how soon are you going to pay me? Do you know how much your bill is? No; that doesn't worry you! You eat, drink, and sleep calmly enough. God feeds the sparrows. Your bill now amounts to two hundred florins and ten kreutzers – it is not worth talking about.'

Those who have not heard any one talk in this way can form no idea of it; love of art, imagination, and the sacred enthusiasm for the beautiful are blasted by the breath of such an attack. You become awkward and timid; all your energy evaporates, as well as your feeling of personal dignity, and you bow respectfully at a distance to the burgomaster Schneegans.

One night, not having a sou, as usual, and threatened with imprisonment by this worthy Mister Rap, I determined to make him a bankrupt by cutting my throat. Seated on my narrow bed, opposite the window, in this agreeable mood, I gave myself up to a thousand philosophical reflections, more or less comforting.

'What is man?' I asked myself. 'An omnivorous animal; his jaws, provided with canines, incisors, and molars, prove it. The canines are made to tear meat; the incisors to bite fruits; and the molars to masticate, grind, and triturate animal and vegetable substances that are pleasant to smell and to taste. But when he has nothing to masticate, this being is an absurdity in Nature, a superfluity, a fifth wheel to the coach.'

Such were my reflections. I dared not open my razor for fear that the invincible force of my logic would inspire me with the courage to make an end of it all. After having argued so finely, I blew out my candle, postponing the sequel till the morrow.

That abominable Rap had completely stupefied me. I could do nothing but silhouettes, and my sole desire was to have some money to rid myself of his odious presence. But on this night a singular change came over my mind. I awoke about one o'clock – I lit my lamp, and enveloping myself in my grey gabardine, I drew upon the paper a rapid sketch after the Dutch school – something strange and bizarre, which had not the slightest resemblance to my ordinary conceptions.

Imagine a dreary courtyard enclosed by high dilapidated walls. These walls are furnished with hooks, seven or eight feet from the ground. You see, at a glance, that it is a butchery.

On the left, there extends a lattice structure; you perceive through it a quartered beef suspended from the roof by enormous pulleys. Great pools of blood run over the flag-stones and unite in a ditch full of refuse.

The light falls from above, between, the chimneys where the weathercocks stand out from a bit of the sky the size of your hand, and the roofs of the neighbouring houses throw bold shadows from storey to storey.

At the back of this place is a shed, beneath the shed a pile of wood, and upon the pile of wood some ladders, a few bundles of straw, some coils of rope, a chicken-coop, and an old dilapidated rabbit-hutch.

How did these heterogeneous details suggest themselves to my imagination? I don't know; I had no reminiscences, and yet every stroke of the pencil seemed the result of observation, and strange because it was all so true. Nothing was lacking.

But on the right, one corner of the sketch remained a blank. I did not know what to put there . . . Something suddenly seemed to writhe there, to move! Then I saw a foot, the sole of a foot. Notwithstanding this improbable position, I followed my inspiration without reference to my own criticism. This foot was joined to a leg – over this leg, stretched out with effort, there soon floated the skirt of a dress. In short, there appeared by degrees, an old woman, pale, dishevelled, and wasted, thrown down at the side of a well, and struggling to free herself from a hand that clutched at her throat.

It was a murder scene that I was drawing. The pencil fell from my hand.

This woman, in the boldest attitude, with her thighs bent on the kerb of the well, her face contracted by terror, and her two hands grasping the murderer's arm, frightened me. I could not look at her. But the man – he, the person to whom that arm belonged – I could not see him. It was impossible for me to finish the sketch.

'I am tired,' I said, my forehead dripping with perspiration; 'there is only this figure to do; I will finish it tomorrow. It will be easy then.'

And I went to bed again, thoroughly frightened by my vision.

The next morning, I got up very early. I was dressing in order to resume my interrupted work, when two little knocks were heard on my door.

'Come in!'

The door opened. An old man, tall, thin, and dressed in black, appeared on the threshold. This man's face, his eyes set close together and his large nose like the beak of an eagle, surmounted by a high bony forehead, had something severe about it. He bowed to me gravely.

'Mister Christian Vénius, the painter?' said he.

'That is my name, sir.'

He bowed again, adding: 'The Baron Frederick Van Spreckdal.'

The appearance of the rich amateur, Van Spreckdal, judge of the criminal court, in my poor lodging, greatly disturbed me. I could not help throwing a stealthy glance at my old worm-eaten furniture, my damp hangings, and my dusty floor. I felt humiliated by such dilapidation; but Van Spreckdal did not seem to take any account of these details; and sitting down at my little table: 'Mister Vénius,' he resumed, 'I come—' But at this instant his glance fell upon the unfinished sketch – he did not finish his phrase.

I was sitting on the edge of my little bed; and the sudden attention that this personage bestowed upon one of my productions made my heart beat with an indefinable apprehension.

At the end of a minute, Van Spreckdal lifted his head.

'Are you the author of that sketch?' he asked me with an intent look.

'Yes, sir.'

'What is the price of it?'

'I never sell my sketches. It is the plan for a picture.'

'Ah!' said he, picking up the paper with the tips of his long yellow fingers.

He took a lens from his waistcoat pocket and began to study the design in silence.

The sun was now shining obliquely into the garret. Van Spreckdal never said a word; the hook of his immense nose increased, his heavy eyebrows contracted, and his long pointed chin took a turn upward, making a thousand little wrinkles in his long, thin cheeks. The silence was so profound that I could distinctly hear the plaintive buzzing of a fly that had been caught in a spider's web.

'And the dimensions of this picture, Mister Vénius,' he said without looking at me.

'Three feet by four.'

'The price?'

'Fifty ducats.'

Van Spreckdal laid the sketch on the table, and drew from his pocket a large purse of green silk shaped like a pear, he drew the rings of it. 'Fifty ducats,' said he, 'here they are.'

I was simply dazzled.

The Baron rose and bowed to me, and I heard his big ivory-headed cane resounding on each step until he reached the bottom of the stairs. Then, recovering from my stupor, I suddenly remembered that I had not thanked him, and I flew down the five flights like lightning; but when I reached the bottom, I looked to the right and left; the street was deserted.

'Well!' I said, 'this is strange.'

And I went upstairs again all out of breath.

II

The surprising way in which Van Spreckdal had appeared to me threw me into a deep wonderment. 'Yesterday,' I said to myself, as I contemplated the pile of ducats glittering in the sun, 'yesterday I formed the wicked intention of cutting my throat, all for the want of a few miserable florins, and now today Fortune has showered them from the clouds. Indeed it was fortunate that I did not open my razor; and, if the same temptation ever comes to me again, I will take care to wait until the morrow.'

After making these judicious reflections, I sat down to finish the sketch; four strokes of the pencil and it would be finished. But here an incomprehensible difficulty awaited me. It was impossible for me to make those four sweeps of the pencil; I had lost the thread of my inspiration, and the mysterious personage no longer stood out in my brain. I tried in vain to evoke him, to sketch him, and to recover him; he no longer accorded with the surroundings than with a figure by Raphael in a Teniers inn-kitchen. I broke out into a profuse perspiration.

At this moment, Rap opened the door without knocking, according to his praiseworthy custom. His eyes fell upon my pile of ducats and in a shrill voice he cried: 'Eh! Eh! So I catch you. Will you still persist in telling me, Mr Painter, that you have no money?'

And his hooked fingers advanced with that nervous trembling that the sight of gold always produces in a miser.

For a few seconds I was stupefied.

The memory of all the indignities that this individual had inflicted upon me, his covetous look, and his impudent smile exasperated me. With a single bound, I caught hold of him, and pushed him out of the room, slamming the door in his face.

This was done with the crack and rapidity of a spring snuff-box.

But from outside the old usurer screamed like an eagle: 'My money, you thief, my money!'

The lodgers came out of their rooms, asking: 'What is the matter? What has happened?'

I opened the door suddenly and quickly gave Mister Rap a kick in the spine that sent him rolling down more than twenty steps.

'That's what's the matter!' I cried, quite beside myself. Then I shut the door and bolted it, while bursts of laughter from the neighbours greeted Mister Rap in the passage.

I was satisfied with myself; I rubbed my hands together. This adventure had put new life into me; I resumed my work, and was about to finish the sketch when I heard an unusual noise.

Butts of muskets were grounded on the pavement. I looked out of my window and saw three soldiers in full uniform with grounded arms in front of my door.

I said to myself in my terror: 'Can it be that that scoundrel of a Rap has had any bones broken?'

And here is the strange peculiarity of the human mind: I, who the night before had wanted to cut my own throat, shook from head to foot, thinking that I might well be hanged if Rap were dead.

The stairway was filled with confused noises. It was an ascending flood of heavy footsteps, clanking arms, and short syllables.

Suddenly somebody tried to open my door. It was shut.

Then there was a general clamour.

'In the name of the law – open!'

I arose, trembling and weak in the knees.

'Open!' the same voice repeated.

I thought to escape over the roofs; but I had hardly put my head out of the little snuff-box window, when I drew back, seized with vertigo. I saw in a flash all the windows below with their shining panes, their flower-pots, their bird-cages, and their gratings. Lower, the balcony; still lower, the street lamp; still lower again, the sign of The Red Cask framed in iron-work; and, finally, three glittering bayonets, only awaiting my fall to run me through the body from the sole of my foot to the crown of my head. On the roof of the opposite house a tortoise-shell cat was crouching behind a chimney, watching a band of sparrows fighting and scolding in the gutter.

One can not imagine to what clearness, intensity, and rapidity the human eye acquires when stimulated by fear.

At the third summons I heard: 'Open, or we shall force it!'

Seeing that flight was impossible, I staggered to the door, and drew the bolt.

Two hands immediately fell upon my collar. A dumpy, little man, smelling of wine, said: 'I arrest you!'

He wore a bottle-green redingote, buttoned to the chin, and a stovepipe hat. He had large brown whiskers, rings on every finger, and was named Passauf.

He was the chief of police.

Five bull-dogs with flat caps, noses like pistols, and lower jaws turning upward, observed me from outside.

'What do you want?' I asked Passauf.

'Come downstairs,' he cried roughly, as he gave a sign to one of his men to seize me.

This man took hold of me, more dead than alive, while several other men turned my room upside down.

I went downstairs supported by the arms like a person in the last stages of consumption – with hair dishevelled and stumbling at every step.

They thrust me into a cab between two strong fellows, who charitably let me see the ends of their clubs, held to their wrists by a leather string – and then the carriage started off.

I heard behind us the feet of all the urchins of the town.

'What have I done?' I asked one of my keepers.

He looked at the other with a strange smile and said: 'Hans – he asks what he has done!'

That smile froze my blood.

Soon a deep shadow enveloped the carriage; the horses' hoofs resounded under an archway. We were entering the Raspelhaus. Of this place one might say:

'Dans cet antre,
Je vois fort bien comme l'on entre.
En ne vois point comme on en sort.'

All is not rose-coloured in this world; from the claws of Rap I fell into a dungeon, from which very few poor devils have a chance to escape.

Large dark courtyards and rows of windows like a hospital, and furnished with gratings; not a sprig of verdure, not a festoon of ivy, not even a weathercock in perspective – such was my new lodging. It was enough to make one tear his hair out by the roots.

The police officers, accompanied by the jailer, took me temporarily to a lock-up.

The jailer, if I remember rightly, was named Kasper Schlüssel; with his grey, woollen cap, his pipe between his teeth, and his bunch of keys at his belt, he reminded me of the Owl-God of the Caribs. He had the same golden yellow eyes, that see in the dark, a nose like a comma, and a neck that was sunk between the shoulders.

Schlüssel shut me up as calmly as one locks up his socks in a cupboard, while thinking of something else. As for me, I stood for more than ten minutes with my hands behind my back and my head bowed. At the end of that time I made the following reflection: 'When falling, Rap cried out, "I am assassinated", but he did not say by whom. I will say it was my neighbour, the old merchant with the spectacles: he will be hanged in my place.'

This idea comforted my heart, and I drew a long breath. Then I looked about my prison. It seemed to have been newly whitewashed, and the walls were bare of designs, except in one corner, where a gallows had been crudely sketched by my predecessor. The light was admitted through a bull's-eye about nine or ten feet from the floor; the furniture consisted of a bundle of straw and a tub.

I sat down upon the straw with my hands around my

knees in deep despondency. It was with great difficulty that I could think clearly; but suddenly imagining that Rap, before dying, had denounced me, my legs began to tingle, and I jumped up coughing, as if the hempen cord were already tightening around my neck.

At the same moment, I heard Schlüssel walking down the corridor; he opened the lock-up, and told me to follow him. He was still accompanied by the two officers, so I fell into step resolutely.

We walked down long galleries, lighted at intervals by small windows from within. Behind a grating I saw the famous Jic-Jack, who was going to be executed on the morrow. He had on a straitjacket and sang out in a raucous voice: *'Je suis le roi de ces montagnes.'*

Seeing me, he called out:

'Eh! Comrade! I'll keep a place for you at my right.'

The two police officers and the Owl-God looked at each other and smiled, while I felt the goose-flesh creep down the whole length of my back.

III

Schlüssel shoved me into a large and very dreary hall, with benches arranged in a semicircle. The appearance of this deserted hall, with its two high grated windows, and its Christ carved in old brown oak with His arms extended and His head sorrowfully inclined upon His shoulder, inspired me with I do not know what kind of religious fear that accorded with my actual situation.

All my ideas of false accusation disappeared, and my lips tremblingly murmured a prayer.

I had not prayed for a long time; but misfortune always brings us to thoughts of submission. Man is so little in himself!

Opposite me, on an elevated seat, two men were sitting, with their backs to the light, and consequently their faces were

in shadow. However, I recognized Van Spreckdal by his aquiline profile, illuminated by an oblique reflection from the
window. The other person was fat, he had round, chubby
cheeks and short hands, and he wore a robe, like Van Spreckdal.

Below was the clerk of the court, Conrad; he was writing
at a low table and was tickling the tip of his ear with the
feather-end of his pen. When I entered, he stopped to look
at me curiously.

They made me sit down, and Van Spreckdal, raising his
voice, said to me: 'Christian Vénius, where did you get this
sketch?'

He showed me the nocturnal sketch which was then in
his possession. It was handed to me. After having examined
it, I replied: 'I am the author of it.'

A long silence followed: the clerk of the court, Conrad,
wrote down my reply. I heard his pen scratch over the paper,
and I thought: 'Why did they ask me that question? That
has nothing to do with the kick I gave Rap in the back.'

'You are the author of it?' asked Van Spreckdal. 'What is
the subject?'

'It is a subject of pure fancy.'

'You have not copied the details from some spot?'

'No, sir, I imagined it all.'

'Accused Christian,' said the judge in a severe tone, 'I ask
you to reflect. Do not lie.'

'I have spoken the truth.'

'Write that down, clerk,' said Van Spreckdal.

The pen scratched again.

'And this woman' – continued the judge – 'this woman
who is being murdered at the side of the well – did you
imagine her also?'

'Certainly.'

'You have never seen her?'

'Never.'

Van Spreckdal rose indignantly; then, sitting down again,
he seemed to consult his companion in a low voice.

These two dark profiles silhouetted against the brightness of the window, and the three men standing behind me, the silence in the hall – everything made me shiver.

'What do you want with me? What have I done?' I murmured.

Suddenly Van Spreckdal said to my guardians: 'You can take the prisoner back to the carriage; we will go to Metzerstrasse.'

Then, addressing me: 'Christian Vénius,' he cried, 'you are in a deplorable situation. Collect your thoughts and remember that if the law of men is inflexible, there still remains for you the mercy of God. This you can merit by confessing your crime.'

These words stunned me like a blow from a hammer. I fell back with extended arms, crying: 'Ah! what a terrible dream!'

And I fainted.

When I regained consciousness, the carriage was rolling slowly down the street; another one preceded us. The two officers were always with me. One of them on the way offered a pinch of snuff to his companion; mechanically I reached out my hand towards the snuff-box, but he withdrew it quickly.

My cheeks reddened with shame, and I turned away my head to conceal my emotion.

'If you look outside,' said the man with the snuff-box, 'we shall be obliged to put handcuffs on you.'

'May the devil strangle you, you infernal scoundrel!' I said to myself. And as the carriage now stopped, one of them got out, while the other held me by the collar; then, seeing that his comrade was ready to receive me, he pushed me rudely to him.

These infinite precautions to hold possession of my person boded no good; but I was far from predicting the seriousness of the accusation that hung over my head until an alarming circumstance opened my eyes and threw me into despair.

They pushed me along a low alley, the pavement of which was unequal and broken; along the wall there ran a yellowish ooze, exhaling a fetid odour. I walked down this dark place with the two men behind me. A little further there appeared the chiaroscuro of an interior courtyard.

I grew more and more terror-stricken as I advanced. It was no natural feeling: it was poignant anxiety, outside of nature – like the nightmare. I recoiled instinctively at each step.

'Go on!' cried one of the policemen, laying his hand on my shoulder; 'go on!'

But what was my astonishment when, at the end of the passage, I saw the courtyard that I had drawn the night before, with its walls furnished with hooks, its rubbish-heap of old iron, its chicken-coops, and its rabbit-hutch. Not a dormer window, high or low, not a broken pane, not the slightest detail had been omitted.

I was thunderstruck by this strange revelation.

Near the well were the two judges, Van Spreckdal and Richter. At their feet lay the old woman extended on her back, her long, thin, grey hair, her blue face, her eyes wide open, and her tongue between her teeth.

It was a horrible spectacle!

'Well,' said Van Spreckdal, with solemn accents, 'what have you to say?'

I did not reply.

'Do you remember having thrown this woman, Theresa Becker, into this well, after having strangled her to rob her of her money?'

'No,' I cried, 'no! I do not know this woman; I never saw her before. May God help me!'

'That will do,' he replied in a dry voice. And without saying another word he went out with his companion.

The officers now believed they had best put handcuffs on me. They took me back to the Raspelhaus, in a state of profound stupidity. I did not know what to think; my conscience itself troubled me; I even asked myself if I really had murdered the old woman!

In the eyes of the officers I was condemned.

I will not tell you of my emotions that night in the Raspelhaus, when seated on my straw bed with the window opposite me and the gallows in perspective, I heard the watchmen cry in the silence of the night: 'Sleep, people of Nuremberg; the Lord watches over you. One o'clock! Two o'clock! Three o'clock!'

Every one may form his own idea of such a night. There is a fine saying that it is better to be hanged innocent than guilty. For the soul, yes; but for the body, it makes no difference; on the contrary, it kicks, it curses its lot, it tries to escape, knowing well enough that its rôle ends with the rope. Add to this, that it repents not having sufficiently enjoyed life and at having listened to the soul when it preached abstinence.

'Ah! if I had only known!' it cried, 'you would not have led me about by a string with your big words, your beautiful phrases, and your magnificent sentences! You would not have allured me with your fine promises. I should have had many happy moments that are now lost forever. Everything is over! You said to me: "Control your passions." Very well! I did control them. Here I am now! They are going to hang me, and you – later they will speak of you as a sublime soul, a stoical soul, a martyr to the errors of Justice. They will never think about me!'

Such were the sad reflections of my poor body.

Day broke; at first, dull and undecided, it threw an uncertain light on my bull's-eye window with its cross-bars; then it blazed against the wall at the back. Outside the street became lively. This was a market-day; it was Friday. I heard the vegetable wagons pass and also the country people with their baskets. Some chickens cackled in their coops in passing and some butter sellers chattered together. The market opposite opened, and they began to arrange the stalls.

Finally, it was broad daylight and the vast murmur of the increasing crowd, housekeepers who assembled with baskets on their arms, coming and going, discussing and marketing, told me that it was eight o'clock.

With the light, my heart gained a little courage. Some of my black thoughts disappeared. I desired to see what was going on outside.

Other prisoners before me had managed to climb up to the bull's-eye; they had dug some holes in the wall to mount more easily. I climbed in my turn, and, when seated in the oval edge of the window, with my legs bent and my head bowed, I could see the crowd, and all the life and movement. Tears ran freely down my cheeks. I thought no longer of suicide – I experienced a need to live and breathe, which was really extraordinary.

'Ah!' I said, 'to live, what happiness! Let them harness me to a wheelbarrow – let them put a ball and chain around my leg – nothing matters if I may only live!'

The old market, with its roof shaped like an extinguisher, supported on heavy pillars, made a superb picture: old women seated before their panniers of vegetables, their cages of poultry and their baskets of eggs; behind them the Jews, dealers in old clothes, their faces the colour of old boxwood; butchers with bare arms, cutting up meat on their stalls; countrymen, with large hats on the backs of their heads, calm and grave with their hands behind their backs and resting on their sticks of hollywood, and tranquilly smoking their pipes. Then the tumult and noise of the crowd – those screaming, shrill, grave, high, and short words – those expressive gestures – those sudden attitudes that show from a distance the progress of a discussion and depict so well the character of the individual – in short, all this captivated my mind, and notwithstanding my sad condition, I felt happy to be still of the world.

Now, while I looked about in this manner, a man – a butcher – passed, inclining forward and carrying an enormous quarter of beef on his shoulders; his arms were bare, his elbows were raised upward, and his head was bent under them. His long hair, like that of Salvator's Sicambrian, hid his face from me; and yet, at the first glance, I trembled.

'It is he!' I said.

All the blood in my body rushed to my heart. I got down from the window trembling to the ends of my fingers, feeling my cheeks quiver, and the pallor spread over my face, stammering in a choked voice: 'It is he! He is there – there – and I, I have to die to expiate his crime. Oh, God! What shall I do? What shall I do?'

A sudden idea, an inspiration from Heaven, flashed across my mind: I put my hand in the pocket of my coat – my box of crayons was there!

Then rushing to the wall, I began to trace the scene of the murder with superhuman energy. No uncertainty, no hesitation! I knew the man! I had seen him! He was there before me!

At ten o'clock the jailer came to my cell. His owl-like impassibility gave place to admiration.

'Is it possible?' he cried, standing at the threshold.

'Go, bring me my judges,' I said to him, pursuing my work with an increasing exultation.

Schlüssel answered: 'They are waiting for you in the trial-room.'

'I wish to make a revelation,' I cried, as I put the finishing touches to the mysterious personage.

He lived; he was frightful to see. His full-faced figure, foreshortened upon the wall, stood out from the white background with an astonishing vitality.

The jailer went away.

A few minutes afterward the two judges appeared. They were stupefied. I, trembling, with extended hand, said to them: 'There is the murderer!'

After a few moments of silence, Van Spreckdal asked me: 'What is his name?'

'I don't know; but he is at this moment in the market; he is cutting up meat in the third stall to the left as you enter from Trabaus Street.'

'What do you think?' said he, leaning toward his colleague.

'Send for the man,' he replied in a grave tone.

Several officers retained in the corridor obeyed this order. The judges stood, examining the sketch. As for me, I had dropped on my bed of straw, my head between my knees, perfectly exhausted.

Soon steps were heard echoing under the archway. Those who have never awaited the hour of deliverance and counted the minutes, which seem like centuries – those who have never experienced the sharp emotions of outrage, terror, hope, and doubt – can have no conception of the inward chills that I experienced at that moment. I should have distinguished the step of the murderer, walking between the guards, among a thousand others. They approached. The judges themselves seemed moved. I raised up my head, my heart feeling as if an iron hand had clutched it and I fixed my eyes upon the closed door. It opened. The man entered. His cheeks were red and swollen, the muscles in his large contracted jaws twitched as far as his ears, and his little restless eyes, yellow like a wolf's, gleamed beneath his heavy yellowish red eyebrows.

Van Spreckdal showed him the sketch in silence.

Then that murderous man, with the large shoulders, having looked, grew pale – then, giving a roar which thrilled us all with terror, he waved his enormous arms and jumped backward to overthrow the guards. There was a terrible struggle in the corridor; you could hear nothing but the panting breathing of the butcher, his muttered imprecations, and the short words and the shuffling feet of the guard, upon the flagstones.

This lasted only about a minute.

Finally the assassin re-entered, with his head hanging down, his eyes bloodshot, and his hands fastened behind his back. He looked again at the picture of the murder; he seemed to reflect, and then, in a low voice, as if talking to himself: 'Who could have seen me,' he said, 'at midnight?'

I was saved!

Many years have passed since that terrible adventure. Thank Heaven! I make silhouettes no longer, nor portraits of burgomasters. Through hard work and perseverance, I have conquered my place in the world, and I earn my living honourably by painting works of art – the sole end, in my opinion, to which a true artist should aspire. But the memory of that nocturnal sketch has always remained in my mind. Sometimes, in the midst of work, the thought of it recurs. Then I lay down my palette and dream for hours.

How could a crime committed by a man that I did not know – at a place that I had never seen – have been reproduced by my pencil, in all its smallest details?

Was it chance? No! And moreover, what is chance but the effect of a cause of which we are ignorant?

Was Schiller right when he said: 'The immortal soul does not participate in the weaknesses of matter; during the sleep of the body, it spreads its radiant wings and travels, God knows where! What it then does, no one can say, but inspiration sometimes betrays the secret of its nocturnal wanderings.'

Who knows? Nature is more audacious in her realities than man in his most fantastic imaginings.

THE THREE SOULS

I

In 1815 I was doing my sixth year of transcendental philosophy in Heidelberg. University life is the life of a lord: you get up at midday: you smoke your pipe: you empty one or two small glasses of schnapps: and then you button your overcoat up to your chin, put on your hat in the Prussian manner over the left ear, and you go quietly to listen, for half an hour, to the well known Professor Hâsenkopf. Everyone is free to yawn or even to go to sleep if that suits him.

When the lecture is over, you go to the inn, stretch your legs under the table; the pretty serving girls rush about with dishes of sausages, slices of ham, and tankards of strong beer. You hum a tune, you drink, you eat. One whistles for the inn's dog Hector, the other grabs Charlotte or Gretel by the waist . . . At times fighting breaks out, cudgel blows shower down, tankards totter, and beer mugs fall. The watch comes and he arrests you and you go and spend the night in jail.

And thus, the days, the months, and the years pass! One meets, in Heidelberg, future princes, dukes, and barons; one also meets the sons of cobblers, schoolmasters, and respectable business men. The young lordlings keep to their own clique, but the rest mingle in brotherly fashion.

I was thirty-two then, my beard was beginning to turn grey; the tankard, pipe, and sauerkraut were going down in my estimation. I felt in need of a change. Such was my melancholy state of mind, when towards the end of the spring of this year, 1815, a horrible event occurred which taught me that I didn't know everything, and that the philosophical career is not always strewn with roses.

Among my friends was a certain Wolfgang Scharf, the most unbending logician that I have ever met. Imagine a small gaunt man, with sunken eyes, white lashes, red hair cut short, hollow cheeks adorned by a bushy beard, and broad shoulders covered in magnificent rags. To see him creeping along the walls, a cob of bread under his arm, his eyes ablaze, his spine arched, you would have thought he was an old tom cat looking for his queen. But Wolfgang thought only of metaphysics. For the past five years he had been living on bread and water in a garret in the old part of the town. Never had a bottle of foaming beer or Rhine wine cooled his ardour for knowledge, never had a slice of ham weighted down the course of his sublime meditations. As a consequence the poor devil was frightening to look at. I say frightening because, in spite of his apparent state of marasmus, there was in his bony frame a terrifying cohesive force. The muscles of his jaws and hands stood out like cords of steel; moreover, his shady look averted pity.

For some reason, this strange being, in the midst of his voluntary isolation, seemed to have time for me. He would come and see me and, seated in my armchair, his fingers shaking convulsively, he would share with me his metaphysical lucubrations. One day he touched on a subject which found me lacking a suitable answer.

'Kasper,' he said to me in a sharp voice, and proceeding through interrogation in the manner of Socrates, 'Kasper, what is the soul?'

'According to Thales it is a sort of magnet. According to Plato, a substance which moves of its own accord. According to Asclepius, an arousal of the senses. Anaximander says that it is a compound of earth and water, Empodocles the blood, Hippocrates a spirit spread through the body. Zeno, the quintessence of the four elements. Xenocrates . . .'

'Good! Good! But what do you think is the substance of the soul?'

'Me, Wolfgang? I say, with Lactantius, that I know nothing about it. I am an Epicurean by nature. Now according to the Epicureans, all judgement comes from the senses; as the soul does not fall under my senses, I am unable to judge.'

'However, Kasper, remark that a crowd of animals such as fishes or insects live deprived of one or more senses. Who knows if we possess all the senses? If there don't exist some which we've never even thought of?'

'It's possible, but in doubt I refrain from passing judgement.'

'Do you think, Kasper, that one can know something without having learnt it?'

'No. All knowledge proceeds from experience or study.'

'But then, my friend, how does it come about that the hen's chicks, as they come out of the egg, start to run about, to take their food by themselves? How does it happen that they recognise the sparrow-hawk in the middle of the clouds, that they hide under their mother's wings? Have they learnt to know their enemy in the egg?'

'It's instinct, Wolfgang. All animals obey instinct.'

'And so it appears that instinct consists of knowing what one has never learnt?'

'Ha!' I exclaimed. 'You are asking too much of me. What can I say?'

He smiled disdainfully, flung the flap of his ragged coat over his shoulder, and went out without saying another word.

I considered him a madman, but a madman of the harmless sort. Who would have thought that a passion for metaphysics could be dangerous?

Things really started to happen when the old cake-seller, Catherine Wogel, suddenly disappeared. This good woman, her tray hanging by a pink ribbon from her stork-like neck, usually presented herself at the inn at about eleven o'clock. The students joked readily with her, reminding her of some childhood escapades, of which she made no secret and laughed fit to split her sides.

'Ha! why yes!' she would say, 'I haven't always been fifty! I've had some good times! Well! afterwards . . . do I regret it? Ah! if only it could all begin again!'

She would breathe a sigh and everyone would laugh.

Her disappearance was noticed on the third day. 'What the devil has become of Catherine?' 'Could she be ill?' 'That's odd, she looked so well the last time we saw her.'

It was learnt that the police were looking for her. As for me, I didn't doubt that the poor old woman, a little too affected by kirsch, had stumbled into the river.

The following morning as I left Hâsenkopf's lecture, I met Wolfgang, skirting the pavements of the cathedral. He had hardly noticed me when he came up to me with his eyes agleam. He said, 'I am looking for you Kasper . . . I am looking for you. The hour of triumph has come . . . you are going to follow me.'

His look, his gesture, his pallor, betrayed extreme agitation. As he seized me by the arm, dragging me towards the square of the Tanners, I could not help an indefinable feeling of fear, without having the courage to resist. The side street which we hurriedly followed plunged behind the cathedral, into a block of houses as old as Heidelberg. The roofs leaning at right angles; the wooden balconies where fluttered the washing of the lower classes; the exterior stairs with their worm-eaten handrails; the hundreds of ragged figures, leaning out of the attic windows and looking eagerly at the strangers who were penetrating their lair, the long poles, going from one roof to the other, laden with bloody hides; then the thick smoke escaping from zigzag pipes at every floor, all this blended together and passed before my eyes like a resurrection of the Middle Ages. The sky was fine, its azure angles scalloped by the old gables, and its luminous rays stretching out now and then over the tumble-down walls, added to my emotion by the strangeness of the contrast.

It was one of those moments when man loses all presence of mind. I didn't even think of asking Wolfgang where we were going.

After the populous neighbourhood where poverty swarms, we reached the deserted square where Wolfgang lived. Suddenly Wolfgang, whose dry, cold hand seemed riveted to my wrist, led me into a hovel with broken windows, between an old shed, abandoned long since, and the stall of the abattoir.

'You first,' he said.

I followed a high wall of dry earth, at the end of which was a spiral staircase with broken steps. We climbed across the debris and, although my friend didn't stop repeating to me in an impatient voice 'higher . . . higher . . .' I stopped at times, gripped by terror, on the pretext of getting my breath and examining the recesses of the gloomy dwelling, but really to deliberate whether it wasn't in fact time to flee.

At last we reached the foot of a ladder whose steps disappeared through a loft in the midst of the darkness. I still ask myself today how I had the rashness to climb this ladder without demanding the slightest explanation from my friend Wolfgang. It appears that madness is contagious.

And so there I was climbing, with him behind me. I got right to the top, I put my foot on the dusty floor, I looked around; it was a huge attic, the roof pierced by three skylights, the grey wall of the gable climbing up on the left to the rafters. There was a small table laden with books and papers in the middle, the beams crossing one another over our heads in the darkness. Impossible to look out, for the skylights were ten or twelve feet above the floor.

I noticed, as my eyes became accustomed to the gloom, a large door with a vent, chest-high, cut in the wall of the gable.

Wolfgang, without a word, made me sit down on a crate which served him as an armchair, and taking up a crock of water in the darkness, drank for a long time, while I looked at him quite bemused.

'We are in the attic of the old abattoir,' he said with a strange smile, putting down his earthenware crock. 'The council has voted funds to build another one outside the town. I have been here for five years without paying any rent. Not a soul has come here to disturb my studies.'

He sat down on some logs piled up in a corner.

'Now then,' he resumed, 'let's get to the point. Are you quite sure, Kasper, that we have a soul?'

'Look here, Wolfgang,' I angrily answered him. 'If you have brought me here to discuss metaphysics, you have made a great mistake. I was just leaving Hâsenkopf's lecture and I was going to the inn to have lunch when you intercepted me. I have had my daily dose of abstraction. It is enough for me. Therefore, explain yourself clearly or let me get back on the track of food.'

'You, then, only live for food,' he said in a sharp tone. 'Do you realise that I have spent days without touching food for the love of science?'

'To each his taste; you live on syllogisms or horned arguments; me, I like sausages and beer.'

He had become quite pale, his lips were trembling, but he mastered his anger.

'Kasper,' he said, 'since you don't wish to answer me, at least listen to my explanations. Man needs admirers and I want you to admire me. I want you to be in some way overwhelmed by the sublime discovery I have just made. It's not asking too much, I think, one hour's attention for ten years of conscientious studies?'

'So be it. I am listening to you, but hurry up!'

A new quivering agitated his face and gave me food for horrifying thought. I was repenting of having climbed the ladder, and I assumed a serious look so as not to infuriate

the maniac further. My meditative physiognomy appeared
to calm him a little, because, after a few moments of silence,
he resumed.

'You are hungry, well here's my bread and here's my
crock. Eat, drink, but listen.'

'You need not trouble, Wolfgang, I shall listen anyway to
you without that.'

He smiled bitterly and continued.

'Not only do we have a soul, a thing accepted since the
beginning of history, but from plant to man, all beings live.
They are animated, therefore they have a soul. You don't
need six years of study under Hâsenkopf to agree with me
that all organised beings have one soul at least. But the more
their organisation perfects itself, the more complicated it gets,
and the more the souls multiply. This is what distinguishes
animate beings from each other. The plant has only one soul,
the vegetable soul. Its function is simple, unique – merely
nutrition, by the air, by means of the leaves, and by the earth
through the roots. The animal has two souls. First of all the
vegetable soul, whose functions are the same as those of the
plant – nutrition by the lungs and intestines, which are true
plants; and the animal soul, so called, which has as its function feeling and whose organ is the heart. Finally man, who
is up to the present the height of earthly creation, has three
souls – the vegetable soul, the animal soul whose functions
are exercised as in the beast, and the human soul which has
its object, reason, and intelligence, and its organ is the brain.
The more the animal nears man in the perfection of its cere-
bral organisation, the more it shares in this third soul, such
as the dog, the horse, the elephant. But alone the man of
genius possesses it in all its fullness.'

At this point Wolfgang stopped and fixed his eyes on me.

'Well,' he said, 'what have you got to say?'

'Well, it's a theory like any other. There is only the proof
missing.'

A sort of frenzied exultation took hold of Wolfgang at this

reply. He leapt up, hands in the air, and exclaimed: 'Yes! Yes! The proof is missing. That is what has been tormenting my soul for ten years. That's what was the cause of so many late nights, of so much moral suffering, so many privations! Because it was on myself, Kasper, that I wanted to experiment first of all. Fasting impressed more and more this sublime conviction on my mind, without its being possible for me to establish any proof of it. But, at last, I have found it. You are going to hear the three souls show themselves, declare themselves . . . you will hear them.'

After this explosion of enthusiasm which gave me the shudders, so much energy did it indicate, so much fanaticism, he suddenly became cold again and, sitting down with his elbows on the table, he resumed, pointing out the lofty wall of the gable.

'The proof is there, behind this wall. I shall show it to you presently. But above all you must follow the progressive step of my ideas. You know the opinions of the classic philosophers on the nature of souls. They accepted four of them, united in man. *Caro*, the flesh, a mixture of earth and water which death dissolves; *Manes*, the spirit, which wanders around tombs – its name comes from *manere*, to remain, to stay; *Umbra*, the shade, more immaterial than *Manes*, it disappears after visiting its relatives; finally *Spiritus*, the spirit, the immaterial substance which climbs up to the gods. This classification appeared right to me; it was a question of breaking down the human being so as to establish the distinct existence of the three souls, an abstraction made from the flesh. Reason told me that each man, before reaching his highest development, must have passed through the state of plant or animal; in other words that Pythagoras had caught sight of the reality, without being able to provide proof of it. Well, as for myself, I wanted to solve this problem. It was necessary to successively extinguish the three souls in myself, then revive them. I had recourse to rigorous fasting. Unfortunately, the human soul, in order to let the animal soul act freely, had to succumb first. Hunger made me lose the faculty of observing myself in the animal state. By exhausting myself I was putting myself in the position of not being able to judge. After a host of fruitless attempts on my own organism I remained convinced that there was only one way of attaining my goal; that was to act on a third person. But who would want to be a party to this type of observation?'

Wolfgang paused, his lips contracted, and brusquely he added: 'I needed a subject at any cost. I decided to experiment on a worthless being.'

At this point I shuddered. This man then was capable of anything.

'Have you understood?' he said.

'Very well; you needed a victim.'

'To study,' he added, coldly.

'And you have found one?'

'Yes! I promised to let you hear the three souls. It will perhaps be difficult now: but yesterday you would have heard them in turn howl, roar, implore, grind their teeth!'

An icy shiver ran through me. Wolfgang, impassive, lit a small lamp which he usually used for his work and went over to the low door on the left.

'Look!' he said, putting his hand forward into the darkness. 'Come near and look, then listen.'

In spite of the most funereal presentiments, in spite of the inward shudder which shook me, lured by the attraction of the mystery, I looked through the vent. Behind the door, extending some three yards back, was a dark pit about ten feet deep. The only door, in or out, was the one through which I was peering. I realised that it was one of those storage spaces built into the ceiling of the abattoir, where butchers piled up the hides from the slaughterhouse so as to let them turn green, before delivering them to the tanners. It was empty and for a few seconds I saw only this hole full of shadows.

'Have a good look,' said Wolfgang in a low voice. 'Don't you see a bundle of clothes gathered together in a corner? It's old Catherine Wogel, the cake-seller, who . . .'

He didn't have time to finish, because a wild piercing cry, similar to that of an enraged cat, made itself heard in the pit. A frightened and frightening shape leapt up, seeming to want to claw its way up the wall. More dead than alive, my brow covered with a cold sweat, I darted backwards, exclaiming: 'It's horrible!'

'Did you hear it?' said Wolfgang, his face lit up by an infernal joy. 'Isn't that the cry of the cat? Ha ha! The old woman, before reaching the human state, was formerly a cat or a panther. Now the beast wakes again. Oh! Hunger, hunger and especially thirst works miracles!'

He wasn't looking at me, he was revelling. A loathsome satisfaction lit up his countenance, his attitude, his smile.

The mewings of the poor old woman had stopped. The madman, having placed his lamp on the table, began to gloat over his 'experiment'.

'She has been fasting for four days. I lured her here under the pretext of selling her a small cask of kirsch. I pushed her into the pit and shut her in. Drunkenness has been the ruin of her. She is now atoning for her excessive thirst. The first two days the human soul was revealed in all its strength. She beseeched me, she implored me, she proclaimed her innocence, saying that she had done nothing to me, that I had no right to do this to her. Then madness took possession of her. She overwhelmed me with reproaches, called me a monster, an inhuman wretch, and so forth. On the third day, which was yesterday, the human soul disappeared completely. The cat brought out its claws. It was hungry; its teeth became long; it started to miaow, to roar. Fortunately we are in a secluded place. Last night the people in the square of the Tanners must have thought there was a real cat fight: there were shrieks that would make one shudder! Now, when the beast is exhausted do you know, Kasper, what will result? The vegetable soul will have its turn. It dies the last. You know, of course, that the hair and nails of corpses still grow under the earth; there even forms in the interstices of the skull a sort of human lichen which is called moss. It is thought to be a mould engendered by the juices of the brain. Finally the vegetable soul itself withdraws. Then, Kasper, the proof of the three souls will be complete.'

These words struck my ears as the reasoning of delirium in the most horrible nightmare. The screeching of Catherine Wogel went through me to the very marrow of my bones. I didn't know myself any more, I was losing my head.

I stood up and grabbed the maniac by the throat, dragging him towards the ladder.

'You wretch!' I said to him. 'Who has given you permission to lay hands on your fellow man? on the creature of God? To satisfy your infamous curiosity? I shall hand you over to justice!'

He was so surprised by my aggression that at first he made no resistance, and let himself be dragged towards the ladder without replying. But suddenly, turning round with the suppleness of a wild animal, he in turn seized me by the neck. His hand, as powerful as a steel spring, raised me off the ground and held me against the wall while with the other he drew the bolt of the door to the pit. Realising his intentions, I made a terrible effort to get free. I set my back athwart the door. But he was endowed with superhuman strength. After a quick and desperate struggle I felt myself lifted up for the second time and hurled into space, while above me echoed these strange words: 'Thus perish rebellious flesh! Thus triumph the immortal soul!'

I had hardly touched the bottom of the pit, bruised and aching all over, when the heavy door closed ten feet above me, shutting off from my eyes the greyish light of the attic.

II

I was caught like a rat in a trap. My consternation was such that I rose to my feet without a moan.

'Kasper,' I said to myself, leaning up against the wall with a strange calmness, 'it is now a matter of devouring the old woman, or being devoured by her . . . Choose! As for wanting to get out of this pit, it's a waste of time. Wolfgang has you in his clutches, he will not let you go. The walls are made of stone and the floor of thick oak planks. No one has seen you cross the square of the Tanners and no one knows you in this district. No one will think of looking for you here. It's all over, Kasper, it's all over. Your last resource is this poor Catherine Wogel, or rather, you are each other's last resource.'

All this passed through my mind like a flash of lightning. When, at that very moment, the pale head of Wolfgang, with his little lamp, appeared at the vent, and when, my hands clasped together through terror, I wanted to beseech him, I realised that I was stammering dreadfully. Not a word came from my trembling lips. He, seeing me like this, began to smile, and I heard him whispering in the silence.

'The coward . . . he beseeches me.'

This finished me. I fell to the ground, and I would have remained in a faint had not the fear of being attacked by the old woman made me come to my senses. However, she still did not move. Wolfgang's head disappeared . . . I heard the maniac crossing his garret, move back the table, cough a little. My ear was so attuned that the slightest noise reached me. I heard the old woman yawning, and, as I turned round, I noticed for the first time her eyes glittering in the dark. At the same time I heard Wolfgang go down the ladder and I counted the steps one by one until the sound died away in the distance. Where had the scoundrel gone to? I did not know, but during all that day and the following night he did not reappear. It was only the following day at about eight o'clock in the evening, just as the old woman and I were howling enough to bring the walls down, that he returned.

I hadn't closed my eyes. I no longer felt fear or rage. I was hungry . . . devouringly hungry. And I knew that the hunger would get even worse.

However, hardly had a faint noise made itself heard in the attic than I became silent and looked up. The vent was lit up. Wolfgang had lit his lamp. Undoubtedly he was going to come and see me. With this expectation, I prepared a touching prayer, but the lamp went out. No one came.

It was perhaps the most frightful moment of my torture. I realised that Wolfgang, knowing that I was not yet exhausted, would not bother to even give me a glance. In his eyes I was only an interesting subject, only ripe for science in two or three days' time – between life and death. I seemed to feel my hair slowly turn grey on my head. Finally my terror became such that I lost all feeling.

At about midnight, I was wakened by something touching me. I leapt up in disgust. The old woman, attracted by hunger, had drawn near. Her hands were fastened on to my clothes. At the same time the screeching of a cat filled the pit and froze me with terror.

I expected a terrible battle to fight her; but the poor wretch was very weak; after all, she was in her fifth day of captivity.

Then Wolfgang's words came back into my mind: 'Once the animal soul is dead the vegetable soul will have the upper hand . . . the hair and nails grow in the grave . . . and the green moss . . . the mould takes root in the interstices of the skull.' I pictured for myself the old woman reduced to this state, her skull covered with mouldy lichen, and myself, lying next to her, our souls spinning their moist vegetation beside each other, in the silence.

This image took such a hold of my mind that I no longer felt the pangs of hunger. Stretched out against the wall, my eyes wide open, I looked in front of me without seeing anything.

And as I was like this, more dead than alive, a vague light shone above in the darkness. I looked up. The pale face of Wolfgang was leaning through the ventilator. He wasn't laughing. He appeared to feel neither joy, satisfaction, or remorse: he was observing me!

Oh! How this face frightened me! Had he laughed, had he enjoyed his vengeance, I would have hoped to bend him . . . but he just observed!

We remained thus, our eyes fixed on each other, one terror stricken, the other cold, calm, attentive, as if facing an inert object. The insect pierced by a needle, which one observes under a microscope, if it thinks, if it understands the eye of man, must have these sort of visions.

I had to die to satisfy the curiosity of a monster. I understood that entreaty would be useless, so I said nothing.

After having looked at me for long enough, the maniac, obviously pleased by his observations, turned his head to look at the old woman. I mechanically followed the direction of his gaze. What I saw haunts me to this day. A haggard head, emaciated, the limbs shrivelled up and so sharp that they seemed to have pierced the rags which covered them. Something mis-shapen, hideous. A dead person's head, the hair scattered around the skull like tall withered grass and, in the midst of all that, shining eyes kindled by fever . . . and two long yellow teeth.

Even more dreadful, I saw two snails already crawling over the skeletal figure. When I had seen all that beneath the wan beam of the lamp, falling like a thread in the midst of the darkness, I closed my eyes with a convulsive shudder, and said to myself: 'That's how I shall be in five days' time.'

When I re-opened my eyes the lamp had been withdrawn.

'Wolfgang!' I exclaimed. 'God's above us . . . God sees us . . . Wolfgang . . . Woe to monsters!'

The rest of the night was spent in terror.

After having dreamed again, in the delirium of the fever, of the chances which were left to me of escaping, and not finding any, suddenly I resolved to die. This determination gave me some moments of calm. I went over in my mind the arguments of Hâsenkopf relating to the immortality of the soul, and, for the first time, I found in them an invincible force.

'Yes,' I exclaimed, 'man's passage through this world is only a time of testing. Injustice, greed, the most deadly passions dominate the heart of man. The weak are crushed by the strong. The poor by the rich. Virtue is but a word on earth. But everything returns to order after death. God sees the injustice of which I am a victim, he will take into account the sufferings that I endure. He will pardon me my immoderate appetites, my excessive love of good living. Before admitting me into his breast he wanted to purify me by rigorous fasting. I offer my sufferings to the Lord.'

However, I must admit to you that in spite of my profound contrition, the longing for the inn and my merry friends, for this good existence which flowed out in the midst of the singing and the excellent wine, made me utter many sighs. I could hear the bubbling of the bottles, the clinking of the glasses, and my stomach would groan like a living person. It formed as it were an extra being inside of me, which protested against the philosophical arguments of Hâsenkopf.

The worst of my sufferings was thirst. It was unbearable at this point; so much so that I sucked the saltpetre on the wall to refresh myself.

When daylight appeared in the vent, vague, uncertain, I suddenly had an extraordinary fit of rage.

'The rogue is there,' I said to myself. 'He has bread, a jug of water, he is drinking . . .!'

Then I imagined him raising to his lips his large jug. I seemed to see torrents of water trickling down his throat. It was a delicious river flowing, flowing endlessly. I could see the wretch's throat swell up with pleasure, rise up, descend voluptuously, his stomach fill up. Anger, despair, indignation, took possession of me and I started to stammer, running around the pit. 'Water . . . water . . . water . . .' And the old woman, coming to life again, repeated behind me like a mad thing, 'Water . . . water . . . water . . .' She followed me, crawling about, her rags flapping. Hell has nothing more terrible.

In the middle of this scene the pale face of Wolfgang appeared for the third time at the vent. It was about eight o'clock. Stopping, I said to him: 'Wolfgang! Listen, let me drink just a mouthful from your jug and I shall allow you to let me die of hunger! I shan't reproach you!' And I cried. 'What you are doing to me,' I resumed, 'is too barbarous. Your immortal soul will answer before God for it. Still, for this old woman, as you so disconcertingly said, it is experimentation on a worthless being. But me, I have studied, and I find your system very good. I am worthy of understanding you. I admire you. Let me just have water. What does it matter to you? One has never come across a conception as sublime as yours. It is certain that the three souls exist! Yes! I want to make it known. I shall be your strongest supporter. Won't you let me have just one mouthful of water?'

Without a reply he withdrew.

My exasperation then knew no limits. I threw myself against the wall hard enough to break my bones. I cursed the wretch in the harshest terms.

In the midst of this fury I suddenly noticed that the old woman had collapsed, and I conceived the idea of drinking her blood. Extreme necessity carries man to excesses that would make one shudder. It is then that the wild beast is aroused in us and all sentiment of justice, of goodwill fades before the instinct of self-preservation.

'What need does she have of blood?' I asked myself. 'Will she not die soon? If I delay all her blood will be dried up!'

A red mist passed before my eyes. Fortunately as I was stooping towards the old woman, my strength left me and I fell beside her, my face in her rags, in a faint.

How long did this absence of feeling last? I do not know, but I was drawn from it by an odd incident, the memory of which will always remain imprinted on my mind. I was drawn from it by the plaintive howling of a dog. This howling, so weak, so piteous, so poignant; cries more moving even than the crying of a man, and which one cannot hear without suffering. I got up, my face bathed in tears, not knowing from where came these cries, so consistent with my own suffering. I listened. Judge my amazement when I realised that it was me who was howling like this.

From then on all sorts of memory fades from my mind. What is certain is that I stayed another two days in the pit, under the maniac's eye, whose enthusiasm on seeing his theory proved was such that he didn't hesitate to summon several of our philosophers to delight in their admiration.

Six weeks later I awoke in a small room in the Rue Plat d'Etain, surrounded by my friends, who congratulated me on having escaped from this lesson in transcendental philosophy.

It was a pathetic moment when Ludwig Bremer brought me the mirror, and, when seeing myself more emaciated than Lazarus as he came out of the tomb, I could not help shedding tears.

Poor Catherine Wogel had given up the ghost.

I cannot even say that justice dealt with this scoundrel Wolfgang. Instead of hanging him, according to his just deserts, after proceedings of six months it was established that this abominable being fell into the category of mystic madman, the most dangerous of all. Consequently he was consigned to a cell in a lunatic asylum where visitors can still hear him hold forth in a curt peremptory voice on the three souls.

He accuses humanity of ingratitude and claims that it should, in all fairness, erect statues to him for his magnificent discovery.

A LEGEND OF MARSEILLES

The origins of this story are obscure. French researchers do not believe it was written by Erckmann–Chatrian. It turned up in The Best Terrible Tales From the French, *anonymous, as were the rest of the stories in the book. Initially assuming they had written it, I have included it here, as it fits in very well with Erckmann–Chatrian's tales. – H. L.*

There is a tradition in Marseilles that on a particular night, about two hundred years ago, all the clocks in that city were put forward one hour – a tradition which is said to have had its origin in the following story.

There lived in the vicinity of that city a Monsieur Valette, a gentleman of ancient family and of considerable fortune. He had married Maria Danville, daughter of the mayor of the city, a young lady, who was, from her beauty, called 'the rose of Marseilles', and who united to every personal charm the most amiable disposition and a most accomplished mind. He had the happiness of seeing himself beloved by the most charming of her sex. M. Valette was blessed with two sons and two daughters, the fair fruit of a happy union; and he dwelt in a beautiful villa in the vicinity of the city, commanding an extensive view of its fine bay – a seat which had been the favourite residence of his ancestors.

As his children grew up, however, he was induced to move to Paris, which place both he and Madame Valette conceived to be more suited to the education of their family, though he was himself fond of rural retirement. The removal of M. Valette and of his family was deplored by his tenantry, to whom he had been as a father, but particularly as M. le Brun, who he had left factor on his estate, was, though a just man, of harsh manners and of a precise and unaccommodating temper.

M. Valette found it necessary in Paris, as all persons of distinction do, to mix with the gay and the fashionable. The time that had been given to the joys of domestic retirement was now consumed in the giddy round of fashion and of amusements, and his open and generous temper led him into a mode of life which but ill accorded with the moderation of his fortune. He made frequent demands upon his factor for renewed remittances; and this man was forced to use rigorous and oppressive measures to procure for his master the necessary means. The scanty vintage of the preceding year had made such demands doubly hard to be obeyed; and Le Brun became as odious to the tenantry as Valette himself had been respected and beloved.

These circumstances were but too little known to Valette, or his generous soul would have revolted from a manner of life which wrung from his tenants almost all their hard-earned substance. One night, as he slept in Paris, the form of his factor appeared to him, covered with blood, informing him that he had been murdered by the tenantry on M. Valette's estate for rigour in collecting his revenue, and his body buried under a particular tree, which it minutely described. The ghost of Le Brun requested, moreover, that he would immediately undertake a journey to Marseilles, and deposit his remains in the grave of his ancestors. To this request Valette assented, and the apparition at once disappeared.

The morning came to dissipate the gloom which the vision of the night had occasioned; and though he had been for some time astonished at the unusual silence of Le Brun, yet he could not help considering the whole as a mere illusion of the imagination. The stories of ghosts he had always considered as fit only for the nursery, and his manly and enlightened mind was wholly unimbued with the least tincture of credulity or superstition. To have taken so distant a journey on such an errand he knew would be interpreted as the height of superstition; and he concealed an incident the very relation of which must have subjected him to the ridicule of his acquaintance.

'You are more thoughtful than usual, father,' said one of his daughters to him next morning at breakfast.

'I am thinking, my dear,' said M. Valette, 'why I have been so long in hearing from Le Brun. I need money, and my demands have not been met.'

Night now came again to usher in that period of reflection which the dissipation of the day had banished, and about the hour of midnight Le Brun again appeared to reproach him for his negligence. There was an evident frown on his countenance, and he inquired of Valette why he had delayed to fulfil his earnest request. Valette again promised immediate obedience, and the night was no longer disturbed by so unwelcome an intruder. Morning came again, the gaiety of which even the voice of sorrow could scarcely resist; and the same train of thoughts occurred to him as on the preceding day.

'It must still be a dream,' said he to himself, 'though a remarkable one certainly. Today will probably bring me the expected letters from Le Brun; and I must yet delay a journey which must subject me at once to ridicule and to inconvenience.' The messengers from the dead seldom petition in vain; and the third night the expected vision appeared with a terrible frown on its countenance, and reproached Valette for his want of friendship to the man whose blood had been spilt in his cause, and for disregarding the peace of his soul. 'If you will grant me my request,' said the phantom, 'I promise to give you twenty-four hours' warning of the time of your own death to arrange your affairs, and to make your peace with God.'

M. Valette promised in the most solemn manner, that he would set off next morning for Marseilles to execute the awful commission; and, with a look of confidence in his words, the apparition of Le Brun disappeared from his sight.

Valette rose next day with the light, and alleging to his family that he had business of the most urgent necessity which called him immediately to Marseilles, he departed, accompanied by a few faithful domestics, to visit the seat of his ancestors after an absence of ten years. There, alas! he found that the murder of Le Brun was but too true. Under the tree that had been so minutely described to him, and which grew in a solitary corner of an adjoining forest, he found the mangled remains, which he caused to be decently interred in the family vault. He in vain, however, made every search for the murderers. The same cause which occasioned the death of the unfortunate Le Brun led the tenants to the most obstinate concealment of the manner of it, and Valette saw, with horror and regret, the misery they had suffered in times of extreme difficulty merely that he might be furnished with the means of extravagance.

'Had I imagined,' he exclaimed, 'that my unsatisfactory pleasures would have cost so dear, I would long since have retired from fashionable life, and sought that happiness in the peaceful seclusion of a beautiful country which was always most congenial to the wishes of my soul. I shall return to my estate,' continued he, 'that my children may learn to relish its beauties, and acquire an attachment to its tranquil pleasures, and to its simple inhabitants. May the blood which has been shed prove a memorable lesson to my sons of the misery of extravagance and the guilt of oppression.'

Impressed with such reflections, M. Valette no sooner returned to Paris than he communicated to his wife the matured and unalterable resolution of his soul. Madame

Valette, having accomplished the principal object of her residence in Paris – the education of her family – assented with
pleasure to a return to those tranquil enjoyments which
were ever dearest to her heart. In little more than a year
they found themselves again in the château of their ancestors, and their return was hailed by a delighted tenantry
– by the widow and the fatherless, by the indigent and the
afflicted. To relieve the distresses of the poor was neither
the least important nor the least pleasant employment of
this family, and on them descended the blessings of those
who had been ready to perish.

About eight years after their return from Paris, the family
mansion demanding repairs, they found it necessary to
remove for some time to Marseilles, where they resided in
the house of M. Danville, the father of Madame Valette.
Time, which wears away even the rocks of the earth, had
effaced the impression of his dream from the mind of Valette,
and cares of a more tender and domestic nature chiefly
occupied his thoughts.

Sitting one night after supper in the midst of his happy
family, a loud and sudden knocking was heard at the gate;
but when the servant went to open it, he found nobody
without. After a short interval the same loud knocking was
again heard, and one of Valette's sons accompanied the
servant to the gate to see who demanded admittance at so
unseasonable an hour. To their astonishment no one was to
be seen there. A third time the knocking was repeated still
louder and louder, and a sudden thought darted across the
mind of Valette. 'I will go to the gate myself,' said he. 'I
believe I know who it is that knocks.'

His presentiment was too truly realised. As he opened the
gate the factor appeared, and whispered to him that next
night at the same time – for it was now the twelfth hour
– he must prepare himself to leave the world. Then, waving
his hand, as if to bid adieu, Le Brun disappeared.

M. Valette returned, pale and ghastly as the phantom he

had seen, to the family circle; and, upon their anxious and urgent inquiries as to the cause of his uneasiness, related for the first time the incident of the dream, and the promised warning he had just received. A sudden gloom and melancholy was spread over the faces of all present. Madame Valette threw her arms round the neck of her husband and embraced him with tears, while his daughters clung round his knees in the utmost distress. M. Danville, however, obstinately declared his incredulity, and considered the whole as one of those unaccountable illusions to which even the strongest minds are sometimes liable. He declared his son-in-law must be the victim of some mental delusion, and although he could not account for his dream, said that this last vision must be mere imagination. No sooner had M. Valette retired to his apartment than M. Danville endeavoured to impress the same opinion on the family of his son-in-law. Apprehensive lest the very imagination of the event might occasion it, or at least be attended by disagreeable consequences, he thought of a device which, as mayor of the city, it was in his power easily to accomplish. This was to cause all the clocks of Marseilles to be put forward one hour, that they might strike the predicted hour of twelve next night when it should be only eleven; so that, if there were really anything in the warning of the ghost, when the time should be believed by Valette to have passed over without any event supervening, he might be persuaded to dissipate the imagination with which he was so deeply impressed.

Next day the unhappy Valette made every effort to arrange his worldly affairs according to his wishes, had his will executed in due legal form, received the sacrament, and prepared himself with all decency and solemnity for the awful event he anticipated. The evening approached. From a large open window which looked into a beautiful garden, and commanded an extensive view into the surrounding country, he saw the sun go down, as he believed, for the last time. For the last time he beheld its blessed light irradiate the blue heavens and gladden the green earth. He thought the myrtles and acacias, as they bowed their limber heads to the breeze, waved him a last adieu. He imagined that the fountains, that threw their drizzling spray on high, played their music with a more plaintive murmur. Now came down upon the world the shadows of night which he believed were to usher him into the darkness of the grave. He beheld the stars twinkle in the azure heaven with a milder radiance than usual. He viewed with tears of affection his wife and his children sitting around him with looks of concealed thoughtfulness and sorrow. 'To leave you, the dearest objects of my affections,' said he, within himself, 'gives to death all its anguish. It were not heaven to be without you. But we part to meet again.'

He considered himself like a criminal doomed to death waiting the hour of his execution, and counting the few remaining moments he had to live.

The lamps were now lighted in the hall, and he sat in the midst of his family and partook of the last supper which, he believed, he was ever to eat upon earth. The clocks of Marseilles tolled the eleventh hour.

'My dearest Maria,' said he to Madame Valette, 'I have now only one hour to live. There is to me but one hour betwixt time and eternity.'

It approached. There was an unusual silence in the company. The twelfth hour struck, when, rising up, he exclaimed: 'Heaven have mercy on me! My time is come.'

He heard the hour distinctly rung out by all the bells in Marseilles.

'The Angel of Death,' said he, 'delays his coming. Could all have been a delusion? No, it is impossible!'

'The ghost,' said M. Danville, in a tone of irony, 'has deceived you. He is one of the lying prophets of Ahab. Are you not yet safe? Consider the whole as a powerful illusion of the imagination, and banish, my friend, a thought which so completely overwhelms you.'

'Well,' rejoined Valette, 'God's will be done! I shall retire to my chamber and spend the night in grateful prayer for so signal a deliverance, for so I must always consider it.'

After having been nearly an hour in his chamber, M. Valette recollected that he had by mistake left unsigned in his library a document of importance to his family, to which is was necessary his name should be affixed. In passing from his bedchamber to the library he had to cross by the head of a flight of stairs, which led immediately down to the cellar where M. Danville kept his choicest wines. At this spot he heard a confused noise of voices below, and instantly ran down to the bottom of the stairs to ascertain the cause. No sooner had he descended than an unseen arm stabbed him to the heart. At this fatal moment the clocks in Marseilles struck one in the morning, or, as it really was, twelve at night – the exact time predicted by Le Brun.

The fact was, the cellar of M. Danville had at that time been broken into by robbers, who, perceiving themselves discovered, saw no other means of escape than by murdering the ill-fated Valette, by whom they had been surprised. These men were the unconscious instruments in the hand of fate. The dagger that stabbed Valette to the heart proved that the decrees of heaven are irresistible, and that there is an hour appointed for all the sons of Adam.

Such is the tradition in Marseilles of how, once upon a time, all the clocks in that city were put an hour forward.

COUSIN ELOF'S DREAM

My cousin, Kaspar Elof Imant, was a man of a melancholy disposition – which means, in other words, he had a bad liver, a little waist, hair of a black-brown, a sharp eye, a long and slightly bent nose, withered cheeks streaked with little red veins, red lips, white teeth, a protruding chin, and little backbone. One might often see him walking, in order to take the air, with shoulders bent, in the Avenue des Plantanes at Birkenfeld. At such times his piercing eyes would acquire a look of abstraction, and the prettiest girls in the place would feel pity for him, although in fact he rejoiced in a yearly rental of five thousand livres and possessed an excellent appetite. They thought he was the victim of some insidious melancholy, and would have done what they could to chase it away.

'That poor M. Elof,' they would say to themselves, 'cannot forget the death of his mother! What he wants is distraction, the sweets of a home to efface the sad memory, a young wife, little children, etc., etc.'

Now Elof was not quite six years old when his mother died, and he was now almost thirty. As for me, I used to tell him of these remarks I heard made concerning him. He would smile, and then suddenly sink into melancholy thought.

Our Aunt Catherine, the wife of Counsellor Weinland, used to give at that time little musical parties, at which one

met a crowd of charming young ladies. I have always thought
that the worthy lady, who took a remarkable interest in
bringing about matches, wished to see her nephews married,
and cultivated what are called 'reciprocal sentiments'.
However that may have been, Elof and I, willingly or unwill-
ingly, had to take our part on these occasions, which were
not a little tiresome to us: what, however, will not one do
for an aunt possessed of three vineyards and of a fine estate
in the neighbourhood of Frankfort? She would ask us to
sing the *duo langouroso* –

> *Ce qu'il me faut à moi . . .*
> *C'est toi! . . . c'est toi! c'est toi! . . .*

with Mademoiselle Ophelia, or Mademoiselle Fridoline – and
we would sing. She would ask us to do the honours of the
whipped-cream and of the *kougelhoff* – and we would do so.
She would tutor us as to our deportment, as to the manner
in which we tied our neckties, or on the turn of our moustaches, and we would listen with the most profound respect.
I would laugh and say on such occasions: 'You are right, my
dear aunt, always right.' Elof would listen, his shoulder
against the piano, looking very miserable, but resigned.

Then the prattle and small-talk would commence, the
counsellor's wife or the baron's wife leading it to the subject
of the absent friends. Did they happen to come in, with what
exclamations of pleasure were they greeted! 'How pleased
we are to see you! Oh! we had quite given you up. We had
ceased to hope, etc., etc.' And the dear friends would
exchange smiles, kisses, embraces!

'He! he! he! Delicious, delicious! Get married then – get
married!'

One evening, however, after the duet, the usual ballad,
and the arietta of *Colibri joli*, some of the ladies, patronesses
of the charity lottery, began to talk about a certain beggar
woman who had recently died at the age of ninety. Madame

Freidag, the baron's wife, dwelt with unction upon this edifying death. Elof, as he sat in a window seat, his head bent down, appeared to listen very attentively. All of a sudden, seizing on a moment of silence, he asked: 'You have doubtless, madam, seen many dead persons while you have been paying your charitable visits during the last twenty years?'

The tone, the look of Elof startled all in the room. I thought there was something strange about him.

'Certainly,' replied the lady, with her face a little flushed.

'And,' went on Elof, 'is it a fact that all dead people have their eyes open?'

'All.'

'And the mouth also?'

'Yes, the mouth too.'

'I thought so,' said Elof, bowing. 'I thought so.' And then he relapsed into his usual abstraction.

These few words produced such an effect upon the party that I saw several of them grow pale. Certainly it was a strange turn for the conversation to take, after the arietta from *Colibri joli*! All felt uneasy, and our worthy aunt, in order to re-establish the merriment, proposed that we should dance a waltz. We did so, but still we could not shake off the strange feeling which had fallen upon us. About eleven o'clock Elof disappeared, and ten minutes after, the last carriage might be heard rattling over the deserted street.

When I went to bid her adieu, my aunt, taking me by the arm, said: 'In Heaven's name, Christian, what is the matter with him! Has Elof gone mad?'

'Ha, ha! my dear aunt, you know what a strange fellow he is, and, after all, what did he say?'

'Well, it is the fault of that woman with her tales of dead and dying folk. Let us think no more about it. Goodnight, Christian.'

I went off full of thought. In the distance twinkled a lamp. I do not know why, but as I came to my lodgings in the

Rue des Capuchins, I felt myself shiver. Before I went to sleep I actually took the extraordinary precaution of looking under my bed. It seemed to me as if some terrible danger were hanging over me. I could not imagine what it could be, but throughout the whole night strange fancies occurred to me. Several times I turned, startled by the rustling of the leaves of the high poplars against my window – listening to the wash of the river Erbach as it swept by the wall of my garden. The shouts of the sailors, the cry of the watchman, seemed to acquire a mysterious significance.

The next morning I was up at five o'clock, I pulled up my Venetian blinds, and listened to the swallows as they twittered on the eaves. All at once I saw Elof afar off, in the empty street. He was walking at a great pace, his hat over his eyes, and his little black cloak drawn tight across his chest. I was about to call out to him, when he turned suddenly to the left, and made his way towards my place. The door of my chamber opened, and there he stood, seemingly not the least surprised to find me up so early.

'Christian,' he said abruptly, 'as archivist of Birkenfeld, I suppose you have the judicial documents of Hundsrück in your charge?'

'Certainly; but sit down.'

'Thanks. How far back do those documents go?'

'A hundred and fifty years – to the reign of Yeri-Peter le Borgne.'

'Well, that is all right. Would you lend me the papers relating to the year 1800?'

'It is impossible. None of the archives must go out of my possession – but I can show you them, if you wish it, in the library of Saint Christophe.'

'That is all I want,' he said, and he commenced to walk up and down impatiently.

'Do you want to go now?'

'Yes, certainly, as quickly as possible.'

'The matter is urgent?'

He stopped short in his walk, and fixed his dark eyes upon me.

'Christian,' he said, 'you shall know all – all. Will you put on your hat?' And he passed it to me.

'Bring the key and let us go.'

This impatience in a man who was generally so calm, and, besides that, the strange questions he had put to Madame Freidag, excited my curiosity. I did what he told me, and we set off at once.

The library of Saint Christophe is an old building in the Romance style, and is said to have been built in the time of Charlemagne. It consists of three high halls, the one above the other. A massive winding stair leads to the top of the building, where, through three loopholes, one can see all the surrounding country as far as eye can reach. In each storey, on each side of the building, are six semicircular windows, little, deep-set, through which the light falls on the large flagstones, while the ceiling is left in deep shadow. In fact it is a barbarous building, which depends for its grandeur upon its height and the associations connected with it. Its position, outside the town, by the side of the river Erbach, gives it an important air. One would scarcely suspect the place was a library, the less so because its heavy oak door remains closed from the first day of the year to that of the feast of Saint Silvester.

We climbed up the winding stairs, lighted here and there by loopholes.

'If these passages are worn,' said I to my companion, 'it is not my fault or that of the savants of Birkenfeld. Since last year, when Count Harvig demanded of me his genea-logical tree, no one has set foot here.'

When we had come to the third storey, while I was putting my key in the lock, Elof seemed to awake from a dream.

'Now I shall see,' he said.

We entered the great empty hall. The sun shone without in all its brilliancy and with all its morning freshness. Through the windows, deep set in the walls, we could catch pretty pieces of landscape – the river, the foaming mills, and the trees, the foliage of which stood out with surprising distinctness. The hall was dark, and the big table was covered with that fine dust which is found in deserted rooms. Elof, looking at the great oaken presses full of papers, uttered a cry of surprise. I pushed the rolling ladder into a dark corner, and said to him: 'What papers do you want?'

'Those of the year 1800.'

'Well, that will be the year eight of the Republic, one and indivisible. We were then a part of the department of the Sarre.'

I commenced to place the ladder. In about five minutes I descended with a big volume under my arm. We seated ourselves in two little walnut-wood armchairs with straight backs, and without pad or cushion, as was the mode in the last century, and I laid my book open upon the table. Any one who had seen us then, seated opposite one another, our shadows thrown on the old walls with their wooden presses, might have taken us for the ghosts of Merlin and the little good-fellow of Liege searching in their conjuring-book. I read the headings. Elof, his eyes sparkling with feverish eagerness, murmured from time to time: 'Go on, go on, it is not there.'

We had in this manner gone through three parts of the volume, and I was getting impatient, when I at last read: 'Extract from the register of the criminal tribunal of the department of the Sarre, the eighth year, in the name of the French people; the criminal tribunal of the department of the Sarre having examined the *acte d'accusation*, dated the 9 Fructidor, against Philippe Gilger, of which the contents are set forth—'

'Ah! Ah!' cried Elof, 'we have it. Read louder, my cousin.'

Elof's look was so fixed that I was troubled by it. The sound of my own voice, re-echoed by the walls, filled me with indefinable terror. I went on: 'The director of the jury of the district of Birkenfeld states that, on the 21st of the month Ventose, Mangel, and Denier, *gens d'armes* of the department of the Sarre, living at Coursel, carrying a mandate of arrest,

issued the 20th of the month Ventose, by the officer of judi-
ciary police in the canton of Grumbach, against Philippe Gilger,
native of Weiswiller, suspected of complicity in robbery and
murder, have conducted to the prison of Birkenfeld the person
of the said Gilger, and remitted the papers concerning him to
the hands of the said jury. As no complaining party appeared
within the two days of adjournment, the director of the jury
has proceeded with the examination relative to the arrest and
detention of the said Gilger, and finds:

'Firstly. That six persons, of whom four belong to Hundsbach,
and two to Schweinschied, returning on the 27th of the month
Frimaire from the fair which had been held the day before
in Birkenfeld, were attacked on the high-road, about nine
o'clock in the morning, by three robbers, one of whom was
Gilger. The robbers, threatening the travellers with pistols and
daggers, extorted from them eighty-five florins.

'Secondly. On the same day, a butcher of Meisenheim,
having passed the night at a farm in Wickenhof, returning
from the same fair at Birkenfeld, was likewise attacked by
the same robbers, and compelled to give them two hundred
and eighty and odd florins.'

A list of many other crimes committed by Gilger and his
companions followed. Elof listened without uttering a word,
which led me to suppose that I had not yet found what he
wanted. At length we came to the twenty-sixth head of the
accusation.

'Twenty-sixthly. The director of the jury states moreover
that, on the 13th of the month Pluviôse, four robbers, armed
with guns, at the head of whom was Philippe Gilger, entered,
between the hours of one and two at night, a mill near to
Birkenfeld, obtaining admission through a skylight, the iron
bar securing which they forced; that the robbers, by these
means, obtained access to the chamber of the miller Pierre
Ringel—'

Elof interrupted me there with a kind of husky cry. I lifted
up my eyes. His pallor alarmed me.

'Yes, yes,' he cried, with a doleful smile. 'That is all right!
Go, on Christian; I am listening.'

In spite of my fear I went on: 'Obtained access to the
chamber of the miller Pierre Ringel, coming to the door of
which, in the interior of the mill, they broke the little glass
window let into the door, and introducing the barrels of
their guns through the opening, forced the miller to hand
them the key. That, when they had entered into the chamber,
they obliged Ringel to deliver up to them his money, his
watch, his pipe marked with the initials P. R.; that, having
searched all the parts of the house, not finding the sums of
money they hoped for, not content with incessantly mocking
the miller, with a thousand imprecations they proceeded to
torture him, placing in his hands a lighted taper; that, in
that extremity Ringel, carried away by pain, beginning to
defend himself, they knocked him down with the butt-end
of their guns, and then threw him out of a window into the
ditch which surrounds the mill, where, however, his body,
in spite of all search, was never found, which makes it
presumed that he was carried away by the stream.

'Twenty-seventh. That on the 18th of the month Ventose,
Philippe Gilger—'

'That is enough,' said Elof. 'All my suppositions are verified. Christian, you shall hear something which will make
your hair stand on end. But let us see the end of the drama
– that which refers to the register of Trèves.'

I turned over several pages and read the declaration of
the jury of accusation of Birkenfeld; the order of arrest, dated
the 11th Fructidor; then the unanimous declaration of the
jury upon the numberless counts of the accusation. At last,
following this declaration, the judgement concluded with
these words:

The criminal tribunal of the department of the Sarre,
after having heard the deputy of the government's
commissary, and having heard his demands according

to law, the accused, and his legal defenders, and having deliberated on the matter:

Condemns Phillipe Gilger to suffer death, conformably, etc . . . mulcts him, moreover, in the costs of the prosecution, etc., etc.

Done, pronounced, and explained in the public court of the tribunal of Trèves, the 23rd of the month Brumaire, in the ninth year of the French Republic, one and indivisible, at six in the morning – Signed: Buchel, president; Bauter, Volbach, Hertzerod, and Warnier, judges of the tribunal, who have all signed the original of the present judgment. To the exact copy, to be joined to the papers, signed: Buchel president, and Warnier registrar.

'What a terrible thing! What a terrible thing!' said Elof. 'That man was innocent.'

'Innocent! How do you know?'

'I know it! I know it! It does not matter how, but I am sure of it.'

He walked up and down the hall with a haggard look on his face, and his long yellow jaws took a greenish hue.

'Ah, that is it, that is it that has weighed upon me for twenty-five years,' said he. 'That is what has made me moody, melancholy.'

Then he came to me, and sitting down in his chair, said to me in a firm, most undoubting voice: 'I do not mean to pretend, Christian, that Gilger was an honest man. All that the act of accusation says is true, with the exception of the murder of the miller. Gilger was a wretched fellow, a robber on the highway; he lived by theft and robbery, but he did not kill Ringel.'

'Who then did kill him?' I asked, astonished at his confident tone.

'Let us see what happened,' said he. 'One the 13th of the month Pluviôse, in the year eight, between one and two in the morning, rain fell in torrents. Ringel, who had been a widower five years, was awake in his room at the back, looking towards the wheel of the mill. He listened to the water foaming in the great ditch, and, not having taken the precaution to lower the sluice before he went to bed, he was afraid he should find the dam somewhat damaged by the current. He was a man about sixty or sixty-five years old, still strong, with grey hair, and of an avaricious disposition. After having listened for some time to the rushing of the water, he rose to strike a light, meaning to turn the handle of the over-fall. At that moment, however, a grating noise struck upon his ear.'

At this point of his story Elof became pale as death, his eyes shone, he bowed his head, and one might have thought that he was listening. I was afraid.

'He heard a grating noise,' said he, drawing a long breath; 'a grating noise in the mill – a sort of sinister grinding, very distinct, which could be heard above the foaming of the water which poured from the spouts and fell in sheets from the roof, above the clatter of the willows lashed by the storm. Then Ringel half-opened the door leading from his room into the mill. He looked for some seconds and saw against the grey background of a skylight to the left several black bent heads. As his sight, through fear, became so powerful that he could see like a cat in the dark, he clearly perceived a stout lever passed between the bars. Three men were using it, and it was this which had made the grinding noise he had heard. He was about to call out for aid when the bar gave way and sprang from the stone. At the same moment two men leapt into the mill. Ringel had only time enough to shut to his door, and recommend his soul to God. For some months past there had been talk of murders committed in the neighbourhood of Birkenfeld, of robberies, of great fires. The Schinderhannes band had visited Hundsrück.

'All these things occurred to the unfortunate man, and he considered he was lost. The rain commenced to cease, and steps could be heard in the mill. The robbers were evidently looking for the owner. Ringel had no weapons. He remembered that his son-in-law slept in the room below, and as loud cries were now heard there, he did not doubt that the robbers had discovered him. The fact is, the son-in-law, Hans Ornacht, had in the beginning escaped by jumping down into the garden, a height of about five-and-twenty feet. The robbers, when they entered, found his window open.'

There was a moment's silence. Elof appeared to be endeavouring to recollect. I asked him how it was he had become acquainted with these particulars, for I did not see how he could have learnt them, the miller having been killed without having told any one what had passed.

'You must know,' replied my cousin, 'that a deadly hatred existed between Pierre Ringel and his son-in-law. The daughter of the miller had been dead some months, leaving a child which ought, naturally, to succeed to the effects of its mother and of its grandfather. Ringel, however, finding himself alone in the world, with a stranger, and not having much affection for the child, which was out at nurse, resolved that he would marry again. He courted an old woman in Nuestadt; and the son-in-law, seeing that it was likely he should lose the mill and all the father-in-law's wealth, conceived the greatest hatred for him.'

'But tell me, Elof, how do you know all this?'

'I know it,' he said gravely, 'and that is enough. Listen to the rest. The greater part of the facts stated in the act of accusation are true, and that proves the penetration of those who prepared it. It is very true that the robbers, after having discovered the room in which Ringel was, broke the window in the door, and threatened to shoot him if he did not give up the key to them. It is quite true that Ringel, not being able to get out of the reach of their guns, which commanded from one side of the room to the other, ended by yielding to the threats of death; that he opened the door, and was horribly maltreated; that, after having been stripped, when the robbers could not find the sums of money which they thought were in the mill, a taper was tied between his fingers in order to force him to say where the treasure lay. Ringel, however, was so avaricious that he would rather have died than give them the information they desired. As for the rest, while one of them struck a light in order to set the taper on fire, disengaging himself from the grasp of the wretches who had hold of his throat, Ringel threw himself out of the window into the ditch of the mill. It was about four o'clock in the morning, and the rain had ceased. He came up to the surface of the water, for he swam excellently, and floated down to the Erbach, the waters of which, swollen by the rain, rushed on with a great roar towards the Rhine. Nothing would have been easier than for the miller to land, but, thinking that there might be robbers on the banks, he was afraid of falling into their hands. He did not wish to land till he came lower down, near to a marshy piece of land covered with reeds, where he was sure no robber could find him. At last, at the end of about twenty minutes, feeling fatigued and chilled to the very marrow of his bones, he tried to gain the bank. At that moment the moon, which had been hitherto covered with clouds, shed a watery light over the country, and the miller, panting, saw, about five feet from him, a man in a boat. He knew him. It was his son-in-law.'

'"Hans," said he, gasping for breath, "it is me. Reach me the oar."'

'But Hans did not answer, and he lifted the oar up. Ringel knew what he meant, and gave a cry of rage and despair. The oar descended on his head. He disappeared; but his vigour was so great that, after a few seconds, he again appeared on the surface. A second blow from the oar killed him. That is how these things happened, Christian. For that deed it was that Gilger was guillotined at Trèves, while the son-in-law, Ornacht, is the owner of the mill, and is esteemed a man of much honesty.'

Elof was silent, and as I looked at him, with my mouth open, it seemed to me that I saw the whole tragedy enacted before my eyes.

'But in heaven's name, cousin,' said I—

'That is not all,' interrupted Elof. 'Yesterday you appeared surprised at the question I addressed to Madame Freidag, whether dead people always have their eyes open.'

'Certainly. I was surprised at that question, and I was not the only one who was so.'

'Ah well, Christian, you shall know why I asked it. In the first place I must tell you I have never seen dead persons. The idea of looking at such is fearful to me. I have only seen one dead man – one only – in a dream, when I was quite a child. He lay amongst some reeds with his mouth and his eyes open. I seemed to see him always – the face white; the big blue eyes turned towards the sky; the body, lifted by the water, moving softly; the arms, stiff, stretched out in the mud, in which play a thousand unclean things – worms, frogs; whilst overhead the long thin leaves of an old willow flutter with every breath of wind. I see that body, abandoned! Around is a deserted country; in the distance are the brown roofs of Birkenfeld; some birds wheel in the air above. To that place, in the morning, I saw a man come down the Erbach in the mist. He came to the body, after having looked around to see that no one was near. He stretched out a long hooked pole from his boat, and with a push sent the body out into the middle of the stream. But dead people float. Then the man tied a big stone to its throat, and it disappeared. That dead man was the miller Ringel, and the other was his son-in-law, the honest Hans Ornacht.'

'Well, but Elof, all this is but a dream.'

'A dream! Remember, Christian, my dream has not deceived me. Dead people have their eyes open and their mouths also. No one had told me that. When I think of dead people – when one speaks to me of the dead, I always see them before me in the fearful guise of that man. Whence does the image proceed? Can it be a memory? No – when these things occurred I was not yet born. Can it be one of those magnetic visions of which the world has heard for more than a century without being able to define what they are? Can it arise from the vital fluid which is called the soul, will, breath, and which transmits itself from one organism to another? How can I tell? However it may be, the fact has never ceased to burden me from my infancy. I will tell you a thing more significant, more incredible – absurd, and nevertheless true. Some days ago, as I walked along the banks of the Erbach, doubting these impressions of mine, and looking on myself almost as a madman, all of a sudden, in spite of my repugnance, it seemed as if something dragged me towards the mill. I went in, hoping that the sight of the interior would dispel my dreams. Well, judge of my surprise when I found everything just as I had imagined it. There was the high timberwork with its cross-beams, the wooden staircase leading to the loft, the millstone, the window with the broken bar – but now secured with a double chain which gives it greater strength – the room which Ringel occupied, and the little window through which he could watch the work going on in the mill – all, everything, even the least things, the most petty details! I was thunderstruck. At that moment a heavy step echoed on the stair. The step troubled me. He came down. I would have liked to fly, but an unknown force held me there. "It is he," I said. It was indeed the man Hans, the son-in-law of Ringel, become old in his turn. He has a bald head, wrinkled jaws, the face furrowed with lines begot by avarice, and perhaps by remorse. He compressed his lips, and then, with a wheedling air, said, smiling: "What can I do for *Monsieur*?"

'"Oh, nothing. I came in from simple curiosity. You have a fine mill here, *Monsieur*. Will you allow me to visit it sometimes?"

'He said nothing but looked at me. Having walked across the lower hall, I went over the little bridge in front, above the sluice, and came to the side of the river. Here is the path – there the reeds. I went on trembling. Big trees, high brambles, scattered rocks, carried me away into the midst of olden dreams. The marsh was dry. I entered it, brushing aside with my feet the long horse-tail and the dry reeds. At length I came to the spot I had so often seen in my dreams. It was there, in that little hollow, that the dead man lay. I stood still and was lost in thought. At length recovering myself, and stamping my foot upon the ground, "Yes, yes," I said, "It was here I saw him." At that moment a slight noise startled me. I turned round. What did I see? The son-in-law, the miller – white, his mouth twitching, his eyes glaring. He had followed me.'

'"What are you doing here?" he asked roughly.

'"Me? Nothing, *Monsieur*. I am looking."

'"Looking! At what do you look?"

'"Oh nothing! I want to see—"

'"There is nothing for one to see here."

'As I was about to reply, he proceeded in an insolent voice: "Go your way."

'The appearance of the man had something terrible in it; a sinister light shone in his countenance. We were alone – night was coming on. I hastened to obey him.

'That is the exact truth, Christian; and although you may tell me that my dream was absurd – that it lacks common sense – all that will not prevent my being assured that it is true. Yes, Hans killed his father-in-law. I am sure of it. I would persist in my declaration under the very knife of the guillotine.'

'But, then, why do you not denounce him?' I asked, rising from my chair. 'Why not tear the mask from the face of this wretched fellow?'

'Denounce him! What are you thinking of, Christian? To denounce him I must have substantial proofs, and such are wanting. If I went and told my dream to the old procurator, Mathias Hertzberg, he would laugh in my face. I should not wonder if he had me seized and put into an asylum. What is a dream in the eyes of your reasonable people? Only a freak of the spirit during a time of sleep. Nothing. Less than nothing!'

'It is true, Elof, it is true. When we cannot comprehend a thing we regard it as absurd – which is much the easier course than getting to the bottom of it. What a great thing is reason!'

We went down the stairs from the library, full of thought. That story had perplexed me.

THE CITIZEN'S WATCH

I

The day before the Christmas of 1832, my friend Wilfred with his counter-bass slung behind him, and I with my violin under my arm, set out from the Black Forest to Heidelberg. There had been a deep fall of snow, so that looking over the wide expanse of deserted country we could discover no trace of the way along which we should go, no road, no path. The bitter wind whistled around with monotonous perseverance, and Wilfred, with his knapsack upon his meagre shoulders, his long legs wide-stretched, the peak of his hat drawn down over his nose, marched on in front of me humming a merry tune from *Ondine*. Once he looked round with a strange smile, and said: 'Comrade, play me the Robin waltz. I should like to dance.'

A laugh followed these words, and the brave fellow again continued his way. I trod in his steps, the snow being nearly up to our knees, and as I went on I found myself becoming by degrees very melancholy.

At length the steeples of Heidelberg peeped up in the distance, and we began to hope that we should arrive there before nightfall. As we pressed on we heard the galloping of a horse behind us. It was about five o'clock in the evening, and big flakes of snow were floating down in the grey light. When the horseman came near to us he pulled in his steed, looking at us out of the corner of his eye. For our part we also looked at him.

Picture to yourself a strongly built man with red whiskers and hair, wearing a fine three-cornered hat, in a brown riding-cloak, and a loose fox-skin pelisse, his hands thrust into furred gloves reaching up to his elbows – an alderman or burgomaster with portly stomach, with a fine valise strapped on the croup of his powerful thick-set horse. Truly a character.

'Hullo, my friends,' said he, disengaging one of his hands from the mittens which hung to his trunk-hose, 'you are going to Heidelberg to play, I suppose.'

Wilfred looked at the stranger, and said shortly: 'What is that to you?'

'Ah, certainly. I have some good advice to give you.'

'Good advice!'

'Yes. If you want it.'

Wilfred took long strides without making any reply, and I, stealing a sidelong glance, thought that the stranger looked just like a great cat, his ears standing up, his eyelids half closed, his moustache bristling, and his air tender and paternal.

'My dear friend,' said he to me, frankly, 'you would do best to return by the way you have come.'

'Why, sir?'

'The illustrious Master Pimenti of Novara is about to give a grand Christmas concert at Heidelberg; all the town will be there, you will not take a kreutzer.'

Wilfred, looking round in a bad temper, said: 'We laugh at your Master Pimenti and all his like. Look at that young man; look at him well. You see he has not yet got a single hair on his chin; he has only played in the little cabins in the Black Forest for the *bourengredel* and the charcoal-burners to dance. Well, this little fellow, with his long fair hair and his big blue eyes, defies all your Italian impostors. His left hand holds in it melodious treasures – treasures of grace and suppleness. His right hand is gifted with the most wonderful

command over the fiddlestick, that heaven in its most boun-
teous mood ever bestowed on man.'

'Ah, ah,' said the other. 'Is that so?'

'It is as I tell you,' cried Wilfred, setting off at his full
speed, and blowing on his red fingers.

I thought he was only making fun of the stranger, who
kept up with us at a gentle trot.

So we went on for about half a league in silence. All of
a sudden the stranger said to us, sharply: 'Whatever may be
your ability, go back again to the Black Forest. We have
enough vagabonds at Heidelberg without your coming to
increase the number. I give you good advice, especially under
the present circumstances. Take it.'

Wilfred was about to make a sharp reply, but the stranger,
putting his horse to the gallop, was already going down the
Elector's Avenue. As he rode on, a company of ravens flew
over the plain, seeming as if they were accompanying him,
and filling the air with their clamour.

We came to Heidelberg at seven o'clock, and we there
found on every wall the big placards of Pimenti.

Grand Concert, Solo, &c.

The same evening while visiting the taverns we met many
musicians from the Black Forest – old comrades, who invited
us to join them. There was old Bruner, the violoncellist; his
two sons, Ludwig and Karl, two good second violins; Henry
Siebel, the clarionet player; the famous Bertha, with her harp;
lastly, Wilfred, with his counter-bass, and myself as first violin.

It was resolved that we should go together, and that after
Christmas we should share like brothers. Wilfred had already
taken for us two a room on the sixth floor of a little inn,
called the Pied-de-Mouton, in the middle of the Holdergrasse,
for four kreutzers a night. It was in truth nothing more than
a garret, but luckily there was an iron stove in it, and so we
lighted a fire there in order to dry our clothes.

While we were sitting down enjoying ourselves eating chestnuts and drinking a flask of wine, behold Annette, the servant, in a little red petticoat, hat of black velvet, her cheeks red, her lips rosy as cherries – Annette comes creeping up the stair, knocks at the door, enters, and throws herself into my arms overjoyed.

I had known the dear girl for a long time, for we came from the same village, and I may tell you that her bright eyes and her pretty ways had completely captivated me.

'I have come to talk with you for a minute,' said she, sitting down upon a stool. 'I saw you come an hour ago, and so here I am.'

Then she commenced to chatter, asking me news about this person and that, till she had asked after all the village, hardly giving me time to reply to her. At length she stopped and looked at me with her sweet expression. We should have sat there till morning if Mother Gredel Dick had not commenced to call out at the foot of the stairs: 'Annette! Annette! Where are you?'

'I am coming, I am coming,' cried the poor child, jumping up.

'She gave me a little tap on the cheek and ran to the door, but before going she stopped.

'Ah,' she cried, coming back again, 'I forgot to tell you. Do you know of it?'

'Of what?'

'Of the death of our pro-rector, Zâhn?'

'Well, what is that to us?'

'Oh, take care, take care, if your papers are not in order. They will be here tomorrow at eight o'clock, to see them. They have been stopping every one, all the world, during the last five days. The pro-rector was murdered in the library of St Christopher's cloister yesterday evening. Last week some one murdered, in a like manner, the old sacristan, Ulmet Elias, of the Rue des Juifs. Some days before, some one killed the old wise woman Christina Haas, and the agate merchant, Seligmann, of the Rue Durlach. Do look well after yourself, my poor Kaspar,' said she tenderly, 'and see that your papers are all right.'

While she was speaking the voice on the stairs kept on crying: 'Annette, Annette, are you coming? Ah, the baggage! to leave me all alone.'

We could also hear the voices of the drinkers as they called for wine, for beer, for ham, for sausages. It was necessary she should go, and Annette ran away as she had come, and we heard her sweet voice: 'Heavens, madam, why do you call so? One would think that the house was on fire!'

Wilfred shut the door, and having sat down again, we looked at one another with some uneasiness.

'That is strange news,' said he. 'Are your papers all right?'

'No doubt they are,' and I handed mine to him.

'Good! Mine are there. I had them looked over before I left. For all that, these murders may be unpleasant for us. I am afraid we shall do no good here, so many families will be in mourning, and, besides, the distraction of the others, the worrying vigilance of the police, the disturbance—'

'Nonsense,' said I. 'You see only the dark side of things.'

We continued to talk of these strange events till it was past midnight. The fire in our little stove lit up every cranny in the roof, the square window with its three cracked panes, the straw mattress spread out near the eaves where the sloping roof met the floor, the black crossbeams, and threw a dancing shadow of the little fir table on the worm-eaten floor. From time to time a mouse, attracted by the warmth, would dart like an arrow along the floor. We heard the wind moaning in the high chimneys, and sweeping the powdered snow off the roofs. I thought of Annette. All was silence.

All of a sudden Wilfred, taking off his waistcoat, said: 'It is time we went to sleep. Let us put some wood on the fire and go to bed!'

'Yes. It is the best thing we can do.'

Saying so, I took off my boots, and in a couple of minutes

we were on the pallet, the coverlet drawn up to our chins, a piece of wood under our heads for a pillow. Wilfred was quickly asleep. The light from the stove came and went. The wind grew fiercer, and I at length slept, in my turn, like one of the blessed.

Towards two o'clock in the morning I was roused by a strange noise. I thought at first that it must be a cat upon the roof, but, placing my ear against the rafters, I was not long in uncertainty. Some one was passing over the roof. I nudged Wilfred with my elbow to wake him.

'Be quiet,' said he, taking my hand. He had heard the noise as well as I. The fire threw around its last gleams, which flickered on the old walls. I was about to get up, when, with one blow of a stone, the fastening of the little window was broken and the casement was thrown open. A white face, with red whiskers, gleaming eyes, and twitching cheeks, appeared, and looked into the room. Our terror was such that we could not even cry out. The man put one leg and then another through the window, and at last jumped into the loft, so lightly, however, that his footsteps made not a sound.

This man, round-shouldered, short, thick-set, his face distorted like that of a tiger on the spring, was no other than the good-natured fellow who had given us advice on our road to Heidelberg. But how changed he was! In spite of the terrible cold he was in his shirt sleeves. He had on a plain pair of breeches. His stockings were of wool, and in his shoes were silver buckles. A long knife, stained with blood, glistened in his hand.

Wilfred and I thought we were lost. He did not seem, however, to see us as we lay in the shadow of the garret, although the flame of the fire was rekindled by the cold air which came in at the window. The man sat down on a stool, and shivered in a strange manner. Suddenly his green yellowish eyes rested on me. His nostrils dilated. He looked towards me for a minute. I had not a drop of blood in my veins. Then he turned away towards the fire, coughed huskily, like a cat, not a muscle of his face moving. At length he took out of his trousers pocket a large watch, looked at it like one seeking the time, and either not knowing what he was doing or designedly, laid the watch upon the table. Then he rose as if uncertain what to do, looked at the window, appeared to hesitate, and went out at the door, leaving it wide open.

I rose to bolt the door, and I could hear the steps of the man as he went down two flights of stairs. A great curiosity overcame my fear, and when I heard him open a window looking into the yard, I turned to an opening in a little turret on the stairs which looked out on the same side. The yard, from this height, looked like a well. A wall fifteen or sixteen feet high divided it in two. To the right of this wall was the yard of a pork-butcher; on the left was that of the inn, the Pied-de-Mouton. It was covered with damp moss and such vegetation as grows in dark corners. The top of the wall could be reached from the window which the man had opened, and from there the wall ran straight on till it reached the roof of a big solemn-looking building at the back of the Bergstrasse. As the moon shone between big snow-clouds, I saw all this in an instant, and I trembled as my eye fell upon the man on the wall, his head bent down, his long knife in his hand, while the wind sighed mournfully around.

He reached the roof in front, and disappeared in at a window.

I thought I was dreaming. For some moments I stood there, my mouth open, my breast bare, my hair flying, the rime from off the roof falling about my head. At last, recovering myself, I went back to our garret, where I found Wilfred, haggard-looking and murmuring a prayer in a low voice. I hastened to put some wood in the stove, and to bolt the door.

'Well?' asked my friend, rising.

'Well,' said I, 'we have escaped. If that man did not see us it is because heaven did not will our death.'

'Yes,' said he. 'Yes. It was one of the murderers whom

Annette spoke about. Good heavens! What a figure, and what a knife!'

He fell back upon the bed. I drained the wine that remained in the flask, and as the fire burnt up and the heat spread itself through the room, and since the bolt on the door seemed strong enough, I took fresh courage.

But the watch was there, and the man might come back for it. The idea made us cold with fear.

'What had we better do?' asked Wilfred. 'It seems to me that our best way would be to go back as quickly as we can to the Black Forest.'

'Why?'

'I do not much care now for double-bass. Do as you wish.'

'But why should we return? What necessity is there for us to leave? We have committed no crime.'

'Hush, hush,' said he. 'That simple word "crime" would suffice to hang us if any one heard us talking. Poor devils like us are made examples of for the benefit of others. People don't care whether they are guilty or not. It will be enough if they find that watch here.'

'Listen, Wilfred,' said I. 'It will do us no good to lose our heads. I certainly believe that a crime has been committed near at hand this night. Yes, I believe it, it is most probable; but in such a case, what ought an honest man to do? Instead of flying he ought to assist in discovering the guilty; he ought—'

'And how – how can we assist?'

'The best way will be to take the watch, give it up to the magistrate, and tell him all that has occurred.'

'Never – never. I could not dare to touch that watch.'

'Very well, then, I will go. Let us lie down now and see if we can get some sleep.'

'I cannot sleep.'

'Well then let us talk. Light your pipe and let us wait for daybreak. I daresay there may be some one up in the inn. If you like, we will go down.'

'I like to remain here better.'

'All right.'

And we sat down beside the fire.

As soon as it was light I went to take up the watch that lay upon the table. It was a very handsome one, with two dials, the one showing the hours and the other the minutes. Wilfred seemed in better spirits.

'Kaspar,' said he, 'after considering the matter over, I think it might be better for me to go to the magistrate. You are too young to manage such matters. You would not be able to explain yourself.'

'As you wish,' said I.

'Yes, it might seem strange that a fellow of my age should send a lad on such an errand.'

'All right. I understand, Wilfred.'

He took the watch, and I could see that his vanity alone urged him on. He would have blushed, no doubt, among his friends at the idea that he was less courageous than myself.

We descended from our garret wrapt in deep thought. As we went along the alley which leads to the Rue Saint Christopher, we heard the clinking of glasses and forks. I recognized the voices of old Brêmer and his two sons, Ludwig and Karl.

'Would it not be well,' I said to Wilfred, 'before going out, to have something to drink?'

At the same time I pushed open the door of the inn. All our friends were there, the violins, the hunting-horns hung up upon the walls, the harp in a corner. We were welcomed with joyful cries, and were pressed to place ourselves at the table.

'Ha,' said old Brêmer, 'good luck to you, comrades. More wind! more snow! All the inns are full of folk, and every flake that falls is a florin in our pockets.'

I saw Annette fresh, beaming, laughing at me with her eyes and lips. The sight did me good. The best cuts of meat were for me, and every time that she came to lay a dish on my right her sweet hand was laid upon my shoulder.

My heart bounded as I thought of the chestnuts we had eaten together. Then the ghastly figure of the murderer passed from time to time before my eyes, and made me tremble. I looked at Wilfred. He was in deep thought. As it struck eight o'clock we were about to part, when the door of the room opened and three tall fellows, with livid faces, with eyes shining like those of rats, with misshapen hats, followed by several others, appeared on the threshold. One of them, with a long nose, formed, as they say, to scent good dishes, a big baton attached to his wrist, approached, and exclaimed: 'Your papers, gentlemen.'

Every one hastened to comply with this command. Wilfred, however, who stood beside the stove, was seized with an unfortunate fit of trembling, and when the police-officer lifted his eye from the paper in order to take a side glance at him, he discovered him in the act of slipping the watch into his boot. The officer struck his comrade on the thigh, and said to him in a joking tone: 'Ha, it seems that we trouble this gentleman!'

At these words Wilfred, to the surprise of all, fell fainting. He sank into a chair, white as death, and Madoc, the chief of the police, coolly drew forth the watch, with a harsh laugh. When he had looked at it, however, he became grave, and turning to his followers: 'Let no one leave,' he cried, in a terrible voice. 'We will take all of them. This is the watch of the citizen, Daniel van den Berg. Attention. Bring the handcuffs.'

The word made our blood run cold, and terror seized on us all. As for me, I slipt under a bench near the wall, and as the officers were engaged in securing poor old Brêmer, his sons, Henry, and Wilfred, who sobbed and entreated, I felt a little hand rest on my neck. It was the pretty hand of Annette, and I pressed it to my lips in a farewell kiss. She took hold of me by the ear, and led me gently, gently. At the bottom of the table I saw the flap of the cellar open. I slipt through it, and the flap closed above me.

All this took but a moment, while all around was in an uproar.

In my retreat I heard a great stamping, then all was still. My poor friends had gone. Mother Gredel Dick, left standing alone upon the threshold, was uttering some peacock-like cries, declaring that the Pied-de-Mouton had lost its good fame.

I leave you to imagine what were my reflections during that day, squatted down behind a cask, cross-legged, my feet under me, thinking that if a dog should come down, or if the innkeeper should take it into her head to come to fill a flask of wine, if a cask should run out and it was necessary to tap another – that any one of these things might ruin me.

All these thoughts and a thousand others passed through my brain. In my mind's eye I already saw old Brêmer, Wilfred, Karl, Ludwig, and Bertha hanging from a gibbet, surrounded by a crowd of ravens, who glutted themselves on them. My hair stood on end at the picture.

Annette, no less anxious than myself, in her fear took care to close the cellar-flap every time she went in and out, and I heard the old dame say to her: 'Leave that flap alone. Are you foolish, that you bother so much about it?'

So the door remained half-open, and from the deep shadow in which I was I saw fresh revellers gather around the tables. I heard their cries, their disputes, and no end of accounts of the terrible band of criminals.

'The scoundrels!' said one. 'Thank heaven, they are caught. What a pest have they been to Heidelberg! One dared not walk in the streets after six o'clock. Business was interrupted. However, it is all over now. In five days everything will be put in order again.'

'You see those musicians from the Black Forest,' cried another, 'are all a lot of scoundrels. They make their way into houses pretending that they come to play. They look around, examine the locks, the chests, the cupboards, the ins and outs, and some fine morning the master of the house is found in his bed with his throat cut, his wife has been murdered, his children strangled, the whole place ransacked from top to bottom, the barn burnt down or something of that kind. What wretches they are! They ought to be put to death without any mercy, and then we should have some peace.'

'All the town will go to see them hanged,' said Mother Gredel. 'It will be one of the best days in my life.

'Do you know, if it had not been for the watch of the citizen Daniel they would never have been discovered. The watch disappeared last night, and this morning Daniel gave notice of its loss to the police. In one hour after, Madoc laid his hand on the whole gang – ha! ha! ha!' and all the room rang with their laughter, while I trembled with shame, rage, and fear by turns.

At last night came, and only a few drinkers sat at the table. The people of the inn had been up late the night before, and I heard the fat mistress gape and say: 'Ah, heavens! when shall we be able to go to bed?'

Only one light remained in the room

'Go to sleep, mistress,' said the sweet voice of Annette. 'I can see very well to all that is wanted until these gentlemen go.'

The topers took the hint, and all left save one, who remained drowsily before his glass.

The watchman at length came round, looked in, woke the man up, and I heard him go out grumbling and reeling till he came to the door.

'Now,' said I to myself, 'that is the last. Things have gone well. Mother Gredel will go to sleep, and little Annette will come to let me out.'

While this pleasant thought passed through my mind I stretched my cramped limbs, when I heard the old innkeeper say: 'Annette, shut up, and do not forget to bar the door. I am going into the cellar.'

It seemed that such was her custom, in order to see all was right.

'The cask is not empty,' stammered Annette, 'there is no necessity for you to go down.'

'Look after your own business,' said the old woman, and I saw the light of her candle as she began to descend.

I had only time to place myself again behind the barrel. The woman, bent down under the low roof of the cellar, went about from one cask to another, and I heard her say: 'Ah, the jade! How she lets the wine drip from the taps! Look! look! I must teach her how to turn a tap better. Did one ever see such a thing! Did one ever see the like!'

Her light threw deep shadows on the damp wall. I drew myself closer and closer.

All of a sudden, when I was imagining that the woman's visit was ended, I heard her sigh – a sigh so deep, so mournful, that I thought something extraordinary must have happened. I raised my head just the least bit, and what did I see? Dame Gredel Dick, her mouth open, her eyes almost out of her head, looking at the foot of the barrel behind which I lay still as a mouse. She had seen one of my feet under the woodwork on which the barrel rested, and she imagined, no doubt, that she had discovered the very chief of the assassins lying hid there in order to throttle her in the night. I at once resolved what to do. Standing up, I said to her: 'Madam, in heaven's name, have pity on me. I am—'

But then, without looking at me, without listening to me, she began to utter her peacock-like cries, cries to stun you, while she began to rush out of the cellar as fast as her extreme stoutness would let her. I was seized with terror, and taking hold of her dress, I threw myself on my knees. That seemed to make matters worse.

'Help! Murder! Oh, heaven! let me go. Take my money. Oh, oh!'

It was terrible.

'Madam,' said I, 'look at me. I am not what you take me for.'

Bah! she was foolish with fright. She raved, she stammered, she bawled in such a shrill voice that if she had been under the earth all the neighbourhood must have been aroused. In such a strait, becoming angry, I pulled her back, jumped before her to the door, and shut it in her face with a noise like thunder, fastening the bolt. During the struggle her light had gone out. Dame Gredel remained in the dark, and her voice was now only heard feebly as if far off.

Exhausted, breathless, I looked at Annette, whose trouble equalled mine. We could not speak, and we listened to the cries as they died away. The poor woman had fainted.

'Oh, Kaspar!' said Annette then, taking my hands in hers, 'what shall we do? Save yourself, save yourself. Some one has perhaps heard the noise. Have you killed her?'

'Killed? Me?'

'Ah well. Run. I will open the door.'

She drew the bolt, and I ran off down the street without so much as even waiting to thank her. How ungrateful! But I was so afraid. The danger was so near.

The sky was black. It was an abominable night, not a star to be seen, not a ray of light, and the wind, and the snow! I ran on for at least half an hour before I stopped to take breath, and then imagine how surprised I was when, on lifting up my eyes, I saw, just in front of me, the Pied-de-Mouton. In my fright I must have run round the neighbourhood; perhaps I had gone round and round. My legs felt heavy, were covered with mud, and my knees shook.

The inn, which had been deserted an hour before, was now as lively as a bee-hive. Lights gleamed from every window. No doubt the place was full of police-officers. Wretched as I was, worn out with cold and hunger, desperate, not knowing where to hide my head, I took the strangest course of all.

'Well,' said I, 'one can but die after all, and one may as well be hanged as leave one's bones in the fields on the way to the Black Forest.' And I went into the inn to give myself up.

Besides the sour-looking fellows, in battered hats, whom I had seen in the morning, and who went and came, ferreted about, and looked everywhere, before a table sat the chief magistrate Zimmer, clothed in black, solemn, with a piercing eye, and by him was his secretary Roth, with his brown periwig, his wise look, and his great eyes big as oyster-shells. No one paid any attention to me, a circumstance which changed my resolution. I sat down in one of the corners of the room, by the great oven, in company with two or three neighbours who had come to see what was going on, and asked in a calm voice for half-a-pint of wine and for something to eat.

Annette was near ruining me.

'Heavens,' she cried, 'is it possible!'

But an exclamation or two amidst such a clatter did not signify. No one noticed it. Having eaten with a good appetite, I listened to the examination of Mother Gredel, who sat in a large chair, her hair all ruffled, and her eyes still wide open with fright.

'What age did the man appear to be?' asked the magistrate.

'About forty or fifty. He was a tremendous man, with black or brown whiskers, I cannot say exactly which. He had a big nose and green eyes.'

'Was there nothing peculiar about his appearance – any blotches or wounds on his face?'

'No. I do not remember any. He had a big mallet and pistols.'

'Very well, and what did he say?'

'He took hold of me by the throat. Happily I cried out so loudly that I frightened him, and then I defended myself with my nails. Ah! when one is about to be murdered, how one can defend oneself?'

'Nothing is more natural, madam, nothing more legitimate. Write that down, M. Roth. The coolness of this good woman has been really wonderful.'

So the deposition went on.

After that they examined Annette, who simply said that she had been so frightened that she really did not notice anything.

'That is enough,' said the magistrate. 'If we require further information we will come again tomorrow.'

All went away, and I asked Mother Gredel to let me have a room for the night. She had not the slightest recollection of me – so much had fear distracted her brain.

'Annette,' she said, 'show the gentleman to the little green room on the third floor. For me, I cannot stand on my feet. Oh heaven! What strange things happen in this world!'

Annette, having lit a candle, led me to the room, and when we were alone together she said to me: 'Ah Kaspar, Kaspar! I should never have believed it of you! I shall never forgive myself for having loved a robber!'

'What, Annette,' cried I, sitting down, despairingly, 'you too! Ah, you have given me the last blow!'

I could have burst into tears, but she saw the wrong she had done me, and, putting her arms around me, said: 'No, no! You do not belong to them. You are too gentle for that, my dear Kaspar. But it is strange – you must have a daring spirit to come here again!'

I explained to her that I was near dying of cold outside, and that that had decided me. We remained some minutes in deep thought, and then she went off for fear Mother Gredel would be after her. When I was alone, having looked out to see that no wall ran near my window, and having examined the bolt on my door, I gave thanks to heaven for having delivered me from so many perils. Then I got into bed, and fell into a deep sleep.

II

The next morning I was up at eight o'clock. The day was dull and misty. When I drew my bed-curtains, I saw that the snow was heaped up upon the window-sill, and that the panes were all frosted. I began to think sorrowfully about my friends. Had they suffered from the cold? How would Bertha and old Brêmer get on? The thought of their trouble grieved me at my heart.

As I was thinking a strange noise rose outside. It approached the inn, and it was not without some fear that I took my place at a window in order to see what it was.

They were bringing the band of supposed robbers to the inn, in order that they might be confronted with Mother Gredel, who was too unwell, after her terrible fright, to go out. My poor comrades came down the muddy street between two files of police-officers, followed by a crowd of lads, howling and whistling like very savages. I can even now see that picture. Poor Brêmer, handcuffed to his son Ludwig; then Karl and Wilfred together; lastly, Bertha, who came by herself, crying in a pitiable manner: 'In heaven's name, gentlemen, in heaven's name, have pity on a poor innocent player on the harp! Fancy me killing, robbing! Oh, heaven, can it be!'

She wrung her hands. The others were sad, their heads bowed down, their hair hanging over their faces.

All the folk in the place congregated in the alley around the inn. The police put all strangers out of it, and shut the door, and the crowd waited eagerly without, standing in the mud, flattening noses against the window-panes.

The greatest stillness reigned in the house, and having dressed myself I opened the door of my room to listen, and to see if I could not learn how matters were going. I heard voices of men as they went and came on the lower landings, which assured me that all the passages were guarded. My door opened on the landing just opposite to the window through which the murderer had fled. I had not before noticed it, but as I stood there, all of a sudden, I perceived that the window was open, that there was no snow upon the sill, and when I came near I saw new traces upon the wall. I shivered when I saw them. The man had been there again! Did he come every night? The cat, the polecat, the ferret, all preying animals, have their one path on which they prey. What a discovery! A mysterious light seemed to illumine my soul.

'Ah,' I cried, 'if I had but a chance to point out the real murderer, my comrades would be saved.'

With my eyes I followed the tracks, which stretched out so clearly to the wall of the neighbouring house.

At that moment I heard some one putting questions. They had opened the door in order to get fresh air. I listened.

'Do you acknowledge having taken part in the murder of the sacristan Ulmet Elias, on the twentieth of this month?'

Then followed some indistinct words.

'Close the door, Madoc,' said the magistrate; 'close the door, madam is unwell.'

I heard no more.

As I leant my head upon the banister, a great conflict took place within me.

'I am able to save my friends,' said I. 'God has pointed out to me the way to render them back to their families. If I fail to do my duty I shall be their murderer – my peace, my honour, will be for ever lost. I shall always look upon myself as the most cowardly, the vilest of mankind!'

For a long time, however, I hesitated, but all of a sudden I resolved. Going down the stairs, I went into the kitchen.

'Have you ever seen that watch?' asked the magistrate of Mother Gredel. 'Remember yourself, madam.'

Without waiting for her to reply, I advanced into the room, and in a firm voice, said: 'That watch, M. Magistrate, I myself have seen in the very hands of the murderer. I identify it. As to the man himself, I can deliver him to you, if you will listen to me.'

There was complete silence around. The police-officers looked at one another astounded. My poor comrades seemed to take courage.

'Who are you, sir?' asked the magistrate.

'I am the friend of these unfortunate prisoners, and I am not ashamed to say it, for all of them, M. Magistrate, all of them, are honest folk, not one of who is capable of committing such a crime as is laid to their charge.'

Again there was silence. Bertha began to weep. The magistrate appeared to collect himself. Then looking fixedly at me, he said: 'Where do you say we can find the murderer?'

'Here, here, M. Magistrate, in this very house. In order to convince you of the truth of what I say, I only beg a minute's private conversation.'

'Very well,' he said, rising.

He made a sign to Madoc, the chief of the police, to follow us, and for the rest to stay behind. We went out.

I rapidly ascended the stairs and they followed me closely. On the third landing I stopped before the window and showed them the tracks of the man in the snow.

'Those are the assassin's traces,' I said. 'He comes along there each night. He went along there at two o'clock yesterday morning. He returned last night, and without doubt he will come again tonight.'

The magistrate and Madoc looked at the marks for some minutes without uttering a word.

'And what grounds have you for saying that those are the traces of the murderer?' asked the magistrate incredulously.

I told them all about the apparition of the man in our garret, I showed them the window from which I had seen him as he fled in the moonlight, which Wilfred had not witnessed as he had remained in bed, and I confessed to them that it was fear alone which had restrained me from telling them all this on the previous night.

'It is strange,' muttered the magistrate. 'This modifies the position of the prisoners very much. But how do you account for the murderer being hidden in the cellar of the inn?'

'That man was myself.'

And I told him all that had passed on the preceding day, from the time my comrades were arrested to the moment of my flight.

'That is enough,' he said.

Turning toward the chief of the police: 'I confess, Madoc,' said he, 'the declarations of these musicians never appeared to me to be conclusive, they were far from satisfying me that they were guilty. Then their papers, at least those of some of them, would establish an alibi such as it would be very difficult to overcome. In the meantime, young man, notwithstanding the apparent truth of your statement, you must remain in our custody until the truth is established. Do not let him out of your sight, Madoc, and take such measures as you think fit.'

The magistrate descended the stairs very thoughtfully, and folded up his papers, without asking another question.

'Conduct the accused back to their prison,' said he, and throwing a contemptuous glance on the fat old innkeeper, he went away, followed by his secretary.

Madoc alone remained with two officers.

'Madam,' said Madoc, 'you must be silent respecting all that has occurred. For the rest, let this young fellow have the room he had yesterday.'

Madoc's look, and the tone in which he spoke, did not admit of reply. Mother Gredel declared she would do whatever he required, so long as he preserved her from the robbers.

'Do not trouble yourself about robbers,' said Madoc. 'We shall remain here all day and all night to keep you safe. Look after your affairs without fear, and to begin with, let us have something to eat. Young man, may I have the pleasure of your company to dinner?'

My position did not admit of my declining his offer, so I accepted the invitation.

We seated ourselves before a ham and a flask of Rhine wine. Some people came in as usual, and tried to obtain information from Mother Gredel and Annette, but they took good care not to speak in our presence, and were very reserved, a matter in them which was very meritorious.

We spent the afternoon in smoking our pipes and in drinking. No one paid us any attention.

The chief of the police, in spite of his extremely upright figure, his piercing eye, his pale lips, and his great eagle nose, was not a bad fellow when he had had something to drink. He told us some tales with much happiness and fluency. He wanted to kiss Annette in the passage. At every joke of his his followers burst out in loud laughter, but as for myself, I was sad and silent.

'Well, young man,' said he to me, laughing, 'cannot you forget the death of your worthy grandmother? What the deuce! We are all mortal. Empty your glass and drive off these miserable thoughts.'

The others joined in, and time passed on amidst a cloud of tobacco smoke, the clinking of glasses, and the tinkling of pewter pots.

At nine o'clock, however, when the watchman had been round, a sudden change came over the scene. Madoc rose and said: 'Ah, then, let us see to our little business; close the door and put the shutters to. Be brisk. As for you, madam and mademoiselle, you had better go to bed.'

These three men, so abominably shabby, looked more like robbers themselves than the preservers of peace and justice. They drew out of their pockets iron bars, at the end of which was a leaden ball, and Madoc, tapping on the pocket of his riding-coat, assured himself that his pistol was there. The next minute he drew it out to put a cap under the hammer.

All this they did with the greatest calmness, and then the chief ordered me to lead them to my garret.

We went up. When we arrived there we found that Annette had taken the trouble to light a fire there. Madoc, muttering curses between his teeth, hastened to throw water over it and extinguish it. Then, pointing to the pallet, he said: 'If you have the heart, you may sleep!'

He sat down with his men at the end of the room near to the wall, and one of them blew out the light.

And I lay there praying to heaven to send the murderer to us.

After a minute or two the silence was so profound that no one could have imagined that there were three men in the room, watching, listening to the slightest noise, like hunters on the track of some timorous beast. I could not sleep, for a thousand horrible thoughts occurred to me. I listened to the clock striking one, two. Nothing happened; no one came.

At three o'clock one of the police-officers moved, and then I thought my man must have come, but all became quiet again. Then I began to think that Madoc must regard me as an impostor; to think how put out he would be, and how he would revenge himself on me the next day; how, wishing to assist my comrades, I had myself run into the toils.

When three o'clock had struck, the time seemed to me to go very quickly. I should have liked the night to have been much longer; time might afford me a loophole of escape.

As I was thinking thus for the hundredth time, all of a sudden, without the least noise, the window opened, and two eyes shone in at the aperture. All was still in the garret.

'The others have gone to sleep,' I thought.

The face stopped there for a moment. Did he suspect something? How my heart beat! The blood ran fast through my veins, but my brow, nevertheless, was cold with fear. I could not breathe.

The face remained there for some seconds, and then he seemed suddenly to make up his mind, and glided into the garret as quietly as of old.

A terrible cry, sharp, ringing, broke the stillness.

'Seize him!'

All the house seemed to ring with the noise of cries, of stamping feet, of husky exclamations, making me shiver with dread. The man shouted, the others panted with their struggle. Then I heard a crash which made the floor creak, the grinding of teeth, the clinking of handcuffs.

'Light,' cried Madoc.

When the light was in, throwing around a blue glare, I could dimly see the police-officers bent over a man in his shirt sleeves. One held him by the throat, the other knelt on his breast. Madoc held his handcuffed hands with a grip which seemed to crush the very bones. The man seemed insensible, save that one of his feet from time to time lifted itself and fell upon the floor again with a convulsive motion. His eyes were almost out of his head, and the froth was on his lips. Hardly had I lighted the candle when the police-officers exclaimed, astonished: 'The citizen!'

All three rose, and I saw them look at one another pale with fright.

The man's eye turned itself to Madoc. He seemed about to speak. In a little while I heard him murmur: 'What a dream! Oh heaven! what a dream!'

Then he drew a long breath, and remained quite still.

I drew near to look on him. It was certainly he, the man who had given us good advice as we were on our way to Heidelberg. Did he know that we should be his ruin; had he some terrible presentiment? He remained perfectly still. The blood trickled from his side over the white floor, and Madoc, recovering himself, bent down beside him and tore his shirt aside from his breast. Then we saw that he had stabbed himself to the heart.

'Ah,' said Madoc, with a sour smile, 'the citizen has cheated the gibbet. He did not let the opportunity slip. You others, stop here while I go and fetch the magistrate.'

He put on his hat, which had fallen off in the struggle, and went out without saying another word.

I remained in the room with the man and the two officers.

At eight o'clock the next day all Heidelberg was acquainted with the wonderful news. It was a strange event in its history.

Who would have suspected Daniel van den Berg, the chief woollen-draper, a man of wealth and position, had these tastes for blood?

The affair was discussed in a thousand different styles. Some said that the rich citizen must have been a somnambulist and irresponsible for his actions – others that he murdered from a mere love of it, for he could not intend to gain anything by his crimes. Perhaps he was both a somnambulist and an assassin also. It is an incontestable fact that the moral being, the will, the soul, whatever you like to name it, does not dominate the somnambulist, but the animal nature, abandoned to itself in such a state, follows naturally the impulse of its instincts whether they be peaceful or sanguinary, and the appearance of Daniel van den Berg, his flat head bulging out behind the ears, his long bristling moustaches, his yellow eyes, all seemed to say that he belonged to the cat tribe – a terrible race, killing for the sake of killing.

However that might be, my comrades were freed.

For five days Annette was famous as a model of devotedness. The son of the burgomaster, Trungott, the plague of his family, even came and asked her to marry him. As for me, I hastened to get back again to the Black Forest, where since that time I have filled the position of leader of the orchestra in the tavern of the Sabre-Vert, on the Tubingian road. If you should happen to pass that way, and if my story has interested you, look in and see me. We will have a bottle or two together, and I will tell you a story which will make your hair stand on end.

THE MURDERER'S VIOLIN

Karl Hâfitz had spent six years in mastering counterpoint. He had studied Haydn, Glück, Mozart, Beethoven, and Rossini; he enjoyed capital health, and was possessed of ample means which permitted him to indulge his artistic tastes – in a word, he possessed all that goes to make up the grand and beautiful in music, except that insignificant but very necessary thing – inspiration!

Every day, fired with a noble ardour, he carried to his worthy instructor, Albertus Kilian, long pieces harmonious enough, but of which every phrase was 'cribbed'. His master, Albertus, seated in his armchair, his feet on the fender, his elbow on a corner of the table, smoking his pipe all the time, set himself to erase, one after the other, the singular discoveries of his pupil. Karl cried with rage, he got very angry, and disputed the point; but the old master quietly opened one of his numerous music-books, and putting his finger on the passage, said: 'Look there, my boy.'

Then Karl bowed his head and despaired of the future.

But one fine morning, when he had presented to his master as his own composition a fantasia of Boccherini, varied with Viotti, the good man could no longer remain silent.

'Karl,' he exclaimed, 'do you take me for a fool? Do you think that I cannot detect your larcenies? This is really too bad!'

And then perceiving the consternation of his pupil, he added: 'Listen. I am willing to believe that your memory is to blame, and that you mistake recollection for originality, but you are growing too fat decidedly; you drink too generous a wine, and, above all, too much beer. That is what is shutting up the avenues of your intellect. You must get thinner!'

'Get thinner!'

'Yes, or give up music. You do not lack science, but ideas, and it is very simple; if you pass your whole life covering the strings of your violin with a coat of grease how can they vibrate?'

These words penetrated the depths of Hâfitz's soul.

'If it is necessary for me to get thin,' exclaimed he, 'I will not shrink from any sacrifice. Since matter oppresses the mind I will starve myself.'

His countenance wore such an expression of heroism at that moment that Albertus was touched; he embraced his pupil and wished him every success.

The very next day Karl Hâfitz, knapsack on his back and baton in hand, left the hotel of The Three Pigeons and the brewery sacred to King Gambrinus, and set out upon his travels.

He proceeded towards Switzerland.

Unfortunately at the end of six weeks he was much thinner, but inspiration did not come any the more readily for that.

'Can any one be more unhappy than I am?' he said. 'Neither fasting nor good cheer, nor water, wine, or beer can bring me up to the necessary pitch; what have I done to deserve this? While a crowd of ignorant people produce remarkable works, I, with all my science, all my application, all my courage, cannot accomplish anything. Ah! Heaven is not good to me; it is unjust.'

Communing thus with himself, he took the road from Brück to Freibourg; night was coming on; he felt weary and footsore. Just then he perceived by the light of the moon an old ruined inn half-hidden in trees on the opposite side of the way; the door was off its hinges, the small window-panes were broken, the chimney was in ruins. Nettles and briars grew around it in wild luxuriance, and the garret window scarcely topped the heather, in which the wind blew hard enough to take the horns off a cow.

Karl could also perceive through the mist that a branch of a fir-tree waved above the door.

'Well,' he muttered, 'the inn is not prepossessing, it is rather ill-looking indeed, but we must not judge by appearances.'

So, without hesitation, he knocked at the door with his stick.

'Who is there? what do you want?' called out a rough voice within.

'Shelter and food,' replied the traveller.

'Ah ha! very good.'

The door opened suddenly, and Karl found himself confronted by a stout personage with square visage, grey eyes, his shoulders covered with a great-coat loosely thrown over them, and carrying an axe in his hand.

Behind this individual a fire was burning on the hearth, which lighted up the entrance to a small room and the wooden staircase, and close to the flame was crouched a pale young girl clad in a miserable brown dress with little white spots on it. She looked towards the door with an affrighted air; her black eyes had something sad and an indescribably wandering expression in them.

Karl took all this in at a glance, and instinctively grasped his stick tighter.

'Well, come in,' said the man; 'this is no time to keep people out of doors.'

Then Karl, thinking it bad form to appear alarmed, came into the room and sat down by the hearth.

'Give me your knapsack and stick,' said the man.

For the moment the pupil of Albertus trembled to his

very marrow; but the knapsack was unbuckled and the stick placed in the corner, and the host was seated quietly before the fire ere he had recovered himself.

This circumstance gave him confidence.

'Landlord,' said he, smiling, 'I am greatly in want of my supper.'

'What would you like for supper, sir?' asked the landlord.

'An omelette, some wine, and cheese.'

'Ha, ha! you have got an excellent appetite, but our provisions are exhausted.'

'You have no cheese, then?'

'No.'

'No butter, nor bread, nor milk?'

'No.'

'Well, good heavens! what *have* you got?'

'We can roast some potatoes in the embers.'

Just then Karl caught sight of a whole regiment of hens perched on the staircase in the gloom, of all sorts, in all attitudes, some pluming themselves in the most nonchalant manner.

'But,' said Hâfitz, pointing at this troop of fowls, 'you must have some eggs surely?'

'We took them all to market this morning.'

'Well, if the worst comes to the worst you can roast a fowl for me.'

Scarcely had he spoken when the pale girl, with dishevelled hair, darted to the staircase, crying: 'No one shall touch the fowls! no one shall touch my fowls! Ho, ho, ho! God's creatures must be respected.'

Her appearance was so terrible that Hâfitz hastened to say: 'No, no, the fowls shall not be touched. Let us have the potatoes. I devote myself to eating potatoes henceforth. From this moment my object in life is determined. I shall remain here three months – six months – any time that may be necessary to make me as thin as a fakir.'

He expressed himself with such animation that the host

cried out to the girl: 'Genovéva, Genovéva, look! The Spirit has taken possession of him; just as the other was—'

The north wind blew more fiercely outside; the fire blazed up on the hearth, and puffed great masses of grey smoke up to the ceiling. The hens appeared to dance in the reflection of the flame while the demented girl sang in a shrill voice a wild air, and the log of green wood, hissing in the midst of the fire, accompanied her with its plaintive sibilations.

Hâfitz began to fancy that he had fallen upon the den of the sorcerer Hecker; he devoured a dozen potatoes, and drank a great draught of cold water. Then he felt somewhat calmer; he noticed that the girl had left the chamber, and that only the man sat opposite to him by the hearth.

'Landlord,' he said 'show me where I am to sleep.'

The host lit a lamp and slowly ascended the worm-eaten staircase; he opened a heavy trap-door with his grey head, and led Karl to a loft beneath the thatch.

'There is your bed,' he said, as he deposited the lamp on the floor; 'sleep well, and above all things beware of fire.'

He then descended and Hâfitz was left alone, stooping beneath the low roof in front of a great mattress covered with a sack of feathers.

He considered for a few seconds whether it would be prudent to sleep in such a place, for the man's countenance did not appear very prepossessing, particularly as, recalling his cold grey eyes, his blue lips, his wide bony forehead, his yellow hue, he suddenly recalled to mind that on the Golzenberg he had encountered three men hanging in chains, and that one of them bore a striking resemblance to the landlord; that he had also those grave eyes, the bony elbows, and that the great toe of his left foot protruded from his shoe, cracked by the rain.

He also recollected that that unhappy man named Melchior had been a musician formerly, and that he had been hanged for having murdered the landlord of The Golden

Sheep with his pitcher, because he had asked him to pay his scanty reckoning.

This poor fellow's music had affected him powerfully in former days. It was fantastic, and the pupil of Albertus had envied the Bohemian; but just now when he recalled the figure on the gibbet, his tatters agitated by the night wind, and the ravens wheeling around him with discordant screams, he trembled violently, and his fears augmented when he discovered, at the farther end of the loft against the wall, a violin decorated with two faded palm-leaves.

Then indeed he was anxious to escape, but at that moment he heard the rough voice of the landlord.

'Put out that light, will you?' he cried; 'go to bed. I told you particularly to be cautious about fire.'

These words froze Karl; he threw himself upon the mattress and extinguished the light. Silence fell on all the house.

Now, notwithstanding his determination not to close his eyes, Hâfitz, in consequence of hearing the sighing of the wind, the cries of the night-birds, the sound of the mice pattering over the floor, towards one o'clock fell asleep; but he was awakened by a bitter, deep, and most distressing sob. He started up, a cold perspiration standing on his forehead.

He looked up, and saw crouched up beneath the angle of the roof a man. It was Melchior, the executed criminal. His hair fell down to his emaciated ribs; his chest and neck were naked. One might compare him to a skeleton of an immense grasshopper, so thin was he; a ray of moonlight entering through the narrow window gave him a ghastly blue tint, and all around him hung the long webs of spiders.

Hâfitz, speechless, with staring eyes and gaping mouth, kept gazing at this weird object, as one might be expected to gaze at Death standing at one's bedside when the last hour has come!

Suddenly the skeleton extended its long bony hand and took the violin from the wall, placed it in position against its shoulder, and began to play.

There was in this ghostly music something of the cadence with which the earth falls upon the coffin of a dearly-loved friend – something solemn as the thunder of the waterfall echoed afar by the surrounding rocks, majestic as the wild blasts of the autumn tempest in the midst of the sonorous forest trees; sometimes it was sad – sad as never-ending despair. Then, in the midst of all this, he would strike into a lively measure, persuasive, silvery as the notes of a flock of gold-finches fluttering from twig to twig. These pleasing trills soared up with an ineffable tremolo of careless happiness, only to take flight all at once, frightened away by the waltz, foolish, palpitating, bewildering – love, joy, despair – all together singing, weeping, hurrying pell-mell over the quivering strings!

And Karl, notwithstanding his extreme terror, extended his arms and exclaimed: 'Oh, great, great artist! oh, sublime genius! oh, how I lament your sad fate, to be hanged for having murdered that brute of an innkeeper who did not know a note of music! – to wander through the forest by moonlight! – never to live in the world again – and with such talents! O Heaven!'

But as he thus cried out he was interrupted by the rough tones of his host.

'Hullo up there! will you be quiet? Are you ill, or is the house on fire?'

Heavy steps ascended the staircase, a bright light shone through the chinks of the door, which was opened by a thrust of the shoulder, and the landlord appeared.

'Oh!' exclaimed Hâfitz, 'what things happen here! First I am awakened by celestial music and entranced by heavenly strains; and then it all vanishes as if it were but a dream.'

The innkeeper's face assumed a thoughtful expression.

'Yes, yes,' he muttered, 'I might have thought as much. Melchior has come to disturb your rest. He will always come. Now we have lost our night's sleep; it is no use to think of rest any more. Come along, friend; get up and smoke a pipe with me.'

Karl waited no second bidding; he hastily left the room. But when he got downstairs, seeing that it was still dark night, he buried his head in his hands and remained for a long time plunged in melancholy meditation. The host relighted the fire, and taking up his position in the opposite corner of the hearth, smoked in silence.

At length the grey dawn appeared through the little diamond-shaped panes; then the cock crew, and the hens began to hop down from step to step of the staircase.

'How much do I owe you?' asked Karl, as he buckled on his knapsack and resumed his walking-staff.

'You owe us a prayer at the chapel of St Blaise,' said the man, with a curious emphasis, 'one prayer for the soul of Melchior, who was hanged, and another for his *fiancée*, Genovéva, the poor idiot.'

'Is that all?'

'That is all.'

'Well, then, good-bye – I shall not forget.'

And, indeed, the first thing that Karl did on his arrival at Freibourg was to offer up a prayer for the poor man and for the girl he had loved, and then he went to The Grape Hotel, spread his sheet of paper upon the table, and, fortified by a bottle of 'rikevir', he wrote at the top of the page *The Murderer's Violin*, and then on the spot he traced the score of his first original composition.

THE CHILD-STEALER

I

In 1815, there was daily to be seen, wandering in the Hesse-Darmstadt quarter of Mayence, a tall emaciated woman, with hollow cheeks and haggard eyes; a frightful picture of madness. This unfortunate woman, named Christine Evig, a mattress-maker, living in the narrow street called Petit Volet, at the back of the cathedral, had lost her reason through the occurrence of a terrible event.

Passing one evening along the winding street of the Trois Bateaux leading her little daughter by the hand, and suddenly observing that she had for a moment let go of the child, and no longer heard the sound of its steps, the poor woman turned and called: 'Deubche! Deubche! where are you?'

Nobody answered, and the street, as far as she could see, was deserted.

Then running, crying, calling, she returned to the port, and peered into the dark water lying beneath the vessels.

Her cries and moans drew the neighbours about her; the poor mother explained to them her agonies. They joined her in making fresh search, but nothing, not a trace, not an indication, was discovered to throw light on this frightful mystery.

From that time Christine Evig had never again set foot

in her home; night and day she wandered through the town, crying in a voice growing feebler and more plaintive: 'Deubche! Deubche!'

She was pitied. Sometimes one, sometimes another kind person gave her food and cast-off clothes. And the police, in presence of sympathy so general, did not think it their duty to interfere and shut Christine up in a madhouse, as was usual at that period.

She was left therefore to go about as she liked, without any one troubling himself concerning her ways.

But what gave to the misfortune of Christine a truly sinister character was that the disappearance of her little daughter had been, as it were, the signal for several events of the same kind; a dozen children disappeared in an astonishing and inexplicable manner, several of them belonging to the upper rank of townspeople.

These events usually occurred at nightfall, when the street-passengers were few, and every one of them was hastening home from business. A wilful child went out to the doorstep of its parent's house, its mother calling after it, 'Karl!' 'Ludwig!' 'Lotelé!' – absolutely like poor Christine. No answer! They rushed in every direction; the whole neighbourhood was ransacked; all was over!

To describe to you the inquiries of the police, the arrests that were made, the perquisitions, the terror of families, would be a thing impossible.

To see one's child die is, doubtless, frightful; but to lose it without knowing what has become of it, to think that we shall never look upon it again, that the poor little being, so feeble and tender, which we have pressed to our heart with so much love, is ill perhaps – it may be calling for us, and we unable to help it – this passes all imagination – exceeds the power of human expression to convey.

Now one evening in the October of that year, 1817, Christine Evig, after having strayed about the streets, had seated herself on the trough of the Bishop's Fountain, her long grey hair hanging about her face, and her eyes wandering dreamily into vacancy.

The servant-girls of the neighbourhood, instead of stopping to chat as usual at the fountain, made haste to fill their pitchers and regain their masters' houses.

The poor mad woman stayed there alone, motionless, under the icy shower in which the Rhine mist was falling. The high houses around, with their sharp gables, their latticed windows, their innumerable dormer-lights, were slowly becoming enveloped in darkness.

The Bishop's Chapel clock struck seven, still Christine did not move, but sat shivering and murmuring: 'Deubche! Deubche!'

At that moment, while the pale hue of twilight yet lingered on the points of the roofs before finally disappearing, she suddenly shuddered from head to foot, stretched forward her neck, and her face, impassable for nearly two years, was lit with such an expression of intelligence, that Counsellor Trumf's servant, who was at the moment holding her pitcher to the spout, turned in astonishment at seeing this gesture of the mad woman's.

At the same moment, a woman, with head bent down, passed along the pavement at the other side of the square, holding in her arms something that was struggling with her, enveloped in a piece of linen cloth.

Seen through the rain this woman was of striking aspect; she was hurrying away like a thief who has succeeded in effecting a robbery, slinking along in the shadow, her rags dragging behind her.

Christine Evig had extended her shrunken left hand, and a few inarticulate words fell from her lips; but suddenly a piercing cry escaped from her bosom: 'It is she!'

And bounding across the square, in less than a minute she reached the corner of the Rue des Vieilles Ferrailles, where the woman had passed out of her sight.

But there Christine stopped, breathless; the stranger was

lost in the darkness of that filthy place, and nothing was to be heard but the monotonous sound of the water falling from the house-gutters.

What had passed through the mad woman's mind? What had she remembered? Had she had some vision – one of those insights of the soul that for a moment unshroud to us the dark depths of the past? I do not know.

By whatever means, she had recovered her reason.

Without losing a moment in pursuing the vanished apparition, the unfortunate woman hurried up the Rue des Trois Bateaux as if carried along by vertigo, and turning at the corner of the Place Gutenberg, rushed into the hall of the provost, Kasper Schwartz, crying in a hoarse voice: 'Monsieur le Prévôt, the child-stealers are discovered! Quick! listen! listen!'

The provost was just finishing his evening meal. He was a grave, methodical man, liking to take his ease after supper. Thus the sight of this phantom greatly disturbed him, and setting down the cup of tea he was in the act of raising to his lips, he cried: 'Good God! am I not to have a single moment's quiet during the day? Can there possibly be a more unfortunate man than I am? What does this mad woman want with me now? Why was she allowed to come in?'

Recovering her calmness at these words, Christine replied in a suppliant manner: 'Ah, monsieur! you ask if there is a being more unfortunate than yourself; look at me – look at me!'

Her voice was broken with tears; her clenched hands put aside the long grey hair from her pale face. She was terrible to see.

'Mad! yes, my God! I have been mad; the Lord, in His mercy, hid from me my misfortune; but I am mad no longer. Oh, what I have seen! That woman was carrying off a child – for it was a child; I am sure of it.'

'Go to the devil, with your woman and child! – go to the devil!' cried the provost. Seeing the unfortunate woman throw herself upon her knees, 'Hans! Hans!' he cried, 'will you come and turn this woman out of doors? To the devil with the office of provost! It brings me nothing but annoyance.'

The servant appeared, and Monsieur Kasper Schwartz pointed to Christine.

'Show her out,' he said. 'Tomorrow I shall certainly draw out a warrant in due form, to rid the town of this unfortunate creature. Thank Heaven we are not without madhouses!'

The mad woman laughed dreamily, while the servant, full of pity for her, took her by the arm, and said gently to her: 'Come, Christine – come!'

She had relapsed into madness, and murmured: 'Deubche! – Deubche!'

II

While these things were passing in the house of the provost, Kasper Schwartz, a carriage came down the Rue de l'Arsenal; the sentinel on guard before the shot-park, recognizing the equipage as that of Count Diderich, colonel of the Imperial regiment of Hilbourighausen, carried arms; a salute answered him from the interior of the vehicle.

The carriage, drawn at full speed, seemed as if going towards the Porte d'Allemagne, but it took the Rue de l'Homme de Fer, and stopped before the door of the provost's house.

As the colonel, in full uniform, got out, he raised his eyes, and appeared stupefied, for the shocking laughter of the mad woman made itself heard outside the house.

Count Diderich was a man about five-and-thirty or forty years of age, tall, with brown beard and hair, and a severe and energetic physiognomy.

He entered the provost's hall abruptly, saw Hans leading Christine, and, without waiting to have himself announced, walked into Monsieur Schwartz's dining-room, exclaiming: 'Monsieur, the police of your district is intolerable! Twenty minutes ago I stopped in front of the cathedral, at the moment

of the Angelus. As I got out of my carriage, seeing the
Countess Hilbourighausen coming down the steps of the
cathedral, I moved on one side to allow her to pass, and
then I found that my son – a child of three years old, who
had been seated by my side – had disappeared. The carriage
door on the side towards the bishop's house was open:
advantage had been taken of the moment when I was letting
down the carriage steps to carry off the child! All the search
and inquiries of my people have been fruitless. I an in despair,
monsieur! – in despair!'

The colonel's agitation was extreme; his dark eyes flashed
like lightning through the tears he tried to repress; his hand
clasped the hilt of his sword.

The provost appeared dumbfounded; his apathetic nature
was distressed at the idea of having to exert himself and
pass the night in giving orders, and going about from place
to place – in short, to recommence, for the hundredth time,
the hitherto fruitless search.

He would rather have put off the business till the next day.

'Monsieur,' replied the colonel, 'understand that I will not
be trifled with. You shall answer for my son with your head.
It is your place to watch over the public security – you fail
in your duty – it is scandalous! Oh that I at least knew who
has struck the blow!'

While pronouncing these furious words, he paced up and
down the room, with clenched teeth and sombre looks.

Perspiration stood on the purple brow of Master Schwartz,
who murmured, as he looked at the plate before him: 'I'm
very sorry, monsieur – very sorry; but this is the tenth! – the
thieves are much more clever than my detectives. What
would you have me do?'

At this imprudent response the colonel bounded with
rage, and seizing the fat provost by the shoulders, dragged
him out of his armchair.

'What would I have you do? Is that the answer you give
to a father who comes to demand of you his child?'

'Let me go, monsieur! – let me go!' roared the provost, choking with alarm. 'In Heaven's name calm yourself! A woman – a mad woman – Christine Evig, has just been here – she told me – yes, I remember – Hans! Hans!'

The servant, who had overheard all at the keyhole, entered the room instantly.

'Monsieur?'

'Fetch back the mad woman.'

'She's still outside, monsieur.'

'Well, bring her in. Pray sit down, colonel.'

Count Diderich remained standing in the middle of the room, and a moment afterwards Christine Evig returned, haggard, and laughing insanely, as she had gone out.

Hans and a servant-girl, curious as to what was passing, stood in the open doorway open-mouthed. The colonel, with an imperious gesture, made a sign to them to go away, then, crossing his arms, and confronting Master Schwartz, he cried: 'Well, monsieur, what kind of intelligence do you expect to obtain from this unfortunate creature?'

The provost moved, as if he were going to speak; his fat cheeks shook.

The mad woman uttered a sort of sobbing laughter.

'Monsieur,' said the provost, at length, 'this woman's case is the same as your own; two years ago she lost her child, and that drove her mad.'

The colonel's eyes overflowed with tears.

'Go on,' he said.

'When she came here a little while ago she appeared to have recovered a spark of reason, and told me—'

Master Schwartz paused.

'What did she tell you, monsieur?'

'That she had seen a woman carrying a child.'

'Ah!'

'Thinking that she was only raving, I sent her away.'

The colonel smiled bitterly.

'You sent her away?' he cried.

'Yes; she seemed to me to have relapsed into her state of madness.'

'*Parbleu*!' cried the count, in a tone of thunder, 'you refuse assistance to this unfortunate woman? You drive away from her her last gleam of hope, instead of sustaining and defending her, as it is your duty to do? And you dare to retain your office! – you dare to receive its emoluments!'

He walked up close to the provost, whose wig trembled, and added, in a low concentrated tone: 'You are a scoundrel! If I do not recover my child, I'll kill you like a dog.'

Master Schwartz, his staring eyes nearly starting from his head, his hands helplessly open, his mouth clammy, said not a word; terror held him by the throat; and besides, he knew not what to answer.

Suddenly the colonel turned his back on him, and going to Christine, looked at her for a few seconds, then, raising his voice: 'My good woman,' he said, 'try and answer me. In the name of God – in the name of your child – where did you see that woman?'

He paused, and the poor woman murmured in a plaintive voice: 'Deubche! – Deubche! – they have killed her!'

The count turned pale, and, carried away by terror, seized the mad woman's hand.

'Answer me, unfortunate creature! – answer me!' he cried.

He shook her; Christine's head fell back; she uttered a peal of frightful laughter, and said: 'Yes – yes – it is done! – the wicked woman has killed it!'

The count felt his knees giving way, and sank rather than sat down upon a chair, his elbows upon the table, his pale face between his hands, his eyes fixed, as if gazing upon some fearful scene.

The minutes passed slowly in silence.

The clock struck ten; the sound made the colonel start. He rose, opened the door, and Christine went out.

'Monsieur,' said Master Schwartz.

'Hold your tongue!' interrupted the colonel, with a with-
ering look.

And he followed the mad woman down the dark street.

A singular idea had come into his mind.

'All is lost,' he said to himself; 'this unhappy woman
cannot reason, cannot comprehend questions put to her; but
she has seen something – her instinct may lead her.'

It is almost needless to add that the provost was amazed.
The worthy magistrate lost not a moment in double-locking
his door; that done, he was carried away by a noble indignation.

'A man like me threatened! – seized by the collar! Aha,
colonel! we'll see whether there are any laws in this country!
Tomorrow morning I shall address a complaint to the Grand
Duke, and expose to him the conduct of his officers,' &c.

III

Meanwhile the colonel followed the mad woman, and by a
strange effect of the excitation of his senses, saw her in the
darkness, through the mist, as plainly as in broad daylight;
he heard her sighs, her confused words, in spite of the
continual moan of the autumn winds rushing through the
deserted streets.

A few late townspeople, the collars of their coats raised to
the level of their ears, their hands in their pockets, and their
hats pressed down over their eyes, passed, at infrequent intervals, along the pavements; doors were heard to shut with a
crash, an ill-fastened shutter banged against a wall, a tile torn
from a housetop by the wind fell into the street; then, again,
the immense torrent of air whirled on its course, drowning
with its lugubrious voice all other sounds of the night.

It was one of those cold nights at the end of October,
when the weathercocks, shaken by the north wind, turn
giddily on the high roofs, and cry with shrilly voices, 'Winter!
– Winter! – winter is come!'

On reaching the wooden bridge Christine leaned over the pier and looked down into the dark muddy water that dragged itself along the canal; then, rising with an uncertain air, she went on her way, shivering and murmuring: 'Oh! Oh! – it is cold!'

The colonel, clutching the folds of his cloak with one hand, pressed the other against his heart, which felt almost ready to burst.

Eleven o'clock was struck by the church of St Ignatius, then midnight.

Christine Evig still went on; she had passed through the narrow streets of l'Imprimerie, of the Maillet, of the Halle aux Vins, of the Vieilles Boucheries, and of the Fosses de l'Evêché.

A hundred times, in despair, the count had said to himself that this nocturnal pursuit would lead to nothing; but, remembering that it was his last resource, he followed her as she went from place to place, stopping, now by a corner-stone, now in the recess of a wall, then continuing her uncertain course – absolutely like a homeless brute wandering at hazard in the darkness.

At length, towards one o'clock in the morning, Christine came once more into the Place de l'Evêché. The weather appeared to have somewhat cleared up; the rain no longer fell, a fresh wind swept the streets, and the moon, now and then surrounded by dark clouds, now and then shining in full brilliancy, shed its rays, smooth and cold as blades of steel, upon the thousand pools of water lying in the hollows of the paving-stones.

The mad woman tranquilly seated herself on the edge of the fountain, in the place she had occupied some hours before. For a long time she remained in the same attitude, with dull eyes, and her rags clinging to her withered form.

All the count's hopes had vanished.

But, at one of those moments when the moon, breaking through the clouds, threw its pale light upon the silent edifices, she rose suddenly, stretched forward her neck, and the colonel, following the direction of her gaze, observed that it was fixed on the narrow lane of the Vieilles Ferrailles, about two hundred paces distant from the fountain.

At the same moment she darted forward like an arrow.

The count followed instantly upon her steps, plunging into the block of tall old buildings that overlook the church of St Ignatius.

The mad woman seemed to have wings; ten times he was on the point of losing her, so rapid was her pace through these winding lanes, encumbered with carts, dung-heaps, and faggots piled before the doors on the approach of winter.

Suddenly she disappeared into a sort of blind alley, pitch dark, and the colonel was obliged to stop, not knowing how to proceed further.

Fortunately, after a few seconds, the sickly yellow rays of a lamp pierced the darkness of the depths of this filthy hole, through a small cracked window-pane; this light was stationary, but now and then it was momentarily obscured by some intervening figure.

Some one was evidently awake in that foul den.

What was being done?

Without hesitation the colonel went straight towards the light.

In the midst of the obstructions he found the mad woman, standing in the mire, her eyes staring, her mouth open, looking at the solitary glimmer.

The appearance of the count did not seem at all to surprise her, only, pointing to the window on the first floor in which the light was seen, she said, 'It's there!' in an accent so impressive that the count started.

Under the influence of this impulsion he sprang towards the door of the house, and with one pressure of his shoulder burst it open. Impenetrable darkness filled the place.

The mad woman was close behind him.

'Hush!' she cried.

And, once more giving way to the unfortunate woman's instinct, the count remained motionless and listened.

The profoundest silence reigned in the house; it might have been supposed that everybody in it was either sleeping or dead.

The clock of St Ignatius struck two.

A faint whispering was then heard on the first floor, then a vague light appeared on a crumbling wall at the back; boards creaked above the colonel, and the light came nearer and nearer, falling first upon a ladder-staircase, a heap of old iron in a corner, a pile of wood; further on, upon a sash-window looking out into a yard, bottles right and left, a basket of rags – a dark, ruinous, and hideous interior.

At last a tin lamp with a smoky wick, held by a small hand, as dry and sinewy as the claw of a bird of prey, was slowly projected over the stair-rail, and above the light appeared the head of an anxious-looking woman, with hair the colour of tow, bony cheeks, tall ears standing almost straight out from the head, light grey eyes glittering under deep brows – in short, a sinister being, dressed in a filthy petticoat, her feet in old shoes, her fleshless arms bare to the elbows, holding a lamp in one hand and in the other a sharp slater's hatchet.

Scarcely had this abominable being glared into the darkness than she rushed back up the stairs with astonishing agility.

But it was too late: the colonel had bounded after her, sword in hand, and seized the old witch by the petticoat.

'My child, wretch!' he cried; 'my child!'

At this roar of the lion the hyaena turned and struck at random with her hatchet.

A frightful struggle ensued; the woman, thrown down upon the stairs, tried to bite; the lamp, which had fallen on the ground, burned there, its wick sputtering in the damp and throwing changing shadows on the dusky wall.

'My child!' repeated the colonel; 'my child, or I'll kill you!'

'You – yes, you shall have your child,' replied the breathless woman in an ironical tone. 'Oh! it's not finished – not – I've good teeth – the coward, to – to strangle me! Ho! – above, there! – are you deaf? – let me go – I'll – I'll tell you all.'

She was nearly exhausted, when another witch, older and more haggard, tottered down the stairs, crying: 'I'm here.'

The wretch was armed with a large butcher's knife, and the count, looking up, saw that she was selecting a place in which to strike him between the shoulders.

He felt himself lost; a providential accident alone could save him.

The mad woman, until then a motionless spectator, sprang upon the old woman, crying: 'It is she! – there she is! Oh, I know her! – she shall not escape me.'

The only answer was a gush of blood, which inundated the landing place; the old woman had cut the unfortunate Christine's throat.

It was the work of a second.

The colonel had time to spring to his feet and put himself on his guard; seeing which the two frightful old women fled rapidly up the stairs and disappeared in the darkness.

The flame of the smoky lamp flickered in the oil, and the count took advantage of its last rays to follow the murderers. But on reaching the top of the stairs, prudence counselled him not to abandon this point of egress.

He heard Christine breathing below, and drops of blood fell from stair to stair in the midst of the silence. It was horrible!

On the other hand, a sound at the back of the den made the count fear that the two women were attempting to escape by the windows.

Ignorance of the place for a moment prevented his moving from the spot on which he was standing, when a ray of light shining through a glass door allowed him to see the two windows of a room looking into the alley lit by a light from without. At the same time he heard, in the alley, a loud voice call out: 'Hallo! – what's going on here? A door open!'

'Come this way! – come this way!' cried the colonel.

At the same moment the light gleamed inside of the house.

'Ah!' cried the voice, 'blood! The devil! – I can't be mistaken – it's Christine!'

'Come here,' repeated the colonel.

A heavy step sounded on the stairs, and hairy face of the watchman, Sélig, with his big otter-skin cap, and his goat-skin over his shoulders, appeared at the head of the stairs, directing the light of his lantern towards the count.

The sight of the uniform astonished the worthy fellow.

'Who's there?' he inquired.

'Come up, my good fellow, come up!'

'Pardon, colonel – but, down below, there's—'

'Yes – a woman has been killed; her murderers are in this house.'

The watchman ascended the few remaining stairs, and, holding up his lantern, threw a light on the place; it was a landing about six feet square, on to which opened the door of the room in which the two women had taken refuge. A ladder on the left hand, leading up to the garret-storey, still further contracted the space.

The count's paleness astonished Sélig. However, he dared not question the colonel, who asked: 'Who lives here?'

'Two women – a mother and daughter; they are called about the market the Jösels. The mother sells butcher's meat in the market, the daughter makes sausage meat.'

The count, recalling the words uttered by Christine in her delirium – 'Poor child! – they have killed it!' – was seized with giddiness, and a cold perspiration burst from his fore-head.

By the most frightful chance he discovered, at the same instant, behind the stairs, a little frock of blue and red tartan, a pair of small shoes, and a black cap, thrown there out of the light. He shuddered, but an invincible power urged him on to look – to contemplate with his own eyes; he approached, therefore, trembling from head to foot, and with a faltering hand raised these articles of dress.

They had belonged to his child!

Some drops of blood stained his fingers.

Heaven knows what passed in the count's heart. For a long while, leaning for support against the wall, with fixed eyes, arms hanging helplessly by his side, and open mouth, he remained as if stunned. But suddenly he sprang against the door with a yell of fury that terrified the watchman. Nothing could have resisted such a shock. Within the room was heard the crashing of the furniture which the two women had piled up to barricade the entrance; the building shook to its foundation. The count disappeared into the obscurity; then came shrieks, wild cries, imprecations, hoarse clamours, from the midst of the darkness.

There was nothing human in it; it was as if wild beasts were tearing each other to pieces in the recesses of their den!

The alley filled with people. The neighbours from all sides rushed into the house, inquiring: 'What's the matter? Are they murdering one another here?'

Suddenly all became silent, and the count, covered with wounds from a knife, his uniform in tatters, came down the stairs, his sword red to the hilt; even his moustaches were blood-stained, and those who saw him must have thought that he had been fighting after the manner of tigers.

What more is there for me to tell you?

Colonel Diderich was cured of his wounds, and disappeared from Mayence.

The authorities of the town considered it judicious to keep these horrible details from the parents of the victims; I learned them from the watchman Sélig himself, after he had grown old, and had retired to his village near Saarbrück. He alone knew these details, having appeared as witness at the secret inquiry which was instituted before the criminal tribunal of Mayence.

THE MAN-WOLF

I

About Christmas time in the year 18—, as I was lying fast asleep at the Cygne Inn at Fribourg, my old friend Gideon Sperver broke abruptly into the room, crying: 'Fritz, I have good news for you; I am going to take you to Nideck, two leagues from this place. You know Nideck, the finest baronial castle in the country?'

Now I had not seen Sperver, who was my foster-father, for sixteen years; he had grown a full beard, a huge fox-skin cap covered his head, and he was holding his lantern close under my nose. It was therefore only natural that I should answer: 'In the first place let us do things in order. Tell me who you are.'

'Who I am? What! Don't you remember Gideon Sperver, the Schwartzwald huntsman? You would not be so ungrateful, would you? Was it not I who taught you to set a trap, to lay wait for the foxes along the skirts of the woods, to start the dogs after the wild birds? Do you remember me now? Look at my left ear, with a frost-bite.'

'Now I know you; that left ear of yours has done it. Shake hands.'

Sperver went on: 'You know Nideck?'

'Of course I do – by reputation; what have you to do there?'

'I am the count's chief huntsman.'

'And who sent you?'

'The young Countess Odile.'

'Very good. How soon are we to start?'

'This moment. The matter is urgent; the old count is very ill, and his daughter has begged me not to lose a moment. The horses are quite ready.'

'But Gideon, look at the weather, it has been snowing three days without cessation.'

'Oh, nonsense; we are not going out boar-hunting; put on your thick coat, buckle on your spurs, and let us prepare to start.'

I could never refuse old Gideon anything; from my childhood he could do anything with me with a nod or a sign; so I equipped myself for the journey.

'I knew,' he said, 'that you would not let me go back without you. The horses are getting impatient. I have had your portmanteau put in.'

'My portmanteau! What is that for?'

'You will have to stay a few days at Nideck, that is indispensable, and I will tell you why presently.'

So we went down into the courtyard. The groom was holding our horses by the bridle. He wished us *bon voyage*, removed his hand, and we were off.

Sperver rode a pure Mecklemburg. I was mounted on a stout cob bred in the Ardennes, full of fire; we flew over the snowy ground. In ten minutes we had left Fribourg behind us.

The sky was beginning to clear up. As far as the eye could reach we could distinguish neither road, path, nor track. Our only company were the ravens of the Black Forest spreading their hollow wings wide over the banks of snow, trying one place after another unsuccessfully for food, and croaking, 'Misery! Misery!'

Gideon galloped on ahead; sometimes as he turned I could see the sparkling drops of moisture hanging from his long moustache. After an hour of this rapid pace Sperver slackened his speed and let me come abreast of him.

'Fritz, I shall have to tell you the object of this journey at some time, I suppose?'

'I was beginning to think I ought to know what I am going about.'

'A good many doctors have already been consulted.'

'Indeed!'

'Yes, some came from Berlin who only asked to see the patient's tongue. Others from Switzerland examined him another way. The doctors from Paris stared at their patient through magnifying-glasses to learn something from his physiognomy. But all their learning was wasted, and they got large fees in reward of their ignorance.'

'Is that the way you speak of us medical gentlemen?'

'I am not alluding to you at all. I have too much respect for you, and if I should happen to break my leg I don't know that there is another that I should prefer to yourself to treat me as patient, but you have not discovered an optical instrument yet to tell what is going on inside of us. If you have indeed such a glass it will be wanted now, for the count's complaint is internal; it is a terrible kind of illness, something like madness. You know that madness shows itself in either nine hours, nine days, or nine weeks?'

'So it is said; but not having noticed this myself, I cannot say that is so.'

'Still you know there are agues which return at periods of either three, six, or nine years. There are singular works in this machinery of ours. Whenever this human clockwork is wound up in some particular way, fever, or indigestion, or toothache returns at the very hour and day.'

'Why, Gideon, I am quite aware of that; those periodical complaints are the greatest trouble we have.'

'I am sorry to hear it, for the count's complaint is periodical; it comes back every year, on the same day, at the same hour; his mouth runs over with foam, his eyes stand out white and staring, like great billiard-balls; he shakes from head to foot, and he gnashes with his teeth.'

'Perhaps this man has had serious troubles to go through?'

'No, he has not. If his daughter would but consent to be married he would be the happiest man alive. He is rich and powerful and full of honours. He possesses everything that the rest of the world is coveting. Unfortunately his daughter persists in refusing every offer of marriage. She consecrates her life to God, and it harasses him to think that the ancient house of Nideck will become extinct.'

'How did his illness come on?' I asked

'Suddenly, ten years ago,' was the reply.

All at once the honest fellow seemed to be recollecting himself. He took from his pocket a short pipe, filled it, and having lighted it: 'One evening,' said he, 'I was sitting alone with the count in the armoury of the castle. It was about Christmas time. We had been hunting wild boars the whole day and had returned at night. It was just as cold as it is tonight, with snow and frost. The count was pacing up and down the room with his chin upon his breast and his hands crossed behind him, like a man in profound thought. From time to time he stopped to watch the gathering snow on the high windows. Everybody at Nideck had been asleep a couple of hours, and not a sound could be heard but the count's heavy spurred boots upon the flags. I remember well that a crow, no doubt driven by a gust of wind, came flapping against the window-panes, uttering a discordant shriek, and how the sheets of snow fell from the windows, and the windows suddenly changed from white to black—'

'But what has all this to do with your master's illness?' I interrupted.

'Let me go on – you will soon see. At that cry the count suddenly gathered himself together with a shuddering movement, his eyes became fixed with a glassy stare, his cheeks bloodless, and he bent his head forward just like a hunter catching the sound of his approaching game. I thought, "Won't he soon go to bed now?" for I was overcome with fatigue. Scarcely had the bird of ill omen croaked its unearthly cry

when the old clock struck eleven. At that moment the count
turns on his heel – he listens, his lips tremble, I can see him
staggering like a drunken man. He stretches out his hands,
his jaws are tightly clenched, his eyes staring and white. I
cried, "My lord, what is the matter?" but he began to laugh
discordantly like a madman, stumbled, and fell upon the
stone floor, face downwards. I called for help; servants came
round. Sébalt took the count by the shoulders; we removed
him to a bed near the window; but just as I was loosening
the count's neckerchief – for I was afraid it was apoplexy –
the countess came and flung herself upon the body of her
father, uttering such heartrending cries that the very remembrance of them makes me shudder.'

Here Gideon took his pipe from his lips, knocked the ashes
out upon the pommel of his saddle, and pursued his tale in
a saddened voice.

'From that day, Fritz, none but evil days have come upon
Nideck, and better times seem to be far off. Every year at
the same day and hour the count has shuddering fits. The
malady lasts from a week to a fortnight, during which he
howls and yells so frightfully that it makes a man's blood
run cold to hear him. Then he slowly recovers his usual
health. He is still pale and weak, and moves trembling from
one chair to another, starting at the least noise or movement,
and fearful of his own shadow. The young countess, the
sweetest creature in the world, never leaves his side; but he
cannot endure her while the fit is upon him. He roars at
her, "Go, leave me this moment! I have enough to endure
without seeing you hanging about me!" It is a horrible sight.
I am at the head of all his retainers, and I would give my
life for his sake; yet when he is at his worst I can hardly
keep off my hands from his throat, I am so horrified at the
way in which he treats his beautiful daughter.'

Sperver looked dangerously wroth for a moment, clapped
both his spurs to his mount, and we rode on at a hard gallop.

I had fallen into a reverie. The cure of a complaint of this description appeared to me more than doubtful, even impossible. It was evidently a mental disorder. To fight against it with any hope of success it would be needful to trace it back to its origin, and this would, no doubt, be too remote for successful investigation.

All these reflections perplexed me greatly. The old huntsman's story, far from strengthening my hopes, only depressed me – not a very favourable condition to insure success. At about three we came in sight of the ancient castle of Nideck on the verge of the horizon. In spite of the great distance we could distinguish the projecting turrets, apparently suspended from the angles of the edifice.

At that moment Sperver drew in his bridle and said: 'Fritz, we shall have to get there before night – onward!'

But it was in vain that he spurred and lashed. The horse stood rooted to the ground, his ears thrown back, his nostrils dilated, his sides panting, his legs firmly planted in an attitude of resistance.

'What is the matter with the beast?' cried Gideon in astonishment. 'Do you see anything. Fritz? Surely—'

He broke off abruptly, pointing with his whip at a dark form in the snow fifty yards off, on the slope of the hill.

'The Black Plague!' he exclaimed with a voice of distress which almost robbed me of my self-possession.

Following the indication of his outstretched whip I discerned with astonishment an aged woman crouching on the snowy ground with her arms clasped about her knees, and so tattered that her red elbows came through her tattered sleeves. A few ragged locks of grey hung about her long, scraggy, red, and vulture-like neck.

Strange to say, a bundle of some kind lay upon her knees, and her haggard eyes were directed upon distant objects in the white landscape.

Sperver drew off to the left, giving the hideous object as wide a berth as he could, and I had some difficulty in following him.

'Now,' I cried, 'what is all this for? Are you joking?'

'Joking? – assuredly not! I never joke about such serious matters. I am not given to superstition, but I confess that I am alarmed at this meeting!'

Then turning his head, and noticing that the old woman had not moved, and that her eyes were fixed upon the same one spot, he appeared to gather a little courage.

'Fritz,' he said solemnly, 'you are a man of learning – you know many things of which I know nothing at all. Well, I can tell you this, that a man is in the wrong who laughs at a thing because he can't understand it. I have good reasons for calling that woman the Black Plague. She is known by that name in the whole Black Forest, but here at Nideck she has earned that title by supreme right.'

And the good man pursued his way without further observation.

'Now, Sperver, just explain what you mean,' I asked, 'for I don't understand you.'

'That woman is the ruin of us all. She is a witch. She is the cause of it all. It is she who is killing the count by inches.'

'How is that possible?' I exclaimed. 'How could she exercise such a baneful influence?'

'I cannot tell how it is. All I know is, that on the very day that the attack comes on, at the very moment, if you will ascend the beacon tower, you will see the Black Plague squatting down like a dark speck on the snow just between the Tiefenbach and the castle of Nideck. She sits there alone, crouching close to the snow. Every day she comes a little nearer, and every day the attacks grow worse. You would think he hears her approach. Sometimes on the first day, when the fits of trembling have come over him, he has said to me, "Gideon, I feel her coming." I hold him by the arms and restrain the shuddering somewhat, but he still repeats, stammering and struggling with his agony, and his eyes staring and fixed, "She is coming – nearer – oh – oh – she comes!" Then I go up Hugh Lupus's tower;

I survey the country. You know I have a keen eye for distant objects. At last, amidst the grey mists afar off, between sky and earth, I can just make out a dark speck. The next morning that black spot has grown larger. The Count of Nideck goes to bed with chattering teeth. The next day again we can make out the figure of the old hag; the fierce attacks begin; the count cries out. The day after, the witch is at the foot of the mountain, and the consequence is that the count's jaws are set like a vice; his mouth foams; his eyes turn in his head. Vile creature! Twenty times I have had her within gunshot, and the count has bid me shed no blood. "No, Sperver, no; let us have no bloodshed." Poor man, he is sparing the life of the wretch who is draining his life from him, for she is killing him, Fritz; he is reduced to skin and bone.'

Gideon was in too great a rage with the unhappy woman to make it possible to bring him back to calm reason. I therefore only begged Sperver to moderate his anger, and by no means to fire upon the Black Plague, warning him that such a proceeding would bring serious misfortune upon him.

'Pooh!' he cried; 'at the very worst they could but hang me.'

'Quite wrong, Sperver, quite wrong. I agree with the Count of Nideck, and I say no bloodshed. Oceans cannot wipe away blood shed in anger. Think of that.'

These words seemed to make some impression upon the old huntsman; he hung down his head and looked thoughtful.

We were then climbing the wooded steeps which separate the poor village of Tiefenbach from the Castle of Nideck.

Night had closed in. Snow was again beginning to fall, heavy flakes dropped and melted upon our horses' manes, who were beginning now to pluck up their spirits at the near prospect of the comfortable stable.

Now and then Sperver looked over his shoulder with evident uneasiness; and I myself was not altogether free

from a feeling of apprehension in thinking of the strange
account which the huntsman had given me of his master's
complaint.

As we ascended the rocky eminence the oaks became
fewer, and scattered birches, straight and white as marble
pillars, divided the dark green of the forest pines, when in
a moment, as we issued from a thicket, the ancient stronghold stood before us in a heavy mass, its dark surface studded
with brilliant points of light.

Sperver pulled up before a deep gateway between two
towers, barred in by an iron grating.

'Here we are,' he cried, throwing the reins on the horses'
necks.

He laid hold of the bell-handle, and the clear sound of a
bell broke the stillness.

After a few minutes a lantern flickered in the deep
archway, showing us in its semicircular frame of ruddy light
the figure of a humpbacked dwarf, yellow-bearded, broad-
shouldered, and wrapped in furs from head to foot. You
might have thought him, in the deep shadow, some gnome
or evil spirit of earth realised out of the dreams of the
Niebelungen.

He came towards us at a very leisurely pace, and laid his
great flat features close against the massive grating, straining
his eyes, and trying to make us out in the darkness in which
we were standing.

'Is that you, Sperver?' he asked in a hoarse voice.

'Open at once, Knapwurst,' was the quick reply. 'Don't
you know how cold it is?'

'Oh! I know you now,' cried the little man; 'there is no
mistaking you. You always speak as if you were going to
gobble people up.'

The door opened, and the dwarf, examining me with his
lantern, with an odd expression in his face, received me with
'*Willkommen, herr doktor,*' but which seemed to say besides,
'Here is another who will have to go away again as the

others have done.' Then he quietly closed the door, whilst
we alighted, and came to take our horses by the bridle.

II

Following Sperver, who ascended the staircase with rapid
steps, I was still able to convince myself that the Castle of
Nideck had not an undeserved reputation.

It was a true stronghold, partly cut out of the rock. Its
lofty vaulted arches re-echoed afar with our steps, and the
outside air blowing with sharp gusts through the loopholes
– narrow slits made for the archers of former days – caused
our torches to flare and flicker. Sperver knew every nook
and corner of this vast place. He turned now to the right
and now to the left, and I followed him breathless. At last
he stopped on a spacious landing, and said to me: 'Now,
Fritz, I will leave you for a minute with the people of the
castle to inform the young Countess Odile of your arrival.'

'Do just what you think right.'

'Then you will find the head butler, Tobias Offenloch, an
old soldier of the regiment of Nideck. He campaigned in
France under the count; and you will see his wife, a
Frenchwoman, Marie Lagoutte, who pretends that she comes
of a high family but, between ourselves, she was nothing
but a *cantinière* in the Grande Armée. She brought in Tobias
Offenloch upon her cart, with one of his legs gone, and he
has married her out of gratitude. You understand?'

'That will do, but open, for I am numb with cold.'

And I was about to push on; but Sperver was not going
to let me off without edifying me upon the history of the
people with whom my lot was going to be cast for a while,
and holding me by the frogs of my fur coat he went on:
'There's, besides, Sébalt Kraft, the master of the hounds; he
is rather a dismal fellow, but he has not his equal at sounding
the horn; and there will be Karl Trumpf, the butler, and

Christian Becker, and everybody, unless they have all gone to bed.'

Thereupon Sperver pushed open the door, and I stood in some surprise on the threshold of a high, dark hall, the guard room of the old lords of Nideck.

My eyes fell at first upon the three windows at the farther end, looking out upon the sheer rocky precipice. On the right stood an old sideboard in dark oak, and on the left a Gothic chimney overhung with its heavy massive mantel-piece, empurpled by the brilliant roaring fire underneath, and ornamented on both front and sides with wood-carvings representing scenes from boar-hunts in the Middle Ages, and along the centre of the apartment a long table upon which stood a huge lamp throwing its light upon a dozen pewter tankards.

At one glance I saw all this; but the human portion of the scene interested me most.

I recognised the major-domo, or head butler, by his wooden leg, of which I had already heard; he was of low stature, round, fat, and rosy, and his knees seldom coming within easy range of his eyesight; a nose red and bulbous like a ripe raspberry; on his head he wore a huge hemp-coloured wig, bulging out over his fat poll; a coat of light green plush, with steel buttons, velvet breeches, silk stock-ings, and shoes garnished with silver buckles. He was standing by the sideboard, with an air of inexpressible satisfaction beaming upon his ruddy features.

His wife, the worthy Marie Lagoutte, her spare figure draped in voluminous folds, her long and sallow face like a skin of chamois leather, was playing with two servants gravely seated on straight-backed armchairs.

Sperver cried, 'Mates, here I am!'

'Ha! Gideon, back already?'

Marie Lagoutte looked up from her cards. The big butler drank off his glass. Everybody turned our way.

'Is monseigneur better?'

The butler answered with a doubtful ejaculation.

'Is he just the same?'

'Much about,' answered Marie Lagoutte, who never took her eyes off me.

Sperver noticed this.

'Let me introduce you to my foster-son, Doctor Fritz, from the Black Forest,' he answered proudly. 'Now we shall see a change, Master Tobie. Now that Fritz has come the abominable fits will be put an end to. If I had but been listened to earlier – but better late than never.'

Marie Lagoutte was still watching us, and her scrutiny seemed satisfactory, for, addressing the major-domo, she said: 'Now, Monsieur Offenloch, hand the doctor a chair; move about a little, do! There you stand with your mouth wide open, just like a fish.'

And the good man, jumping up as if moved by a spring, came to take off my cloak. 'Permit me, sir,'

'You are very kind, my dear lady.'

'Give it to me. What terrible weather! Ah, *monsieur*, what a dreadful country this is.'

'So monseigneur is neither better nor worse,' said Sperver, shaking the snow off his cap; 'we are not too late, then. Ho, Kasper! Kasper!'

A little man, who had one shoulder higher than the other, and his face spotted with innumerable freckles, came out of the chimney corner. 'Here I am!'

'Very good; now get ready for this gentleman the bedroom at the end of the long gallery – Hugh's room; you know which I mean.'

'Yes, Sperver, in a minute.'

'And you will take it with you, as you go, the doctor's knapsack. Knapwurst will give it to you. As for supper—'

'Never you mind. That is my business.'

'Very well, then. I will depend upon you.'

The little man went out, and Gideon, after taking off his cape, left us to go and inform the young countess of my

arrival. I was rather overpowered with the attentions of
Marie Lagoutte.

'Give up that place of yours, Sébalt,' she cried to the
kennel-keeper. 'You are roasted enough by this time. Sit
near the fire, *monsieur le docteur*; you must have very cold
feet. Stretch out your legs; that's the way.' Then, holding
out her snuff-box to me: 'Do you take snuff?'

'No, dear madam, with many thanks.'

'That is a pity,' she answered, filling both nostrils. 'It is
the most delightful habit.' She slipped her snuff-box back
into her apron pocket, and went on: 'You are come not a
bit too soon. Monseigneur had his second attack yesterday;
it was an awful attack, was it not, Monsieur Offenloch?'

'Furious indeed,' answered the head butler gravely.

'It is not surprising,' she continued, 'when a man takes
no nourishment. Fancy, *monsieur,* that for two days he has
never tasted broth!'

'Nor a glass of wine,' added the major-domo, crossing his
hands over his portly, well-lined person.

'Time was,' remarked the master of the hounds in a dismal
voice, 'time was when monseigneur hunted twice a week;
then he was well; when he left off hunting, then he fell ill.'

'Of course it could not be otherwise,' observed Marie
Lagoutte. 'The open air gives you an appetite. The doctor
had better order him to hunt three times a week to make
up for lost time.'

There was a few moments' silence, during which I could
hear the wind beating against the window-panes, and rush,
sighing and wailing, through the loopholes into the towers.

Sébalt sat with legs across, and his elbow resting on his
knee, gazing into the fire with unspeakable dolefulness.
Marie Lagoutte, after having refreshed herself with a fresh
pinch, was settling her snuff into shape in its box, while I
sat thinking on the strange habit people indulge in of pressing
their advice upon those who don't want it. At this moment
the major-domo rose.

'Will you have a glass of wine, doctor?' said he, leaning over the back of my armchair.

'Thank you, but I never drink before seeing a patient.'

He opened his eyes wide and looked with astonishment at his wife.

'The doctor is right,' she said. 'I am quite of his opinion. I prefer to drink with my meat, and to take a glass of cognac afterwards.'

Marie Lagoutte had hardly finished when Sperver opened the door quietly and beckoned me to follow him.

I bowed to the 'honourable company', and as I was entering the passage I could hear that lady saying to her husband: 'That is a nice young man. He would have made a good-looking soldier.'

Sperver looked uneasy, but said nothing. I was full of my own thoughts. Soon Gideon brought me into a sumptuous apartment hung with violet-coloured velvet, relieved with gold. A bronze lamp stood in a corner, its brightness toned down by a globe of ground crystal; thick carpets, soft as the turf on the hills, made our steps noiseless. It seemed a fit abode for silence and meditation.

On entering Sperver lifted the heavy draperies which fell around an ogee window. I observed him straining his eyes to discover something in the darkened distance; he was trying to make out whether the witch still lay there crouching down upon the snow in the midst of the plain; but he could see nothing, for there was deep darkness over all.

But I had gone on a few steps, and came in sight, by the faint rays of the lamp, of a pale, delicate figure seated in a chair not far from the sick man. It was Odile of Nideck.

At the sight of this fair creature, a sense of music and harmony swept sadly through my soul, with faint impressions of the old ballads of my childhood – of those pious songs with which the kind nurses of the Black Forest rock to peaceful sleep our infant sorrows.

She rose.

'You are very welcome, *monsieur le docteur*,' she said with touching kindness and simplicity; then, pointing with her finger to a recess where lay the count, she added, 'There is my father.'

I bowed respectfully and without answering, for I felt deeply affected, and drew near to my patient.

Sperver, standing at the head of the bed, held up the lamp with one hand, holding his fur cap in the other. Odile stood at my left hand. The light fell softly on the face of the count.

At once I was struck with a strangeness in the physiognomy of the Count of Nideck, and in spite of all the admiration which his lovely daughter had at once obtained from me, my first conclusion was, 'What an old wolf!'

And such he seemed to be indeed. A grey head covered with short, close hair, strangely full behind the ears, and drawn out in the face to a portentous length, the narrowness of his forehead up to its summit widening over the eyebrows, which were shaggy and met, pointing downwards over the bridge of the nose, imperfectly shading with their sable outline the cold and inexpressive eyes; the short, rough beard, irregularly spread over the angular and bony outline of the mouth – every feature of this man's dreadful countenance made me shudder, and strange notions crossed my mind about the mysterious affinities between man and the lower creation.

But I resisted my first impressions and took the sick man's hand. It was dry and wiry, yet small and strong; I found the pulse quick, feverish, and denoting great irritability. What was I to do?

I stood considering; on the one side stood the young lady, anxiously trying to read a little hope in my face; on the other Sperver, equally anxious and watching my every movement. A painful constraint lay, therefore, upon me, yet I saw that there was nothing definite that could be attempted yet.

I dropped the arm and listened to the breathing. From time to time a convulsive sob heaved the sick man's heart, after which followed a succession of quick, short respirations. A kind of nightmare was evidently weighing him down – epilepsy, perhaps, or tetanus. But what could be the cause of origin?

I turned round full of painful thoughts.

'Is there any hope, sir?' asked the young countess.

'Yesterday's crisis is drawing to its close,' I answered; 'we must see if we can prevent its recurrence.'

'Is there any possibility of it, sir?'

I was about to answer in general medical terms, not daring to venture any positive assertions, when the distant sound of the bell at the gate fell upon our ears.

'Visitors,' said Sperver.

'Go and see who it is,' said Odile, whose brow was shaded with anxiety. 'How can one be hospitable to strangers at such a time? It is hardly possible!'

But the door opened, and a rosy face, with golden hair, appeared in the shadow, and said in a whisper: 'It is the Baron of Zimmer-Bluderich, with a servant, and he asks for shelter in the Nideck. He has lost his way among the mountains.'

'Very well, Gretchen,' answered the young countess, kindly; 'go and tell the steward to attend to the Baron de Zimmer. Inform him that the count is very ill, and that this alone prevents him from doing the honours as he would wish. Wake up some of our people to wait on him, and let everything be done properly.'

Nothing could exceed the sweet and noble simplicity of the young châtelaine in giving her orders. These thoughts passed through my mind whilst admiring the grace and gentleness in every movement of Odile of Nideck; I could recall nothing to my recollection equal to this ideal beauty.

'Go, now, Gretchen' said the young countess, 'and make haste.'

The attendant went out, and I stood a few seconds under the influence of the charm of her manner.

Odile turned round, and addressing me, 'You see, sir,' said she with a sad smile, 'one may not indulge in grief without a pause; we must divide ourselves between our affection within and the world without.'

'True, madam,' I replied; 'souls of the highest order are for the common property and advantage of the unhappy – the lost wayfarer, the sick, the hungry poor – each has his claim for a share.'

The deep-fringed eyelids veiled the blue eyes for a moment, while Sperver pressed my hand.

Presently she pursued: 'Ah, if you could but restore my father's health!'

'As I have had the pleasure to inform you, madam, the crisis is past; the return must be anticipated, if possible.'

'Do you hope that it may?'

'With God's help, madam, it is not impossible; I will think carefully over it.'

Odile, much moved, came with me to the door. Sperver and I crossed the ante-room, where a few servants were waiting for the orders of their mistress. We had just entered the corridor when Gideon, who was walking first, turned quickly round, and, placing both his hands on my shoulders, said: 'Come, Fritz; I am to be depended upon for keeping a secret; what is your opinion?'

'I think there is no cause of apprehension for tonight.'

'I know that – so you told the countess – but how about tomorrow?'

'Tomorrow?'

'Yes; don't turn round. I suppose you cannot prevent the return of the complaint; do you think, Fritz, he will die of it?'

'It is possible, but hardly probable.'

'Well done!' cried the good man, springing from the ground with joy; 'if you don't think so, that means that you are sure.'

And taking my arm, he drew me into the gallery. We had

just reached it when the Baron of Zimmer-Bluderich and his groom appeared there also, marshalled by Sébalt with a lighted torch in his hand. They were on their way to their chambers, and those two figures, with their cloaks flung over their shoulders, their loose Hungarian boots up to their knees, the body closely girt with long dark-green laced and frogged tunics, and the bear-skin cap closely and warmly covering the head, were very picturesque objects by the flickering light of the pine torch. They disappeared through a side passage.

Gideon took a torch from the wall, and guided me through quite a maze of corridors, aisles, narrow and wide passages, under high vaulted roofs and low-built arches; who could remember? There seemed no end.

'Here is the hall of the margraves,' said he; 'here is the portrait-gallery, and this is the chapel, where no mass has been said since Louis the Bold became a Protestant.'

All these particulars had very little interest for me.

After reaching the end we had again to go down steps; at last we happily came to the end of our journey before a low massive door. Sperver took a huge key out of his pocket, and handing me the torch, said: 'Mind the light – look out!'

At the same time he pushed open the door, and the cold outside air rushed into the narrow passage. The torch flared and sent out a volley of sparks in all directions. I thought I saw a dark abyss before me, and recoiled with fear.

'Ha, ha, ha!' cried the huntsman, 'you are surely not afraid, Fritz? Come on; don't be frightened! We are upon the parapet between the castle and the old tower.' And my friend advanced to set me the example.

The narrow granite-walled platform was deep in snow, swept in swirling banks by the angry winds.

Perhaps, I thought within myself, the witch is looking up at us, and that idea gave me a fit of shuddering. I drew closer together the folds of my horseman's cloak, and with my hand upon my hat, I set off after Sperver at a run; he was raising the light above his head to show me the road, and was moving forward rapidly.

We rushed into the tower and then into Hugh Lupus's chamber. A bright fire saluted us here with its cheerful rays; how delightful to be once more sheltered by thick walls!

I had stopped while Sperver closed the door, and contemplating this ancient abode, I cried: 'Thank God! We shall rest now!'

'With a well-furnished table before us,' added Gideon. 'Don't stand there with your nose in the air, but rather consider what is before you – cold meats and hot wines, that's what I like. Kasper has attended to my orders like a real good fellow.'

Gideon spoke the truth. The meats were cold and the wines were warm, for in front of the fire stood a row of small bottles under the gentle influence of the heat.

At the sight of these good things my appetite rose in me wonderfully. But Sperver, who understood what is comfortable, stopped me.

'Fritz,' said he, 'don't let us be in too great a hurry; we have plenty of time; the fowls won't fly away. Your boots must hurt you. After eight hours on horseback it is pleasant to take off one's boots, that's my principle. Now sit down, put your feet into these slippers, take off your cloak, and throw this lighter coat over your shoulders. Now we are ready.'

And with his cheery summons I sat down with him to work, one on each side of the table, remembering the German proverb; 'Thirst comes from the evil one, but good wine from the Powers above.'

III

We ate with the vigorous appetite which ten hours in the snows of the Black Forest would be sure to provoke.

The fire crackled, the forks rattled, teeth were in full

activity, bottles gurgled, glasses jingled, while outside the wintry blast, the high moaning mountain winds, were mournfully chanting the dirge of the year, that strange wailing hymn with which they accompany the shock of the tempest and the swift rush of the grey clouds charged with snow and hail, while the pale moon lights up the grim and ghastly battle scene.

But we were snug under cover, and our appetite was fading away into history. Sperver had filled his mug with wine; he presented it to me, saying, 'To the recovery of my noble master, the high and mighty lord of Nideck.'

A feeling of satisfied repletion stole gently over us, and we felt pleased with everything.

I fell back in my chair and began dreamily to consider what sort of place I had got into.

It was a low vaulted ceiling cut out of the live rock, almost oven-shaped, and hardly twelve feet high at the highest point. At the farther end I saw a sort of deep recess where lay my bed on the ground, and consisting, as I thought I could see, of a huge bear-skin above, and I could not tell what below, and within this yet another small niche with a figure of the Virgin Mary carved out of the same granite, and crowned with a bunch of withered grass.

'You are looking over your room,' said Sperver. '*Parbleu!* It is none of the biggest or grandest, not quite like the other rooms in the castle. We are now in Hugh Lupus's tower, a place as old as the mountain itself, going as far back as the days of Charlemagne. In those days, as you see, people had not yet learned to build arches high, round, or pointed. They worked right into the rock.'

'Well, for all that, you have put me in strange lodgings.'

'Don't be mistaken, Fritz; it is the place of honour. It is here that the count put all his most distinguished friends. Mind that: Hugh Lupus's tower is the most honourable accommodation we have.'

'And who was Hugh Lupus?'

'Why, Hugh the Wolf, to be sure. He was the head of the family of Nideck, a rough-and-ready warrior, I can tell you. He came to settle up here with a score of horsemen of halberdiers of his following. They climbed up this rock – the highest rock amongst these mountains. You will see this tomorrow. They constructed this tower, and proclaimed, "Now we are the masters! Woe befall the miserable wretches who shall pass without paying toll to us! We will tear the wool off their backs, and their hide too, if need be. From this watch-tower we shall command a view of the far distance all round. The passes of the Rhéthal, of Steinback, Roche Plate, and of the whole line of the Black Forest are under our eye. Let the Jew pedlars and the dealers beware!" And the noble fellows did what they promised. Hugh the Wolf was at their head. Knapwurst told me all about it sitting up one night.'

'Who is Knapwurst?'

'That little humpback who opened the gate for us. He is an odd fellow, Fritz, and almost lives in the library.'

'So you have a man of learning at Nideck?'

'Yes, we have, the rascal! Instead of confining himself to the porter's lodge, his place, all the day over he is amongst the dusty books and parchments belonging to the family. He comes and goes along the shelves of the library just like a big cat. Knapwurst knows our story better than we know it ourselves. He would tell you the longest tales, Fritz, if you would only let him.'

'So then, Gideon, you call this tower, Hugh's tower, the Hugh Lupus tower?'

'Haven't I told you so already? What are you so astonished at?'

'Nothing particular.'

'But you are, I can see it in your face. You are thinking of something strange. What is it?'

'Oh, never mind! It is not the name of the tower which surprises me. What I am wondering at is, how it is that you,

an old poacher, who had never lived anywhere since you
were a boy but amongst the fir forests, between the snowy
summits of the Wald Horn and the passes of the Rhéthal –
you who, during all your prime of life, thought it the finest
of fun to laugh at the count's gamekeepers, and to scour the
mountain paths of the Schwartzwald, and beat the bushes
there, and breathe the free air, and bask in the bright
sunshine amongst the hills and valleys – here I find you, at
the end of sixteen years of such a life, shut up in this red
granite hole. That is what surprises me and what I cannot
understand. Come, Sperver, light your pipe, and tell me all
about it.'

The old poacher took out of his leathern jacket a blackened pipe; he filled it at his leisure, gathered up in the
hollow of his hand a live ember, which he placed upon
the bowl of his pipe; then with eyes dreamily cast up to
the ceiling he answered meditatively: 'Old falcons, gerfal-
cons, and hawks, when they have long swept the plains,
end their lives in a hole in a rock. Sure enough I am
fond of the wide expanse of sky and land. I always was
fond of it; but instead of perching by night upon a high
branch of a tall tree, rocked by the wind, I now prefer
to return to my cavern to drink a glass, to pick a bone
of venison, and dry my plumage before a warm fire. The
Count of Nideck does not disdain Sperver, the old hawk,
the true man of the woods. One evening, meeting me by
moonlight, he frankly said to me, "Old comrade, you hunt
only by night. Come and hunt by day with me. You have
a sharp beak and strong claws. Well, hunt away, if such
is your nature; but hunt by my licence, for I am the eagle
upon these mountains, and my name is Nideck!"'

At that moment there was a shock that made the door
vibrate; Sperver stopped and listened.

'It is a gust of wind,' I said.

'No, it is something else. Don't you hear the scratching
of claws? It is a dog that has escaped. Open, Lieverlé!' cried

the huntsman, rising; but he had not gone a couple of steps when a formidable-looking hound of the Danish breed broke into the tower, and ran to lay his heavy paws on his master's shoulders, licking his beard and his cheeks with his long tongue, uttering all the while short barks and yelps expressive of his joy.

Sperver had passed his arm round the dog's neck, and turning to me, said: 'Fritz, what man could love me as this dog does? Do look at this head, these eyes, these teeth!'

He uncovered the animal's teeth, displaying a set of fangs that would have pulled down and rent a buffalo. Then repelling him with difficulty, for the dog was redoubling his caress: 'Down, Lieverlé. I know you love me. If you did not, who would?'

Never had I seen so tremendous a dog as this Lieverlé. His height attained two feet and a half. He would have been a most formidable creature in an attack. His forehead was broad, flat, and covered with fine soft hair, his eye was keen, his paws of great length, his sides and legs a woven mass of muscles and nerves, broad over the back and shoulders, slender and tapering towards the hind legs. But he had no scent. If such monstrous and powerful hounds were endowed with the scent of the terrier there would soon be an end of game.

Sperver had returned to his seat, and was passing his hand over Lieverlé's massive head with pride, while enumerating to me his excellent qualities. Lieverlé seemed to understand him.

'See, Fritz, that dog will throttle a wolf with one snap of his jaws. For courage and strength, he is perfection. He is not five years old, but he is in his prime. I need not tell you that he is trained to hunt the boar, Every time we come across a herd of them I tremble for Lieverlé; his attack is too straightforward, he flies on the game as straight as an arrow. That is why I am afraid of the brutes' tusks. Lie down, Lieverlé, lie on your back!'

The dog obeyed, and presented to view his flesh-coloured sides.

'Look, Fritz, at that long white seam without any hair upon it from under the thigh right up to the chest. A boar did that. I sewed up his belly in spite of his howling and yelling, for he suffered fearfully; but in three days he was already licking his wound, and a dog who licks himself is already saved. You remember that, Lieverlé, hey! and aren't we fonder of each other now than ever?'

I was quite moved with the affection of the man for that dog, and of the dog for his master, they seemed to look into the very depths of each other's souls. The dog wagged his tail, and the man had tears in his eyes.

Sperver went on: 'What amazing strength! Do you see, Fritz, he has burst his cord to get to me – a rope of six strands; he found out my track and here he is! If he were to grip you by your breeches you would not get away so easily!'

'Nor any one else, I suppose.'

I was still contemplating the dog, when, suddenly recollecting our broken conversation, I went on: 'Now, Sperver, you have not told me everything. When you left the mountains for the castle was it not on account of the death of Gertude, your good, excellent wife?'

Gideon frowned, and a tear dimmed his eye; he drew himself up, and shaking out the ashes of his pipe upon his thumbnail, he said: 'True, my wife is dead. That drove me from the woods; I could not look upon the valley of Roche Creuse without pain. I turned my flight in this direction; I hunt less in the woods, and I can see it all from higher up, and if by chance the pack tails off in that direction I let them go. I turn back and try to think of something else.'

Sperver had grown taciturn. With his head drooped upon his breast, his eyes fixed on the stone floor, he sat silent. I felt sorry to have awoken these melancholy recollections in him. Then, my thoughts once more returning to the Black Plague grovelling in the snow, I felt a shivering of horror.

How strange! Just one word had sent us into a train of unhappy thoughts. A whole world of remembrances was called up by a chance.

I know not how long this silence lasted, when a growl, deep, long, and terrible, like distant thunder, made us start.

We looked at the dog. With head raised high, ears cocked up, and flashing eye, he was listening intently – listening to the silence as it were, and an angry quivering ran down the length of his back.

Sperver and I fixed on each other anxious eyes; yet there was not a sound, not a breath outside, for the wind had gone down; nothing could be heard but the deep protracted growl which came from deep down the chest of the noble hound.

Suddenly he sprang up and bounded impetuously against the wall with a hoarse, rough bark of fearful loudness. The walls re-echoed just as if a clap of thunder had rattled the casements.

Lieverlé, with his head low down, seemed to want to see through the granite, and his lips, drawn back from his teeth, displayed two close rows of fangs white as ivory. Still he growled. For a moment he would stop abruptly with his nose snuffling close to the wall, next the floor, then he would rise again in fresh rage, and with his forepaws seemed as if he would break through the granite.

We watched in silence without being able to understand what caused his excitement. Another yell of rage more terrible than the first made us spring from our seats.

'Lieverlé! What possesses you? Are you going mad?'

He seized a log and began to bang the wall, which only returned the dead, hard sound of solid rock. There was no hollow in it; yet the dog stood in the posture of attack.

'Decidedly you must have been dreaming bad dreams,' said the huntsman. 'Come, lie down, and don't worry us any more with your nonsense.'

At that moment a noise outside reached our ears. The

door opened, and the fat honest countenance of Tobias
Offenloch with his lantern in one hand and his stick in the
other, his three-cornered hat on his head, appeared, smiling
and jovial, in the opening.

'*Salut! l'honourable compagnie!*' he cried as he entered: 'what
are you doing here?'

'It was that rascal Lieverlé who made all that row. Just
fancy – he set himself up against that wall as if he smelt a
thief. What could he mean?'

'Why *parbleu*! he heard the dot, dot of my wooden leg,
to be sure, stumping up the tower-stairs,' answered the jolly
fellow, laughing.

Then setting his lantern on the table: 'That will teach you,
friend Gideon, to tie up your dogs. You are foolishly weak
over your dogs – very foolishly! Just this minute I met Blitzen
in the long gallery; he sprang at my leg – see there are the
marks of his teeth in proof of what I say; brute of a hound!'

'Tie up my dogs! That's rather a new idea,' said the
huntsman. 'Dogs tied up are good for nothing at all; they
grow too wild. Besides, was not Lieverlé tied up, after all?
See his broken cord.'

'What I tell you is not on my own account. When they
come near me I always hold up my stick and put my wooden
leg foremost.'

Tobias sat down and with both elbows on the table, his
eyes expanding with delight, he confided to us that just now
he was a bachelor.

'You don't mean that!'

'Yes, Marie Anne is sitting up with Gertrude in monseigneur's anteroom.'

'Then you are in no hurry to go away?'

'No, none at all. I should like to stay in your company.'

'How unfortunate that you should have come in so late!'
remarked Sperver; 'all the bottles are empty.'

The disappointment of the discomfited major-domo
excited my compassion. The poor man would so gladly have

enjoyed his widowhood. But in spite of my endeavours to repress it a long yawn extended wide my mouth.

'Well, another time,' said he, rising. And he took his lantern. 'Good night, gentlemen.'

'Stop – wait for me,' cried Gideon. 'I can see Fritz is sleepy; we will go down together.'

'Very gladly, Sperver; on our way we will have a word with Trumpf, the butler. He is downstairs with the rest, and Knapwurst is telling them tales.'

'All right. Good night, Fritz.'

'Good night, Gideon. Don't forget to send for me if the count is taken worse.'

'I will do as you wish. Lieverlé, come.'

They went out, and as they were crossing the platform I could hear the Nideck clock strike eleven. I was tired out and soon fell asleep.

IV

Daylight was beginning to tinge the only window in my dungeon tower where I was roused by the distant notes of a hunting horn.

There is nothing more sad and melancholy than the wail of this instrument when the day begins to struggle with the night.

Leaning upon my elbow I lay listening to the plaintive sound, which suggested something of the feudal ages. The contemplation of my chamber, the ancient den of the Wolf of Nideck, with its low, dark arch, threatening almost to come down to crush the occupant; and further on that small leaden window, just touching the ceiling, more wide than high, and deeply recessed in the wall, added to the reality of the impression.

I arose quickly and ran to open the window.

There presented itself to my astonished eyes such a

wondrous spectacle as no mortal tongue, no pen of man, can describe – the wide prospect that the eagle, the denizen of the high Alps, sweeps with his far-reaching ken every morning at the rising of the deep purple veil that overhung and horizon by night – mountains farther off! mountains far away! and yet again in the blue distance – mountains still, blending with the grey mists of the morning in the shadowy horizon! – motionless billows that sink into peace and still- ness in the blue distance of the plains of Lorraine. Such is a faint idea of the mighty scenery of the Vosges, boundless forests, silver lakes, dazzling crests, ridges, and peaks projecting their clear outlines upon the steel blue of the valleys clothed in snow. Beyond this, infinite space!

I stood mute with admiration. At every moment the details stood out more clearly in the advancing light of morning; hamlets, farmhouses, villages, seemed to rise and peep out of every undulation of the land. A little more attention brought more and more numerous objects into view.

I had leaned out of my window rapt in contemplation for more than a quarter of an hour when a hand was laid lightly upon my shoulder; I turned round startled, when the calm figure and quiet smile of Gideon saluted me with: '*Guten Tag*, Fritz! Good morning!'

Then he also rested his arms on the window, smoking his short pipe.

We sat long contemplating and meditating over this grand spectacle. From time to time the old poacher, noticing me with my eyes fixed upon some distant object would explain: 'That is the Wald Horn; this is the Tiefenthal; there's the fall of the Steinbach; it has stopped running now; it is hanging down in great fringed sheets, like the curtains over the shoulder of the Harberg – a cold winter's cloak! Down there is a path that leads to Fribourg; in a fortnight's time it will be difficult to trace it.'

I could not tear myself away from so beautiful a prospect. A few birds of prey, with wings hollowed into a graceful curve sharp-pointed at each end, the fan-shaped tail spread out, were silently sweeping round the rock-hewn tower, herons flew unscathed above them, owing their safety from the grasp of the sharp claws and the tearing beak to the elevation of their flight.

Not a cloud marred the beauty of the blue sky; all the snow had fallen to earth; once more the huntsman's horn awoke the echoes.

'That is my friend Sébalt lamenting down there,' said Sperver. 'He knows everything about horses and dogs, and he sounds the hunter's horn better than any man in Germany.

'Poor Sébalt! He is pining away over monseigneur's illness; he cannot hunt as he used to do. His only comfort is to get up every morning at sunrise and play the count's favourite airs. He thinks he shall be able to cure him that way!'

Sperver, with the good taste of a man who appreciates beautiful scenery, had offered no interruption to my contemplations; but when, my eyes dazzled and swimming with so much light, I turned round to the darkness of the tower, he said to me: 'Fritz, it's all right; the count has had no fresh attack.'

These words brought me back to a sense of the realities of life.

'Ah, I am very glad!'

'It is all owing to you, Fritz.'

'What do you mean? I have not prescribed yet.'

'What signifies! You were there; that was enough.'

'You are only joking, Gideon! What is the use of my being present if I don't prescribe?'

'Why, you bring him good luck!'

I looked straight at him, but he was not even smiling!

'Yes, Fritz, you are just a messenger of good; the last two years the lord had another attack the next day after the first, then a third and a fourth. You have put an end to that. What can be clearer?'

'Well, to me it is not so very clear; on the contrary, it is very obscure.'

'We are never too old to learn,' the good man went on. 'Fritz, there are messengers of evil and there are messengers of good. Now that rascal Knapwurst, he is a sure messenger of ill. If ever I meet him as I am going out hunting I am sure of some misadventure; my gun misses fire, or I sprain my ankle, or a dog gets ripped up! – all sorts of mischief come. So being quite aware of this, I always try and set off at early daybreak, before that author of mischief who sleeps like a dormouse has opened his eyes; or else I slip out by a back way by the postern gate. Don't you see!'

'I understand you very well, but your ideas seem to me very strange, Gideon.'

'You, Fritz,' he went on, without noticing my interruption – 'you are a most excellent lad; Heaven has covered your head with innumerable blessings; just one glance at your good-natured smile is enough to make any one happy. You positively bring good luck with you. I have always said so, and now would you like to have a proof?'

'Yes, indeed I should. It would be worth while to know how much there is in me without my having any knowledge of it.'

'Well,' said he, grasping my wrist, 'look down there!'

He pointed to a hillock at a couple of gunshots from the castle.

'Do you see there a rock half-buried in the snow, with a ragged brush by its side?'

'Quite well.'

'Do you see anything near?'

'No.'

'Well, there is a reason for that. You have driven away the Black Plague! Every year at the second attack there she was holding her feet between her hands. She bore a curse with her. This morning the very first thing I did was to get up here. I climbed up the beacon tower; I looked all round;

the old hag was nowhere to be seen. I looked up and down, right and left, and everywhere; not a sign of the creature anywhere. She had scented you evidently.'

And the good fellow, in a fit of enthusiasm, shook me warmly by the hand, crying with unchecked emotion: 'Ah, Fritz, how glad I am that I brought you here! The witch *will* be sold, eh?'

'So, Sperver,' I said, 'the count has spent a good night?'

'A very good one.'

'Then I am very well pleased. Let us go down.'

We again traversed the high parapet, and I was now better able to examine this way of access, the ramparts of which arose from a prodigious depth; and they were extended along the sharp narrow ridge of the rock down to the very bottom of the valley. It was a long flight of jagged precipitous steps descending from the wolf's den, or rather eagle's nest, down to the deep valley below.

Gazing down I felt giddy, and recoiling in alarm to the middle of the platform, I hastily descended down the path which led to the main building.

We had already traversed several great corridors when a great open door stood before us. I looked in and descried, at the top of a double ladder, the little gnome Knapwurst, whose strange appearance had struck me the night before.

The hall itself attracted my attention by its imposing aspect. It was the receptacle of the archives of the house of Nideck, a high, dark, dusty apartment, with long Gothic windows, reaching from the angle of the ceiling to within a couple of yards from the floor.

There were collected along spacious shelves, not only all the documents, title-deeds, and family genealogies of the house of Nideck, but all the chronicles of the Black Forest, the collected works of the old Minnesinger, and great folio volumes from the presses of Gutenberg and Faust. The deep shadows of the groined vaults, their arches divided by massive ribs, and descending partly down the cold grey walls, reminded one of the gloomy cloisters of the Middle Ages. And amidst these characteristic surroundings sat an ugly dwarf on the top of his ladder, with a red-edged volume upon his bony knees, his head half-buried in a rough fur cap, small grey eyes, wide misshapen mouth, humps on back and shoulders, a most uninviting object, the familiar spirit of this last refuge of all the learning belonging to the princely race of Nideck.

But a truly historical importance belonged to this chamber in the long series of family portraits, filling almost entirely one side of the ancient library. All were there, men and women; from Hugh the Wolf to Yeri-Hans, the present owner; from the first rough daub of barbarous times to the perfect work of the best modern painters. My attention was naturally drawn in that direction.

Hugh Lupus, a bald-headed figure, seemed to glare upon you like a wolf stealing round the corner of a wood. His grey bloodshot eyes, his red beard, and his large hairy ears gave him a fearful and ferocious aspect.

Next to him, like the lamb next to the wolf, was the portrait of a lady of youthful years, with gentle blue eyes, hands crossed on the breast over a book of devotions, and tresses of fair long silky hair encircling her sweet countenance with a glorious golden aureola. This picture struck me by its wonderful resemblance to Odile of Nideck.

I had examined this picture attentively for some minutes when another female portrait, hanging at its side, drew my attention reluctantly away. Here was a woman of the true Visigoth type, with wide low forehead, yellowish eyes, prominent cheek-bones, red hair, and a nose hooked like an eagle's beak.

That woman must have been an excellent match for Hugh, thought I, and I began to consider the costume, which answered perfectly to the energy displayed in the head, for the right hand rested upon a sword, and an iron breastplate enclosed the figure.

I have some difficulty in expressing the thoughts which passed through my mind in the examination of these three portraits. My eye passed from the one to the other with singular curiosity.

Sperver, standing at the library door, had aroused the attention of Knapwurst with a sharp whistle, which made that worthy send a glance in his direction, though it did not succeed in fetching him down from his elevation.

'Is it me that you are whistling to like a dog?' said the dwarf.

'I am, you vermin! It is an honour you don't deserve.'

'Just listen to me, Sperver,' replied the little man with sublime scorn; 'you cannot spit so high as my shoe!' which he contemptuously held out.

'Suppose I were to come up?'

'If you come up a single step I'll squash you flat with this volume!'

Gideon laughed, and replied: 'Don't get angry, friend; I don't mean to do you any harm; on the contrary, I greatly respect you for your learning; but what I want to know is what you are doing here so early in the morning, by lamp-light? You look as if you had spent the night here.'

'So I have: I have been reading all night.'

'Monsieur Knapwurst,' I began very respectfully, 'would you oblige me by enlightening me upon certain historic doubts?'

'Speak, sir, without any constraint; on the subject of family history and chronicles I am entirely at your service. Other matters don't interest me.'

'I desire to learn some particulars respecting the two portraits on each side of the founder of this race.'

'Aha!' cried Knapwurst with a glow of satisfaction lighting up his hideous features, 'you mean Hedwige and Huldine, the two wives of Hugh Lupus.'

And laying down his volume he descended from his ladder to speak more at his ease. When he had arrived at my side he bowed to me with ceremonious gravity. Sperver stood behind us, very well satisfied that I was admiring the dwarf of Nideck. In spite of the ill-luck which, in his opinion, accompanied the little monster's appearance, he respected and boasted of his superior knowledge.

'Sir,' said Knapwurst, pointing with his yellow hand to the portraits, 'Hugh of Nideck, the first of his illustrious race, married, in 832, Hedwige of Lutzelbourg, who brought to him in dowry the counties of Giromani and Haut Barr, the castles of Geroldseck, Teufelshorn, and others. Hugh Lupus had no issue by his first wife, who died young, and in rather suspicious circumstances, in the year of our Lord 837. Then Hugh, having become lord and owner of the dowry, refused to give it up, and there were terrible battles between himself and his brothers-in-law. But his second wife, Huldine, whom you see there in a steel breastplate, aided him by her sage counsel. It is unknown whence or of what family she came, but for all that she saved Hugh's life, who had been made prisoner by Frantz of Lutzelbourg. He was to have been hanged that very day, and a gibbet had already been set up on the ramparts, when Huldine, at the head of her husband's vassals, whom she had armed and inspired with her own courage, bravely broke in, released Hugh, and hung Frantz in his place. Hugh had married his wife in 842, and had three children by her.'

'So,' I resumed pensively; 'the first of these wives was called Hedwige and the descendants of Nideck are not related to her?'

'Not at all.'

'Are you quite sure?'

'I can show you our genealogical tree; Hedwige had no children; Huldine, the second wife, had three.'

'That is surprising to me.'

'Why so?'

'I thought I traced a resemblance.'

'Oho! Resemblance! Rubbish! cried Knapwurst with a

discordant laugh. 'See – look at this wooden snuff-box, in it you see a portrait of my grandfather, Hanswurst. His nose is as long and as pointed as an extinguisher, and his jaws like nutcrackers. How does that affect his being the grand-father of me – of a man with finely-formed features and an agreeable mouth?'

'Oh no! – of course not.'

'Well, so it is with the Nidecks. They may some of them be like Hedwige, but for all that Huldine is the head of their ancestry. See the genealogical tree. Now, sir, are you satis-fied?'

Then we separated – Knapwurst and I – excellent friends.

V

'Nevertheless,' thought I, 'there is the likeness. It is not chance. What is chance? There is no such thing; it is nonsense to talk of chance. It must be something higher!'

I was following my friend Sperver, deep in thought, who had now resumed his walk down the corridor. The portrait of Hedwige, in all its artless simplicity, mingled in my mind with the face of Odile.

Suddenly Gideon stopped, and, raising my eyes, I saw that we were standing before the count's door.

'Come in, Fritz,' he said, 'and I will give the dogs a feed. When the master's away the servants neglect their duty; I will come for you by-and-by.'

I entered, more desirous of seeing the young lady than her father; I was blaming myself for my remissness, but there is no controlling one's interest and affections. I was much surprised to see in the half-light of the alcove the reclining figure of the count leaning upon his elbow and observing me with profound attention. I was so little prepared for this examination that I stood rather dispossessed of self-command.

'Come nearer, *monsieur le docteur*,' he said in a weak but

firm voice, holding out his hand. 'My faithful Sperver has often mentioned your name to me; and I was anxious to make your acquaintance.'

'Let us hope, my lord, that it will be continued under more favourable circumstances. A little patience, and we shall avert this attack.'

'I think not,' he replied, 'I feel my time drawing near.'

'You are mistaken, my lord.'

'No; Nature grants us, as a last favour, to have a presentiment of our approaching end.'

'How often I have seen such presentiments falsified!' I said with a smile.

He fixed his eyes searchingly upon me, as is usual with patients expressing anxiety about their prospects.

I stood my examination firmly and successfully, and the count seemed to regain confidence; he again pressed my hand, and resigned himself calmly and confidently to my treatment.

Not until then did I perceive Mademoiselle Odile and an old lady, no doubt her governess, seated by her bedside at the other end of the alcove.

They silently saluted me, and suddenly the picture in the library reappeared before me.

'It is she,' I thought, 'Hugh's first wife. There is the fair and noble brow, there are the long lashes, and that sad, unfathomable smile.'

I was pursuing these reflections when the lord of Nideck began to speak: 'If my dear child Odile would but consult my wishes I believe my health would return.'

I looked towards the young countess; she fixed her eyes on the floor, and seemed to be praying silently.

'Yes,' the sick man went on, 'I should then return to life; the prospect of seeing myself surrounded by a young family, and of pressing grandchildren to my heart, and beholding the succession to my house, would revive me.'

At the mild and gentle tone of entreaty in which this was

said I felt deeply moved with compassion; but the young lady made no reply.

In a minute or two the count, who kept his watchful eyes upon her, went on: 'Odile, you refuse to make your father a happy man? I only ask for a faint hope. I fix no time. I won't limit your choice. We will go to court. There you will have a hundred opportunities of marrying with distinction and with honour. Who would not be proud to win my daughter's hand? You shall be perfectly free to decide for yourself.'

'My dear father,' said Odile, as if to evade any further discussion, 'you will get better. Heaven will not take you from those who love you. If you but knew the fervour with which I pray for you!'

'That is not an answer,' said the count drily. 'What objection can you make to my proposal? Is it not fair and natural? Am I to be deprived of the consolations vouchsafed to the neediest and most wretched? You know I have acted towards you openly and frankly.'

'You have, my father.'

'Then give me your reason for your refusal.'

'My resolution is formed – I have consecrated myself to God.'

The eyes of the count kindled with an ominous fire. I tried to make the young countess understand by signs how gladly I would hear her give the least hope, and calm his rising passion; but she seemed not to see me.

'So,' he cried in a smothered tone, as if he were strangling, 'so you will look on and see your father perish? A word would restore him to life, and you refuse to speak that one word?'

'Life is not in the hand of man, for it is God's gift; my word can be of no avail.'

'Those are nothing but pious maxims,' answered the count scornfully, 'to release you from your plain duty. But has not God said, "Honour thy father and thy mother?"'

'I do honour you,' she replied gently. 'But it is my duty not to marry.'

I could hear the grinding and gnashing of the man's teeth. He lay apparently calm, but presently turned abruptly and cried: 'Leave me; the sight of you is offensive to me!'

And addressing me as I stood by agitated with conflicting feelings: 'Doctor,' he cried with a savage grin, 'have you any violent malignant poison about you to give me – something that will destroy me like a thunderbolt? It would be a mercy to poison me like a dog, rather than let me suffer as I am doing.'

His features writhed convulsively, his colour became livid.

Odile rose and advanced to the door.

'Stay!' he howled furiously, 'stay till I have cursed you!'

So far I had stood by without speaking, not venturing to interfere between father and daughter, but now I could refrain no longer.

'Monseigneur,' I cried, 'for the sake of your own health, for the sake of mere justice and fairness, do calm yourself; your life is at stake.'

'What matters my life? What matters the future? Is there a knife here to put an end to me? Let me die!'

His excitement rose every minute, I seemed to dread lest in some frenzied moment he should spring from the bed and destroy his child's life. But she, calm though deadly pale, knelt at the door, which was standing open, and outside I could see Sperver, whose features betrayed the deepest anxiety. He drew near without noise, and bending towards Odile: 'Oh, *mademoiselle*!' he whispered, '*mademoiselle*, the count is such a worthy, good man. If you would but just say only, "Perhaps – by-and-by – we will see."'

She made no reply and did not change her attitude.

At this moment I persuaded the lord of Nideck to take a few drops of laudanum; he sank back with a sigh, and soon his panting and irregular breathing became more measured under the influence of a deep and heavy slumber.

Odile arose, and her aged friend, who had not opened her lips, went out with her. Sperver and I watched their slowly retreating figures. There was a calm grandeur in the step of the young countess which seemed to express a consciousness of duty fulfilled.

When she had disappeared down the long corridor Gideon turned towards me.

'Well, Fritz,' he said gravely, 'what is your opinion?'

I bent my head down without answering. This girl's incredible firmness astonished and bewildered me.

VI

Sperver's indignation was mounting.

'There's the happiness and felicity of the rich! What is the good of being master of Nideck, with castles, forests, lakes, and all the best of the Black Forest, when an innocent-looking damsel comes and says to you in her sweet soft voice, "Is that your will? Well, it is not mine. Do you say I must? Well, I say no, I won't." Is it not awful? Come on, Fritz; let us be off. I am suffocating here; I want to get into the open air.' And the good fellow, seizing my arm, dragged me down the corridor. We were going down the stairs which led into the hall, when, at a turn in the corridor, we found ourselves face to face with Tobias Offenloch, the major-domo, in a great state of palpitation.

'Halloo!' he cried, closing our way with his stick right across the passage; 'where are you off to in such a hurry? What about our breakfast?'

'Breakfast! Which breakfast do you mean?' asked Sperver.

'What do you mean by pretending to forget what breakfast? Are not you and I to breakfast this very morning with Doctor Fritz?'

'Aha! so we are! I had forgotten all about it.'

And Offenloch burst into a great laugh which divided his jolly face from ear to ear.

'Ha, ha! This is rather beyond a joke. And I was afraid of being too late! Come, let us be moving. Kasper is upstairs waiting. I ordered him to lay the breakfast in your room; I thought we should be more comfortable there. Goodbye for the present, doctor.'

'Are you not coming up with us?' asked Sperver.

'No, I am going to tell the countess that Baron de Zimmer-Bluderich begs the honour to thank her in person before he leaves the castle.'

'The Baron de Zimmer?'

'Yes, that stranger who came yesterday in the middle of the night.'

'Well, you must make haste.'

'Yes, I shall not be long. Before you have done uncorking the bottles I shall be with you again.'

And he hobbled away as fast as he could.

The mention of breakfast had given a different turn to Sperver's thoughts.

'Exactly so,' he observed, turning his back; 'the best way to drown all your cares is to drink a draught of good wine. I am very glad we are going to breakfast in my room. Here we are, Fritz. Just listen to the wind whistling through the arrow slits. In half-an-hour there will be a storm.'

He pushed the door open; Kasper seemed very glad to see us. That little man had flaxen hair and a snub nose. Sperver had made him his factotum. He now stood with a napkin over his arm, and was gravely uncorking the long-necked bottle of Rhenish.

'Kasper,' said his master, as soon as he had surveyed this satisfactory state of things, 'Kasper, I was very well pleased with you yesterday; everything was excellent. Today I am quite as well satisfied. You shall have the honour of filling our glasses. I mean to raise you step by step, for you are a very deserving fellow.'

Kasper looked down bashfully and blushed; he seemed to enjoy his master's praises.

We took our places, and were just going to attack the boar's head when Master Tobias appeared, followed by no less a personage than the Baron of Zimmer-Bluderich, attended by his groom.

We rose from our seats. The young baron advanced to meet us with head uncovered. It was a noble looking head, pale and haughty, with a surrounding of fine dark hair. He stopped before Sperver.

'*Monsieur*,' said he, 'I am come to ask you for information as to this locality. Madame la Comtesse de Nideck tells me that no one knows these mountains so well as yourself.'

'That is quite true, monseigneur, and I am at your service.'

'Circumstances of great urgency oblige me to start in the midst of the storm,' replied the baron, pointing to the window-panes thickly covered with flakes of snow. 'I must reach Wald Horn, six leagues from this place!'

'That will be a hard matter, my lord, for all the roads are blocked up with snow.'

'I am aware of that, but necessity obliges.'

'You must have a guide, then. I will go, if you will allow me, to Sébalt Kraft, the head huntsman at Nideck. He knows the mountains almost as well as I do.'

'I am obliged to you for your kind offers but still I cannot accept them. Your instructions will be quite sufficient.'

Sperver bowed, then advancing to a window, he opened it wide. A furious blast of wind rushed in, driving the whirling snow as far as the corridor, and slammed the door with a crash.

'Gentlemen,' said Sperver with a loud voice to make himself heard above the howling winds, and with arm extended, 'you see the country mapped out before you. Here you can see the peak of the Altenberg. Farther on behind that white ridge you may see the Wald Horn, beaten by a furious storm. You must make straight for the Wald Horn.

From the summit of the rock, called Roche Fendue, you will see three peaks, the Behrenkopp, the Geierstein, and the Trielfels. It is by this last one at the right that you must proceed. There is a torrent across the valley of the Rhéthal, but it must be frozen now. In any case, if you can get no further, you will find on your left, on following the bank, a cavern halfway up the hill, called Roche Creuse. You can spend the night there and tomorrow, if the wind falls, you will see the Wald Horn before you. Only be careful to go right round the base of the Behrenkopp, for you could not get down the other side. It is a precipice.'

During these observations I was watching the young baron, who was listening with the closest attention. No obstacle seemed to alarm him. The old groom seemed not less bent upon the enterprise.

Just as they were leaving the window a momentary light broke through the grey snow-clouds – just one of those moments when the eddying wind lays hold of the falling clouds of snow and flings them back again like floating garments of white. Then for a moment there was a glimpse of the distance. The three peaks stood out behind the Altenberg. The description which Sperver had given of invisible objects became visible for a few moments; then the air again was veiled in ghostly clouds of flying snow.

'Thank you,' said the Baron. 'Now I have seen the point I am to make for; and, thanks to your explanations, I hope to reach it.'

Sperver bowed without answering. The young man and his servant, having saluted us, retired slowly and gravely.

Gideon shut the window, and addressing Master Tobias and me, said: 'The deuce must be in the man to start off in such horrible weather as this. I could hardly turn out a wolf on such a day as this. However, it is their business, not mine. I seem to remember that young man's face and his servant's too. Now let us drink! Maître Tobie, your health!'

I had gone to the window, and as the Baron Zimmer and

his groom mounted on horseback in the middle of the court-yard, in spite of the snow which was filling the air, I saw at the left in a turret, pierced with long Gothic windows, the pale countenance of Odile directed long and anxiously towards the young man.

'Fritz! What are you doing?'

'I am only looking at those stranger's horses.'

'Oh, the Wallachians! I saw them this morning in the stable. They are splendid animals.'

The horsemen galloped away at full speed, and the curtain in the turret-window dropped.

VII

Several uneventful days followed. My life at Nideck was becoming dull and monotonous. Every morning there was the doleful bugle-call of the huntsman, whose occupation was gone; then came a visit to the count; after that breakfast, with Sperver's interminable speculations upon the Black Plague, the incessant gossiping and chattering of Marie Lagoutte, Maître Tobias, and all that pack of idle servants. The only man who had any kind of individual existence was Knapwurst, who sat buried up to the tip of his red nose in old chronicles all the day long, careless of the cold so long as there was anything left to find out in his curious researches.

Still the disorder of Yeri-Hans, lord of Nideck, was taking its usual course, and this gave my only occupation any serious interest. All the particulars which Sperver had made me acquainted with appeared clearly before me; sometimes the count, waking up with a start, would half rise, and supported on his elbow, with neck outstretched and haggard eyes, would mutter, 'She is coming, she is coming!'

Then Gideon would shake his head and ascend the signal-tower, but neither right nor left could the Black Plague be discovered.

After long reflection upon this strange malady I had come to the conclusion that the sufferer was insane. The strange influence that the old hag exercised over him, his alternate phases of madness and lucidity, all confirmed me in this view.

Medical men who have given especial attention to the subject of mental aberrations are well aware that periodical madness is of not infrequent occurrence. In some cases the illness appears several times in the year, in others at only particular seasons of the year.

'The Count of Nideck is suffering from such an attack,' I said; 'unknown chains unite his fate with that of the Black Plague. Who can tell?' thought I; 'that woman once was young, perhaps beautiful!'

And my imagination, once launched, carried me into the interesting regions of romance; but I was careful to tell no one what I thought. If I had opened out those conjectures to Sperver he would never have forgiven me for imagining that there could have been any intimacy between his master and the Black Plague; and as for Mademoiselle Odile, I dared not suggest insanity to her.

The poor young lady was evidently most unhappy. Her refusal to marry had so embittered the count against her that he could scarcely endure to have her in his presence. He bitterly reproached her with her ingratitude and disobedience, and expatiated upon the cruelty of ungrateful children. Sometimes even violent curses followed his daughter's visits. Things at last were so bad that I thought myself obliged to interfere. I therefore waited one evening on the countess in the ante-chamber and entreated her to relinquish her personal attendance upon her father. But here arose contrary to all expectations, quite an unforeseen obstacle. In spite of all my entreaties she steadily insisted on watching by her father and nursing him as she had done hitherto.

'It is my duty,' she repeated, 'and no arguments will shake my purpose,' she said firmly.

'Madam,' I replied as a last effort, 'the medical profession, too, has its duties, and an honourable man must fulfil them even to harshness and cruelty; your presence is killing your father.'

I shall remember all my life the sudden change in the expression of the face of Odile.

My solemn words of warning seemed to cause the blood to flow back to the heart; her face became white as marble, and her large blue eyes, fixed steadily upon mine, seemed to read into the most secret recesses of my soul.

'Is that possible, sir?' she stammered; 'upon your honour, do you declare this? Tell me truly!'

'Yes, madam, upon my honour.'

There was a long and painful silence, only broken at last by these words in a low voice: 'Let God's will be done!'

And with downcast eyes she withdrew.

The day after this scene about eight in the morning, I was pacing up and down in Hugh Lupus's tower, thinking of the count's illness, of which I could not foretell the issue, when three discreet taps upon my door turned my thoughts into another channel.

'Come in!'

The door opened, and Marie Lagoutte stood within, dropping me a low curtsey.

This old dame's visit put me out, and I was going to beg her to postpone her visit, when something mysterious in her countenance caught my attention. She had thrown over her shoulders a red-and-green shawl; she was biting her lips, with her head down, and as soon as she had closed the door she opened it again, and peeped out, to make sure that no one had followed her. I was quite puzzled.

'*Monsieur le docteur*,' said the worthy lady, advancing towards me, 'I beg your pardon for disturbing you so early in the morning, but I have a very serious thing to tell you.'

'Pray tell me all about it, then.'

'It is the count.'

'Indeed!'

'Yes, sir, you know that I sat up with him last night.'

'I know. Pray sit down.'

She sat before me in a great armchair. 'Doctor,' she resumed, with her dark eyes upon me, 'you know I am not timid or easily frightened. I have seen so many dreadful things in the course of my life that I am astonished at nothing now.'

'I am sure of that, ma'am.'

'Well,' the good woman resumed, 'last night, between nine and ten, just as I was going to bed, Offenloch came in and said to me, "Marie, you will have to sit up with the count tonight." At first I felt surprised. "What! Is not *mademoiselle* going to sit up?" "No, *mademoiselle* is poorly, and you will have to take her place." Poor girl, she is ill; I knew that would be the end of it, I told her so a hundred times. So I took my knitting, said good night to Tobias, and went into monseigneur's room. Sperver was there waiting for me, and went to bed; so there I was, all alone.

'About half-past ten,' she went on, 'I was sitting near the bed, and from time to time drew the curtain to see what the count was doing; he made no movement; he was sleeping as quietly as a child. It was all right until eleven o'clock, then I began to feel tired. I did not think anything was going to happen, and I said to myself, "He is sure to sleep till daylight." About twelve the wind went down; the big windows had been rattling, but now they were quiet. I got up to see if anything was stirring outside. It was all as black as ink; so I came back to my armchair. I took another look at the patient; I saw that he had not stirred an inch, and I took up my knitting, but in a few minutes more I began nodding, nodding, and I dropped right off to sleep. I had been asleep an hour, I suppose, when a sharp current of wind woke me up. I opened my eyes, and what do you think I saw? The tall middle window was wide open, the curtains were drawn, and there in the opening stood the count in his white night-dress, right on the window-sill.'

'The count?'

'Yes.'

'Nay, it is impossible; he cannot move!'

'So I thought too; but that is just how I saw him. He was standing with a torch in his hand; the night was so dark and the air so still that the flame stood quite straight.'

I gazed upon Marie with astonishment.

'First of all,' she said, after a moment's silence, 'to see that long, thin man standing there with his bare legs, I can assure you it had such an effect upon me! I wanted to scream; but then I thought, "Perhaps he is walking in his sleep; if I shout he will wake up, he will jump down, and then—" So I did not say a word, but I stared and stared till I saw him lift up his torch in the air over his head, then he lowered it, then up again and down again, and he did this three times, just like a man making signals; then he threw it down upon the ramparts, shut the window, drew the curtains, passed before me without speaking, and got into bed muttering some words I could not make out.'

'Are you sure you saw all that, ma'am?'

'Quite sure.'

'Well it is strange.'

'I know it is; but it is true. Ah! it did astonish me at first, and then when I saw him get into bed again and cross his hands over his breast just as if nothing had happened, I said to myself, "Marie, you have had a bad dream; it cannot be true;" and so I went to the window, and there I saw the torch still burning; it had fallen into a bush near the third gate, and there it was shining just like a spark of fire. There was no denying it.'

Marie Lagoutte looked at me a few moments without speaking.

'You may be sure, doctor, that after that I had no more sleep; I sat watching and ready for anything. Every moment I fancied I could hear something behind the armchair. I was not afraid – it was not that – but I was uneasy and restless. When morning came, very early I ran and woke Offenloch and sent him to the count. Passing down the corridor I noticed that there was no torch in the first ring, and I came down and found it near the narrow path to the Schwartzwald; there it is!'

And the good woman took from under her apron the end of a torch, which she threw upon the table.

I was confounded.

How had that man, whom I had seen the night before feeble and exhausted, been able to rise, walk, lift up, and close down that heavy window? What was the meaning of that signal by night? I seemed to myself to witness this strange, mysterious scene, and my thoughts went at once to the Black Plague. When I aroused myself from this contemplation of my own thoughts, I saw Marie Lagoutte rising and preparing to go.

'You have done quite right,' I said as I took her to the door, 'to tell me of these things, and I am much obliged to you. Have you told any one else of this adventure?'

'No one, sir, such things are only told to the priest and the doctor.'

'I see you are a very wise, sensible woman.'

These words were exchanged at the door of my tower. At this moment Sperver appeared at the end of the gallery, followed by his friend Sébalt.

'Fritz!' he shouted, 'I have got news to tell you.'

'Oh come!' thought I, 'more news! This is a strange condition of things.'

Marie Lagoutte had disappeared, and the huntsman and his friend entered the tower.

VIII

On the countenance of Sperver was an expression of suppressed wrath, on that of his companion bitter irony.

'Yes,' cried Sperver, 'I have got strange things to tell you.'

He threw himself in a chair, seizing his head between his clenched hands, while dismal Sébalt calmly drew his horn over his head and laid it on the table.

'Now Sébalt,' cried Gideon, 'speak out.'

'The witch is hanging about the castle.'

This piece of intelligence would have failed to interest me before seeing Marie Lagoutte, but now it struck me forcibly. There certainly was some mysterious connection between the lord of Nideck and that old woman.

'Just wait a moment, friends,' said I to Sperver and his comrade. 'I want to know, first of all, where does this Black Pest come from?'

Sperver stared at me with astonishment.

'Come from? Who can tell that?'

'Very well, you can't. But when does she come within sight of Nideck?'

'As I told you, ten days before Christmas, at the same time every year.'

'And how long does she stay?'

'A fortnight or three weeks.'

'Is she ever seen before? not even on her way? nor after?'

'No.'

'Then we shall have to catch her, seize her,' I cried. 'This is contrary to nature. We must find out where she comes from, what she wants here, what she is.'

'Lay hold of her!' exclaimed Sperver; 'seize her! Do you mean it?' and he shook his head. 'Fritz, your advice is good enough in its way, but it is easier said than done. I could very easily send a bullet after her, but the count won't consent to that measure; and as for catching in any other way than by powder and shot, why, you had better go first and catch a squirrel by the tail! Listen to Sébalt's story, and you shall judge for yourself.'

The master of the hounds, sitting on the table with his legs crossed, fixed his eyes mournfully upon me, and began his tale.

'This morning, as I was coming down from the Altenberg, I followed the road to Nideck. The snow filled it up entirely. I was going on my way, thinking of nothing particular, when I noticed a foot-track; it was deep down, and went across the road. The person had come down the bank and gone up on the other side. It was the very track of the Black Pest! I know the old woman by her foot better than by her figure, for I always go, sir, with my eyes on the ground. I know everybody by their tracks; and as for this one, a child might know it.'

'What, then, distinguishes this foot so particularly?'

'It is so small that you could cover it with your hand; it is finely shaped, the heel is rather long, the outline clean, the great toe lies close to the other toes, and they are all as fine as if they were in a lady's slipper. It is a lovely foot. Twenty years ago I should have fallen in love with a foot like that. Whenever I come across it, it has such an effect on me! No one would believe that such a foot could belong to the Black Plague.

'Well, I recognised that track and started off in pursuit. I was hoping to catch the creature in her lair, but I will tell you the way she took me. I climbed up the bank by the roadside, only two gunshots from Nideck. I go along the hill, keeping the track on my right; it led along the side of the wood in the Rhéthal. All at once it jumps over the ditch into the wood. I struck to it, but, happening to look a little to my left, I saw another track which had been following the Black Plague. I stopped short; was it Sperver's? or Kasper Trumpf's? or whose? I came to it, and you may fancy how astounded I was when I saw that it was nobody from our place! I know every foot in the Schwartzwald from Fribourg to Nideck. That foot was like none of ours. It must have come from a distance. The boot – for it was a kind of well-made, soft gentleman's boot, with spurs, which leave a little print behind them – the boot was not round at the toes, but square. The sole was thin, and bent with every step, and it had no nails in it. The walk was rapid, and the short steps were like those of a young man of twenty to five-and-twenty.'

'Who can this be?' Sperver exclaimed.

Sébalt raised his shoulders and extended his hands, but said nothing.

'Who can have any object in following the old woman?' I asked

'No one on earth can tell,' was the reply.

'I kept following the track; it went up the next ridge through the pine-forest. When it doubled round the Roche Fendue I said to myself, "Ah, you accursed plague! if there were much game of your sort there would not be much sport." So we all three arrived – the two tracks and I – at the top of the Schnéeberg. There the wind had been blowing hard; the snow was knee-deep. I got to the edge of the torrent of the Steinbach, and there I lost the track. I halted, and I saw that after trying up and down in several directions, the gentleman's boots had gone down the Tiefenbach. That was a bad sign. I looked along the other side of the torrent, but there was no appearance of a track there – none at all! The old hag had paddled up and down the stream to throw any one off the scent who should try to follow her. Where was I to go to? – right, or left, or straight on? Not knowing, I came back to Nideck.'

'You haven't told us about her breakfast,' said Sperver.

'No, I was forgetting. At the foot of Roche Fendue I saw there had been a fire; there was a black place; but it was as cold as ice. Close by I saw a wire trap in the bushes. It seems the creature knows how to snare game. A hare had been caught in it; the print of its body was still plain, lying flat in the snow. The witch had lighted the fire to cook it.'

At this Sperver cried indignantly: 'Just fancy that old witch living on meat while so many honest folks in our villages have nothing better than potatoes to eat! That's what upsets me, Fritz! Ah! if I had but—'

But his thoughts remained untold; he turned deadly pale,

and all three of us, in a moment, stood rigid and motionless, staring with horror at each other's ghastly countenances.

A yell – the howling cry of the wolf in the long, cold days of winter – the most fearful and harrowing of all bestial sounds – that fearful cry was echoing through the castle not far from us! It rose up the spiral staircase, it filled the massive building as if the hungry, savage beast was at our door!

Travellers speak of the deep roar of the lion troubling the silence of the night amidst the rocky deserts of Africa; but the vast snowy deserts of the North too have their characteristic cry – a strange, lamentable yell that seems to suit the character of the dreary winter scene. That voice of the Northern desert is the howl of the wolf!

The instant after this awful sound had broken upon the silence followed another formidable body of discordant sounds – the baying and yelling of sixty hounds – answering from the ramparts of Nideck. The whole pack gave voice at the same moment and, dominating over all, the long, dismal, prolonged note of the wolf's monotonous howl; his was the leading part in this horrible concert!

Sperver sprang from his seat and turning to us he cried: 'Fritz! Sébalt! – come, come quickly!'

We flew down the steps four at a time and rushed into the fencing-school. Here we heard the cry of the wolf alone, prolonged beneath the echoing arches; the distant barking and yelling of the pack became almost inaudible in the distance; the dogs were hoarse with rage and excitement, their chains were getting entangled together.

Sperver drew the keen blade of his hunting-knife. Sébalt did the same; they preceded me down the gallery.

Then the fearful sounds became our guide to the sick man's room. Sperver spoke no more; he hurried forward. Sébalt stretched his long legs. I felt a shuddering horror creep through my whole frame – a horrible presentiment of something shocking and abominable came over us.

As we approached the apartments of the count we met

the whole household afoot – gamekeepers, huntsmen, kennel-keepers, scullions were all mingled and jostling each other, asking: 'What is the matter? Where are those cries coming from?'

Without stopping we ran into the passage which led into the count's bedroom, where we met poor Marie Lagoutte, who alone had had the courage to penetrate thither before us. She was holding in her arms the young countess, who had fainted; she was carrying her away as fast as she could.

At last we had reached the count's chamber. The howling came from behind his door. We stole fearful glances at one another without attempting to account for the hideous noise, or explaining the presence of such a wild guest in the house.

Sperver hastily pushed the door open, and, knife in hand, was darting into the room; but he stood arrested on the threshold, motionless as a stone.

Never have I seen a picture of horror as he displayed standing there, his eyes starting from his head, and his mouth wide open and gasping for breath. I gazed over his shoulder, and the sight that met my eyes made the blood run chill as snow in my veins.

The lord of Nideck, crouching on all fours upon his bed, with his arms bending forward, his head carried low, his eyes glaring with fierce fires, was uttering loud protracted howlings!

He was the wolf!

That low receding forehead, that sharp-pointed face, that foxy-looking beard, bristling off both cheeks; the long meagre figure, the sinewy limbs, the face, the cry, the attitude, declared the presence of the wild beast half-hidden, half-revealed under a human mask!

At times he would stop for a second and listen attentively with head awry, and then the crimson hangings would tremble with the quivering of his limbs, like foliage shaken by the wind; then the melancholy wail would open afresh.

Sperver, Sébalt, and I stood nailed to the floor; we held our breath, petrified with fear.

Suddenly, the count stopped. As a wild beast scents the wind, he lifted his head and listened again.

There, there, far away, down among the thick fir-forests, whitened with dense patches of snow, a cry was heard in reply – weak at first; then the sound rose and swelled in a long protracted howl, drowning the feebler efforts of the hounds: it was the she-wolf answering the wolf!

Sperver, turning round awe-stricken, his countenance pale as ashes, pointed to the mountain, and murmured low: 'Listen – there's the witch!'

And the count still crouching motionless, but with his head now raised in the attitude of attention, his neck outstretched, his eyes burning, seemed to understand the meaning of that distant voice, and a kind of fearful joy gleamed in his savage features.

At this moment, Sperver, unable or unwilling to restrain himself any longer, cried in a voice broken with emotion: 'Count – what are you doing?'

The count fell back thunderstruck. We rushed into the room to help. It was time. The third attack had commenced, and it was terrible to witness!

IX

The lord of Nideck was dying. What can science do in presence of the great mortal strife between Death and Life? At the supreme hour when the invisible wrestlers are writhed together body to body and limb to limb, panting, each in turn overthrowing and overthrown, what avails the healing art? One can but watch, and tremble, and listen!

Towards midnight the Count of Nideck seemed almost gone; the agony of death was at hand; the broken, weakened pulse indicated the sinking of the vital powers; then it might return to a more active state but there seemed no hope.

My only duty left was to stay and see this unhappy man die. I was exhausted with fatigue and anxiety; whatever art could do I had tried.

I told Sperver to sit up, and if need be close his master's eyes in death. The poor faithful fellow was in the utmost distress; he reproached himself with his involuntary cry: 'Count – what are you doing?' and tore his hair in bitter repentance.

I went away alone to Hugh Lupus's tower, having had scarcely any time to take food, but I did not feel the want of it.

There was a bright fire on the hearth; I threw myself dressed upon the bed, and sleep soon came to relieve my weight of apprehension.

I was sleeping with my face turned towards the fire, and as it often happens, the flame fitfully rising and falling threw a fluttering, flickering light like those of ruddy flapping wings against the walls, and wearied still more my dropping eyelids.

Lost in a dreamy slumber, I was half opening my eyes to see the cause of these alternate lights and shadows, when the strangest sight surprised me.

Close by the hearth, hardly revealed by the feeble light of a few dying embers, I recognised with dismay the dark profile of the Black Plague! She sat upon a low stool, and was evidently warming herself.

At first I thought myself deceived by my senses, which would have been natural enough after the exciting scenes of the last few days; I raised myself upon my elbow, gazing with my eyes starting with fear and horror.

It was she indeed! I lay horrified, for there she sat calm and immovable, with her hands clasped over her skinny knees, just as I had seen her in the snow, with her long scraggy neck outstretched, her hooked nose, her compressed lips.

How had the Black Pest got here? How had she found her way into this high tower crowning the dangerous precipices? Everything that Sperver had told me of this mysterious being seemed to be coming true! And now the unaccountable behaviour of Lieverlé, growling so fiercely against the wall, seemed clear as the daylight. I huddled myself close up into the alcove, hardly daring to breathe, and staring upon this motionless profile.

The old woman stirred no more than the rock-hewn pillars on each side of the hearthstone, and her lips were mumbling inarticulate sounds.

My heart was palpitating, my fears increased momentarily during the long silence, made more startling by the motionless supernatural figure that sat there before me.

This had lasted a quarter of an hour when, the fire catching a splinter of fir-wood, a flash of light broke out, the shaving twisted and flamed, and a few rays of light flared to the end of the room.

That luminous jet was sufficient to show me that the creature was clothed in an old dress of rich purple silk as stiff as cardboard, with a violet pattern; there was a massive bracelet upon her left wrist, and a gold arrow stuck through her thick grey hair twisted over the back of her head. It was like an apparition out of the ages past.

Still the Plague could have had no hostile intentions towards me, or she might easily have taken advantage of my sleep to have put them in execution.

That thought was beginning to give me some confidence, when suddenly she rose from her seat and with slow steps approached my bed, holding in her hand a torch which she had just lighted. I then observed that her eyes were fixed and haggard.

I made an effort to rise and cry aloud, but not a muscle of my body would obey my wishes, not a breath came to my lips; and the old woman, bending over me between the curtains, fixed her stony stare upon me with a strange unearthly smile. I wanted to call for help, I wanted to drive her from me, but her petrifying stare seemed to fascinate and paralyse me, just as that of the serpent fixed the little bird motionless before it.

Suddenly she turned her head, went round upon her heel, listened, strode across the room, and opened the door.

At last I recovered a little courage; an effort of will brought me to my feet; I darted after her footsteps; she with one hand was holding her torch on high, and with the other kept the door open.

I was about to seize her by the hair, when at the end of the long gallery, under the Gothic archway of the castle leading to the ramparts, I saw – a tall figure.

It was the Count of Nideck! The Count, whom I had thought a dying man, clad in a huge wolf-skin thrown with its upper jaw projecting grimly over his eyes like a visor, the formidable claws hanging over each shoulder, and the tail dragging behind him along the flags.

He wore stout heavy shoes, a silver clasp gathered the wolf-skin round his neck, and his whole aspect, but for the ice-cold deathly expression of his face, proclaimed the man born for command – the master!

I had the presence of mind to throw myself into the embrasure of the window.

The count entered my room with his eyes fixed on the old woman and his features unrelaxed. They spoke to one another in hoarse whispers, so low that I could not distinguish a word. But there was no mistaking their gestures. The woman was pointing to the bed.

They approached the fireplace on tiptoe. There in the dark shadow of the recess at its side the Black Plague, with a horrible smile, unrolled a large bag.

As soon as the count saw the bag he made a bound towards the bed and kneeled upon it with one knee; there was a shaking of the curtains, his body disappeared beneath their folds, and I could only see one leg still resting on the floor, and the wolf's tail undulating irregularly from side to side.

They seemed to be acting a murder in ghastly pantomime. No real scene, however frightful, could have agitated me more than this mute representation of some horrible deed.

Then the old woman ran to his assistance, carrying the bag with her. Again the curtains shook and the shadows crossed the walls, but the most horrible of all was that I fancied I saw a pool of blood creeping across the floor and slowly reaching the hearth. But it was only the snow that had clung to the count's boots, and was melting in the heat.

I was still gazing upon this dark stream, feeling my dry tongue cleave to the roof of my mouth, when there was a great movement; the old woman and the count were stuffing the sheets of the bed into the sack, they were thrusting and stamping them in with just the same haste as a dog scratching at a hole, then the lord of Nideck flung this unshapely bundle over his shoulder and made for the door; a sheet was dragging behind him, and the old woman followed him torch in hand. They went across the court.

My knees were almost giving way under me; they knocked together for fear. I prayed for strength.

In a couple of minutes I was on their footsteps, dragged forward by a sudden irresistible impulse.

I crossed the court at a run, and was just going to enter the door of the tower when I perceived a deep but narrow pit at my feet, down which went a winding staircase, and there far below I could see the torch describing a spiral course around the stone rail like a little star; at last it was lost in the distance.

Now I also descended the first steps of this newly discovered staircase, directing my course after this distant light; suddenly it vanished. The old woman and the count had reached the bottom of the precipice.

Soon I came to the last step; I looked around me and discovered a narrow streak of moonlight shining under a low door, I kicked a way through these obstacles, clearing the snow away with my feet, and then found that I was at the very foot of the keep – Hugh's donjon tower.

Who would have supposed that such a hole would have led up into the castle? Who had shown it to the old woman?

The vast plain lay spread before me bathed in a light almost equal to that of day. On the right lay extended wide the dark line of the Black Forest with its craggy rocks, its gullies, its passes stretching away as far as the sight could reach.

The night air was keen and sharp, but perfectly calm, and I felt myself awakened to the highest degree.

My first examination of the horizon was for the figures of the count and his strange companion. I soon distinguished their tall dark forms standing out sharply against the star-spangled purple heavens. I nearly overtook them at the bottom of the ravine.

The count was moving with deliberate steps, the imaginary winding-sheet dragging slowly after him. There was an automatic precision in the movements of both.

I kept six or eight yards behind them down the hollow road to the Altenberg, now in the shade, now in the full light, for the moon was shining with astonishing brilliancy.

I could have wished to turn back, but some invisible power impelled me onwards to follow this funeral procession in pantomime. Even to this day I fancy still I can see the rough mountain path through the Black Forest, I can hear the crisp snow crackling under foot, and the dead leaves rustling in the light north wind; I can see myself following those two silent beings, but I cannot understand what mysterious power drew me in their footsteps.

At last we reached the forest, and advanced amongst the tall bare-branched beeches.

Sometimes I fancied I could hear steps behind me; I turned sharply round but could see no one.

We had just reached the long rocky ridge that forms the

crest of the Altenberg; behind it flows the torrent of the
Schnéeberg, but in winter no current is visible; scarcely does
a mere thread of its blue waters trickle under the thick crust
of ice. Here the deep solitude is broken by no murmuring
brooks, no warblings of birds, no thunder of the waterfall.
In the vast unbroken solitudes the awful silence is terrible.

The Count of Nideck and the old woman found a gap in
the face of the rock, up which they mounted straight with
marvellous celerity, whilst I had to pull myself up by the
help of the bushes.

Hardly had they reached the ridge of the crags, which
came almost to a point, when I was within three yards of
them, and I beheld beyond a dreadful precipice of which I
could not see the bottom. At the left hung in the air like a
vast sheet the fall of the Schnéeberg, a mass of ice. That
resemblance to an immense wave taking the precipice at
one bound, that mere semblance of movement amidst the
stillness and immovableness of death, and the presence of
those two speechless creatures pursuing their ghastly work
with automatic precision, added to the terror with which I
already trembled.

The count had laid down his burden; the old woman and
he took it up together, swung it for a moment over the edge
of the precipice, then the long shroud floated over the abyss,
and the imaginary murderers in silence bent forward to see
it fall.

That long white sheet floating in the air is still present
before my eyes.

The white burden disappeared in the dark depths of the
precipice. At last the cloud which had long been threatening
to cover the moon's bright disc veiled her and her rays ceased
to shine.

The old woman, holding the count by the hand and
dragging him forward with hurried steps, came for a moment
into view.

The cloud had overshadowed the moon, and I could not

move out of their way without danger of falling over the precipice.

After a few minutes, during which I lay as close as I could, there was a rift in the cloud. I looked out again. I stood alone on the point of the peak with the snow up to my knees.

Full of horror and apprehension, I descended from my perilous position, and ran to the castle in as much consternation as if I had been guilty of some great crime.

As for the lord of Nideck and his companion, I lost sight of them.

X

I wandered around the castle of Nideck unable to find the exit from which I had commenced my melancholy journey. Lost in the snow, I ran to and fro panting and alarmed, and unable to judge which way to direct my steps.

At last, exhausted, my beard a mass of ice, my ears nearly frost-bitten, I discovered the gate and rang the bell with all my might.

It was then about four in the morning. Knapwurst made me wait a terribly long time. His little lodge cut in the rock remained silent; I thought the little humpbacked wretch would never have done dressing; for of course I supposed he would be in bed and asleep.

I rang again.

This time his grotesque figure appeared abruptly, and he cried to me from the door in a fury: 'Who are you?'

'I? – Doctor Fritz.'

'Oh, that alters the case,' and he went back into his lodge for a lantern, crossed the outer court where the snow came up to his middle, and staring at me through the grating, he exclaimed: 'I beg your pardon, Doctor Fritz; I thought you would be asleep up there in Hugh Lupus's tower. Were *you* ringing? Now that explains why Sperver came to me about midnight to ask if anybody had gone out. I said no, which was quite true, for I never saw you going out.'

'But pray, Monsieur Knapwurst, do for pity's sake let me in, and I will tell you about that by-and-by.'

'Come, come, sir, a little patience.'

And the hunchback, with the slowest deliberation, undid the padlock and slipped the bars, whilst my teeth were chattering, and I stood shivering from head to foot.

'You are very cold, doctor,' said the diminutive man, 'and you cannot get into the castle. Sperver has fastened the inside door, I don't know why; he does not usually do so; the outer gate is enough. Come in here and get warm. You won't find my little hole very inviting, though. It is nothing but a sty, but when a man is as cold as you are he is not apt to be particular.'

Without replying to his chatter I followed him in as quickly as I could.

We went into the hut, and in spite of my complete state of numbness, I could not help admiring the state of picturesque disorder in which I found the place.

The whole edifice consisted of but one apartment, furnished with a very uninviting bed, which the dwarf did not often take the trouble to make, and two small windows with hexagonal panes, weather-stained with the rainbow tints of mother-of-pearl. A large square table filled up the middle, and it would be difficult to account for the massive oak slab being got in unless by supposing it to have been there before the hut was built.

On shelves against the wall were rolls of parchment, and old books great and small. Wide open on the table lay a fine black-letter volume, bound in vellum, clasped and cornered with silver. Besides there was nothing but two leathern armchairs, bearing on them the unmistakable impression of the misshapen figure of this learned gentleman.

I need not stay to do more than mention the small cast-iron stove, with its low, open door wide open, and throwing out now and then a volley of bright sparks; and to complete the picture, the cat arching her back, and spitting threateningly at me with her armed paw uplifted.

'So you went out last night, doctor?' inquired my host, after we had both installed ourselves, and while I had my hands in a warm place upon the stove.

'Yes, pretty early,' I answered. 'I had to look after a patient.'

This brief explanation seemed to satisfy the little hunchback, and he lighted his blackened boxwood pipe, which was hanging over his chin.

'You don't smoke, doctor?'

'I beg your pardon, I do.'

'Well, fill any one of these pipes. I was here,' he said, spreading his yellow hand over the open volume. 'I was reading the chronicles of Hertzog when you came.'

'Ah, that accounts for the time I had to wait! Of course you stayed to finish the chapter?' I said, smiling.

He owned it, grinning, and we both laughed together.

'But if I had known it was you,' he said, 'I should have finished the chapter another time.'

There was a short silence, during which I was observing the very peculiar physiognomy of this misshapen being – those long deep wrinkles that moated in his wide mouth, his small eyes with the crow's feet at the outer corners, that contorted nose, bulbous at its end, and especially that huge double-storeyed forehead of his. The whole figure reminded me not a little of the received pictures of Socrates.

The snow was melting away from my legs, the balmy warmth of the stove was shedding a pleasant influence over my feelings, and I felt myself reviving in this mixed atmosphere of tobacco smoke and burning pine wood.

Knapwurst gravely laid his pipe on the table, and reverently spreading his hand upon the folio, said in a voice that seemed to issue from the bottom of his consciousness: 'Doctor Fritz, here is the law of the prophets!'

'How so? What do you mean?'

'Parchment – old parchment – that is what I love! These old yellow, rusty, worm-eaten leaves are all that is left to us of the past, from the days of Charlemagne until this day. The oldest families disappear, the old parchments remain. Where would be the glory of the Hohenstauffens, the Leiningens, the Nidecks, and so many families of renown? Where would be the fame of their titles, their deeds of arms, their magnificent armour, their expeditions to the Holy Land, their alliances, their claims to remote antiquity, their conquests once complete, now long ago annulled? Where would be all those grand claims to historic fame without these parchments? Nowhere at all.

'All in those distant times, while knights and squires rode out to war, and fought and conquered or fought and fell over the possession of a nook in a forest, or a title, or a smaller matter still, with what scorn and contempt did they not look down upon the wretched little scribbler, the man of mere letters and jargon, half-clothed in untanned hides, his only weapon an inkhorn at his belt, his pennon the feather of a goosequill! How they laughed at him, calling him an atom or a flea, good for nothing! Well, what has happened? That flea has kept them in the memory of men longer than their castles stood, long after their arms and their armour had rusted in the ground. I love those old parchments. I respect and revere them. Like ivy, they clothe the ruins and keep the ancient walls from crumbling into dust and perishing in oblivion!'

Having thus delivered himself, a solemn expression stole over his features, and his own eloquence made the tears of moved affection to steal down his furrowed cheeks.

I was surprised, and said, 'Monsieur Knapwurst, do you know Latin?'

'Yes, sir,' he answered, but without conceit, 'both Latin and Greek. I taught myself. The count, hearing me drop a Latin quotation once, was astonished and said, "When did you learn Latin, Knapwurst?' 'I taught myself, monseig-neur.' He asked me a few questions, to which I gave pretty good answers. '*Parbleu!*' he cried, 'Knapwurst knows more than I do; he shall keep my records.' So he gave me the keys of the archives; that was thirty years ago. Since that time I have read every word.'

'So he is a very good master, is he?'

'Oh, Doctor Fritz, he is the kindest-hearted master!' cried the dwarf, with hands clasped. 'He has but one fault. He has no ambition. Why, he might have been anything he pleased. Think of a Nideck, one of the very noblest families in Germany! He had but to ask to be made a minister or a field-marshal. Well! he desired nothing of the sort. When he was no longer a young man he retired from political life. Except that he was in the campaign in France at the head of a regiment he raised at his own expense, he has always lived far away from noise and battle; plain and simple, and almost unknown, he seemed to think of nothing but his hunting.'

These details were deeply interesting to me. The conver-sation was of its own accord taking just the turn I wished it to take.

'So the count has never had any exciting deeds in hand?'

'None, Doctor Fritz, none whatever; and that is a pity. A noble excitement is the glory of great families. It is a misfor-tune for a noble race when a member of it is devoid of ambition; he allows his family to sink below its level.'

I was astonished; for all my theories upon the count's past life were falling to the earth.

'Still, Monsieur Knapwurst, the lord of Nideck has had great sorrows, has he not?'

'Such as what?'

'The loss of his wife.'

'Yes, you are right there; his wife was an angel; he married her for love. She was a Zaân, one of the oldest and best nobility of Alsace, but a family ruined by the Revolution.

The Countess Odile was the delight of her husband. She died of a decline which carried her off after five years' illness. Every plan was tried to save her life. They travelled in Italy together but she returned worse than she went, and died a few weeks after their return. The count was almost broken-hearted, and for two years he shut himself up and would see no one. Time at last calmed his grief, but there is always a remainder of grief,' said the hunchback, pointing with his finger to his heart; 'you understand very well, there is still a bleeding wound. The count would not marry again; all his love is given to his daughter.'

'So the marriage was a happy one throughout?'

'Happy! Why it was a blessing for everybody.'

I said no more. It was plain that the count had not committed, and could not have committed, a crime. I was obliged to yield to evidence. But, then, what was the meaning of that scene at night, that strange connection with the Black Pest, that fearful acting, that remorse in a dream, which impelled the guilty to betray their past atrocities? I lost myself in vain conjectures.

By that time the icy numbness which had laid hold of me had nearly passed away, and I was enjoying that pleasant sense of relief which follows great fatigue when by the chimney corner in a comfortable easy-chair, veiled in wreaths of tobacco smoke, you yield to the luxury of repose.

So we sat for a quarter of an hour.

At last I ventured to remark: 'But sometimes the count gets angry with his daughter?'

Knapwurst started, and fixing a sinister, almost a fierce and hostile eye upon me, answered: 'I know, I know!'

I watched him narrowly, thinking I might learn something now in support of my theory, but he simply added ironically: 'The towers of Nideck are high, and slander flies too low to reach their elevation!'

'No doubt; but still it is a fact, is it not?'

'Oh yes, so it is; but after all it is only a craze, an effect of his complaint. As soon as the crisis is past all his love for *mademoiselle* comes back. I assure you, sir, that a lover of twenty could not be more devoted, more affectionate, than he is. That young girl is his pride and his joy. A dozen times have I seen him riding away to get a dress, or flowers, or what not, for her. He went off alone, and brought back the articles in triumph, blowing his horn. He would have entrusted so delicate a commission to no one, not even to Sperver, whom he is so fond of. Mademoiselle never dares express a wish in his hearing lest he should start off and fulfil it at once. The lord of Nideck is the worthiest master, the tenderest father, and the kindest and most upright of men. Those poachers who are for ever infesting our woods, the old Count Ludwig would have strung them up without mercy; our count winks at them; he even turns them into gamekeepers. Look at Sperver! Why, if count Ludwig was alive, Sperver's bones would long ago have been rattling in chains; instead of which he is head huntsman at the castle.'

All my theories were now in a state of disorganisation. I laid my head between my hands and thought a long while. Knapwurst, supposing that I was asleep, had turned to his folio again.

The grey dawn was now peeping in, and the lamp turning pale. Indistinct voices were audible in the castle. Suddenly there was a noise of hurried steps outside, I saw some one pass before the window, the door opened abruptly, and Gideon appeared at the threshold.

XI

Sperver's pale face and glowing eyes announced that events were on the move. Yet he was calm, and did not seem surprised at my presence in Knapwurst's room.

'Fritz,' he said briefly, 'I am come to fetch you.'

I rose without answering and followed him. Scarcely were

we out of the hut when he took me by the arm and drew me on to the castle.

'Mademoiselle Odile wants to see you,' he whispered.

'What! Is she ill?'

'No, she is much better, but something strange is going on. This morning about one o'clock, thinking that the count was nearly breathing his last, I went to wake the countess; with my hand on the bell my heart failed me. "Why should I break her heart?" I said to myself. "She will learn her misfortune only too soon; and then to wake her up in the middle of the night, weak and frail as she is, after such shocks, might kill her at a stroke." I resolved I would take it all on myself. I returned to the count's room. I looked in – not a soul was there! Impossible! the man was in the last agonies of death. I ran into the corridor like a madman. No one was there! Into the long gallery – no one! I lost my presence of mind, and rushing again into the young countess's room, I rang again. This time she appeared, crying out: 'Is my father dead?" "No." "Has he disappeared?" "Yes, madam. I had gone out for a minute – when I came in again—" "And Doctor Fritz, where is he?" "In Hugh Lupus's tower." "In *that* tower?" She started. She threw a dressing-gown around her, took her lamp, and went out. I stayed behind. A quarter of an hour after she came back, her feet covered with snow, pale and cold! She set her lamp upon the chimney-piece and looked at me fixedly, said: "Was it you who put the doctor into that tower?" "Yes, madam." "Unhappy man! you will never know the extent of the harm you have done." I was about to answer, but she interrupted me: "No more; go and fasten every door and lie down. I will sit up. Tomorrow morning you will find Doctor Fritz at Knapwurst's, and bring him to me. Make no noise, and mind, you have seen nothing and know nothing!"'

'Is that all, Sperver?' I asked.

He nodded gravely.

'And about the count?'

'He is in again. He is better.'

We had got to the antechamber. Gideon knocked at the door gently, then he opened it, announcing: 'Doctor Fritz.'

I took a pace forward, and stood in the presence of Odile. Sperver retired, closing the door.

A strange impression crossed my mind at the sight of the young countess standing pale and still, leaning upon the back of an armchair, her eyes of feverish brightness, and robed in a long dress of rich velvet. But she stood calm and firm.

'Doctor,' she said, motioning me to a chair, 'pray sit down; I have a very serious matter to speak to you about.'

I obeyed in silence. In her turn she sat down and seemed to be collecting her thoughts.

'Providence or an evil destiny, I know not which, has made you witness of a mystery in which lies involved the honour of my family.'

So she knew it all! I sat confounded and astonished. 'Madam, believe me, it was but chance—'

'It is useless,' she interrupted; 'I know it all, and it is frightful!' Then, in a heartrending appealing voice, she cried: 'My father is not a guilty man!'

I shuddered, and with hands outstretched cried: 'Madam, I know it; I know that the life of your father has been one of the noblest.'

Odile had half-risen from her seat, as if to protest, by anticipation, against any supposition that might be injurious to her father. Hearing me myself taking up his defence, she sank back again, and covering her face with her hands, the tears began to flow.

'God bless you sir!' she exclaimed. 'I should have died with the very thought that a breath of suspicion was harboured against him.'

'Ah! madam, who could possibly attach any reality to the action of a somnambulist?'

'That is quite true sir, I had had that thought myself, but

appearances – pardon me – yet I feared – still I knew Doctor
Fritz was a man of honour.'

'Pray, madam, be calm.'

'No,' she cried, 'let me weep on. It is such a relief; for
ten years I have suffered in secret. Oh, how I suffered! That
secret, so long shut up in my breast, was killing me. I should
soon have died, like my dear mother. God has had pity upon
me, and has sent you, and made you share it with me. Let
me tell you all, sir, do let me!'

She could speak no more. Sobs and tears broke her voice.
At length she lifted her beautiful head; she wiped her tear-
stained cheeks, and she resumed in slow and melancholy
tones:

'When I go back into the past, sir, when I return to my
first impressions, my mother's is the picture before me. She
was a tall, pale, and silent woman. She was still young at
the period to which I am referring. She was scarcely thirty,
and yet you would have thought her fifty. Her brow was
silvered round with hair white as snow; her sharp, clear
profile – her lips ever closed together with an expression of
pain – gave to her features a strange character in which
pride and pain seemed to contend for the mastery. There
was nothing left of the elasticity of youth in that aged woman
of thirty – nothing but her tall upright figure, her brilliant
eyes, and her voice, which was always as gentle and as sweet
as a dream of childhood. She often walked up and down
for hours in this very room, with head hanging down, and
I, an unthinking child, ran happily along by her side, never
aware that my mother was sad, never understanding the
meaning of her deep melancholy.'

Odile smiled bitterly and went on: 'Sometimes I would
happen, in my noisy play, to disturb my mother in her silent
walk; then she would stop, look down, and, seeing me at
her feet, would slowly bend, kiss me with an absent smile,
and then again resume her interrupted walk and her sad
gait. Since then, sir, whenever I have desired to search back

in my memory for remembrances of my early days that tall, pale woman has risen before me, the image of melancholy. There she is,' pointing to a picture on the wall, 'there she is! – not such as illness made her as my father supposes, but that fatal and terrible secret. See?'

I turned round, and as my eye dwelt upon the portrait the lady pointed to, I shuddered.

It was a long, pale, thin face, cold and rigid as death, and luridly lighted up by two dark, deep-set eyes, fixed, burning, and of a terrible intensity.

'I know not how my mother made that terrible discovery,' added Odile, 'but she became aware of the mysterious attraction of the Black Pest and their meetings in Hugh Lupus's tower; she knew it all – all! She never suspected my father – ah no! – but she perished away by slow degrees under this consuming influence! and I myself am dying.'

'One night,' she went on, 'I was only ten – and my mother, with the remains of her superhuman energy, for she was near her end that night, came to me when I lay asleep. It was in winter, her stony cold hand caught me by the wrist. I looked up. In one hand she held a flaming torch, with the other she held me by the arm. Her robe was sprinkled with snow. There was a convulsive moment in all her limbs and her eyes were fired with a gloomy light through the long locks of white hair which hung in disorder round her face. She said, "Odile, my child, get up and dress! You must know it all!" Then taking me to Hugh Lupus's tower she showed me the open subterranean passage. "Your father will come out with the she-wolf; don't be frightened, he won't see you." And presently my father, bearing his funereal burden, came out with the old woman. My mother took me in her arms and followed; she showed me the dismal scene on the Altenberg of which you know. "Look, my child," she said, "you must, for I – am going to die soon. You will have to keep that secret. You alone are to sit up with your father," she said impressively, "you alone. The honour of your family depends upon you!" And so we returned. A fortnight after, my mother died, leaving me her will to accomplish and her example to follow. I have scrupulously obeyed her injunctions as a sacred command, but oh, at what a sacrifice! I have been obliged to disobey my father and to rend his heart. If I had married I should have brought a stranger into the house and betrayed the secret of our race. No one in this castle knows of the somnambulism of my father, and but for yesterday's crisis, which broke down my strength completely and prevented me from sitting up with my father, I should still have been its sole depository. God has decreed otherwise, and has placed the honour and reputation of my family in your keeping. You will keep that secret sir, I know you will keep it, because it is your duty to do so. But I expect more than this of you, much more, and this is why I consider myself obliged to tell you all!'

She rose slowly from her seat.

'Doctor Fritz,' she resumed in a voice which made every nerve within me quiver with deep emotion, 'my strength is unequal to my burden; I bend beneath it. I need a helper, a friend. Will you be that friend?'

'Madam,' I replied, rising from my seat, 'I gratefully accept your offer of friendship. I cannot tell you how proud I am of your confidence; but still, allow me to unite with it one condition.'

'Pray speak, sir.'

'I mean that I will accept that title of friend with all the duties and obligations which it shall impose upon me.'

'What duties do you mean?'

'There is a mystery overhanging your family; that mystery must be discovered and solved at any cost. That Black Pest must be apprehended. We must find out where she comes from, what she is, and what she wants!'

'Oh, but that is impossible!' she said with a movement of despair.

'Who can tell that, madam? Perhaps Divine Providence

may have had a design connected with me in sending Sperver to fetch me here.'

'You are right, sir. God never acts without consummate wisdom. Do whatever you think right. I give my approval in advance.'

I raised to my lips the hand which she tremblingly placed in mine, and went out full of admiration for this frail and feeble woman, who was, nevertheless, so strong in the time of trial.

XII

An hour after the conversation with Odile, Sperver and I were riding hard, and leaving Nideck rapidly behind us. Lieverlé accompanied us, flying alongside of us like an arrow from the bow. A whirlwind seemed to sweep us in our headlong way.

The towers of Nideck were far away, and Sperver was keeping ahead as usual when I shouted: 'Halloo, comrade, pull up! Halt! Before we go any farther let us know what we are about.'

He faced round.

'Only just tell me, Fritz, is it right or is it left?'

'No; that won't do. It is of the first importance that you should know the object of our journey. In short, we are going to catch the hag.'

A flush of pleasure brightened up the long sallow face of the old poacher, and his eyes sparkled.

'Ha, ha!' he cried. 'I knew we should come to that at last!'

And he slipped his rifle round from his shoulder into his hand.

This significant action roused me.

'Wait, Sperver; we are not going to kill the Black Pest, but to take her alive. I declare to you that the life of this woman is bound up with that of your master. The ball that hits her hits your lord.'

Sperver gazed at me in astonishment.

'Is this really true, Fritz?'

'Positively true.'

There was a long silence; Sperver sat motionless, his hand still upon his gun.

'Well, let us try and catch her alive. We will put on gloves if we have to touch her, but it is not so easy as you think, Fritz. She tramps everywhere, and lives in a hole wherever she pleases. She has a sure foot, a keen eye, and can scent you a couple of miles off. How are you going to catch her then? If we only had one end of her trail, who knows but with courage and perseverance—'

'As for her trail, don't trouble about that; that's my business.'

'What do you know about following up a trail?'

'Why should not I?'

'Oh, if you are so sure of it, and you know more about it than I do, of course march on, and I'll follow!'

The old hunter was vexed that I should presume to trespass upon his special province; therefore, I turned sharply to the left, sure of coming across the woman's trail, who, after having left the count at the postern gate, must have crossed the plain to reach the mountain.

Sperver rode behind me now, whistling rather contemptuously, and I could hear him now and then grumbling but in a moment I heard him utter an exclamation of surprise; then, fixing a keen eye upon me, he said: 'Fritz, you know more than you choose to tell.'

'How so, Gideon?'

'The track that I should have been a week finding, you have got it at once. Come, that's not all right!'

'Where do you see it, then?'

'Oh, don't pretend to be looking at your feet.'

And pointing out to me at some distance a scarcely perceptible white streak in the snow: 'There she is!'

Immediately he galloped up to it; I followed in a couple

of minutes; we had dismounted, and were examining the track of the Black Pest. The huntsman knelt on the ground. I was all ears; he was closely examining. 'It is a fresh track,' he pronounced, 'last night's. It is a strange thing, Fritz, during the count's last attack that old witch was hanging about the castle.'

Then examining with greater care: 'She passed here between three and four o'clock this morning.'

'How can you tell?'

'It is quite a fresh track; there is sleet all round it. Last night, about twelve, I came out to shut the doors; there was sleet falling then, there is none upon the footsteps, therefore she has passed since.'

'That is true enough, Sperver, but it may have been made much later; for instance, at eight or nine.'

'No, look, there is frost upon it! The fog that freezes on the snow only comes at daybreak. The creature passed here after the sleet and before the fog – that is, about three or four this morning.'

I was astonished at Sperver's exactitude. He rose from his knee, clapping his hands together to get rid of the snow, and looking at me thoughtfully, as if speaking to himself, said: 'It is twelve, is it not, Fritz?'

'A quarter to twelve.'

'Very well; then the old woman has got seven hours' start on us. We must follow upon her trail step by step; on horseback we can do it in half the time, and, if she is still going, about seven or eight tonight we have got her, Fritz. Now then, we're off.'

And we started afresh upon the track. It led us straight to the mountains.

Galloping away, Sperver said: 'If good luck only would have it that she had rested an hour or two in a hole in a rock, we might be up with her before the daylight is gone.'

'Let us hope so, Gideon.'

'Oh, don't think of it. The old she-wolf is always moving;

she never tires; she tramps along all the hollows in the Black Forest. We must not flatter ourselves with vain hopes. If, perhaps, she has stopped on her journey, so much the better for us; and if she still keeps going, we won't let that discourage us.'

A burning ardour hurried us on in pursuit; my blood was at fever heat; I was determined to stand at no obstacle in laying hold of this extraordinary being. The snow was flying in our rear; sometimes splinters of ice, bitten off by the horse-shoes, like shavings of iron from machinery, whizzed past our ears.

Lieverlé, in a high state of enthusiasm and excitement, took bounds sometimes as high as our horses' backs, and I could not but tremble at the thought that when we came up at last with the Pest he might tear her in pieces before we could prevent him.

But the old woman gave us all the trouble she could; on every hill she doubled, at every hillock there was a false track.

'After all, it is easy here,' cried Sperver, 'to what it will be in the wood. We shall have to keep our eyes open there!'

We had just reached the edge of a pine-forest. In woods of this description the snow never reaches the ground except in the open spaces between the trees, the dense foliage intercepting it in its fall. This was the difficult part of our enterprise. Sperver dismounted to see our way better, and placed me on his left so as not to be hindered by my shadow.

Here were large spaces covered with dead leaves and the needles and cones of the fir-trees, which retain no footprint. It was, therefore, only in the open patches where the snow had fallen on the ground that Sperver found the track again.

It took us an hour to get through the thicket. At last we descended a valley to the left and Gideon, pointing to the track of the she-wolf outside the edge of the brushwood, triumphantly remarked: 'There is no feint in this sortie, for once. We may follow this track confidently.'

'Why so?'

'Because the Pest has a habit every time she doubles of going three paces to the right; then she retraces her steps four, five, or six in the other direction, and jumps away into a clear place. But when she thinks she has sufficiently disguised her trail she breaks out without troubling herself to make any feints.'

We galloped off again. The track of the she-wolf now passed on to the heights of the forest by so steep an ascent that several times we had to dismount and lead our horses by the bridle.

'There she is, turning to the right,' said Sperver. 'In this direction the mountains are craggy; perhaps one of us will have to lead both horses while the other climbs to look after the trail. But don't you think the light is going?'

The landscape now was assuming an aspect of grandeur and magnificence. Vast grey rocks, sparkling with long icicles, raised here and there their sharp peaks like breakers amidst a snowy sea.

Unfortunately the horses were beginning to tire; they sank deeper in the snow and no longer neighed joyfully. And added to this the endless mazes of the Black Forest wearied us too. The old woman affected this solitary region greatly; here she had trotted round a deserted charcoal-burners' hut; farther on she had torn out the roots that projected from a moss-grown rock; there she had sat at the foot of a tree, and that very recently – not more than two hours since, for the track was quite fresh – and our hope and our ardour rose together. But the daylight was slowly fading away!

At five o'clock it was almost dark. Sperver halted and said: 'Fritz, my lad, we have started a couple of hours too late. The she-wolf has had too long a start. In ten minutes it will be as dark as a dungeon. The best way would be to reach Roche Creuse, which is twenty minutes' ride from here, light a good fire, and eat our provisions and empty our flasks. When the moon is up we will follow the trail again, and unless the old hag is the foul fiend himself, ten to one we shall find her dead and stiff with cold against the foot of a tree, for nothing can live after such a tremendous tramp in weather like this. Sébalt is the best walker in the Black Forest, and he would not have stood it. Come Fritz, what is your opinion?'

'I am not so mad as to think differently. Besides, I am perishing with hunger!'

'Well, let us start again.'

He took the lead and passed into a close and narrow glen between two precipitous faces of rock. The fir-trees met over our heads; under our feet ran a mere thread of the stream, and from time to time some ray from above was dimly reflected in the depths below and glinted with a dull leaden light.

The darkness was now such that I thought it prudent to drop my bridle on Rappel's neck. The steps of our horses on the slippery gravel awoke strange discordant sounds like the screaming of monkeys at play. The echoes from rock to rock caught up and repeated every sound, and in the distance a tiny space of deep blue widened as we advanced; it was the issue from the glen.

I was beginning to feel the keen air moving upon my face, for we were approaching the outlet of the gorge, when all at once a red light struck the rock a hundred feet above us, purpling the dark green of the fir-trees and lighting up the wreaths of snow.

'Ha!' cried Sperver, 'we have got her at last!'

My heart leaped; we stood closely pressed, the one against the other.

The dog growled low and deep.

'Cannot she escape?' I asked in a whisper.

'No; she is caught like a rat in a trap. There is no way out but this, and everywhere all round the rocks are two hundred feet high. Now, vile hag, I hold you!'

He alighted in the ice-cold stream, handing me his bridle.

I caught in the silence the click of the lock of his gun, and that slight noise threw me into a tremor of apprehension.

'Sperver, what are you about?'

'Don't be alarmed; it is only to frighten her.'

'Very well, then, but no blood. Remember what I told you – the ball which strikes the Pest slays the count!'

'Don't trouble yourself,' was the answer.

He went away without further parley. I could hear the splash of his feet in the water, then I saw his tall figure emerge at the opening of the dark glen, black against a purple background. He stood five minutes motionless. Attentive, bending forward. I looked and listened, still moving onward. As he returned I was but a few yards from him.

'Hark!' he whispered mysteriously. 'Look there!'

At the end of the hollow, scooped out perpendicularly like a quarry in the mountain side, I saw a bright fire unrolling its golden spires beneath the vault of a cave, and before the fire sat a man with his hands clasped about his knees, whom I recognised by his dress as the Baron de Zimmer-Bluderich.

He saw motionless, his forehead resting between his hands. Behind him lay a dark gaunt form extended on the ground. Farther on, his horse, half lost in the shade, reared his neck, gazed on us with eyes fixed, ears erect, and nostrils distended.

I stood rooted to the ground.

How did the Baron happen to be in that lonely wilderness at such a time? What did he want here? Had he lost his way?

The most contradictory conjectures were passing in confusion through my excited brain, and I could not tell what conclusion to arrive at, when the baron's horse began to neigh, and the master raised his head.

'Well, Donner, what is the matter now?' said he.

Then he, too, directed his gaze our way, straining his eyes through the darkness.

That pale face with its strongly-marked features, thin lips, and thick black eyebrows meeting together, and forming a deep hollow on the brow in the form of a long vertical wrinkle, would have struck me with admiration at any other time; while now an inexplicable anxiety laid hold of me, and I was filled with vague apprehensions.

Suddenly the young man exclaimed: 'Who goes there?'

'I, monseigneur,' answered Sperver, coming forward. 'Sperver, chief huntsman to the lord of Nideck.'

A flash shot from the baron's quick eye, not a muscle of his countenance quailed. He rose to his feet, gathering his pelisse over his shoulders. I drew towards me the horses and the dog, and this animal suddenly began howling fearfully.

Sperver and the Baron stood at a distance of fifty yards from each other, the first immovable in the midst of the deep glen, his gun unslung from his shoulder, the other erect upon the level platform outside of the cave, carrying his head high, fixing on us a haughty eye and a proud look of superiority.

'What do you want here?' he asked aggressively.

'We are looking for a woman,' replied the old poacher, 'a woman who comes every year prowling about Nideck, and our orders are to take her.'

'Has she stolen anything?'

'No.'

'Has she committed murder?'

'No, monseigneur.'

'Then what do you want with her? What right have you to pursue her?'

'And you – what right have you over her?' answered Sperver with an ironical smile. 'See, there she is. I can see her at the bottom of the cave. What right have you to meddle with our affairs? Don't you know that we are here in the domains of Nideck, and that we administer justice and execute our own decrees?'

The young man changed colour, and said coldly: 'I have no account to render to you.'

'Beware,' replied Sperver. 'I am here on behalf on the lord Yeri-Hans. I am in the execution of my duty, and you are putting yourself in the wrong.'

'Your duty!' cried the young man bitterly. 'If you talk about your duty you will oblige me to do mine!'

'Well, do it!' cried the huntsman, whose features were becoming disturbed with anger.

'No,' replied the baron, 'I am not responsible to you, and you shall not come here!'

'That's what we shall soon see!' said Sperver, drawing nearer to the cave.

The young man drew his hunting-knife. Perceiving this menacing action, I was about to dart between them, but happily the hound which I was holding by his collar slipped from me with a violent shock and threw me to the ground. I thought the baron would be lost, but at that instant a wild shriek rose from the dark bottom of the cavern, and as I rose to my feet I saw the old woman standing erect before the fire, her tattered garments hanging loosely about her, her grey and tangled locks floating wildly in the wind; she flung her bony arms in the air and uttered prolonged piercing howls like the cry of agony of the hungry wolf in the long cold nights of winter.

Never in my life have I seen a more fearful apparition. Sperver, motionless, his eyes riveted on the fearful object before him, and his mouth open with astonishment, stood as if rooted to the earth. But the powerful dog, surprised himself at this unexpected sight, stood still for a moment; then, his back bristling in preparation for a mighty leap, he made a rush with a deep, impatient growl which made me tremble. The platform before the cave was about eight or nine feet from the level where we stood, or he would have reached it at a single bound. The baron flung himself before the woman with a piercing cry, 'My mother!' then the dog took another spring, and Sperver, quick as lightning, raised his gun, and brought down the poor animal dead at the young man's feet.

When the smoke of the explosion had cleared away I saw Lieverlé lying outstretched at the foot of the rock, and the woman fainting in the arms of the young man. Sperver, pale with concentrated rage and excitement, and eyeing the young baron darkly, dropped the butt of his gun to the ground, his features discomposed, and his eyes half-hid in his gloomy frown.

'Seigneur de Bluderich,' he cried, with his hand extended, 'I have killed my best friend to save the life of that unhappy woman, your mother! Thank God that her life is bound up with that of the Count of Nideck! Take her away! Take her hence, and never let her return here again; if you do I cannot answer for what old Sperver may be driven to do!'

Then, with a glance at the poor dog: 'Oh! Lieverlé, Lieverlé!' he cried, 'was it to end thus? Come Fritz, let us go. I cannot stay here. I might do something that I should have to repent of!'

And, laying hold of Fox by the mane, he was going to throw himself into the saddle, but suddenly his feelings of distress overcame all restraint, and bowing his head upon his horse's neck, he burst into sobs and tears, and wept like a child.

XIII

Sperver had gone, bearing the body of poor Lieverlé in his cloak. I had declined to follow; my sense of duty kept me by this unhappy woman. Besides, I must confess I was curious to see a little more closely this strange mysterious being, and therefore as soon as Sperver had disappeared in the darkness of the glen. I began to climb up to reach the cavern. There I beheld a strange sight.

Extended upon a large cloak of white fur lay the aged woman in a long ragged robe of purple, her fingers clutching her breast, a golden arrow through her grey hair.

Never shall I forget the figure of this strange woman; her vulture-like features distorted with the last agonies of death, her eyes set, her gasping mouth, were fearful to look upon.

The baron, on his knees at her side, was trying to restore her; but I saw at a glance that the wretched creature was dying, and it was not without a profound sense of pity that I took her by the arm.

'Leave madam alone – don't touch her,' cried the young man with irritation.

'I am a surgeon, monseigneur.'

He looked in silence at me for a moment, then rising, said: 'Pardon me, sir; pray forgive my hasty language.'

He trembled with excitement, scarcely yet subdued, and presently he went on: 'What is your opinion, sir?'

'It is over – she is dead!'

Then, without speaking another word, he sat upon a large stone, with his forehead resting upon his hand and his elbow on his knee, his eyes motionless, as still as a statue.

I sat near the fire, watching the flames rising to the vaulted roof of the cave, and casting lurid reflections upon the rigid features of the corpse.

We had sat there for an hour as motionless as statues, each deep in thought, when, suddenly lifting his head, the baron said: 'Sir, all this utterly confounds me. Here is my mother – for twenty-six years I thought I knew her – and now an abyss of horrible mysteries opens before me. You are a doctor; tell me, did you ever know anything so dreadful?'

'Monseigneur,' I replied, 'the Count of Nideck is afflicted with a complaint strikingly similar to that from which your mother appears to have suffered. If you feel enough confidence in me to communicate to me the facts which you have yourself observed, I will gladly tell you what I know myself; for perhaps this exchange of our experiences might supply me with the means to save my patient.'

'Willingly, sir,' he replied, and without any further prelude he informed me that the Baroness de Bluderich, a member of one of the noblest and oldest families in Saxony, took, every year towards autumn, a journey into Italy, with no attendant besides an old man-servant, who possessed her entire confidence; that man, being at the point of death, had desired a private interview with the son of his old master, and prompted, no doubt, by the pangs of remorse, he told the young man that his mother's visit to Italy was only a pretense to enable her to make, unobserved, a certain excursion into the Black Forest, the object of which was unknown to himself, but which must have had something fearful in its character, since the baroness returned always in a state of physical prostration, ragged, half dead, and that weeks of rest alone could restore her after the hideous labours of those few days.

This was the purport of the old servant's disclosures to the young baron, who believed that in so doing he was only fulfilling his duty.

The son, anxious at any sacrifice to know the truth of this account, had, that very year, ascertained it, first by following his mother to Baden, and then into the gorges of the Black Forest. The footsteps which Sébalt had tracked in the woods were his.

When the baron had thus imparted his knowledge to me, I thought I ought not to conceal from him the mysterious influence which the appearance of the old woman in the neighbourhood of the castle exercised over the count, nor the other circumstances of this unaccountable series of events.

We were both amazed at the extraordinary coincidence between the facts narrated, the mysterious attraction which these beings unconsciously exercised the one over the other, the tragic drama which they performed in union, the familiarity which the old woman had shown with the castle, and its most secret passages, without any previous examination of them; the costume which she had discovered in which to carry out this secret act, and which could only have been rummaged out of some mysterious retreat revealed to her by the strange instinct of insanity. They plainly re-enacted a murder and the attendant disposal of a dead body – but of whom? I was to find out in time.

But the darkness of night was beginning to yield to the pale tints of early dawn. A neighing of horses was heard far up the defile; then, with the first rays of dawn, we distinguished a sledge driven by the baron's servant; its bottom was littered with straw; on this the body was laid.

I mounted my horse and rode after the sledge to the exit from the defile where they drove off in the direction of Hirschland and I rode towards the towers of Nideck.

At nine I was in the presence of Mademoiselle Odile, to whom I gave a faithful narrative of all that had taken place.

Then repairing to the count's apartments, I found him in a very satisfactory state of improvement. He felt very weak, as was to be expected after the terrible shocks he had gone through, but had returned to the full possession of his clear faculties, and the fever had left him the evening before. There was, therefore, every prospect of a speedy cure.

A few days later, seeing the old lord in a state of convalescence, I expressed a desire to return to Fribourg, but he entreated me so earnestly to stay at Nideck, and offered me terms so honourable and advantageous that I felt myself unable to refuse compliance with his wishes.

XIV

I shall long remember the first boar-hunt in which I had the honour to join with the count, and especially the magnificent return home in a torchlight procession after having sat in the saddle for twelve hours together.

I had just had supper, and was going into Hugh Lupus's tower, when passing Sperver's room, whose door was half open, shouts and cries of joy reached my ears. I stopped, when the most jovial spectacle burst upon me. Around the massive oaken table beamed twenty square rosy faces, bright and ruddy with health and fun.

The hob and nobbing of the glasses gave out an incessant tinkling and clattering. There was sitting Sperver with his bossy forehead, his moustaches bedewed with Rhenish wine, his eyes sparkling, and his grey hair rather disordered; at his right was Marie Lagoutte, on his left Knapwurst. He was raising aloft the ancient silver-gilt and chased goblet dimmed with age.

Knapwurst, squatting in his armchair, with his head on a level with Sperver's elbow, looked like a big pumpkin. Then came Tobias Offenloch, and farther on loomed the melancholy long face of Sébalt, who was peeping with a sickly smile into the bottom of his wine-glass; then all the other servants.

The light of the lamp shed over the whole scene its amber-coloured hue and left in the shade the old grey and time-stained walls. The vaulted roof was ringing with the joyous shouts of laughter.

As soon as Sperver caught sight of me, he held out his hand: 'Fritz,' said he, 'we only wanted you. It is a long time since I felt so comfortable as I do tonight. You are welcome, old boy!'

As I gazed upon him with surprise – for since the death of Lieverlé I had never seen him smile – he added more seriously: 'We are celebrating the return of monseigneur to his health, and Knapwurst is telling us stories.'

All the guests turned my way, and I was saluted with kindly welcomes on all sides.

I was dragged in by Sébalt, seated near Marie Lagoutte, and found a large glass of Bohemian wine in my hand before I could quite understand the meaning of it all.

The old hall was echoing with merry peals of laughter, and Sperver, throwing his arm round my neck, shouted:

'Here is my son! He and I – I and he – until death! Here's the health of Doctor Fritz!'

Knapwurst, standing as high as he was able upon the seat of his armchair, leaned towards me and held me out his glass. Marie Lagoutte and Sèbalt repeated, 'Your health, Doctor Fritz!' Then there was a moment's silence. Every guest drank. Then, with a single clash, every glass was set vigorously upon the table.

'Bravo!' cried Sperver.

Then, turning to me: 'Fritz, we have already drunk to the health of the count and of Mademoiselle Odile; you will do the same.'

Twice had I to drain the cup before the vigilant eyes of the whole table. Then I too began to look grave. Could it have been drunken gravity?

Sperver kept on humming and laughing. Suddenly putting his hand upon the dwarf's misshapen back, he cried: 'Silence! Our friend Knapwurst is going to tell us again a new legend he has uncovered from his parchments.'

'Won't you have another instead?' asked the hunchback.

'No. I like this best.'

'I know better ones than that.'

'Knapwurst,' insisted the huntsman, raising his finger impressively, 'I have reasons for wishing to hear the same again and no other. Cut it shorter if you like. There is a great deal in it. Now, Fritz, listen!'

The dwarf rested his elbows on the table, and started.

'Bernard Hertzog relates that the burgrave Hugh, surnamed Lupus or the Wolf, when he was old, used to wear a cowl, which was a kind of knitted cap that covered in the crest of the knight's helmet when engaged in fighting. When the helmet tired him he would take it off and put on the knitted cowl, and its long cape fell around his shoulders.

'Up to his eighty-second year Hugh still wore his armour, though he could hardly breathe in it.

'Then he sent for Otto of Burlach, his chaplain, his eldest

son Hugh, his second son Berthold, and his daughter the red-haired Bertha, wife of a Saxon chief named Bluderich, and said to them: "Your mother Huldine, the she-wolf, has bequeathed you her claws; her blood flows, mingled with mine, in your veins. In you the wolf's blood will flow from generation to generation; it shall weep and howl among the snows of the Black Forest. Some will say, 'Hark! The wind howls!' others, 'No, it is the owl hooting!' But not so; it is your blood, mine, and the blood of the she-wolf who drove me to murder Hedwige, my wife before God and the Church. She died under my bloody hands! Cursed be the she-wolf! for it is written, 'I will visit the sins of the fathers upon the children.' The crime of the father shall be visited upon the children until justice shall have been satisfied!"

'Then old Hugh the Wolf died.

'From that dreary day the north wind has howled across the wilds, and the owl has hooted in the dark, and travellers by night know not that it is the blood of the she-wolf weeping for the day of vengeance that will come, whose blood will be renewed from generation to generation – so says Hertzog – until the day when the first wife of Hugh, Hedwige the Fair, shall reappear at Nideck under the form of an angel to comfort and to forgive!'

Then Sperver, rising from his seat, took a lamp and demanded of Knapwurst the keys of the library, and beckoned to me to follow him.

We rapidly traversed the long dark gallery, then the armoury, and soon the archive-chamber appeared at the end of the great corridor.

All noises had died away in the distance. The place seemed quite deserted.

Once or twice I turned round, and could then see with a creeping feeling of dread our two long fantastic shadows in ghostly fashion writhing in strange distortions upon the high tapestry.

Sperver quickly opened the old oak door, and with torch

uplifted, his hair all bristling in disorder, and excited features, walked in the first. Standing before the portrait of Hedwige, whose likeness to the young countess had struck me at our first visit to the library, he addressed me in these solemn words: 'Here is she who was to return to comfort and pity me! She has returned! At this moment she is downstairs with the old count. Look well, Fritz; do you recognise her? Is it not Odile?'

Then turning to the picture of Hugh's second wife: 'There,' he said, 'is Huldine, the she-wolf. For a thousand years she has wept in the deep gorges amongst the pine forests of the Schwartzwald; she was the cause of the death of poor Lieverlé; but henceforward the lords of Nideck may rest securely, for justice is done, and the good angel of this lordly house has returned. The curse is at an end.'

SOURCES

First, a list of those books, in English and French, of Erckmann–Chatrian's short stories that were published in Britain and America, and are worth reading:

Confessions of a Clarionet Player (Ward, Lock, 1874)
Contes Fantastique (in French) (Blackie, 1901)
The Man-Wolf (Ward, Lock, 1876)
The Polish Jew (Ward, Lock, 1873)
Popular Tales and Romances (Ward, Lock, 1872)
Stories of the Rhine (Ward, Lock, 1875)
The Story of a Campaign in Kabylia (Ward, Lock, 1874)
Strange Stories (Appleton, 1880 (USA))
The Wild Huntsman (Ward, Lock, 1877)

Readers should also be aware of *The Best Terrible Tales from the French* (Gibbings, 1891), which contains several Erckmann–Chatrian stories, completely uncredited. Ward, Lock did not seem to have pounced on Gibbings, as the book was reissued, still anonymous, by William Reeves in 1912.

Before listing the sources of the stories in this book, two things should be made clear. First, Erckmann–Chatrian stories appeared under various titles, and I have listed those alternative titles that I know. Second, loose ends were left flapping in many Erckmann–Chatrian stories, whether due to the quality of translation, or the authors' carelessness, I do not know. I have tied them up where possible. If you can discover where, well done. If you can't, then I did a good job. Dates in brackets show the year of the original French publication.

'The Invisible Eye' (1857): from *The Polish Jew* (alternative title 'Second Sight');

'The Owl's Ear' (1860): new translation by Eithne Fearnley-Whittingstall of a story from *Contes Fantastique* (alternative titles: 'The Inventor' and 'An Unknown Inventor');

'The White and the Black' (1860): from *Stories of the Rhine*;

'The Burgomaster in Bottle' (1849): from *The Polish Jew*;

'My Inheritance' (1860): from *Contes Fantastique*. This version comes from an undated (1920s) anthology, *The Masterpiece Library of Short Stories* (alternative title: 'Uncle Christian's Inheritance);

'The Wild Huntsman' (1866): from *The Wild Huntsman* (alternative title 'The Forest House', as which it appeared as the title story of a book issued by Sampson Low in 1871). This has been slightly edited;

'Lex Talionis' (1860): from *The Polish Jew*;

'The Crab Spider' (1860): new translation by Eithne Fearnley-Whittingstall of a story from *Contes Fantastique* (alternative titles: 'The Waters of Death' and 'The Spider of Guyana');

'The Mysterious Sketch' (1860): from *Strange Stories*;

'The Three Souls' (1859): new translation by Eithne Fearnley-Whittingstall of a story from *Contes Fantastique*;

'A Legend of Marseilles': from *The Best Terrible Tales from the French*;

'Cousin Elof's Dream' (1859): from *The Best Terrible Tales from the French* (alternative title: 'Retro Sight');

'The Citizen's Watch' (1859): from *Contes Fantastique* and *The Best Terrible Tales from the French* (alternative titles: 'The Dean's Watch' and 'The Man Cat');

'The Murderer's Violin' (1860): from *The Wild Huntsman*;

'The Child-Stealer' (1862): from *Stories of the Rhine*;

'The Man-Wolf' (1860): from *The Man-Wolf*. This has been slightly edited.

ACKNOWLEDGEMENTS

The Invisible Eye has a long history, and I owe a lot to various people for their help along the way. In chronological order:

Eithne Fearnley-Whittingstall, for her splendid translations of some of these stories;

Thom Tessier and Phil Edwards, who produced the first edition in 1981 from the decks of the sinking ship that was Millington;

Mike Ashley, for help with biographical details;

The late Richard Dalby, who supplied 'The Mysterious Sketch' for the first edition, and 'The Burgomaster in Bottle' for this one. His help with biographical details, and his information from French sources, have been invaluable for both editions;

David Brawn and Georgie Cauthery at HarperCollins, whose infectious enthusiasm for this kind of book has been so welcome.